LEATHER
AND
LACE

LEATHER AND LACE

BY

DIANN MILLS

BARBOUR
PUBLISHING

Dedication:
This book is dedicated to my critique partners
Kathleen Y'Barbo and Louise Gouge.
I treasure our friendship.

ISBN 1-59789-127-4

For more information about DiAnn Mills, please access the author's Web site at the following Internet address:
http://diannmills.com

Published by Barbour Publishing, Inc., P.O. Box 719, Uhrichsville, Ohio 44683, www.barbourbooks.com

Our mission is to publish and distribute inspirational products offering exceptional value and biblical encouragement to the masses.

 Member of the
Evangelical Christian
Publishers Association

Printed in the United States of America.

BLESSED IS THE MAN THAT WALKETH NOT IN
THE COUNSEL OF THE UNGODLY, NOR STANDETH IN
THE WAY OF SINNERS, NOR SITTETH IN THE SEAT
OF THE SCORNFUL.

PSALM 1:1

PROLOGUE

It's a perfect time to ride out of here. They won't be back for hours, maybe not till tomorrow with this storm coming. A good rain will hide my tracks. . .make it harder to trail me.

Casey O'Hare scanned the early morning horizon and watched the mounting storm clouds gather, roll, and spread across a blue-black sky. A brisk wind from the east swept up small sticks and leaves, tossed them lightly, then plunged them to the ground. In the distance, lightning flashed a jagged path across the sky. No rumble of thunder, just a warning of what lay ahead.

The fresh, earthy smell of rain teased her nostrils. Heavy drops hammered onto the dry ground faster and faster, as though daring her to escape this savage life. Riding in the open during a thunderstorm would be dangerous, but so was day-to-day survival with a gang of outlaws.

She could do it alone. She could stop the wishing and dreaming and change her sordid life. *I will not become like them.* Somewhere in this wide country was a place called home—and she'd find it.

CHAPTER 1

Fugitive Casey O'Hare had gone days without food but never without her gun. She knew how to call an outlaw's bluff and when to listen. She recognized desperation in wanted men and could smell trouble by the turn of the wind. But her senses turned to sickening dread when she found herself looking into the steel barrel of a Winchester .44.

With an inward gasp, she studied the man towering over her. The stranger could be one more man on the run. He could be hungry for the reward. Or he could have orders to shoot her on sight. Glancing above the ominous man's head to the cold, starless Utah night, Casey tasted bitter, gut-wrenching fear.

Is he alone?

"Evenin'." She mustered the courage to smile. "You look right cold. Sit yourself by my fire."

"I might." He didn't budge. "Soon as I take care of a few things." His gloved finger rested a hair's breadth from the trigger. Too close for her to jump him. A fresh sprinkling of snow reflected from the firelight and sparkled like silver across the top of the rifle barrel. He stuck his snow-caked boot under her Winchester, lying across her lap, and lifted it into his hand.

9

"Have some coffee, mister. It'll warm you up. Mighty cold t'night. Take my mug. I've got another one." She searched his shadowed features for something that might call his identity to mind. Remote hideaways and grim corners triggered nothing in her memory, and she'd always taken pride in remembering a face.

Keeping her hands in full view, she reached for the coffeepot teetering on the crackling fire and poured the strong brew. Tossing it in his face crossed her mind, but the rifle under her chin reined in the thought. "Here you are. Hope you aren't hungry. I'm fresh out of grub."

"No thanks."

Her gaze lifted above the rifle to the shadowy figure looming above the blaze. Flames danced high enough to touch on his silhouette yet provided too little light to scrutinize his every detail. Beneath a snow-dusted, wide-brimmed hat pulled down tightly over his eyes glared a face as dismal as nature's call to the winter night. Ice clung to his amber-colored mustache and beard. Casey recalled a man frozen to death who looked friendlier than this one.

"Mind if I get another mug from my saddlebag?"

"I'll get it." He reached for her saddlebag and pulled out her Colt and derringer. "No mug here." He hunkered down onto a stack of drying wood and shifted the aim of his rifle from her face to her chest.

"I must have left it somewhere."

"Give me the knife in your boot. Nice and easy-like."

She obliged and let him think he had her—for now. While he gulped the hot coffee, she tugged at the worn army blanket around her neck.

She inched closer to the fire and watched the red orange flames lick greedily at the dry wood. The popping and snapping broke the silence like an old man who'd settled down to ease his bones.

How do I get out of this one? Who is he?

"Good coffee." His voice rose barely above the sputtering fire.

In the firelight, she saw his piercing eyes—deep turquoise, as hard as the stone, and matching in color. She'd never seen eyes like his; she'd have remembered. Not once did his intense stare leave her face or show a trace of emotion. "State your business, mister."

"Jenkins's men got caught up in the snow, but come daybreak, they'll be back on your trail."

"Did Jenkins send you after me? Are you after his reward?"

"Neither," he said.

"The law?"

"No."

"Have I wronged you?"

"No, ma'am. I'm passing on a word of warning. If I can read your trail in the dark and snow, they won't have any trouble come morning."

"Guess I'd best be getting out of here." She hesitated a moment more. "Look, mister, I need my rifle. Without it, you're marking my grave."

"I'm keeping it," he said. "Do you know the way down out of these hills?"

"I'll find it." She kicked at a loose log on the fire. "And I don't need your help."

"I'm not asking. I'm telling."

"Why? You got a fondness for Brown's Park and gettin' caught in a snowstorm?"

"I have my reasons." He spat his words like venom.

"Let's get one thing straight," she said. "I don't intend to let Jenkins catch up with me, or let a judge sentence me to hang, or lace a man's pocket with bounty money. You belong to one of them. And you'd better not be around when I find out who you are."

He chuckled. "I never say anything I don't mean, and I don't doubt you'd blow a hole right through me. I want Jenkins for myself, and by sticking with you, I'm bound to get him."

Must be a money-grubbing bounty hunter. She shivered. With a price on her head, she didn't see a bounty hunter holding any better credentials than an outlaw. She should have shot Jenkins when she'd had the chance. More so, she shouldn't have gotten mixed up with a gang of outlaws in the first place. Seemed like her life had gone from one bad decision to another—except this last one to leave it all behind.

"Do you have a name? I need to call you something," she said.

"Morgan."

"I reckon you already know me."

"Casey O'Hare, Davis Jenkins's woman." Morgan wrapped his gloved fingers around the coffeepot.

"I'm not his woman, never was, never will be."

A hint of amusement flashed across his face and sparked an angry flame within her. He poured a second cup of coffee. "You're prettier than the stories and the wanted posters, but the fire's the same. Must be the red hair."

She stared hard into the stranger's face. His mouth curved into a slight smile. Casey observed what she could see of his face in the shadows and searched for a defined mark of deceit, but she saw only a clever stranger. Could this Morgan be an angel sent to deliver her or the devil setting her up for a kill?

Perhaps the beard and mustache were meant to disguise a man she'd otherwise recognize. Mr. Morgan wouldn't be the first to hide this way. He could conceal his looks easier than she with her long hair and the fact she was a woman outlaw in a territory full of wanted men.

A wolf howled. Casey shuddered as several more answered. If the wild animals didn't devour her, she'd surely freeze to death. Seemed like her life had been forever preyed upon by someone or something.

Good folks said a person like her couldn't shake her past. But she knew better. She'd lose Casey O'Hare in some secluded town where no one would recognize her.

"How do I know you aren't one of them?" she asked.

"You don't, but I'll tell you what I do know." He handed her the empty mug, and she filled it for herself. "I've heard plenty through more than a half-dozen men about how Davis Jenkins set his gang after the woman who refused to stay with him. Those claims are over six weeks old." He glared into her face. "By this time, he might very well want you dead. You and I both know Jenkins always gets what he wants, no matter what the cost."

Casey felt the icy air as she looked up to meet the gaze of this stranger who appeared too confident for her ease of mind. "I don't hold much stock in rumors. Only fools rely on hearsay in this part of the country, and they rarely live to remedy their mistakes."

"I'm no fool, and I know where they're camped."

"So how far off are they?" She wrapped her freezing gloved hand around the hot mug. His finger still rested on the Winchester's trigger.

"Depends on the weather. I saw 'em earlier today. Can't miss Jenkins with that ugly scar running down his face."

"What kind of man tracks down another in this snow and cold? Most men wouldn't risk their life for the likes of him."

"I don't claim to be a smart man, just vengeful."

"Makes me think I'm better off alone."

"But you're not, and I'm telling you that we're camping by the Green River tomorrow night."

Maybe you are, but I have other plans.

"Why did you run off?" Morgan asked. "Word is he treated you fair."

She bit back another caustic remark. "I said I'm not his woman, which is the reason he wants me back. It has nothing to do with money, another man, or any other lie you've heard. He'll not rest until I'm either with him or dead."

"I don't believe a word of it. A lover's spat. That's all. What happened? Is the law paying more money for his hide than yours? Or did he find out you had another man?"

"I didn't ask you to believe me."

"You've been a part of this gang since you were fourteen. Now you tell me there's never been anything between you and Jenkins?"

"You're talking through your hat."

He laughed. "Fancy words from someone who has a gun on them."

"I'm not afraid of you."

"You should be, since I know a whole lot about you."

"Where did you get your information?"

"I happened to be in Billings when you shot a man in self-defense."

"The sheriff called it murder."

"You were nothing more than a kid, and the man pulled a gun on you. Besides, you didn't kill him."

She knew that man died; she saw the wanted poster. "Sounds like you watched the whole thing or had firsthand news."

"I told you before, I was in Billings. Remember the heat and the storm that stopped the posse?"

A vague recollection taunted her mind—a young woman in a light blue dress and a man dressed in a dark suit. . .shiny boots. "What were you doing in Billings?"

"Getting married."

Maybe this man did know a lot about her. But why? "Why aren't you home with her?"

"She's dead."

"No young'uns?"

Morgan's eyes narrowed. "I'll ask the questions."

Casey held her tongue. No point in making him mad.

"Tim's riding with 'em," Morgan said. "I saw him with Jenkins yesterday. In fact, he and the boss looked real friendly."

"Leave my brother out of this." She clenched her fists. How had Morgan learned so much about her? Newspapers seldom printed the truth, and wanted posters never got any of it right. Too late to change anything; only remorse sealed her fate.

Casey emptied the coffee grounds onto the frozen earth. *Just like my life—useless. I despise this miserable emptiness. I hate sleeping with one hand on a gun and always having to look over my shoulder.* Casey took a deep breath. *Soon this will be behind me, or I'll die trying to free myself from the whole sorry lot of them.*

"We'd best get going," Morgan said. "We're wasting time, and I don't entertain the thought of another blizzard coming through."

She studied the stranger's face, then turned her attention to the looming blackness behind him. Could *they* be hiding among those trees that seemingly stretched to the sky? Were they laughing and thinking about what they'd do to her? She shook her head and refused to dwell on Jenkins and the others; the nightmares would drive her mad.

Right now she needed to concentrate on this Morgan fellow and how to outsmart him. Until then, she'd be traveling down an icy mountain path, weary and nursing the pain of wretched memories.

"We're wasting time, girl. I have plans."

A gust of bone-chilling wind whipped across her face and took her breath away.

CHAPTER 2

Daylight stole through the clouds in shades of dusty pink and purple as Casey and Morgan inched their way down the treacherous, narrow trail laden with ice and snow. Steep, glassy canyon walls stood between them and Willow Creek, hours more of gripping the reins and relying on the sure-footedness of her spotted gelding.

At times, her horse stumbled to his knees, then slowly struggled from the quicksand of snow to carry her on. Led by the faint light of a quarter moon and the stranger ahead of her, Casey wondered if she'd ever shake free of this night. The thought of plunging over the side of a cliff kept her rigid in the saddle and breathing deeply. If they ever reached Willow Creek, she'd find a way to break free of Morgan during the eight-mile trek south to Green River.

The gelding shook his head. "Easy, Stoney." She patted his neck and pulled her bandanna down from her nose and mouth. "You're doing good."

Her chest ached from fighting the cold and trying to breathe the thin, high mountain air, and her eyes stung from lack of sleep and watching the trail. If only she could have slept a few hours before beginning this descent. Fear of frostbite needled at her, and she wished she had a little kerosene to rub on her hands—hard to pull a trigger without fingers.

Her mind twisted with the unknown identity of the man who was using her to get to Jenkins. No need to ask why; the outlaw had hurt and killed more folks than many saw in a lifetime. One haunting memory after another crept in unbidden, but those memories were why she'd rather die than go back to the gang.

Sunrise lifted over the horizon, a flicker of color giving rise to a myriad of candles blending into one across the eastern sky. The cliffs behind them and the lower elevation brought warmer temperatures, while trees, bent with the weight of winter, gladly shed their crystal cocoons. With the hint of warmer temperatures, Casey anticipated budding plants and lush patches of green. This might be April's last grim reminder of winter.

If only her bleak past held the same promise of spring. She had a price on her head, and too many men carried bullets with her name on them. But soon all of that would be behind her. Still, the truth nagged her like a hurting tooth; she'd have to deceive good people to escape the past. Sometimes the dirt clung to her no matter how hard she scrubbed.

"How are you doing?" Morgan turned in the saddle to peer at her. "Thawed out yet?"

"When I can feel my hands, I'll let you know."

"You haven't complained since we left."

"What would you want me to say? Thanks for the good company?"

He tipped his hat and turned back to the trail. Morgan had something she craved: the strength of knowledge. *What if Jenkins does catch up with me?* The mere thought seared her soul. His ugly snarl and low, contemptuous laugh echoed from every direction.

She scanned the area around them. Jenkins's scarred face flashed across her mind, features she'd never forget. Some women thought him fine looking with his dark eyes and thick black hair, but when he drank, his right eye jerked about like a mad dog.

I've got to quit worryin' on him. Morgan's the danger here.

At the banks of Willow Creek, they stopped to dismount and water the horses. The cool morning air brushed across her face, smelling fresh and clean. White-capped water gurgled and rushed over rocks as if chased by what her ma had called a banshee. She knew the feeling.

Casey stretched her aching back. The night had been hard—too cold and dangerous. She removed her gloves and massaged her hands. "We made it," she said and carefully examined Stoney's legs to check for injuries.

"You had your doubts?"

"Plenty of times."

"I never took you for one who scared easily."

"I don't. I've been on the run for a long time, and I've been in some pretty tight spots. But nothing like the blizzard we left in the mountains. As far as I'm concerned, fighting nature is a lot harder than outthinking a man."

"I'll be sure to remember those words of wisdom." He grinned.

He's a pleasing man when he smiles, but looks are deceiving. Perfectly straight white teeth were framed by up-turned lips, and she saw a dimple high on his left cheek. Most of the men she encountered were toothless, either from fights or a rotten mouth. But none could be trusted.

"If you're after Jenkins's reward, he'll thank you and blow a hole through your heart."

"I imagine so, if that's what I planned," he said. "I told you before. I'm doing this for selfish reasons. Jenkins and I have a score to settle. . .and you're the bait. Though if you feel grateful for the guide down the mountains, you can cook breakfast. I don't know about you, but I'm hungry."

She glanced around at the open space, a clear target for anyone. "It's a deal, except I don't like the idea of being the worm on your hook." The doubts about him lingered like a pesky burr. "I don't feel like announcing our breakfast to the whole country, either."

"Yes, ma'am." His turquoise eyes sparkled. It angered her. "I know a spot where we can see up or down the creek. Does that suit you better?"

"Much better." Was he testing her, and if so, for what?

She wanted to know his business now, but patience might save her skin. The snow-covered mountains behind them had nearly won. How amazing that something so beautiful could be so dangerous. She turned and smiled. Folks said the same thing about her. She used to like hearing them, but not anymore.

"They're most likely stirring up there with no idea you made it out during the night. Jenkins is cunning, and only God knows where they really are. We best eat and push on. Whereabouts you headed?"

She nearly laughed at his attempt to gain information. "Not sure." She tucked a few strands of hair under her hat. "In the beginning, I only wanted to get away, but I can't decide in which direction. West to California or on to Oregon sounds good, or even back east where the country's civilized."

"Somehow, I don't think you'd fit into city life."

"You're probably right." She stole another look at the mountains. Oh, how she'd like to believe she'd left the misery behind. "But I have to go somewhere, and I need to make up my mind."

"Why not Texas?"

"Most wanted faces end up there or in Arizona. I'd like to think I'm different."

"It's a big territory. You could lose yourself in some remote town and start all over again."

"I suppose you're right. I've been there a few times and liked what I saw. You could ride for days from the spindly pines in the east to the dry plains of the far west. There isn't much law, though—almost as wild as here."

"Texas Rangers have cleaned it up."

"Thanks. Sounds like my kind of place." She laughed, and he joined her. For a moment, she relaxed. "Do you always hand out good advice to outlaws?"

"I'm only suggesting. Of course, I'm partial. Can't think of anywhere else on this earth I'd rather be, especially the hill country between Austin and San Antonio."

"Do you have family there?" They talked easily, almost as though they were friends.

"Some," he said. "My folks were originally from this part of the country, near Vernal, but they moved to Texas after the war."

Now I see why you know this area so well. Suspicion settled into her bones. Vernal lay about twenty-five miles south, a rough town known for its ability to hide the worst of men. Its well-deserved reputation could have easily driven out a respectable family or caused a bounty hunter to set down roots. Before this was all over, she'd find out who Morgan was.

"Did Tim know when you left?" he asked.

She questioned whether to answer him. Finally she figured she had nothing to lose. "No."

"Just wondered." Morgan pointed to a spot several yards to the right of them. "We'll be fine back in the brush. I can fish if you'll build a fire."

Once Casey had gathered enough kindling and wood, she reached into her saddlebag for a precious match to light it, then nursed along the flame. Nearly sick with exhaustion, she sat on a log and closed her eyes. Her weakened condition had dulled her mind, but she had to keep her wits. The smell of burning wood tugged at her senses, and she remembered dried beef and hard biscuits the morning before. Her stomach craved food. . .her mind craved her guns. . .her heart craved freedom.

She warmed her hands over the flames and went through the motions of making coffee—the last of it. The comforts of a home sounded mighty grand, and she thought back to the last time she ate a decent meal, slept in a real bed, or enjoyed the luxury of a tub bath. Most likely at a brothel while the gang enjoyed the ladies. At least a real home now had substance and meaning. Sitting motionless, she fought the urge to sleep. Birds sang around her like a mama humming a lullaby. In an effort to stay awake, she pulled a hairbrush from her saddlebag and began to ease out every tangle she could find. The thought of searching through Morgan's saddlebags for a gun nudged her, but she figured he had one eye on her and a revolver strapped to his belt. A quick glimpse in his direction confirmed her suspicions.

"Watching me, are you?" she called.

"That's my job."

Frustration inched through her. He had to rest sometime. A short while later, the smell of roasting fish yanked at her stomach. She could have eaten it raw.

They ate in silence. She preferred it—gave her time to plan a way out of this mess. Morgan yawned. When he slept, she'd make her move.

"Let's get out of here," he said.

"Don't you want to rest awhile? The horses are wore out."

"I said we're getting out of here." He doused the fire, and she saw a change in him. Hard. Cold. Hate.

Jenkins must have been on his mind.

They headed downstream toward Green River. The two rode side by side; neither spoke.

"Just who are you?" she finally asked.

"A man bent on ridding innocent folks of Davis Jenkins, and you're going to help me."

"How you going to do it?"

"Told you before. Use you as bait. Trade you for a chance to get Jenkins out in the open."

The picture that crossed her mind wasn't pretty. "What did he do to you?"

She waited for a reply. Nothing. Morgan reminded her of a mountain cat stalking his prey until the right moment to go in for the kill. But she had to give him credit: He was clever. For that trait, he'd earned her respect.

As the sun brightened, the water shimmered in a deep shade of bluish green—such a splendid sight after the preceding day's dismal white—and they passed bare trees broken only by an occasional pine. All around the sweet, fragrant smells of new plants filled her nostrils. Her spirits lifted, and she wasn't sure why. One man trailed her, and another held her captive. Maybe she'd crossed the line into madness.

Last night, she vowed she wouldn't be camping this night along the Green River, but things had changed. She hated not being in control. Of course, once Jenkins made it down the mountain, he'd be right behind them. Then she'd learn the truth about how Morgan planned to pull Jenkins into the open. Why hadn't he shot the animal when he saw him and Tim riding together? Maybe she'd find the answer to that, too.

Jenkins was a driving fool, relentless and easily agitated when he wanted something. He thought nothing of pushing horses and men till they dropped. When the time came to find fresh mounts, he'd steal from a nearby ranch or from other outlaws who might have horses hidden in a canyon. The frightening thought spurred her on.

With a heavy heart, she turned her attention to the peaceful countryside. Twisted pine trees grew monumental against a backdrop of slate-gray rock, timeless in a territory governed by lawless men. Somehow the beauty of nature clashed with the upheaval, or maybe it merely offered a reprieve for those who seldom took the time to appreciate its beauty.

"Brown's Park has been a favorite spot for horse thieves ever since those days following the Civil War," Morgan said, breaking the silence.

"I didn't know it had been used that long."

"It borders on the Wyoming and Utah territories and the state of Colorado. Seems to stop lawmen cold and keeps them confused as to jurisdiction. Just think about all the hideaways where outlaws can winter stolen animals."

Did Morgan think she was stupid, or was he nervous and just talking? Of course she knew those spots. She'd been to most of them.

About a mile south flowed Crouse Creek. Casey anticipated meeting up with familiar faces at the crossing. The creek ranked as the most secluded spot in Brown's Park. Unfortunately, some of the most detestable creatures known to humankind roamed there. Would Morgan want to wait there for Jenkins? She had to think of something soon. From the corner of her eye, she saw he'd slung her rifle over the other side of his saddle. At the first chance, she'd get it and break loose.

"Do you want to go wading?" Morgan asked.

She shivered at the thought. "We nearly froze to death last night, and now you want to catch your death of cold?"

"It might wake us up."

"I'd rather find a place to sleep." She lifted her hat, then tucked her hair up before plopping it back on. "Providing I live through this, are you going to let me go?"

"I could use the reward."

Too bad he had her knife, too.

"I like this time of year best," he said. "It might be the sight of things growing or winter passing, but whatever it is, the weather makes me feel lazy."

"I don't want to be lazy yet."

"Didn't you just say you wanted to find a place to sleep?"

"I'll sleep when I don't have to run from somebody." *And Jenkins is not the only one I need to watch out for.*

He stared at her oddly, and a nerve twitched in his cheek. "Casey, during those years with Jenkins, did you ever spend much time in one place?"

She laughed at his ludicrous question. "No, but I did think on it."

The two rode farther downstream and forded the river. The water splashed up cold against her legs, and soon she chilled to the bone. Suddenly Casey felt uneasy. She noticed Morgan had glanced back more than once. Foreboding bit at her heels. Jenkins must be close behind.

CHAPTER 3

In the distance, the shouts of men echoed from upstream. Casey drew in a ragged breath and strained to listen.

"Jenkins is making better time than I expected." Morgan pulled his chestnut mare to a halt. "But we need to throw 'em. I know of a cave farther downstream that's hidden beneath a ledge of rock. Have you been there?"

"No, and I've ridden up and down this riverbank with Jenkins plenty of times."

They crossed on through cold water to the opposite bank and rode on toward a wall of brown and gray rock covered by sparse growth. She studied each crack and tree that jutted from the side, but her trained eyes couldn't find the cave.

He cocked his rifle and dismounted. "We need to lead the horses."

Casey slid from Stoney and followed Morgan through a narrow path lined with brush to the cave's opening. Morgan picked up a limb and handed it to her. She used it as a brush to cover their tracks, thinking about the times she'd done this very thing to hide from lawmen. Inside the cool and dank quarters, she blinked several times until her eyes adjusted to the darkness. With the horses, they barely had room to turn around. She hated closed-in places; they always made her anxious. The smell of the animals coupled with mustiness aroused a whirlpool of recollections. In the past, she'd hidden from the law, not Jenkins. And he'd outsmarted every posse and lawman in the country.

Morgan pointed to a bramble and leaf-covered slice of rock. "We can see the river's edge from there." He pushed away just enough of the obstruction for them to see the outside.

Long moments trickled by while they stared at the riverbank.

"Are you thinking this is what I planned?" he asked.

She looked beyond the opposite creek bank for signs of Jenkins before answering. "Looks that way to me. Not sure, though. You're a peculiar man." She noted his square jaw and concluded it gave him a determined look, but for what? "Have you led me into a trap?"

"Not intentionally. I never planned to get you or me killed."

"The bait always loses. So what do we do now?"

"Wait a few more minutes. From the prickling on the back of my neck, it won't be long."

Within moments, Casey saw the first signs of the gang riding into view. Her heart slammed relentlessly against her chest. If Jenkins had ridden such a short distance behind them, then they must have started down the mountain last night. Suspicions about Morgan's motives tugged at her mind. The two men must have talked before Morgan stepped into her campsite. Her gaze rested on her rifle and the saddlebag that held her Colt and derringer.

"Odd how they picked up our trail right after we broke camp," she said.

"Think what you want."

Nothing in his expression revealed deceit. Although he didn't show signs of fear, she'd seen that emotion bring out other types of reactions in a man—anger, overconfidence, or loss of good sense.

"I wish I knew how they got here so fast." Casey craned her neck to count how many men rode in pursuit. "Or maybe I don't want to know."

Morgan continued to study the men. "I know you don't have any reason to trust me, but if I'm one of them, why are we hiding?"

"You tell me."

Not a muscle flinched. "Time will prove my words."

"So it will."

Silence seemed deafening. The waiting, the endless waiting.

"I've met men twice your size who weren't nearly as tough," Morgan said.

"Or as mean when I'm riled." She started to say more, but the sight of those she knew by name riding along the opposite riverbank caused the words to die in her throat.

Casey inwardly shuddered. Through the brush, she viewed her brother beside Jenkins. What part would Tim play if Jenkins discovered them? Surely he felt some sort of compassion for her. In the years they'd ridden with Jenkins, Casey had watched her brother change from a kind, misguided young man to a ruthless killer. No surprise he rode with them.

Her gaze moved from her brother to Jenkins. The outlaw sat tall and proud, as though he led an army brigade instead of a gang of outlaws. She well recognized his coal-black hair and the way he carried his rifle across the saddle.

The whole bunch rode in pursuit of one woman. She didn't want to think about what might happen if they caught her. . .or if they already had. Panic rose and burned in her chest, and her stomach curdled worse than day-old milk. It couldn't be much more than noon, but the whole mad race from Jenkins could be over.

"I guess Jenkins knows about this cave after all," she said. "He has the eyes of an eagle and the tactics of an angry rattler."

"Most likely so."

"Is there a way out?"

"Just through the front, the way we came in." He rubbed a bristled chin. "And I thought I was clever."

In that instant Casey wanted to believe Morgan spoke the truth.

"If only Jenkins rode within rifle range," she said. "But I'm not so sure I want any of them on this side of the river."

"Gunfire would send the rest in our direction with little time for us to get away."

Neither spoke about the gang choosing to rush them or smoke them out. The thought invited either a dance with death or a mercilessly slow torture. How long could they hold them off in a rock coffin?

The outlaws rode alongside the Green River until they disappeared. Not once did Jenkins's gaze cast a shadow on the cave. Caution stopped her from believing she was safe. After all, Morgan had *his* plans.

Silently, Casey waited, still expecting the band to leap out from nowhere. She noted the afternoon sun begin its slow descent and send dazzling jewels across the water. It glistened brilliantly as though the world lay in peace.

"They're back," Morgan said.

The gang rode upstream on the cave's side. Her blood ran cold. Jenkins most likely enjoyed this cunning game of wit. *Think. I have a man on the outside who wants me dead, and one in the inside who I can't trust.*

The hollow faces filed by. She could almost smell the leather and the unwashed bodies mixed with cheap whiskey. Some of them she'd known since the beginning; others only a short while. She'd dug out bullets from a few and helped bury their partners, but all were ready to take their orders from Jenkins. *I shouldn't have been so proud—should have slept with a few of them or promised to run off with 'em.*

They rode slowly along the river's edge several yards in front of the cave. Each one looked as if he'd given up hope of finding her. Mumbling and cursing rose above the splashing of water and the calls of nature. Once she thought Tim stared straight into the overhanging rock. Jenkins, however, kept his sight fixed on the river, appearing to concentrate on its ripple and flow.

Casey willed her heart to slow. She suddenly realized the closeness of the man beside her. His breath, warm against her face, and his presence unnerved her. If he wanted to kill Jenkins, now was the chance. Uncomfortable, she stepped back. Then, somehow, she found herself lost in the vortex of his eyes. Logic told her to break free of his visual hold, but instead, she sunk her heart into forbidden turquoise pools.

"They're not leaving," she whispered. "It's all a game."

"Casey," Morgan said, "don't you wonder why you and I have ended up like this together?"

She turned from him. "I don't have time to think on it. I'm more concerned about coming out of this alive." She shook with the tension flaring between them.

"Mark my word. There's a reason." He lowered his rifle yet maintained his watch. "And I don't know why, either."

"Thought you wanted Jenkins. I'm the bait, remember?"

"That's exactly what I told you." He stared back at the men and groaned. "They're camping in front of us."

Alarm threatened to strangle her. Already she could sense Jenkins's murderous hands around her neck. Whether he planned to wait for nightfall or force them out at his whim made little difference. She'd turn her gun on herself before facing his fury.

"What do you think?" She swallowed her staggering emotions.

"Pick them off one by one? Let them know we're ready and have it out now before we collapse from lack of sleep or water?" She brushed back a loose strand of hair from her face. "I want to face them now. I'm tired, too tired to think or reason. You have a chance to shoot Jenkins and still get out of here alive. I'll hold them off."

"I'm here for whatever happens. I'm not leaving you to that animal."

Who was this man? "A mule has more sense than you do. Stick with me, and you'll end up dead. Save the heroics. What happened to your plan?"

"We'll think of something," Morgan said. "We've come too far to risk getting killed because they think they have us."

"And they don't?"

"Not yet." He studied the terrain. "Where's your spunk, girl? I thought you had more fight in you than this." He took a passing glance at their horses. "You know, I'd gamble on them thinking we'd wait till dark to sneak out of here."

She paced across the dirt floor of the cave and watched a lizard scamper up the wall. "You're talking hours away. Jenkins could get very impatient by then."

"True. What do you say we let them get their horses unsaddled and make a run for it?"

What did they have to lose? "So you're going to get him when we ride out?"

He nodded.

"I've got friends in Vernal. We could hide out a few days."

"I still know a few folks there," he said. "Unless you have a better idea."

She shook her head. "Running is part of my life, and as long as someone is after me, I'll keep running."

Staring up at the rock ledge masking the cave's opening, she felt a renewal of energy. Jenkins had two guards posted at opposite ends of the riverbank, with Tim seated adjacent to the cave. The outlaws' horses glistened with sweat.

"We're outnumbered, but their horses are spent. I think we can outrun them." Morgan's jaw tightened. He reached for her rifle along with the Colt and derringer. "This isn't the way I planned to return these."

"And it's not the way I wanted them back, either." She slipped the revolver into her gun belt, dropped the derringer into her coat pocket, and tightened her fingers around the stock barrel of the rifle. The familiarity did little to boost her confidence.

Staring at the water's edge, she recalled similar situations and remembered the anxious gut fear. But she'd always been in Jenkins's company, not against him.

The outlaws relaxed by the riverbank. Some reached for a chaw of tobacco and a bottle of whiskey; some filled their canteens with water. From the sordid laughter, she knew which ones bragged about their reputations. Only Jenkins and the guards held their weapons in hand.

"We need some wood," Jenkins shouted.

"What for?"

"Burn out Casey and Morgan." He pointed to the cave.

"You—" Casey whipped her attention to Morgan.

"He knows I'm trailing him. So does your brother."

"How's come I never heard of you?"

"Maybe Jenkins doesn't tell his woman everything."

She wanted to spit on him.

Jenkins stepped behind two of the men.

"I see you're hiding from me," Morgan called out.

"And have you pick me off?" Jenkins laughed. "Can't believe my luck. Got you both."

"That's what you think," Morgan said.

Jenkins laughed again. "Gonna get mighty hot in there."

Morgan swung his attention her way. "Are you ready?"

Casey clenched her fists in an effort to dispel the anger and fear snaking up her spine. "Sure. Don't have much choice."

"Only the hand of God can help us now."

"He may help you, but I haven't done anything good to get His attention."

"God doesn't help us because we deserve it."

She startled. "What are you, a preacher?"

"Far from it. I just know who's in control."

Moments later, the two stepped from the cave and swung up onto their saddles. Two black-billed magpies flew from a tree above them as if they understood the turmoil threatening to explode. A desire to live raced through her veins as desperate as the escape from the overhanging rock to open ground. *I will not become like them.* How many times had she told herself that very thing over the years? She spurred her horse on behind Morgan's mare and shut out all thoughts but the flight to freedom.

Instantly, Jenkins's guards were alerted. Rifle fire split the air. Bullets whizzed past them; one whistled near her ear. *Tim, how can you be a part of this?* The shouts and curses of excited men filled the air. She heard Morgan's rifle and wondered where the bullet landed.

All too soon, the pounding of horse hooves broke the peacefulness of the afternoon. It sounded like drums signaling out a war cry. Morgan stole a look back, then urged his mare faster down the riverbank. Without hesitation, Casey raced behind. Instinct took over her actions and buried her fear. From the shouts behind them, many of the men pressed closer than safety allowed. She leaned against Stoney's neck and clung to the hope of the gang's horses tiring first.

Morgan's horse climbed steadily up a path of rock. He seemed to know exactly where it led. The thought bothered her, but she didn't have time to contemplate his knowledge except to recall that he'd once lived in these parts. The path wound around rock as perilous as the icy trail from the night before.

The steep ascent came to a sharp fork. Morgan stopped for a moment and took another look behind them. "Casey, you take the right, and I'll wind up to the left." He pointed to a high ridge on her side. "I'll meet you there. Listen for my rifle to signal them coming. With both of us firing from opposite directions, it should throw them long enough for us to get an edge."

"Did you get Jenkins?"

"Not sure."

She nodded and dug her heels into the horse's sides. What kind of man risked his life for a female outlaw—unless money ruled his good sense?

Her gelding picked its way to higher ground. She willed herself to stay calm, to collect her thoughts, and to stay alert.

Sometime, somehow during the last few hours, she'd begun to depend upon Morgan. She couldn't pinpoint when, but time would tell if she paid for it with her life. Could she be so tired that exhaustion had altered her good judgment?

With death nipping at her heels, Casey questioned if God really existed. Morgan certainly seemed to know more about the subject than she did. Her mother had trusted in God, and she died in peace. Many a time, Casey had tended to Jenkins's men when they lay dying. They became twisted, ugly distortions of men, clinging to life and afraid of the unknown. She didn't want to end up like that.

Morgan. . . She was afraid to trust him and afraid not to. He waved his rifle, then fired, and Casey returned the signal. Jenkins ascended the rocky path and neared the fork. *Morgan didn't get you.* She tried to catch a glimpse of Tim's face, but his wide-brimmed hat shielded his face. She didn't want him dead, but she feared he wouldn't hesitate to shoot her.

Morgan squeezed another shot, and it bounced off rock, causing Jenkins's horse to startle. The animal screamed in protest, then reared. The outlaw fell and rolled into a crevice. Like a snake. She raised her rifle and fired, but he disappeared in the shadows. The other men scattered as best they could in view of the narrow path. All Casey could do was fire into the lower rock walls. The outlaws rapidly returned their own fire, but she knew they could only speculate where she and Morgan were located.

"Move back." Tim's voice echoed to the men.

Casey held her breath. Jenkins must be hurt or better yet dead. She calculated how long before any of them headed up the steep path again on both sides of the fork.

Morgan motioned for her to climb higher. She urged her horse up to the meeting ground. As she guessed, the narrow trail wound around to a small rock clearing. Before she had a moment to consider their next move, a rifle shot pierced the air, then another. Morgan rode into the clearing slumped over his horse and fell. Crimson rivers oozed from his thigh and chest. One of the men had gotten to him before he reached the clearing.

Casey raced to Morgan's still body and jumped from her gelding. She didn't know where the few tears she shed came from. She'd seen enough hole-filled men. But the rare display of emotion slipped over her cheeks: blinding, stinging tears full of regret. She laid her ear against his chest and ignored the blood staining her face and hands. A faint heartbeat gave her hope. A weak moan escaped his lips. For certain, he barely held on to life. Her gaze swept around the clearing. No one. Where did the shots come from?

She yanked out an old shirt and a bottle of Tim's whiskey from her saddlebag. She'd taken it one night when he was mean drunk, never expecting she'd find a purpose for it.

Casey dropped to her knees beside Morgan and carefully opened his shirt. Bits of cloth lay embedded in the open flesh, and she carefully picked them out. The hole in his upper chest lay dangerously close to his heart, and the bullet had sunk deep. Tearing her old shirt into strips, she poured whiskey over the largest piece. She dabbed at the wound with the wet cloth and gasped at the profuse bleeding. All the while, she glanced about, looking for Jenkins and his men to overtake them.

Why couldn't you have been more careful? Her hands trembled as she worked. *You shouldn't have tangled with the likes of me in the first place. No matter what the reason.* She glanced at Stoney. This was her chance to get away. Morgan wasn't worth trying to figure out, and he lay dying anyway.

But she'd decided weeks ago to live a decent life. Leaving him might have been what the old Casey would do. . . .

She steadied herself, then hastily mixed a mud paste of dirt and whiskey and applied it to Morgan's chest. Ofttimes it stopped the bleeding.

"I couldn't have been worth this much trouble," she whispered. "Why didn't you listen to me in the cave? I was the bait, remember?"

His face grayed—a frightening indication of death. His breathing grew shallow, then faded to nothing. Again she placed her ear near his heart. A faint sound of life.

The echo of hoofbeats startled her. Her gaze darted from Morgan to the area around them for signs of Jenkins. She refused to leave the injured man, but helplessness gripped her just the same. Snatching up her rife, she prepared for the worst.

CHAPTER 4

"Casey!"

She held her breath and watched Tim ride up beside her. His hardened life had chiseled so many lines in his face. The once-boyish features were now rigid and drawn.

"Did you think you could really get away?" He swung his leg over the saddle and took long strides toward her. His pale blue eyes blazed, and his jaw tightened. It wouldn't be the first time he had hit her. He snatched her rifle from her hands.

"Tim, help me." She swallowed hard. He hated whining. "He's dying."

"I've already done more than you deserve." He grabbed her arm, but she jerked free. "And you owe me for all this trouble."

"Please." Heat flooded her face.

"Don't beg, 'cause I ain't listening."

Casey hated what the outlaw life had done to them. "I'm not begging. I'm asking for help."

He cursed. "I ain't helping you with nothin'. All you've ever done is cause me trouble since the day I lit out on my own and you followed."

She reached deep within her to find strength. "Then don't tell Jenkins where I am. Let me get out of your life for good."

"Jenkins ain't finding nobody. His leg's got a hole in it and broke. But I'm bringing you back." He stepped forward, and she moved just beyond his reach. "You're his woman whether you like it or not."

"Let me get away from all this. You won't ever have to deal with me again." *Just turn around and ride away.*

"Hey, Tim," a familiar voice echoed from the trail below. "Have you found 'em?"

She lifted her chin and captured his gaze.

"Tim," the man shouted again. "You got Casey and that feller she's with?"

He narrowed his eyes. Every part of him seethed with loathing. Moments ticked by. "No need. The two are gone." He tossed her rifle at her feet. Without a word, he mounted his horse and headed back down the rocky path.

Casey unclenched her fists, unaware that her fingertips had been digging into her palms. She took a deep breath and turned her attention to Morgan. The sight of torn flesh didn't cause her to cringe. She'd grown used to it from mending the knife wounds and bullet holes of Jenkins's men.

"I've seen worse," she whispered. Who was she trying to convince? Death had a stranglehold on the man.

She wrapped pieces of her shirt around his chest while blood dripped onto the dirt and rock beneath him. She'd learned about herbs and remedies from Franco, a Mexican who used to ride with Jenkins. He'd taught her well, even the language. Franco wanted her to leave the gang and go with him to Mexico, but Jenkins got wind of it and shot him. No matter. She didn't have any of those remedies with her now.

Morgan wouldn't live long without help. She'd risked this much, and she refused to let him die.

Once, he opened his eyes, and she saw a flicker of recognition. But a moan escaped his lips, and he drifted back into unconsciousness. Already the makeshift bandage seeped blood.

While Casey treated Morgan's leg, she neither heard a sound nor saw any movement from his limp form. The ashen color of his skin and his uneven breathing filled her with dread. What if the bullet had punctured his lung? No blood spilled from his mouth and nose. Good. Maybe there was hope.

We can't stay in this clearing.

She could only imagine the outlaw leader's rage when he learned of their escape. He wouldn't waste any time sending men after them or raising the reward. She'd caused Jenkins a lot of grief, and now he nursed a bullet wound and a broken leg. His misfortune might slow him down long enough for them to escape—if Morgan lived. But what about the others? They were a greedy lot and eager to land a stake in Jenkins's money.

Casey shuddered. With Jenkins laid up, that left Tim to lead the gang. How long would her brother stall them? She didn't want to think of another meeting with him. He'd change his mind for sure.

Stoney nuzzled up against her and rubbed his soft nose against her hand. She patted him gently. Strange how the horse's touch calmed her nerves.

She fretted over how to get Morgan to Vernal. Her gaze swung from the unconscious figure to his horse. She had no choice but to build a travois. Glancing about, she saw several broken limbs left from the heavy winter snows. It had to be enough, for she couldn't risk dragging up pieces of wood from below. Using Morgan's rope, she tied together a wooden frame between two trailing poles, then fixed his blanket on top. Tugging and pulling, she positioned the injured man onto the travois, certain she'd killed him in the process. At least in his current state, he couldn't feel the pain. She covered him with her blanket and used her rope to tie him securely.

They had miles to cover, and she didn't want to think about Morgan dying along the way. When they reached Vernal, Doc would tend to him. He boasted of a lucrative practice in mending the bullet- and knife-ravaged bodies of many men—good and bad.

Unfortunately, Jenkins also needed Doc to yank out a bullet and set his broken leg, and she sure didn't need the outlaws getting there first. The thought made her weak, dizzy.

❧❧❧

White-hot pain seared every inch of Morgan's body, as though he'd been branded and a fiery poker prodded at his open wounds. His mind swam in a haze that floated in and out. At first he fought the unconsciousness, but when his mind numbed, he didn't hurt. Didn't feel like screaming. Jenkins had succeeded in killing him. The outlaw had won. Only a breath of time stood between Morgan and God. He groaned with the intensity of the pain. Whatever dragged him along had hit something. More torture? He tried to focus on what he could remember. The unseen outlaw. . .the agony in his body. His mind cleared slightly, long enough for the torture to wield its sword into his chest and leg.

Oh God, release me from this pain. Take me to You.

Casey O'Hare. He hadn't cared what happened to her until he saw her courage in the face of death. All he wanted was a way to trap Jenkins. He'd banked on the outlaw agreeing to an exchange for her and stepping out in the open. The four-year search would finally come to an end, but the haunting in his soul told him he still wouldn't rest. Hate had driven him for so long that he wasn't sure he wanted the pursuit to end. He'd survived on revenge; without it, he had no reason to go on.

What happened instead staggered him. They'd been trapped, and when she offered to stay behind, he realized he couldn't send a woman to her death—not even an outlaw. How well he understood the price she'd pay for leaving Jenkins. No woman deserved his torture. Still, a nagging question needled him. Why had she stayed seven years with an outlaw gang?

Morgan struggled to talk. He had to warn her. . .convince her to leave him behind before one of the Jenkins gang caught up with them. . .pray for her. . . . He could do that. She needed help to start her life over; the kind of help only God could give.

Was she guilty of everything he'd read and heard? Didn't matter now. He was heading to his Maker. *Help her, I beg of You.*

Blackness swirled in his mind, and he faded into blissful darkness.

The trail to Vernal led straight south through dry canyons where nary a soul existed, not an easy path to venture with a badly wounded man. Time played an important part in whatever happened. If only she had medicinal herbs. She'd cleaned Morgan's torn flesh with whiskey, then bound the wounds tight. Nothing more she could do.

A moan from Morgan caused her to stop and check on him.

"Don't you dare die on me." Casey wanted to shake him. "You're a strong man. You can make it."

In a distant but not forgotten corner of her mind, she recalled the frail figure of her mother praying over Tim's fevered young body. He'd gotten pneumonia in the wet and cold while looking for their drunken pa. Ma had kneeled beside him for hours, and Tim had recovered.

Casey looked up into the late afternoon sky, a cloudless canopy of deepening blue. Tears flowed freely over her cheeks for a man who appeared more dead than alive. Could this be the reason why the two of them had met? Did Morgan sense his destiny?

Oh God, I haven't prayed since I was a little girl, and I don't know if You have any idea who I am, but if You're really there, would You listen for a moment? This man's dying because he tried to help me. I'm not sure what kind of man he is, but he's done an honorable thing by me. What I'm asking is for You to please spare him. I'd be greatly obliged. Amen. She paused. *And, God, no matter what happens—whether he lives or dies—I'm finished with the past. My ma taught me how to live right, and I know she's with You now. So if You don't mind, I'd like for You to please tell her I'm changing my ways. Maybe someday Tim will, too. Thank You, God, for listening.*

Casey wiped the wetness from her cheeks. Something about this man made her react like a female, a trait she'd long since ignored. She inspected the ropes that secured Morgan to the travois and thought about all the men she'd seen die. Glancing once more into the heavens, she sighed and hoped there lived a God who heard prayers.

Casey rode with a firm hold on the rope leading Morgan's horse. Her fingers grew numb from the grip; her palms laid raw against the rough rope. She'd tucked her gloves inside a saddlebag when they became too cumbersome each time she stopped to check on Morgan. The profuse bleeding and his uneven breathing told a grim story. He clung to life by a mere thread.

She attempted to toss aside a sickening thought. Had Morgan been betrayed by Jenkins? Was her opinion of the dying man based on fool's ground? Surely not. Surely she had not been blinded by the dream of freedom and the possibility of a man she could trust.

For most of the journey, Morgan remained unconscious. In rare moments, low, guttural sounds rose to his lips. At those times, she stopped to moisten his lips with water and wipe droplets of sweat from his face, sweat that came from the battle he was fighting. He resembled a mangled animal: bloody and helpless. She agonized if her efforts were killing him or helping him cling to life.

My fault. My fault.

Normally the solitude of the open country offered a reprieve from an angry world. This time she ignored it all and focused on the critical matters ahead. Finding Doc to care for Morgan stood foremost in her mind. Once Morgan was treated and the danger had passed, she'd leave Vernal for the sake of those two men. No one, absolutely no one, would ever risk his life for her again.

With the slow progress, she continuously focused her attention in all directions for signs of Jenkins's men. The threat of being discovered tarried in the air, and her head felt like someone kept hitting her with a closed fist. Sleep, she needed sleep.

Casey's mind raced with loathsome memories of Jenkins. She shook her head and refused to dwell on the past. In the beginning, Tim had tried to protect her; then he became like one of them. He'd come to her aid today, but he wouldn't again. She could feel it in her bones.

Her gaze rested on the figure behind her. She wanted to believe Morgan was different from Jenkins. The outlaw stood for all the dark and contemptuous parts of her past, while Morgan offered hope. But they could have been working together and something had gone wrong. She desperately craved for Morgan to be a good man, but she couldn't afford to be stupid. Stupid got you killed. She had to be ready for the truth, as ugly as it might be.

A faint cry from Morgan interrupted her thoughts. "Casey," he whispered.

She reined in Stoney and hurried to his aid. "Leave me," he said between gasps. "I'll. . .slow you down."

"No, sir. We're in this together. Jenkins was shot, and his leg's broke. So we have a head start. We're okay for now, and besides, I've got to get you to a doctor."

He mouthed the word. "Vernal?"

"Yes, and we're nearly there."

It took several long moments for him to form his words. More beads of sweat rolled down his face. She brushed them away with her fingertips. "Won't make it. . . . Leave me."

"No." She checked the blood-soaked bandages and noted his colorless face in the evening shadows. "You just hush and save your strength."

She mounted her horse, and Stoney trudged ahead. Soon darkness wrapped its cloak around them and concealed the pair from the daggers of night. A clear sky filled with glimmering stars, and a slice of moon offered a silver path. Every step inched them closer to safety.

In the wee hours of the morning, the two arrived in Vernal. The town resounded with drunken men and laughter, and the crack of rifle fire sparked a wave of anxiety. Were they waiting at Doc's, hiding in the blackness and waiting for her to appear? She dismounted and cautiously led the horses in the hope that one of Jenkins's men wouldn't emerge from the faceless voices.

Only Morgan's needs kept her planting one foot in front of the other. He was the driving force that pushed her on past the extreme exhaustion and hunger warring against her body. Each time she felt like giving in to fatigue, she recalled the deeds of the injured man tied to the travois. And her mind wrestled with the whole matter again.

She slipped within the shadows of the main street and pulled both mounts through a pathway wide enough for a wagon. It turned sharply to the left and down a dark, narrow street to Doc's house. Rifle in hand, cocked and ready, she peered around for one of Jenkins's gang, the men she knew by name and deed.

Standing motionless, Casey studied the small frame house belonging to Doc. When reasonably assured no one shared the surroundings, she mounted the steps to the porch, silently cursing their creaking. She rapped lightly, then harder when Doc didn't answer. Only silence greeted her. She kicked the door, partly in anger and partly in frustration. A bellowing voice responded.

"I've got a badly injured man." She stared into the darkness behind her and wondered if another pair of ears heard her plea. Her voice lowered. "He's been shot in the chest and lost a lot of blood."

Doc cleared his throat. "He's most likely dead."

"Doc, this is Casey O'Hare. Please, open up." Not prone to emotion, she knew any more words were locked in her throat. She took a breath. "I don't think this man is an outlaw. He got hurt trying to help me."

"All right," Doc said. "The whole town has heard how you left Jenkins."

She swung around, expecting the click of a trigger and a bullet etched with her name on it. In the next instant, she fought the urge to blow a hole through the door. "Are you going to open up or not?"

"Oh, I guess I'll see what I can do. Bring him in."

Casey looked back at the sad remains of Morgan. "I need you to give me a hand. I've got him tied to a travois."

She heard Doc utter a long string of complaints—"How is a man supposed to get any sleep," and "I'm not about to get myself killed over any outlaw dispute." The latch lifted. He towered in the doorway and lifted high a kerosene lantern.

Barefoot and bare chested with suspenders holding up loose-fitting trousers, Doc presented a less than welcoming figure. His shoulder span reminded her of a grizzly. For certain, his size alone caused most men to think twice about crossing him.

Doc cut Morgan from the wooden frame and lifted him into his arms. "Best hide those horses in the shed behind my stable," he said over his shoulder. "It's empty right now, but there's extra feed and water. I wouldn't want any of Jenkins's men finding your horses." He handed her the lantern. "Get on out of here. I've got plenty of work to do. This man is more dead than alive." His voice thundered, but that was Doc's way.

"One of Jenkins's men may be here to fetch you." She hoped the warning didn't change his decision to treat Morgan. "Jenkins's leg's broke, and he's been shot."

Doc nodded and disappeared into the small house. She stared after him a good bit before turning her attention to the horses. The animals needed to be fed and rubbed down. Besides, what could she do for Morgan?

Her heart plummeted with the realization of just how quickly Jenkins could find them. In one fleeting breath, she considered running, but her commitment to the injured man robbed her normal way of thinking. She couldn't leave him with Doc, not just yet. For now, she must stay in Vernal until Morgan took a turn for the best, or she learned he was one of them, or he died. The not knowing clawed at her heart.

Morgan had mentioned Vernal when talking about his family, said he had a few friends there but didn't say what kind. The decent folk stayed off by themselves. They avoided the wanted men and didn't deal with them unless forced to. Past emotions, past deeds, and a yearning for a clear conscience stopped her from contemplating that the injured man might walk among the corrupt. She wanted to believe he had the same values as she yearned to find. Then again, she'd never learn the truth if he died.

CHAPTER 5

Casey stole into the bedroom where Doc labored over Morgan. A yellow glow from a lantern lit up the blood-soaked cloths on both sides of Morgan's chest, and a pan on the floor held another blood-soaked cloth. The harsh, acidic smell of carbolic spray met her nostrils and burned her eyes. The odor was characteristic of Doc. A few years back, she'd heard him say it kept his instruments clean and free from dirt that could cause infection. She'd seen a few other doctors who worked in filth. They said cleaning everything was a waste of time and money, but they lost a lot more of their patients than Doc ever did.

"Did you wash up?" A sable and silver beard covered Doc's face, and the same color of coarse hair sprouted from every exposed portion of his body. He did look and sound like a grizzly.

"Yes, sir."

"Hold this lantern over him," Doc said. "He's lost too much blood, girl, and I still need to yank out that bullet."

She snatched up the light. Morgan looked bad, really bad. She thought he must be dead, but Doc wouldn't be working so hard if he was.

Doc's huge fingers wrapped around a two-pronged instrument.

"I want that lantern right over the hole." He adjusted the light to suit him, then dug through the raw flesh. A few moments later, he released a heavy sigh and pulled out a bloody piece of lead. It landed with a *ping* in a pan. He proceeded to stitch up Morgan's chest and then bandaged it. The process intrigued her, but doctoring always had. Doc didn't speak or lift his gaze until he finished.

"What do you know about this man?" He picked up the blood-soaked instruments and tossed them into the pan with the bullet. "You can set that lantern on my dresser."

"Not much." She obliged him, then studied Doc's face. "He was after Jenkins, but he ended up saving my life. You know him, don't you?"

"I might." He wiped his hands on a clean cloth. "In my profession, it's best not to offer much information. Could prove dangerous."

Casey stared into Morgan's pale face. "It's hard to trust anyone, Doc, and when you do, well, someone gets hurt." She hesitated. "Is he going to make it?"

Doc picked up the pan and walked into the next room, where he lifted a hot kettle of water from the stove and poured it over the instruments. "Hard to say, Casey. He's strong and a fighter, but it'll take several hours before we know. Right now, both of you need to get some sleep. There's nothing more you or I can do for him but wait."

"Jenkins might be here anytime about his bad leg."

Lines creased Doc's brow. "You aren't going to do anyone any good in your condition. Tomorrow morning we'll work out this mess." He took another clean cloth and dipped it into a bucket of water. Wiping her cheek, he shook his head. "I'm not looking at this blood a moment longer. At first I thought it might be yours." He swiped at the other cheek. "I'd like to offer you better sleeping quarters than the floor, but he has my extra bed. If Jenkins does need my attention, I'll have the other room free."

She rinsed and dried her hands. The calluses stained from dirt and blood stared back at her. Some things never came clean. "The floor is just fine, Doc. Believe me, I'm just grateful for what you've done. Helping me with him and knowing Jenkins is after us puts you in a real nasty position."

"I've been there before." For the first time, he smiled. "Jenkins isn't going to bother me. If he does, who's left to piece together the rotten bunch around here?"

She liked Doc. The first time she'd met him, nearly three years ago, one of Jenkins's men had gotten shot. The fellow died while Doc tried to remove a bullet. She remembered the sweat dripping from his forehead as he worked to save the man's life. The droplets hadn't been from fear of the outlaw leader but from the intense effort to keep the man alive. Doc had impressed her as a man of honor and respect, something she craved even then.

"I've heard rumors." He filled the kettle with fresh water from a bucket. "And I wish you luck. You've a good head on your shoulders and an obvious sense of right and wrong. If you didn't, you wouldn't be trying to get away." He studied her face in the shadows. "You aren't having a baby, are you?"

The thought revolted her. "No, Doc."

"Just needed to make sure."

She understood. If she carried the outlaw's baby, Jenkins wouldn't kill her. If a baby wasn't his, he'd peel the flesh from her body.

Casey watched Doc open the cookstove, stir the embers, and add firewood. With his massive shoulders and arms, his efforts looked like child's play.

"I'll make it through this." She leaned against the doorway. "I don't have much choice. Jenkins will kill me, given the first opportunity."

"I thought he only wanted you back."

"Maybe at first. I imagine the thought of me getting away has him powerful mad."

He slammed the top of the stove, and the sound startled her, reminding her of gunfire.

"Too bad Morgan didn't finish him off for you," Doc said as he headed into Morgan's room.

Her gaze flew to his back. "I didn't tell you his name. In fact, I wondered if he'd given me his real one. Guess you know more about him than I do."

He turned and eyed her curiously. "Maybe so. I haven't seen him in quite a spell. Knew his folks well. That man lying in there is a whole sight better than the likes of Jenkins and his bunch. He comes from a good family—educated, churchgoin' folk." He shook his head. "Right now, I wish I could do more for him. I tell you this. He's one of the finest men I've ever known."

Exhaustion tore through her, but she craved to hear more. "What else can you tell me?"

He scratched his bearded cheek. "Ah, I'll let him tell you when he's feeling better." His words rang with finality. "Right now, you come with me." He headed into the room where Morgan lay, and she followed like a child who knew better than to disobey. He pulled out two neatly folded quilts from a leather-strapped trunk.

Most likely somebody's payment for his doctoring. Unfortunately, she didn't have any money and nothing to give in trade. Both thoughts worried her.

Doc fashioned a pallet on the floor beside the bed. She couldn't remember feeling so tired, but she ought to be sitting by Morgan's side and tending him. She glanced up at Doc as he examined the bandages, clean and unstained with blood.

"If you don't lie down and get some rest, I'm going to have two patients." Doc's tone would have caused the worst of men to take notice. "The circles under your eyes could bury a man."

She merely nodded, too weary to respond. Suddenly the room

began to spin, and the horrible pounding in her head nearly blinded her. In one stride, Doc caught her before she tumbled to the floor.

Through the haziness clouding her mind, she sensed Doc tugging at her boots. She wanted to focus on his previous words about Morgan. *What did he say? Morgan is one of the finest men he's ever known?*

Casey woke with stinging, sleep-robbed eyes. Groggy and disoriented, she stretched sore muscles and pieced together the events of her last waking hours. Light filtered in through the closed window blinds. Panic raced through her. What time was it?

She rose slowly from the floor, dizzy with the telltale signs of extreme hunger and the weakness accompanying it. She grabbed the iron bedpost and battled a surge of blackness. Morgan, what had happened to him? She had to make sure he was still alive.

She blinked away her mind's confusion and focused on the man's face. He seemed to be asleep, and his coloring looked better. His forehead felt cool. Morgan had survived the night.

She searched the room for her boots. Usually she slept fully clothed, a habit formed years ago to protect herself from Jenkins and the other outlaws who craved women like babies craved milk. Casey spied her boots at the foot of the bed. *Doc.*

The tantalizing smell of food tugged at her stomach. She listened at the door, and when silence greeted her, she slowly opened it. The aroma of eggs, biscuits, potatoes, fried ham, and real coffee nearly made her crazy. Her attention focused on a plate on the cookstove, heaped high with the food. Beside it sat a coffeepot and a full mug of steaming coffee, certainly not the dirt-tasting brew she often made by the fire.

Doc paused from reading a newspaper at the table. In the daylight, he didn't look nearly as menacing, but his huge frame spilled over the chair. "I heard you get up. The food and coffee are hot and ready. Are you rested?"

"Yes, sir, and I'm starved." She smiled. "Thanks. I feel so much better."

"There's water in the basin, and any other business can be taken care of out back." He frowned. "You're skinnier than a fence post."

"I know, Doc. I'll take care of myself real soon. What about Morgan? How's he doing?"

"He's holding his own, and that's a good sign. The crucial hours have passed." He folded his newspaper and stood from the chair. "I've given him something to make him sleep for a couple more hours."

"I appreciate everything you've done. I couldn't begin to list it all."

Doc shook his head. "Don't you go bawlin' on me. It's my job to heal, and I'm glad I could help. Now go take care of things so you can eat. You're as white as Morgan. And there's plenty more food if that doesn't fill you up."

She snatched up her hat from a hook near the front door and twisted her hair up underneath it. She tucked in each strand, then lowered the brim over her eyes. As she strode past the cookstove, she grabbed a biscuit and bit into it hungrily. Never had anything tasted so fine.

<hr />

Casey positioned her jeans and shirt over the cookstove and patted them impatiently. They needed to dry faster. One small bloodstain refused to fade from her shirt; a grim reminder of the preceding day. She yanked on the piece of rope holding up Doc's pants around her waist, thinking she'd drown in his clothes. The amount she'd rolled up at the ankles could have made her a dress—not that she owned any.

My, she felt good with hot food in her stomach and a clean body from a hot bath—it felt like the sun beating down warm after a cold spell. Morgan still slept, but Doc said he was holding on well.

She glanced about the room for signs of Morgan's or her belongings. Earlier she'd removed her hat from the hook near the front door and placed it in the bedroom where Morgan slept. Only the drying clothes remained in view.

Soon she must make plans to leave Vernal. When Morgan woke and she saw his recovery, she'd be gone. Without any money, she wondered how she'd pay for the doctoring and medicine. Her only choice was to send it once she found work.

Casey slipped into a huge rocker near the stove and drew her knees up to her chest. It must have been constructed especially for Doc, because the size of it swallowed her up. Closing her eyes, she ran her fingers through damp hair in an effort to speed up its drying.

"You're quiet." Doc rubbed his stubbly chin.

"Oh, I'm just thinking." A smile for Doc came easily. If only Tim had half this man's qualities, then maybe he'd leave Jenkins, too.

"About what, may I ask?"

"Um, nothing in particular, mostly thinking about life. Right this minute I want to believe I'm safe. Morgan's still alive. Jenkins isn't at your door. I'm fed and clean. Looks to me like everything is just fine." She nodded her head.

"Doesn't take much to please you." he said. "If it didn't mean facing outlaws, I'd ask you to stay. Marry you up. Maybe I could put some meat on your bones."

"Make me fat and sassy?" Casey closed her eyes and leaned back against the rocker. "I think you just want someone to cook and clean for you."

"And keep me company and probably do a little nursing when all of the chores are done." Doc chuckled.

She waved her arms in mock ridicule of his suggestion. "Chores?

I don't do chores. Besides, I haven't made a bed in years."

"Then what do you do?" He leaned forward on his chair, obviously enjoying their bantering.

"I'm always on the run or waiting to be on the run." *But your offer is tempting, too tempting.*

"Guess I could be a traveling doctor. We'd make quite a pair, Miss Casey."

"Yes, indeed we would." She captured the warm glow of his soft brown eyes. She could stay here, but it wouldn't be fair to Doc. A woman needed to love a man before she married him. "Doc, you saved Morgan's life. He'd be dead by now if it wasn't for you." She poked her finger through a cinder hole in the knee of the trousers. "But I'm not sure exactly how I can pay the bill. I can't stick around and work for you with Jenkins after me."

"Did I ask for money? As I recall, I asked you to hold the lantern." He folded his arms across his barrel chest. "Besides, there aren't any charges."

"You can't make a living treating folks for free. And I don't believe in charity."

"Doctoring is my job, my life. If I'd gone into this to make money, I'd be in a different part of the country, not Vernal."

Casey laughed as she looked into his round face. "I promise I'll send you money as soon as I get work, but I've got to get out of here real soon."

"You're not rested enough." He wagged his thick finger at her, as though the little girl in her should cower at his demands. "You'll be sick and have no one to take care of you."

"I'll be fine." She massaged the back of her neck. "As soon as Morgan wakes up and I know he's out of danger, I'm leaving."

Doc stood and paced the floor. "I don't suppose there's any use in arguing with you. I declare, you are the most stubborn woman I've ever met. Makes me want to tie you up." He towered over her, and she grinned. "If you're bent on leaving, there's got to be a way I can help."

Casey shook her head. "Thanks, but I'll be just fine." A thought struck her. "Yes, there is something."

He raised a brow.

"A Bible, Doc. Do you have a Bible?"

He eyed her strangely. "Well, as a matter of fact, I do. What do you want with it?"

"To read. I want to read it." Her own words startled her. With her limited knowledge of the Good Book, she knew God had answered her prayers about Morgan. Maybe there were a few other things she needed to know.

A wry smile spread over his ample cheeks. "Let me fetch it for you." He disappeared into the bedroom where Morgan lay and returned with a worn, black leather book. With his huge hand, he wiped the dust from the cover as though the contents were pure gold. "This belonged to my father. I reckon I don't get it out enough."

She reached for it with both hands and carefully laid it in her lap. "Thanks. I'll be real careful." She ran her fingers over the rough grain of the binding. A bit of fear assaulted her. She understood her life had not been as this book directed. Slowly she opened it and gingerly leafed past the pages of personal information about Doc's family until she found the listing of all the Old and New Testament books. Confused, she glanced up into his face. "Where should I begin? My ma used to read stories to me and Tim before she got sick and lost her eyesight. I remember her telling us about three men in a lion's den, baby Jesus, and a blind man getting healed."

Doc took in a deep breath. "I believe it was Daniel in the lion's den and three men in a fiery furnace. But anyway, it depends on what you're looking for."

"I want to be certain God is really there, or if we're on our own from the day we're born to the day we die."

"What are your feelings about God right now, this very minute?" Doc kneeled on the floor beside the rocker. The big man looked humble, the sound of his voice solemn.

"I'm not sure. Maybe I want to believe because I'm so miserable with my life and so scared about the future. I remember when Morgan got shot, I asked God to spare him. I told Him I wanted to change, and I planned to live right whether Morgan lived or not. Now he's doing much better, and I'm grateful. I want to trust and believe like my ma, but I don't have any idea where to begin."

Doc nodded and lifted the Bible from her lap. "I suppose you could start at the beginning with the creation. Hmm, that would probably be the best. Yes, read the book of Genesis, then go to the first book in the New Testament called Matthew."

"What's this all about?"

He licked his forefinger and turned the pages. "I'm no preacher, but the Old Testament is full of trustworthy accounts about how God helped the Jewish people. He blessed them when they were obedient and punished them when they weren't. They were His chosen people, His children. All the way through the Old Testament, He speaks about a man sent from God who would save the people from their sins. In Matthew," he pointed at the book, "Jesus is born. He was God's Son."

"So is the New Testament all about Jesus?"

"Yes, His life, His teachings, and those who followed Him."

"Like the stories I remember my ma telling."

"I imagine so."

"What happened to this Jesus?" she asked. "Ma took sick about the time I should have been paying attention, and I couldn't tell whether she was serious or the fever made her talk strange."

"His own people killed Him."

"Why?" It made no sense that folks would kill someone who came to help. "Didn't God send Him?"

"Yes, but they didn't like what Jesus said. Those folks chose to keep living wrong rather than change."

"Sounds like a number of men I know." She stared at the Bible in his hands and eased her feet to the floor. Curiosity seemed to get the best of her. "Doc, how did you learn so much about God?"

He patted her shoulder and placed the Bible in her lap. "My father was a circuit ridin' preacher, and a good one. He devoted his whole life to telling folks about the Lord. In fact, he didn't take care of himself. Took sick when I was sixteen years old and died. I blamed God and decided I wanted to heal people's bodies, not their souls. Funny thing, you can't do one without the other."

With those words, her respect for Doc grew another notch. "How long did it take for you to figure it all out?"

"Too long." He laughed and stuck his thumbs in his suspenders. "Still don't have all the answers. You go ahead and read. I'm going to check on our patient."

She wanted to follow, but he'd let her know when Morgan awoke. Settling back into the rocker, she thought about Doc's life—believing in God and practicing medicine in a town full of lawless men. He had a special kind of faith, the kind she desperately wanted. She wondered what God thought about outlaws and all the things she'd done. Most likely He didn't have much use for her, but she'd like to give it a try. Maybe this Bible had a list of what she was supposed to do. And she could get started right away on doing good things for folks instead of being one of those who hurt them.

"Casey," Doc called from the other room. "You'd best step in here."

CHAPTER 6

A chill raced up Casey's spine. She closed Doc's Bible and once more ran her fingers across the rough binding. She'd viewed dead men before, men she'd grown to care for, and she could do it again. Rising to her feet, she laid the Bible on the chair.

"Casey." Doc's tone was urgent.

"I'm coming." She hated her reaction to Morgan, a man she barely knew. He even admitted to using her. But the bullets in his body spoke of something else. Only one other man had ever made her feel that way, and he was dead.

Her boots clicked across the wooden floor to Doc's side. He smiled. "Morgan wants to talk to you."

His eyes were open, but his pallor shook her senses as though she *did* look into the face of a dead man.

"You're alive." She wanted to laugh and cry at the same time.

His eyelids fluttered, but he managed a slight grin. "You crazy girl. . . . How did you get me here?"

She wondered where he found the strength to speak. "Made a travois and tied you to it. I've done easier things, but I was too stubborn to let you die."

He wet his lips. "I wanted. . .to."

"Oh, I remember." Her whole body relaxed. "You begged me to leave you."

A twinge of pain swept across his face, and he gasped at its severity. "I. . .bet I did. I—I feel like I fell over a cliff and bounced all the way down."

Casey touched her finger to his lips. "Please, you're too weak to waste your time on words. Rest, and do what Doc says."

"She's right." Doc's gruffness layered every word. "I'm going to let Casey spoon-feed you some clear soup and have you take a dose of laudanum, but understand it's gonna take time to get you back on your feet again. You're one lucky—"

A pounding at the door stopped Doc's orders in midair. Without a word, Casey hurried into the kitchen. Her body quivered as she snatched up her drying clothes and coffee mug before scurrying back into the room with Morgan. She stuffed the items, along with her rifle, under the bed. In seconds, she had her gun belt strapped to her waist and the Colt in her hand. Doc took the bowl of broth and eased the door shut. Shadows closed in around her. Again the hammering against the door thundered in her ears, and she heard a haunting voice.

"Open up, Doc."

Her heart hammered against her chest until she feared Tim might hear.

She stole across the room and waited. The idea of shooting her own brother sickened her, but she could threaten.

Her gaze flew to Morgan, who peered at her through the narrowed slits of his eyes. Tim would pump one bullet after another into him. She stepped across the room and covered his head.

"Doc, if you're in there, open up."

"Who's there?" Doc asked, and Casey realized he searched for any traces of what might have been left behind.

"Tim O'Hare."

"What's the problem?"

The front door creaked open.

"Jenkins got a bullet in his leg, and it's busted. The bone's sticking out. Hurting him powerful bad." Tim sounded tired, and that meant a short temper.

"Where is he?"

"Outside of town, about two hours' ride from here. I tried bringing him in, but he's carrying on like a madman."

The familiar agitation in her brother's words caused her to shudder. He couldn't be trusted when he was riled.

"Just let me get my bag and pack a few things."

"Make it fast. I'm tired of hearing Jenkins bellyache."

Doc must have lifted his black medical bag onto the table. From the sound of clinking bottles, she assumed he was rummaging through its contents.

"I have splints and bandages, but I need to get extra laudanum from my bedroom," he said.

Casey cringed at the thought of the painkiller on Doc's dresser. Normally it would be in the other room where he treated folks. Would Tim suspect anything? She backed behind the door. Her hand wrapped around the handle of the Colt. Odd how something she knew so well could be what she despised the most. Her palm rested on the butt, worn by use.

Doc opened the door, and Tim's tall silhouette cast an eerie shadow across the wooden planks. Even in the dimly lit room, Morgan's body could be clearly seen.

"Who's your patient, Doc?" Tim asked.

"She isn't a patient. I do have a personal life."

"Well, I'll be." Tim said with a heavy dose of sarcasm. "Excuse me, ma'am."

Doc rummaged through the medicinal items on his dresser. "I'll be back in a few hours, honey." He leaned over Morgan's covered head and planted a kiss atop the blanket, then turned to Tim. "Does Jenkins appear to have an infection?"

He shook his head. "Cut real bad, but nothing festerin'. Say, have you seen my sister?"

"Casey? Why? Did you send her to fetch me?"

"Naw. She lit out and is traveling with some man. He got himself hurt, so I figured they'd have headed here." Tim leaned on one leg. How well she knew the stance. " 'Course he might have died."

"True. Check the undertaker or the saloons. I heard quite a bit of commotion last night." Doc walked toward the open door. "I need to saddle up my horse."

Casey held her breath. She recalled Doc's earlier request to stable her and Morgan's horses in an empty shed across the way. *Thank you.*

The front door squeaked shut with the same grating irritation as when it opened. A moment later, the only sound came from a clock ticking on the dresser. Time. Doc had bought her time.

As much as she wanted to leave Vernal, Morgan needed tending until Doc returned. After latching the front door, Casey carried the rocker from the kitchen to Morgan's bedside and then gently uncovered his head. She contemplated whether or not to light the kerosene lamp. After much deliberation, she set a faintly lit lamp on the floor beside the bed and hoped no one could see the light through the shade covering the single window. Wrapping a quilt around her shoulders, she eased into the rocker and watched Morgan's face for signs of distress.

The longer she sat, the wearier she became. Sore tired, she labeled it. Every part of her body ached, even after the hours she'd slept the previous night. Sometimes she thought she could sleep for days. But not now.

I need to sort things out. . .figure out where to go, what to do.

No matter how she looked at the situation, staying in Vernal invited trouble. Each moment she lingered became a death threat for Morgan and Doc. The truth, plain and simple, echoed silently throughout the room. She'd seen enough men die in her day, and she vowed not one more grave would be dug for her sake. She knew little about Morgan, but he'd earned her respect. She'd gone over these things before. No point wasting breath to figure another way out of this mess or the answers to the questions about Morgan.

Casey touched his forehead. No fever. He rested so easily, peacefully. A smile tugged at her lips. She eased back into the rocker and laid the quilt over her lap. Soon her body gave in to sleep.

The next morning at daybreak, Casey awoke with a start. Her intentions of keeping a vigil for Morgan had vanished when she'd succumbed to sleep. Standing, she opened the bedroom door to let in a shaft of early morning light. Doc snored in the next room.

Quietly, she placed wood in the cookstove and made coffee. Before the town came to life, she'd be gone. A short while later, she sat in the rocker beside Morgan's bed and nursed a hot cup of coffee. A bit of sadness settled on her at the thought of leaving Morgan and Doc. She shook her head. Nonsense notions.

Casey studied Morgan's bearded face while he slept. Many a lonely night lay ahead when she would want to recall his every line and feature. Amber hair hung to his shoulders, with a touch of curl to the ends that softened his rugged looks. Wiry, knotted sideburns were trimmed somewhat even, as though he disciplined himself to keep a part of civilization alive. Tightly twisted eyebrows capped his deep-set eyes, which now sank back into his head, leaving a cavernous pit below them. No matter that they were closed; she'd always remember the intensity of his turquoise eyes.

"Those circles could bury a man." Now she knew what Doc meant.

She wanted to stroke Morgan's cheek, to feel the coolness of his skin just once before he opened his eyes. Yet how would she explain her foolishness if he awoke? Doc praised him as a good man, but those words didn't necessarily mean Morgan was good for her.

Casey turned and cautiously slipped her fingers through the side of the window shade to view the outside world. The sun's announcement of morning cast an orange tint to the area around her—not quite real, as though she could relax for a moment. Perhaps the town looked more ordinary than sinister, without any signs of lawless men. Of course, all of them were sleeping away the previous night's activities. She heard a stirring and glanced back to see Morgan watching her.

"What's. . .going on?" he asked.

"Nothing. It's quiet out there." She stepped closer to his side.

"Too bad we're hiding. We could lift the shades and let in some light."

"I have a feeling most of Doc's patients are lying low from somebody."

"True, but this room is like a tomb."

"A safe cave," she said.

He attempted to move his arms and groaned.

"Lie still, or you'll start bleeding." Casey set her coffee on the dresser and adjusted the blanket around his neck.

When he tried to raise his arms again, she pinned them to his side. "Don't try to move, or I'll tie you to this bed."

"I think you tried that before."

"And I managed just fine, didn't I?"

He glared up at her. "Tough lady, aren't you?"

"Don't rile me. This lady packs a gun."

"And I'm in no shape to fight." He took a labored breath. "Has Doc said how long I'll be laid up?"

She crossed her arms. "You won't like this. He told me yesterday that it'll take at least a month."

"A month. He's crazy. I have things to do." He started to lift himself up again, but his face registered a stab of pain.

Her temper flared like a spark took to kindling. "You nearly died, and the hole in your chest is going to take awhile to heal. Doc doesn't need to stitch you up again, and I won't be here to nurse you."

"What do you mean?"

"I have to leave before the morning's out. It's only a matter of time before Jenkins catches up with me. He's already got men out looking. Don't imagine he'd be real happy with Doc tending to you or hiding me. The longer I stay here, the more dangerous it is for both of you." She turned her attention to the outside, fully suspecting Jenkins's men to be armed and keeping a watchful eye on Doc's house. *I'm so tired of this.*

"Use your head, girl. You can't ride out alone. As soon as I'm able, we'll go together."

She shook her head and stubbornly kept her focus on the empty street. Tears threatened to spill over her cheeks, but she swallowed them instead. Tears were for weak females, not hardened women. "I've made up my mind."

"What can I say to change it?"

"Nothing."

"I don't want to lose you to Jenkins's vengeance." He coughed, and she spun around to see if there was blood. She saw nothing.

An awkward silence rose between them, and she turned back to the window. *If only I could believe you. I must be more of a fool than I thought.* "There'll be plenty of opportunities for you to find Jenkins.

Besides, looks like you slowed him down for quite a spell."

"I did get him."

She nodded. "One of his legs is broke and has a hole in it. You can catch him all by yourself. Don't need me at all. Both of you will be getting around about the same time."

"Jenkins isn't what I'm afraid of losing."

"You're not making sense."

"Of course I am, and you know it."

"I won't risk your life or anyone's ever again," she said. "The past is over. I left it in the mountains. Staying here with you and Doc is clearly selfish."

"Look at me and not that blasted street." For a weak man, Morgan had no problem spitting out his words. "Even if I asked you to stay with me?"

She didn't dare turn around. "It's impossible. In fact, it's stupid."

"Where are you heading? Jenkins might have the roads blocked."

She paced the length of his bed. Only a fool would share such plans. "I don't know."

"Arizona, Mexico, California?"

Casey met his dour temperament with all of the determination she could muster. "If I did know, I'd keep it to myself. It's best we part and you not know my whereabouts."

"That is the most illogical statement I've ever heard." Morgan's pale face reddened.

Their disagreement built a wall between them. At a loss for words, she stared emotionlessly above his head, a trait she'd practiced for years. *Don't feel. Soon you'll forget.*

"You're being bullheaded about this. I'll not let you leave without me! Do you understand?" Morgan attempted to pull up from the pillow, but instead he gasped for air.

She forced herself not to tend to him. "I'm leaving, and nothing you can say or do will stop me." Although she meant the words to sound sharp, tenderness laced them like a fine lady's handkerchief against rough, calloused skin.

"Your stubbornness is going to get you killed," he managed to say through clenched teeth. "Or worse."

"There's nothing worse than being killed." She stepped back. Touching him battled with her good sense.

"Yes, there is. As a woman, you know exactly what I mean."

She chose not to answer him until she won control over her emotions. "Morgan, you can heal without me. I'd just get jumpy and irritable over every little noise." She tapped her fingers on the iron bed frame.

The lines deepened across his brow. Any other man would have passed out with the arguing. "How many men can you trust before you get to where you're going?"

"Probably none."

"So who's going to help you?"

"I don't need anyone."

Neither of them spoke for several long moments. "How will I know if you're all right?" His tone softened as though he'd accepted her plans.

She took a deep breath. "I need to write Doc about some things. He'll let you know I'm all right. Please rest, and I'll wake you before I leave."

"That's real nice of you, Casey. Me and Doc will have a party."

She shoved aside her fragile feelings and left him.

"I'm not done talking yet."

She kept right on walking. If she stopped, she'd lose sight of what really mattered. Odds were she'd never see him again anyway. Earlier that morning she'd mentally pieced together a southern route to Robber's Roost. From there, she'd decide which way to go.

As soon as she readied her gelding, Doc joined her. "Jenkins was mad and drunk last night. By the time I set his leg and dug out that bullet, he was madder and drunker. He upped the reward on you, then dared the rest of his gang to go after it. None of his men are going to waste any time getting here," Doc said. "Your leaving is against my better judgment, but you face more danger by staying in Vernal. You be careful." Doc yanked on the girth. "I'll be praying for God to guide and protect you. Run on in and tell Morgan good-bye."

Inside the house, she took one last glance at the tidy kitchen, the clean table, and the absence of a woman. She remembered Doc's offer to marry her. He would, too. She didn't doubt it for a minute, but the idea of a man putting up with her past was too much for her to think on.

At the sight of Morgan sleeping, she considered leaving without saying good-bye. She hesitated, then touched his shoulder. As he slowly opened his eyes, she smiled with years of regret tugging at her heart. Uncomfortable with their farewell, she stood with her hands behind her back, her revolvers strapped to her hips.

"You're much prettier when you smile." Morgan managed a weak grin.

"I'm leaving now."

"What about us?" he asked. "Do you want to walk away from what started in the mountains?"

"I'm getting away from Jenkins. No need to worry about me." She shifted from one foot to another.

"You're escaping from him, but are you also running from me? Believe me, I know there's something between us, Casey. And you can't deny it, either."

She swallowed hard. Something in the back of her mind shouted bounty hunter. It made sense, too. "Don't do this. Don't confuse me." She took a step back toward the door. "I'm going to forget about you.

My life is heading in a different direction, and I'm doing what I feel is right for everyone."

"What is good and right is the two of us finding out what happened in the mountains." His words were stronger, or perhaps his returning strength bolted behind them.

She shook her head. "You must be getting a fever, 'cause you're talking out of your head. When you're better, you'll see I've made the right decision. I haven't forgotten what you did for me or that you entered my camp to use me for bait. It won't take long for you to remember those motives and what drove you into the mountains in the first place." Her words ended abruptly, for Doc stepped in from the outside. "Good-bye, Morgan."

"God be with you" echoed in her ears.

CHAPTER 7

At the sound of Casey's voice, Stoney tossed his head and responded like an old friend. An extra leather pouch had been slung over her full saddlebags. In fact, nothing else could be stuffed inside any of them.

"What did you put in my bags?" She patted the bulges.

"Provisions." Doc looped his fingers inside his suspenders.

"I don't have the money to pay for this. Doc, I can't even pay for Morgan's care, and now you give me more things?"

He offered a wry smile. "No need to worry. Tim took care of it."

"Tim?" Casey's eyes widened, and she took in the area around her.

"Yeah, he said he owed you. He told me a story about you not taking money from the jobs they did." Doc stroked the gelding's neck as though Tim's words were common knowledge.

"True. And I can't take this, either. He stole the money to buy these provisions." She started to lift the bags from the saddle, but Doc stopped her.

"Best you have the provisions to survive than Tim to squander it on women and gambling. A good bit of the money is left, and I placed it in the saddlebag on the bottom, left side."

"Keep the money for Morgan's care."

"And have Tim O'Hare after me? I'm smarter than that, sweet lady." He touched her shoulder. "I also put a small gift in the top saddlebag."

"From you?" Apprehension settled upon her. She despised being indebted to anyone.

"It's an extra Bible. A rancher gave it to me for birthing a baby. I don't need two."

Overwhelmed, she hugged the big man. "Thank you. I'll take good care of it. You have my word." She swung up into the saddle. A part of her wanted to stay and face Jenkins. It would be over then. But she didn't have the guts to shoot it out with him. She'd rather learn what the Bible said about such things.

Casey grasped Doc's huge hand. "I'll miss you." She started to add that she'd also miss his cooking, his gruff mannerisms, and his long talks, but a lump formed in her throat. A sense of urgency surfaced. She'd probably never see Doc or Morgan again. She might not see noon.

<hr />

Morgan fought the sleep drawing him into a world where healing took place and reality seemed irrelevant. He was madder than a riled rattler with the realization that Casey had left. He'd known the infamous lady for only a few days, and when he hadn't been unconscious, he'd despised her. How did one woman get under a man's skin so quickly?

He'd known all along that she had a rare beauty: red-brown hair that reminded him of a desert sunset and pale blue eyes veiled behind thick, dark lashes. When he walked into her campsite, she looked out of place, as though an angel had taken residence in a man's world.

An angel or a demon? He knew the rumors. A bounty hunter from Missouri said Jenkins had found her in a brothel. One report said Casey and Tim stumbled onto the gang by accident, and Jenkins had to have her. Whatever the truth, she ran from him now.

Morgan saw the grit in her eyes in the mountains of Utah when he shoved his Winchester under her chin. If she feared him, she didn't show it. The calm speech and soft voice indicated a woman of confidence. He'd expected Casey O'Hare to use her beauty to wiggle out of his hold, but instead she challenged him with a sharp mind—repeatedly. How else could she have survived all those years with Jenkins? She'd lived among one of the most hardened gangs in American history. Casey might have noble intentions of ridding her life of Davis Jenkins, but without help, that animal would catch her for sure.

Forget her. She's not worth it. Look at what she's done over the years.

Yet she'd put her life on the line for him. Took care of him when anyone else would have left him to die. Risked her life with Jenkins hot on her trail. Morgan had learned just enough to drive him crazy, just enough to wonder if his best-laid plans were wrong. The God he acknowledged in good and needy times might be trying to tell him something. . .or warn him. If he'd have stuck to God's ways these past four years, then maybe he could decipher the message.

Six hours passed, and still the confusion of what began in the mountains of Utah and continued up until this morning in Vernal tore at Casey's heart. She lifted her tear-stained face to the late morning sun and willed the bittersweet memories of Morgan to fade.

This is insane. I hardly know the man. How could I let him torment me so? He had no right to confuse me this way—saying things that most likely meant nothing to him.

She hated to think his reasons for asking her to stay were to trap Jenkins, to satisfy lust, or to earn a bounty. Certainly the past seven years had taught her to be a better judge of character.

She shoved her raging thoughts aside and attempted to dwell on the future. Living in the past invited an early grave, and the only way to clear distance between her and Jenkins was to take advantage of the present. She didn't need Morgan. . .just like she hadn't needed Franco. Now why did she think of him? He'd been dead over three years.

Casey shook her head in hopes of dispelling painful regrets. She patted the full saddlebags. Guilt possessed her in one breath for the way Tim got the money, and thankfulness claimed her in another because maybe he cared for her after all.

My poor wayward brother. How much more I want for you.

He'd never been able to save much, but then neither did most of the outlaws. Even Jenkins talked about the ranch he'd one day own in Mexico. They all talked big about buying ranches, cattle, and horses, then settling down, but few managed to hold on to anything except their horses and guns—and seldom their lives. Instead, they all spent their money on horses, fancy saddles, guns, liquor, poker games, brothels. . . .

For Tim, it was always, "I'll quit after the next job." But that last job never happened. In the beginning, when she and Tim left home to escape Pa's beatings, all Tim wanted was to earn a few dollars and take care of Casey.

"I'm joining up with the Jenkins gang," he'd announced one night while they camped near the border of Missouri and Kansas. "I talked to a few of his men in town, and they could use another gun."

"That's wrong, Tim. We're doing fine by ourselves."

"We need the money."

"But you could get killed or sent to prison."

He pressed in close to her as though someone other than the darkness could hear. "I promised Ma I'd take care of you. I'll ride with 'em for a few jobs, just long enough to save a little money. Then we'll head to California or Oregon and buy us a pretty stretch of land."

Casey stared into the face of her seventeen-year-old brother and searched for the right words to change his mind.

"Have I ever lied to you?" he asked.

"No. But what would I do while you rode with them?"

He smiled, that boyish grin that always melted her heart. "They said you could cook for 'em. Nothing else."

And she had believed him.

When would it end? The blood and the victims of selfish greed. The sound of a cocked rifle. The smell of gunfire. The taste of violence. The feeling of fear and despair that twisted her gut. She dug her heels into Stoney's sides. *Keep moving. Soon it will be over. Soon. . .*

Casey remembered the Bible tucked into the saddlebag. Beginning tonight, she'd read by firelight, and the thought gave her something to look forward to. Surely the answers plaguing her miserable life were written within those pages. Sometimes she felt like a prairie twister, ready to tear up everything in her path. The anger frightened her as though she might end up like Tim.

"If you can't handle this, then work for Rose," Tim had said when she asked him last winter to leave the gang.

"Sell myself for the next meal?" Casey asked. "Working in a brothel? At least here I'm only fighting off one man."

"Then quit whining. I'm tired of hearing it. You want a better life? Stop fighting Jenkins, and he'll take care of you."

"I'd rather be dead."

"Suit yourself."

As twilight crept in around her, much like the old quilt she used to hide under during storms when she was a kid, Casey urged Stoney up through the aged formation of weathered rock. She recalled from past rides through the area how it changed magnificently in color from red and white to yellow and black: the beauty of a land totally suspended in time.

Tomorrow I'll see the beauty on the other side of the cliffs. The realization brought a spark of hope, fueling all her secret dreams, like wearing a dress and not a gun belt. She knew large patches of deep green pine and waving blades of grass stretched for miles. Beautiful. Utterly breathtaking. Perhaps solitude was the best form of freedom.

Weary, she stopped for the night and gathered enough wood to build a small fire. As soon as she finished eating leftover biscuits and bacon from the morning, she opened the Bible to Genesis and read by the flickering flames.

"In the beginning God created the heaven and the earth. . . ." She read through the creation and on to the struggle between Adam and Eve's sons. Reading about Cain killing Abel tugged at her conscience. She had read as far as Noah when her eyes closed.

The following morning, Casey ignored the rumbling in her stomach to put miles behind her. She picked her way down through low brush and bluish-gray rock lining Nine Mile Canyon. The dry, bleached terrain spread nearly five times longer than its title.

Carved into the stone walls were the signs of an ancient Indian civilization. *Are you haunted? What stories are engraved in your rock?* She stared at the tall, silent tombs. *I'm not afraid. I've more to fear from men.*

Nine Mile Canyon eventually evened out onto the flats of the lower Colorado Plateau. Casey rested Stoney and took in one of the most majestic views of the country. Shielding her eyes from bright sun rays, she glanced eastward to see huge rock strongholds that stood as stepping-stones to higher mountains.

Slowly her gaze moved to the south. She dreaded the ride ahead through parched territory where rattlesnakes and scorpions would be her only companions. Deep gullies, jagged rock, and dry riverbeds invited death to all who attempted to find their way through the rock guarding the Green River.

Many a gang led a posse into a dry canyon here, only to leave them to die from lack of food or water. Tim had once said the smartest men were outlaws, and the most cunning of lawmen had once been on the run. Jenkins had been a young officer for the Confederacy; he never liked losing.

For five days, Casey wound through the treacherous, often confusing canyon lands. She camped near the Yampa and Dirty Devil rivers, then rode on again only to face extreme isolation across the barren flats, west to where the Green and Colorado rivers came together. Only the nighttime ritual of Bible reading offered any element of peace.

Someday life will be better. I'll find my promised land.

She dreaded the next hundred miles. Buzzards circled the sky, and desert fever threatened anyone who braved forward. Luckily the springs flowed freely, and she didn't have to battle the blazing heat.

At last she reached the part of her journey where the surroundings abounded in rich, earthy hues. Sand and clay formed the orange-red dry land, while greenish-gray sage, twisted pines, and junipers rose from remote spots. At times the clouds in the distance seemed to be outlined in tints of red, or perhaps she merely saw a reflection of the clay-baked earth.

I can't head into Robber's Roost. How stupid of me to consider it. Every man there will be looking for Jenkins's reward. I can sleep a few more nights with my saddle as a pillow.

She studied the lookout points on all sides of the circular-shaped hideaway, knowing more than one pair of eyes watched from behind huge rocks. Scanning the horizon line where two flat-topped buttes faced east and north, Casey hid her hair beneath her hat. Perhaps none of them would recognize the lone rider. Foolish thought. She had better sense. They already knew her horse, had heard the rumors.

Lifting her rifle high, she waved to where she knew guards positioned themselves. They'd seen her coming for miles, but the formality of a signal offered them respect, if there could be honor among desperadoes.

Morgan had been right. For a woman, there were worse things than dying.

Forty miles to the west lay Hanksville, thirty miles south lay Dandy Crossing, and fifty-five miles to the north flowed the Green River. Although she faced indecision as to which direction to continue, she held no notions of heading east into more barren territory. Riding through a graveyard had little appeal.

Morgan talked of Texas. The country was an outlaw's refuge with miles upon miles of huge, free territory, especially for those who wanted a fresh start.

The decision made, Casey rode southeast to Santa Fe along the Old Spanish Trail for another nearly five hundred miles. She wondered about hostile Indians, but they couldn't be worse than Jenkins.

In Santa Fe, she walked into a hotel. A young man barely old enough to shave scowled at her. "I'd like a room, please," she said.

"Figured that." The kid wiped his nose with the sleeve of his shirt. "Gotta have the money up front."

Casey lifted the saddlebag from her shoulder and dug out a few bills. "How much?"

"Depends."

Casey lifted a brow and met his gaze. How the kid had lived

this long amazed her. Jenkins would have finished him right there. "Depends on what?"

"If you're runnin' from the law or something else."

Casey leaned on the wooden enclosure separating them. "So my money buys me protection from the sheriff or an angry husband?"

"Whatever you need." He slid her a cocky half smile.

"Neither. I need a room, now. Do I look up your pa, or are we doing business?"

The kid winced for a brief second, but she caught it. "My pa's gone."

"Then I suggest you take care of me before I let you find out who you're riling."

The kid's features hardened, and the look reminded her of a younger Tim. He turned the register her way, and she scribbled in Shawne Flanagan—a mixture of her middle name and her mother's maiden name.

She took a bath, washed her clothes, and slept for twelve hours straight. With a full stomach—more food than she'd eaten in days—she sought out a mercantile.

"Mornin'," a thin, gray-haired, matronly lady said. "How can I help you?"

Casey glanced down at her worn jeans and shirt, grateful she'd washed them. "I need a traveling dress."

The woman offered a generous smile. "I have just the one for you—perfect color for your pretty hair and just right for traveling." She nodded her head to punctuate her words. "Right this way."

In the back of the store, Casey saw the ladies' clothing. The mercantile had six ready-made dresses, more than she had ever seen at one time—unless she counted the scant clothing the girls at Rose's Place wore. The owner selected a dark blue dress with the collar, cuffs, and sashes in cream. Beneath a long, fitted, double-breasted jacket trimmed in midnight-blue buttons rested a deep purple skirt gathered in the back with a bustle. Fine. So very fine.

Trembling like a frightened child, Casey slipped into a back room and tried on the dress along with a suitable petticoat and the other intimate clothing that she'd worn only once when contemplating working for Rose. That lasted until the first greasy-looking man touched her.

Shaking her head to rid the memories, she glanced at the fabric hugging her thin body. *I look like a real lady.*

She emerged from the storage room, her skirts rustling as she'd always dreamed.

"You are lovely." The woman clasped her hands in front of her. "And I have a hat, too." She produced a curved-brimmed hat with a sprinkling of cream, dark blue, and purple flowers entwined with a cream ribbon. She tied it beneath Casey's chin and snatched up a mirror. "See for yourself."

Casey had only imagined such splendor. Outlaws were notoriously dirty and tattered. Visions of her ragged underclothes painted an unpleasant picture of her life up to now. She inhaled deeply. "I'll take the dress and the hat, and the proper undergarments."

This worrisome path of life had come to a fork in the road, and for the first time she wanted to ride in the right direction.

A short while later, she left the mercantile, made her way to the livery, and sold her beloved Stoney. Parting with him made her feel like she'd lost a friend, but it had to be done. She wept most of the night, almost as much as when Ma died.

The following day, Casey boarded the Atchison, Topeka, and Santa Fe Railroad heading south to El Paso for a lonely three hundred miles. She used the name Shawne Flanagan again, believing Tim would never tell Jenkins. Her brother did care; he'd proved it by leaving money with Doc. Storing her rifle and Colt in a newly purchased trunk, she shoved the derringer into her dress pocket and carried Doc's Bible. She wore her new clothes and pulled her hair back into a fashionable bun, allowing a few curly tendrils to trail down her neck and around her face.

She studied every man in her path. A lump from inside a jacket or at the hip indicated a revolver. She searched for a lawman's badge or the cautious glance of an outlaw. Either could recognize her. Either could end her charade.

The seats on the train quickly became uncomfortable, almost as bad as endless days in the saddle. Although she didn't have to cook, some of the meals tasted worse than dirt coffee and burnt beans. The soot from the windows settled on her clothes and infuriated her. She wanted to continue looking like a fine lady.

From the hot, dusty border town of El Paso, the Southern Pacific rambled east into the immense, wild lands of Texas.

The first time she stepped down from the train, a deputy with hair graying at his temples stood at the depot. His thumbs hooked into his gun belt. Every point of his star glittered. He observed passengers greeting family and friends while some waited for the porter to produce their trunks.

Is he looking for me? She swallowed hard. Her legs suddenly felt like lead. The deputy tipped his hat, and Casey stumbled and nearly fell. Within the hour, she had another ticket.

Days ventured into weeks as Casey wandered from one town to the next. She'd stay a few days in one place. At the first hint of someone recognizing her, she'd board the next train. Her traveling dress quickly became soiled, so she purchased a simple wrapper of heavy cotton, much cheaper than her blue traveling dress. The fabric featured green and gold stripes on a brown background, and it buttoned down the front to the top of a ruffled hem. A nudging at her heart made her wonder if Morgan would approve. She shrugged.

Restless and fearful, she couldn't relax until she found the right town to call home. Her money dwindled. She'd have to find work soon. Rose would advise her to do what came naturally.

CHAPTER 8

Three weeks after Morgan cheated death, he saddled his horse and said good-bye to Doc. He fought the pain in his chest and leg to climb out of Doc's bed, tug on his boots, clean his rifle, and continue his unrelenting search for the outlaw. The hate was like a fire threatening to consume him, for now he had another reason to stop Jenkins: Casey O'Hare.

Morgan realized how Jenkins's evil mind worked. The thought pierced what little bit remained of his heart and soul, while confusion about his staggering feelings for Casey left him frustrated. *It's because she's a woman, that's all. Can't protect herself from a whole gang of outlaws.* So he vowed to push on, but sometimes he wondered where it all would end.

"I'll wire you money as soon as I get to a bigger town," Morgan said to Doc as he saddled his horse.

"Seems like you and Casey are more concerned about paying me than getting well." Doc stood wide-legged in the middle of the stable with his arms folded across his massive chest. "You don't have your strength back yet."

Morgan avoided the big man's stare. "I need to move on."

"To find Casey?"

"Maybe."

"You think that's smart?"

Morgan flipped his saddlebag over the saddle and faced Doc. "No, but I can't seem to talk myself out of it."

"Are you after the woman or still bent on getting Jenkins?"

"If I had the answer to that, I'd still be sittin' on your front porch talking about heading home to Texas."

"So it's both. God help you, Morgan. Does Casey know?"

Aggravated to the point of hollering, Morgan hurried through his last preparations. Doc was his friend, not his enemy. "I didn't tell her."

"She's a good girl, not what other folks think," Doc said. "Oh, I know she's got herself mixed up in a few messes, but she deserves a chance to live a good life."

Morgan nodded. "I've looked at this thing inside out, and I know I have to find her. Not sure why. But I know why I have to stop Jenkins."

"Hate's trying to kill you, and it almost did this time."

Morgan pulled himself up onto the saddle. His upper leg ached, and the effort strained at his chest.

"I see the pain on your face. Rest up two more weeks. By then, we might hear from her."

"Can't. I have to find them both."

"Then where you headed?"

"Arizona. Got me a hunch." Morgan reached down and shook Doc's hand. "You saved my life, Doc. I owe you."

"Then find Casey before Jenkins does."

What would I do if I did find her?

Casey closed the Bible and then her eyes. So much she didn't understand. The words and ideas all jumbled together into one huge puzzle, almost like a map that had been torn and some of the pieces lost.

The train rumbled on. Its rhythmic sound lulled her to near sleep. West Texas was as hot and dry as Arizona and New Mexico. No place looked like where she wanted to settle down. Money ran low, and she didn't want to spend it all for fear she'd have to find refuge in a hurry. Trains were expensive. Buying food was expensive. She'd make better time traveling by horseback, and she'd long since regretted purchasing the store-bought dress and wrapper. Decision made, Casey took a deep breath and patted the derringer in her pocket. Someday she'd throw it away. But not today. Probably not tomorrow.

Rifle fire pierced the air. She startled and peered out the window. Nothing. Had she been thinking about the gang and thought she heard gunfire? Two more rifle shots echoed. Visions of the past blew past her mind like a dust storm. The train pulled to a grinding halt, like a powerful horse snorting and pawing at the bit. Two dirty men boarded the train from the rear, both wearing bandannas and carrying Winchesters. They wore the mean look of hunger, not for food but for those things that belonged to other folks. One poked his rifle barrel under a man's hat, then lifted it into his hands. Realization hit her hard. For the first time, she was on the receiving end of outlaws. She stole a quick glance at the two; they didn't look like any of Jenkins's men. Would they recognize her?

"Jewelry, watches, and money," one of the outlaws said. "No one gets hurt as long as we get what we want."

She'd pinned her money in the lining of her dress, except for a small amount in her Bible. That should suit them. When the two walked by, she avoided peering up into their faces. The second man told a woman to stop her sniveling. He sounded familiar, and then Casey remembered. He'd ridden with Jenkins for a short while before joining up with the James gang.

"Put it all in here." The man held his hand open.

Casey opened her Bible and pulled out the small amount. Her heart thudded like a scared rabbit. He snatched it up and kept walking. She inhaled sharply. No more chances. She'd not ride another train.

Once the outlaws left, her thoughts turned to the people around her. A woman cried. A mother clung to her baby. The faces of men paled. It didn't matter that she hadn't robbed anyone or stuck a gun in someone's face. She knew the kind of men who'd rather take from hardworking folks than get an honest job. Greed spurred them on just as she grasped for peace and freedom.

Casey's mouth went dry. She massaged her arms. The wanted posters were right. She deserved whatever happened to her—either at the end of a rope or a bullet. Maybe she should turn herself in and rid this country of one more outlaw.

At least working for Rose wasn't against the law.

Rose Meadows. Casey doubted if that was her real name, but it sounded good to the men who stood in line for her—and her ladies. Rose said she once worked at the Bird Cage in Tombstone, and that's where she learned her trade.

"Come see me when you've had your fill of Jenkins," Rose said. "Don't worry about him. If he gives you any trouble, I'll cut him a percent of what you make."

The idea of Jenkins and Rose getting a share of her pay while she worked her backside seemed no better than riding with the outlaws. But at sixteen years old, after he'd blackened both of her eyes for refusing him, she'd agreed to Rose's business arrangement.

One night was all it took. Rose painted Casey's face and lips, then dressed her in a blue sleeveless "gown" that dipped low in the front and was tight across the middle. Casey came down the steps with the rest of the girls into the smoky bar only to hear the lewd remarks and applause of drunken men. One paid the price for her, and she led him upstairs. When the door closed and she took a whiff of his breath and unwashed body, she grabbed her old clothes and headed back to the gang. That's when she taught herself how to throw a knife with her left and right hand. From then on, a knife rested in both boots.

Now at twenty-one years old, she'd only been with one man—Jenkins—and each time he forced himself on her, she hated him a little more.

As the days and weeks continued, her mind lingered on Morgan, the man who had nearly died to save her life. He'd captured a part of her that she believed could never be caught—her heart. Had he healed? Was he safe? Many a restless night she wrestled with his identity. If she knew the truth about him, she could deal with it. But wondering about where he came from and his reasons for tracking down Jenkins occupied too much of her time.

After the train robbery, Casey got off at the next town and headed straight to the livery. The owner had a fine-looking zebra-dun stallion for sale. She rubbed her hands over his legs, all the while talking to him softly. No horse could ever replace Stoney; the gelding seemed to sense her moods.

"You sure you can handle this one?" the owner asked. "A fine-looking lady like you should have a gentle horse. I've got a good mare in the back."

"Oh, I can handle this one. Does he have a name?"

"Stampede."

"Good name."

The livery owner laughed. "I gave it to him 'cause when he takes a notion to run, he doesn't leave anything behind but dust—and sometimes me." He scratched his chin. "Sure hate for you to get hurt."

She patted Stampede's neck. "I'll be careful."

A little dealing and the man threw in a saddle, blanket, and bridle. She rolled up her dress and other lady's clothes and stuffed them into a leather bag. Some would have said keeping these clothes was foolish, but having them made her feel that soon she'd wear them again. She wrapped them around her Bible.

Before she headed out of town, Casey made one more stop. At the local mercantile, she bought jeans, a shirt, a soft roll hat, a blue scarf, socks, and a pair of boots.

"Do you need anything else?" the slightly graying woman asked. "Provisions?"

Casey mentally counted the pitiful amount of money she had left. "Yes, ma'am. I do."

A portly man with a balding head shuffled from the back room of the mercantile. "Maude, we need to get that last shipment unloaded."

"That and a whole lot of other chores."

He looked up. "Excuse me, miss, didn't see you there."

"Try using your spectacles. No wonder the drawer comes up short." Maude shook her head. "We need some help for a couple of weeks, Hank."

"I'll ask around. Can't pay much."

"Hush about such things," Maude said.

A thought raced through Casey's mind, and she slowly turned to face the older gentleman. "Did you say for a couple of weeks?"

"Yes. Do you know of somebody?" He reached in his shirt pocket and placed his spectacles on his nose. He peered at her. "You're not from around here, are you?"

Casey's pulse quickened. "No, sir. I'm passing through, but I could use a job for a few weeks."

"It would be hard work going through boxes and putting things on the shelves," Maude said. "And most everything is dirty."

"I'm not afraid of the work. Is there a boardinghouse in town?"

"My brother owns the only one," Maude said. "Although since my sister-in-law died, the cooking isn't so good."

She wondered if what little money in her pocket would pay for a room and food.

"Maybe this gal could help out with a few things in exchange for a place to stay," Hank said.

"You trying to work the poor girl to death? Mercy, Hank, the good Lord needs to hit you up alongside the head sometimes."

"That's all right," Casey said. "I'd do whatever was needed."

"Well, get that settled and come on back. We can get you started right away." Hank stuck his thumbs under his suspenders. "I think the Lord is smilin' on us today, Maude."

Maude pressed her lips together. "Let's hope it's not at the expense of working this poor girl to death. What's your name, miss?"

"Shawne. Shawne Flanagan. Thank you for helping me. I'm beholden to you."

"We're Hank and Maude Stevens. You'll be working mostly in the back. Won't be much opportunity to meet other folks," Maude continued.

"I do fine by myself."

Casey struck up a deal with the owner of the boardinghouse. She'd cook breakfast each morning before going to work at the mercantile and clean up the kitchen after she finished in exchange for her room. And the livery man could keep Stampede until she was ready to leave town.

For the first time in Casey's life, she had a respectable job. A warm feeling rose up inside her. Was this what decent felt like? She hoped Maude and Hank wouldn't ask personal questions. Casey caught her breath. The name of the town. . .Deer Creek. Odd name for a place in dry West Texas.

A week later found Casey helping Hank stock the shelves and put the items in "departments," as Maude called them.

"Where you going once you leave town?" Hank stood and huffed.

LEATHER
LACE

His rounded stomach seemed to get in the way of lifting the bags of flour from the storage room to the shelves behind the counter.

Casey sensed her face reddening. "St. Louis."

"Got kin there?"

"I think so." She knew he meant well, but the questions pounded at her conscience. Lying broke one of the Ten Commandments.

"Me and the missus been talking. Are you running from a husband?"

Casey offered a faint smile. "Something like that."

"I knew it. Is he after you?"

She nodded and set a jug of molasses on the shelf. *Hank, please stop.*

"I'm sorry. You gonna be all right?"

"Yes, sir."

"Maude and I've been praying for you."

A can of beans slipped from her fingers to the floor. "Thank you." The thought of deceiving these good people made her feel dirty, the kind of filth that lye soap wouldn't scrub off.

Hank snatched up the can of beans and righted it on the shelf. "Would you like to go to church with me and Maude tomorrow?"

"I'm sorry, but I have work to do at the boardinghouse."

"Maude's brother needs a lesson on his Christian duty."

"Maybe I can go next week." Not even Jenkins would think to look for her in a church. She could see the newspaper headlines now: CASEY O'HARE STEPS INSIDE CHURCH. The roof would likely fall in.

A few days later, Casey stepped back from the shelves to admire how nice the store looked. The containers were stacked neatly, and she loved the smell of spices and coffee. In one corner were tools. Beside those were pots and pans. In another corner, ready-made clothes, boots, and shoes stood crisp and inviting. Casey tried to imagine the type of people who'd buy them. She'd be content to spend the rest of her life working for Hank and Maude. Even the cooking and cleaning at the boardinghouse weren't too hard.

The past no longer stood foremost in her thoughts, because other decent things took over. If only she could rid her mind of Morgan.

"Shawne, dear, would you take these yard goods back with the others?" Maude asked.

Casey gathered up two bolts of what Maude called "calico" and made her way to the middle of the store. One bolt had a pretty blue pattern, but Casey favored the green color of the second bolt. The bell above the door jingled. Two men walked in. Both wore gun belts and the hungry look of greed. She recognized both of them.

Stepping back into the shadows, she turned, straightened the bolts, and listened.

"Howdy. How can I help you?" Hank asked.

Tell 'em to leave.

Heavy boots thudded across the wooden floor. With the click of a revolver's hammer, Casey turned back around.

"You can empty your money into this bag." The gunman shoved a leather bag into Hank's face.

Casey eyed the gunman at the counter while the second man kept vigil at the door.

Maude gasped. Her hand flew to her mouth.

"Don't worry, dear," Hank said and patted her hand. He opened the cash register and began pulling out bills.

"You get over here." The man at the door wielded a Smith and Wesson with an ivory grip in Casey's direction. He eyed her strangely.

He recognizes me. She inched forward in the hope that she looked too frightened to move. Maude's face paled, and Hank didn't look well, either. They'd been nothing but kind to her since the day she walked into their mercantile. She moved closer to the counter and the gunman.

Twelve feet. Six feet. Four feet. The man at the door continued to stare a hole through her.

Reaching into her dress pocket, Casey whipped out her derringer and sent a bullet into the man's wrist. Blood spurted on the counter and onto Hank's shirt and suspenders.

The gunman dropped his revolver, and Casey snatched it up. She tossed the derringer to Hank. Shock crested the outlaw's face. In a split second she turned to the man at the door and sent a bullet into his shoulder.

"Casey O'Hare." The man grabbed his shoulder and lifted his revolver.

She sent another bullet into the man's firing arm, just below his elbow.

"I knew I recognized you."

"A lot of good it did. You won't be robbing anyone for a while."

"You're as good as dead. Jenkins will find out about this."

"Then you'd better get out of here fast, because this gunfire will have the sheriff here real quick."

"Then we'll tell him who you are," the gunman at the counter said.

Casey laughed. "Guess we'll all hang together." She lifted the revolver. "Get out of here, before all you'll need is the undertaker."

The two made their way to the door, and she slammed it shut. With a deep breath she faced her friends.

CHAPTER 9

Casey laid the Smith and Wesson on the counter beside the cash register and reached behind for a rag. She couldn't look at Hank and Maude. Not yet anyway.

"Blood always stains," she said and proceeded to scrub off the splotches on the wooden counter. Satisfied that it was clean, she proceeded to the floor and bent to wipe up the little pools of blood. An eerie silence beat down on her. She knew she should say something, but what? *I'm an outlaw. I've deceived you. I carry a Bible in my saddlebag, and I'm faster with my Colt than most men can blink. Cross me wrong, and I'll pin you to a tree with a knife.*

The bell rang over the door, and the sheriff entered, nearly knocking her down.

"I'm sorry, miss." He righted her, and she stood numb and ready for whatever happened next. The man was young, as evidenced by his spindly attempt at a handlebar mustache.

"Heard shots," the sheriff said. "Are you all right?" He saw the blood-soaked rag in Casey's hand, and his gaze flew to Hank.

"We're all right," Hank said. "A couple of men came in here and demanded the money." Hank picked up the Smith and Wesson. "He tried to use this on me, but I knocked it out of his hand and—"

"Used it on him?" The sheriff's eyes widened.

Hank shrugged. "Had to protect these women."

The sheriff took long steps to face Hank. He stuck out his hand. "You're a brave man, and I'm proud to call you a friend."

"Thank you. I didn't do any different than any other man. I needed to take care of those I care about." He wrapped his arm around Maude's waist. "I'm no hero—just an old man with not much sense."

Maude's eyes pooled with tears, and she pulled a handkerchief from her pocket to dab the wetness. The sight yanked at Casey's heart. The innocent were always the ones to get hurt.

"Well, if everything is fine here, I'd better round up a couple of deputies and get after those two."

Hank nodded. "My guess is they'll be ridin' slow."

The sheriff tipped his hat to Maude and Casey, then hurried from the mercantile. She had to say something. With the bloodstained rag in her hand, she took a deep breath.

"Thank you for not turning me in," she said to Hank. "I'm sorry you had to learn this way."

Maude sniffed. "Would we ever have heard the truth?"

Casey shook her head. "My work ends in three days, and I would have been out of here."

"If you're a part of the Jenkins gang, then what did that outlaw mean?" Hank asked.

"I ran from him, all of them." Why did she suddenly ache all over? Even her throat stung like she'd swallowed dirt. "I want to start my life over. . .live decent."

"So the law and the gang's after you?" Hank went on.

"Yes."

"But you lied to us," Maude said. "I thought you were this kind and sweet young woman."

"I believe she is," Hank said. His hand was still wrapped around his wife's waist. "She risked her life to save our store and our lives. That says enough for me."

Casey moistened her lips. "Then you'll let me ride out of here without telling the sheriff?"

"Yes." Hank spoke quickly.

"Miss Maude?"

Tears flowed down the older woman's cheek. "I don't understand this afternoon, not any of this. All those things I read in the news-papers. And the wanted posters. . ."

"In the short time she's been here, have you seen anything from this gal that looked like she was an outlaw?"

Maude sighed. "No. Nothing."

"If it makes a difference," Casey said, "I never killed or robbed anyone, but I did shoot a man in Billings when he pulled a gun on me. I heard he's fine. Please don't argue over me, 'cause I've done plenty of other things that I'm ashamed of."

Maude dabbed her eyes again. "I won't breathe a word to anyone."

"Again, I'm beholden to you. You showed me how to live respect-able." Casey glanced around at the neatly stocked shelves. "I wish I could stay here forever and forget about the past, but that's foolishness."

Maude stepped from behind the counter. "You won't ever make it unless you have a relationship with the Lord."

"I have a Bible. . .been reading it."

"That's not enough. You have to ask Jesus to forgive you and turn your life over to Him."

"Like turning my life over to the law?"

Maude nodded. "Except with God, you have the promise of heaven."

"Does this have to do with Him dying on the cross for our sins?" When Maude agreed, Casey shook her head. "I can't do that yet. Too many things are unsettled. My life isn't much good."

"But you don't have to do anything—"

Casey waved her had. "Maybe someday when all this is behind me. Right now I have to get my things and ride out of here. Those two men won't waste any time telling the sheriff who I am."

"I'll go fetch your horse." Hank hesitated. "When you get to where you're going, will you write us?"

"I promise." Strange how a couple of weeks could make her feel so close to these good people. But Maude's request would have to wait. When Casey was good enough, she'd take care of talking to God about things. Until then, she'd keep riding and reading.

<hr/>

Days later, Casey sat rigid in the saddle and scanned the hill country near San Antonio. She'd grown weary of endless days in rain and blistering heat and short nights under the stars. More than once, she considered riding into some town and turning herself in to the sheriff. The idea of a hanging always stopped her.

She'd journeyed through desert and prairie lands and on through the area Morgan had spoken about. The green territory was familiar, but looking at it as a part of him caused her to appreciate each hill and valley. She wiped the sweat from her face with a dirty bandanna and tasted dirt through parched lips. Her back felt as wet as if she'd jumped into a river with her clothes on. Enough of this. She turned Stampede northwest.

The zebra-dun stallion lived up to his name. He loved to run, which had suited her just fine when she left Deer Creek. At first she fretted over whether the sheriff had caught up to those two outlaws.

They'd tell him for sure where to find her, and if they got away, they'd waste no time finding Jenkins. The gang and the law could be closing in on her. But then she realized worrying about it only made her stomach churn and her head hurt. She'd keep riding until some remote town looked safe.

Every morning she thought of Morgan, and he stayed in her dreams when the world gathered its blanket of darkness.

"I've made him something near perfect," she said to Stampede. "But dreams settle a body down better than nightmares."

The beauty surrounding the rich area of central Texas captured her senses. Wild petunias in bright purplish blue sprawled nearly two feet tall. Pink prairie verbenas sprang up in clusters beside streams and in open fields. She marveled at the midsummer display of color, ranging from pale pink to blue and bright yellow. Towering live oaks and mesquite trees provided shade from the hot sun, and she sensed something different about the area. This was new territory to her, since the gang hadn't ridden any farther south than Fort Worth.

Then, when she least expected it, memories of Jenkins flooded her mind and tortured her soul. Casey shuddered and willed her body to relax. Even the sweet smell of nature in bloom did nothing to ease the past.

The first time he forced himself on her, she had been fourteen years old, a kid too young and too naive to have much sense. She and Tim had been with the gang for about two months. Every day she begged her brother to leave, but the tales of money and notorious outlaws were too much temptation. The gang camped along the Missouri River a few miles from Jefferson City, where they grew anxious for whiskey and women. Jenkins rode out with them, and she seized the opportunity to take a bath and wash her hair.

When Casey stepped out of the water, Jenkins stood alone on the bank. Even now, as she remembered struggling to get away, the unbidden moment attacked her senses.

"Where you goin'?" he'd said with a laugh.

"My clothes." Casey swallowed her tears but not her fear.

He glanced toward the small pile to the right of him. "Oh, you can have 'em later." He stepped closer, and she backed into the water. "I've been wonderin' what was under them jeans. Now I can see for myself."

She backed farther until the water was up to her neck. "Please leave me alone."

"Can't do that." He pulled his gun from his waist. "Out of the water, girl."

He hurt her, bruised her in places no one would ever see, and when he was done, he threw her clothes at her.

"There you are. And this won't be the last time you and me get together."

"I'll tell Tim."

His eye twitched, and he grabbed her face. "One word and that no-count brother of yours is dead. Understand?"

When she didn't answer, he squeezed her face. "Keep your mouth shut, and don't try to leave. Ya understand?"

She nodded.

"And from now on you ride with us, Casey girl." He ran his fingers through her damp hair. "I like this." He bent to kiss her, but she spit in his face.

A mistake.

"What happened to your face?" Tim later demanded.

"I fell when a snake was after me." That wasn't far from the truth.

The vile smell of Jenkins's breath, his hands on her bruised flesh, and all the sounds of nature disappeared. Some things could never be forgotten. Some women might have given in to Jenkins and his way of life, but she refused. Call it stubborn; call it uppity; call it remembering her ma's kind nature. She hated every moment of those seven years. And the only reason she stayed was fear.

Casey dug her heels into Stampede's sides and let the stallion fly.

Warm nights gave way to warmer mornings, and by afternoon the temperature heated up again. Casey remembered this part of Texas rarely saw snow, which sounded better than the subzero temperatures of the North, especially the winters in the Utah, Idaho, Montana, Wyoming, and Dakota territories. Watching the seasons change had been a splendid sight, but a warmer climate suited her bones.

As the miles lay behind her and the forests grew thick and green, she began to look for a small quaint town to call her own. She bathed in the sparkling creeks feeding off the Brazos River and passed huge clusters of tall, spindly pine. Choosing to travel back roads, she avoided anyone who might cause her harm, but now and then she met a traveler and asked where they were bound or where they'd been.

Surely she could hide from all those who wanted her dead.

Morgan dusted off the sides of his jeans and stomped the miles of dirt from his boots. He'd been to Arizona and New Mexico, and now he was back in Texas. He'd searched for Casey and Jenkins since May, and here it was July. He still limped after a long day in the saddle, and the comforts of home sounded good. The hotel near the livery in Houston advertised a good meal, a bed, and a bath. He sorely needed all three. Come tomorrow evening, he planned to ride toward his ranch and see how he could help his mother and family. Leaving her to run his place was another one of those things that needed to change. She'd sold the ranch to him some years back, but he'd wanted her to stay, along with his younger brother and sister. Now she ran the place like a man because he was out chasing Jenkins. What a good son he'd turned out to be.

Bone-tired, Morgan reflected on the days since leaving Vernal, sleeping little and pondering. . .always wondering what to do. How to end the vendetta? How to go on with his life? How to forget Casey? The answers lay in returning to the Lord, but he rode on in search of another way, his own way.

At times he prayed. At times he cursed the God who gave him life. Sometimes he wept. It just came more easily to ride mile after mile, to run away from the demons hot on his trail. When sleep refused to ease his pain, he stared up at the sky and remembered the full moon and the many stars the night he led Casey down from the snow-covered mountain. Then the torment began again. He barely knew this woman. He should hate her.

Anxious for an end to it all, Morgan considered putting a bullet in his head. But he feared facing God as much as he feared the moment-by-moment nightmares.

I'm a coward. Don't even have the guts to finish it.

All of his anguish had brought him to Houston. A part of him said his mother deserved a son who didn't look like he'd driven cattle for weeks on end. He'd clean up and ride on north to see her. Maybe talk, really talk about his past.

Morgan knew this city had a preacher on the west side of town—a man who had a reputation for having answers. Perhaps if this man explained why God had allowed things to happen, Morgan could go on. He could step over the line and be a man again. He might even find his faith in God.

After checking his horse at the livery and taking a bath, he made his way to a white board church. The door opened easily, as though inviting him inside. A twinge of guilt whispered to him that he wasn't worthy to step inside. And logic agreed.

Raised stained-glass windows and a nice cross-breeze made it pleasant. He removed his hat and walked down front. His boots creaked across the wooden floor, as though telling him he might have waited too long. A Bible rested on the pulpit, and he picked it up. Not certain where to turn, he held it in his hands. Some folks believed just holding the Good Book cured them of diseases and problems. He didn't believe that, but he did know the power of God's Word.

"Need some help?"

Morgan lifted his gaze to a tall man standing in the doorway. The sun illuminated his figure. Morgan nearly spooked.

"Are you the preacher?" He wasn't the man Morgan expected.

"Yes, sir. Do you have need of me?"

"I might." The preacher made his way toward him. He didn't have the years of wisdom Morgan craved. A white-haired preacher like the one from home suited him better.

"No man steps inside an empty church unless he has a heart to match."

"You don't know anything about it."

"We could talk." The preacher walked closer. "You look mighty troubled."

"Do you always call it like you see it?"

"Yes, sir, I do. Straight to the point."

Morgan hesitated. Already he'd abandoned the reason why he came here in the first place. "I'll just head on out."

"I can leave," the preacher said. His lanky frame reminded Morgan of a cowhand. His light brown hair hung to his shoulders.

"That's not necessary. Got a few things to do." Morgan placed the Bible back in its place and stepped away from the pulpit.

"Nothing's as important as getting right with God."

Morgan stopped. "I'd like to believe that."

"Are you running from the law?"

"No."

"Then you must be running from God. Best you take care of it here and now."

Morgan didn't like the preacher's cocky attitude. He preferred a man of God who wasn't so pushy.

"I've made you mad," the preacher said. "Good. We're getting somewhere. As a believer—and I think you are—you can't run anywhere that God won't find you. In the worst of places, He'll show up and surprise you."

"And if a man is angry about something God's done?" Morgan asked.

"God doesn't get involved with evil. We have plenty of that around us." The preacher held up his hands. "I know what you're going to say. God has the power to stop anything. Mister, whatever's eating at you will destroy you. The only answer is to turn back to God. He's allowed something to happen in your life, something you can't push aside. Understand the good is from God, and evil is from the devil. And for some things, we won't have the answers till Judgment Day."

"It's complicated." Morgan swallowed hard. His knees weakened, and he desperately wanted to leave.

"Complicated for us, but not for Him."

Morgan stopped in the middle of the aisle and met the young preacher eye to eye. The color of his gaze was dark, nearly black, like Morgan felt. The simple words spoken by the man of God had been said before but never with such clarity. Or maybe he finally heard. *Some things we won't have the answers for till judgment day.*

"Give Him the problem. You don't have to carry it," the preacher said.

Living with the guilt and hate had turned Morgan's heart into stone.

"Would you like for me to pray with you?"

The preacher was the unlikeliest person for Morgan to turn to for advice—not to mention prayer. "I'll be thinking on it." He brushed past the man to the door.

The preacher chuckled. "Doesn't make any sense to me why a man would want to go on bein' miserable when he has a chance to find peace."

Morgan's hand touched the door. Sunshine burst ahead of him, but behind him were shadows—always shadows loomed behind him. Wasn't this why he'd ridden for days? Cried like a child and begged for a sign? Had he grown so hard that hunting down Jenkins meant more than life? More than finding Casey? More than the God of his youth? He wanted to cover his ears and stop the agony raging through his soul, but the questions came from his heart.

He whirled back around and made the trek down the aisle, past the preacher, to the altar.

CHAPTER 10

Morgan stayed in Houston with the preacher for nearly a month. For once, he wasn't planning how to kill Jenkins. No longer tormented by a voracious need to find Jenkins, he helped out at the small church and reflected upon the past four years. Doing things for others made him happy, and he caught himself laughing, really laughing. This had to be real peace.

With a freedom in his soul not evident in years, Morgan realized his hate-fueled vendetta never would have been satisfied by killing Jenkins. The loathing for the outlaw had given him a reason to get up every morning. If Jenkins had been killed, Morgan would no longer have had a reason to live. His demons never would have let him go. The preacher helped him face the truth about himself and seek forgiveness. What happened four years ago was not his fault, but he could help Casey escape the same fate. The pain of regret left him determined to be a different man. He'd treated his family and God shamefully. Surely the future held more than the past.

Now he understood how Casey must feel; her longing for a free life gave her strength. He no longer concerned himself as to why they'd met or even why the attraction. Its frail beginnings felt warm and almost forbidden. The thought shook him to his toes. Perhaps his need to help her stemmed from the same desire to live for tomorrow and discard the filth from yesterday. If so, that was enough.

I've become a philosopher. Must have been the coming-to-Jesus meeting with the preacher. Morgan prayed the insight would also give him wisdom.

He set his sights on finding Casey, but first he needed reconciliation with his family. After a week, he posted a letter to his mother that he'd be home soon and had much to tell her. Then he sent another one to Doc in Vernal, being careful not to mention names. He wrote:

> *Wire me if you know of our lady's whereabouts. I need to find her before anyone else does. Remember our parting conversation? God finally has my attention. The past is behind me. I'm in Houston for a few more weeks, then will move on to see my mother near Kahlerville.*

A week later, Morgan received a telegram from Doc.

> *Not heard from our lady. Rumors aren't good. Please find her.*

Late one July morning, amid dripping sweat that soaked the back of her shirt and flooded her mind with discouragement, Casey met a boy riding a mule near the outskirts of a rural town. He greeted her with a wide grin and a face dotted with peach-colored freckles. Hair the color of straw fell across his forehead and around huge ears. Bare feet emerged like wings from the sides of the sway-backed animal.

"Fine mule you have there." She forced a smile.

"Thank you, sir." He raked back the hair from his face and patted the animal's neck. "Your horse is real fine."

Her smile proved genuine. "His name is Stampede. Likes to run."

"My pa would like him. He loves good horseflesh."

"Can you tell me the name of the town up ahead?"

"Kahlerville."

"Does your town have a preacher?"

"We sure do." He sat taller on the mule.

"Does he live there, or is he the traveling kind?" A spurt of something livened her spirit. Maybe it was the innocence of the boy.

"Oh, Reverend Rainer and his wife live right beside the church. In a parsonage. That's what ya call the house where a preacher lives."

"You don't say. I didn't know that. Does he preach a good sermon?"

With a tug to his outstretched ear, the boy contemplated her question. "Well, I don't always listen real good like I should, but my pa says Reverend Rainer is better than most. A lot of folks come on Sundays and Wednesday night prayer meetings, if that helps."

"Is your sheriff law abiding?"

The boy nodded. "We don't have any outlaws, and if we did, my pa says we'd string 'em up."

Casey smiled. "Sounds like a fine town."

"My pa calls it sleepy 'cause nothing ever happens, but that suits my ma."

"Thank you. I may pay your town a visit."

The boy disappeared, and Casey wondered if Kahlerville could be *her* town. But a tough sheriff might recognize her. Or would he? If his reputation scared away those who broke the law, then the likelihood of an outlaw settling in Kahlerville seemed small. . . making it a potentially safe place to live.

She was so tired of running and being called "sir." Life seemed no easier than riding with Jenkins, except this way she had a chance to live better. She followed the same road lined with huge oaks into town and rode down through the center of activity. One side of the street held a barber-undertaker, a boardinghouse, and a general store that had the sign POST OFFICE. A bit of melancholy met her at the thought of Hank and Maude. A small building clearly marked LAW OFFICE caught her attention. The opposite side of the street marked the sheriff's office and a two-story bank building. She laughed. Clever banker.

She shielded her eyes from the sun's glare and spotted a newspaper and telegraph office, the newest of the buildings. Several feet outside of town, beyond a cluster of pine trees, stood a two-story saloon. She'd never had a liking for whiskey. She'd tried it twice, and both times, she'd gotten sick. Two ladies sunned themselves from a second-story window and waved as she rode by. The red- and purple-trimmed building obviously housed entertainment for citizens of the sleepy town.

Casey looked beyond the edge of town and viewed a livery and blacksmith. *A growing town, not too large.* For a moment she wondered if Morgan's hometown looked anything like this, but he'd indicated that he lived west from where she roamed.

She rode on past the business establishments to where the road wound to the right and then curved sharply back to the left. Off to the left in a grove of pine trees nestled a small church and a neatly kept two-story frame home. Both appeared to have received a recent coat of whitewash. Everything in this part of Texas looked green and pretty. Between the house and the church, a tall man labored over a picket fence. The pounding of his hammer echoed through the morning air like a woodpecker bent on making its place in the world. The man stopped long enough to pull a nail from his pocket. So intent were his efforts that he apparently didn't notice the lone rider.

The sound of children's laughter captured her attention, and she turned to see a schoolhouse set back even farther from the main road on the right. Ah, noontime. In her curiosity with Kahlerville, she'd ignored the rumbling in her stomach, and she seldom took time for anything but water in the mornings. The entire picturesque scene flooded her with a sense of peace and safety. Maybe she didn't belong here at all, but she wanted a place to call home.

Tying her horse to a hitching post in the churchyard, she observed that the man had discovered her; he waved at her with a little less fervor than the two ladies at the saloon. Finding a burst of courage, she seized the opportunity to greet him while walking his way.

"Morning, sir. I'm looking for Reverend Rainer."

"That's me. What can I do for you?"

He looked about sixty years old with silver hair and soft gray eyes that radiated warmth. Perspiration beaded his face, and she noticed several lines etched across his forehead, revealing a man consumed with care.

Casey removed her hat so as not to leave any doubt of her gender. "My name is Shawne Flanagan," she said. "I met a young boy outside of town who directed me to you. I've just ridden in and hoped you could help me."

"Certainly." He wiped his sweat-beaded face on the arm of his blue shirt. "Would you like to come inside?"

"Oh, no, sir. I'm much too dirty." Casey moistened her lips and wished she'd changed into her dress, but then she wouldn't look proper sitting atop a horse. If the reverend judged her based on clothing and cleanliness, she'd already failed. At least she'd removed her gun belt and stored her Colt in the saddlebag. "Please excuse the way I look. I've been traveling for a long time, and this clothing is more practical." All the while, she searched his gray eyes for disapproval.

"Nonsense; you look fine to me. I'm ready for a cool drink of water. How about you?"

She followed him to a covered well and silently watched as he lowered, then raised a bucket. The rope creaked and groaned, but soon the bucket surfaced, full of clear, cool water. The two shared a dipper, and Casey relaxed slightly with the preacher's easy talk of the weather.

"Are you certain you wouldn't like to come inside?" he asked.

She shook her head. "I'm comfortable right here, and I don't want to take you away from your chores."

He chuckled. "Young lady, I'd much rather talk any day than mend fence."

They laughed together, and Casey realized the time had come to speak her mind. "Sir, as I said before, I just rode into town, and I'm wondering if you could recommend a place to stay and any available work."

Reverend Rainer appeared to contemplate her request. His gaze focused on the dirt road back into town. "Let me think. Work isn't plentiful for a young woman. The boardinghouse is run by some good folks. What kind of work have you done?"

"I've done cooking. Truthfully, I'd do about anything respectable." *Why didn't I bathe before coming here?*

He paused for a moment. "Have you done any nursing?"

"Yes, sir. I've taken care of sick folks."

"And you said you can cook?"

"Yes, sir." *I've cooked everything from squirrel to rattler.*

"Can you come back by here this afternoon before supper? I may have something for you."

Thoroughly pleased with the twist of events, she formed an easy smile. "Thank you, Reverend. I'll be here."

As she rode Stampede to the livery stable, her spirits lifted. For the first time in many days, encouragement wove a trail of hope around her heart. She made arrangements for her stallion and gathered up her saddlebags to visit the boardinghouse. A short while later, Casey soaked in a warm bath and fought the sleep it invited. Her eyelids refused to stay open, and the thought of a real bed with clean linens tugged at her senses, but the prospect of sleeping past the appointed hour and keeping Reverend Rainer waiting didn't settle well.

After a polite inquiry to the owners of the establishment, Casey was led to the kitchen, where she used an iron to smooth out the wrinkles of her blue traveling dress. She'd rather have tackled an angry mama bear. Thank goodness Rose had taught her a few womanly chores. Clean, neatly dressed, and her hair piled high and pinned into place, Casey felt much better about her second meeting with Reverend Rainer. She made her way down the stairs of the boardinghouse and ran straightway into the sheriff, a tall man with hair and eyes as dark as Jenkins's. The star on his chest fixed in her mind.

"Afternoon, ma'am." He tilted his hat.

She held her breath and smiled. "Afternoon." Someday she planned to look a lawman in the eye and not fret about being recognized. And someday she planned to pack away the derringer in her dress pocket. . . and the knives in her boots.

This time she walked to the parsonage and endured the heat. Birds sang and insects chirped, but nothing soothed the fluttering of butterflies in her stomach. Whether her nervousness came from her brief meeting with the sheriff or talking to Reverend Rainer about work, she had to shake off the trembling inside her. If this job didn't work out, she'd ride on to Mexico and maybe South America. But she wanted to give the town a try.

A short while later, Casey stood on the wide front porch of the Rainer home and rapped lightly on the door. Everything looked newly painted, from the steps to the heavily carved front door, all in the cloud white she'd noticed earlier. An assortment of potted green plants lined the perimeter of the porch, except on the west side where a swing eased back and forth in a light breeze. A tabby cat slept on a braided rug, oblivious to Casey's presence. She bent to scratch its head, and the animal barely opened its eyes to acknowledge her.

Smoothing her dress, Casey took a deep breath and waited for the reverend. Now she felt like a proper lady. All she had to do was act like one. Someday she'd be one. A lot of "somedays" had floated through her mind this afternoon.

Reverend Rainer opened the door with a feed sack apron wrapped around his waist. He'd rolled up the sleeves of a white shirt past his elbows, and flour coated his forearms. With a towel in one hand, he proceeded to wipe the white dusting from his exposed hands and arms.

"Excuse me," he said. "I thought I'd be finished before you arrived."

"Would you like me to come back later?" Where was his wife?

"Certainly not." A warmness in his gray eyes relaxed her. "I've looked forward to our visit since noon."

As he reached to rub his nose, a fine mist of flour covered his nostrils, and she couldn't help but laugh. "I'm sorry," Casey said. "I'm forgetting my manners."

"Nothing of the sort." He chuckled. "Cooking is not what I do best. I've learned a lot of things in these aging years of mine, but mastery of the kitchen is not one of them. The only thing I can make is biscuits, and the Good Book says that 'man does not live by bread alone.'" He wiped the white powder from his face and ushered her inside. "Do come in, Miss Flanagan. Would you like to sit in the parlor?"

"Why don't we talk in the kitchen?" A fresh fluttering of nervousness attacked her. "You probably need to finish what you've started."

"That sounds good to me. We could continue our discussion while I roll out biscuits."

Casey liked the reverend's kind face, although his eyes reminded her of an eagle, somewhat piercing, as if he knew a secret. For certain, he looked out of place in an apron. She considered taking more than a passing glance at the furnishings but thought better of it. She had no idea what folks were supposed to talk about with a preacher, other than God things. The idea of drowning in silence needled at her.

In the kitchen, he pulled out a chair from the table, and she sat on the edge just as she'd seen some ladies do during the past few weeks. "You have a fine home," she said.

"Thank you. Several members of our church painted it last week. They did a good job." The reverend paused. Picking up the rolling pin, he cleared his throat. "I'm not used to delivering speeches in an apron, but I'll do my best." He eased the pin across the dough. "Let me begin by saying my wife is upstairs sleeping. She's been ill for some time now. When she wakens I'll introduce you."

"I'll look forward to it." Casey folded her hands in her lap. Noting the exquisitely carved oaken table and chairs before her, she complimented him on the fine furniture.

"My wife's father made this for us many years ago. I fully intended to learn how to craft furniture until the War between the States broke out. I felt God's call to the ministry and served the entire time as a soldier and chaplain. So I began carving names into the Book of Life instead of wood into furniture." He paused and stared out the window. His face suddenly aged. "Now I don't need to take up your entire afternoon with small matters. You asked me if I knew of someplace respectable for you to work."

"Yes, sir, I did." Casey's heart pounded even faster.

"Well, I've been thinking and praying and talking to Sarah this afternoon. Sarah's my sweet wife. We may very well have a possible solution. Goodness, where are my manners? Sarah would be appalled. Would you like a cup of coffee? I know I could use one."

He wiped his hands on the apron before waiting for an answer and poured the fresh, hot liquid into a delicate china cup ribbed in gold.

Casey's fingers trembled, and she willed them to cease. The ladies she'd observed on the trains didn't shake; she dared not, either.

"I make my coffee a little strong," he said.

"I prefer it strong." She lifted the cup to her lips. It tasted of brew made with part grounds and part dirt. Familiar but horrible. "It's delicious."

"Now I know better, but thanks just the same."

He pulled out a chair for himself and sat across from her. Taking a deep breath, the reverend began again. "Miss Flanagan, I desperately need help here. I told you before about my wife sleeping. You see, she's confined to bed. As much as I love her and want to take good care of her, I can't seem to get anything done. The house needs attention, my cooking is terrible, and my sermons are suffering. The ladies from church are gracious to bring food and come to visit, but I need someone who can take care of Sarah and the house on a regular basis."

Reverend Rainer stood again, and for a moment, she thought he resembled an old Indian chief with his silver hair and high cheekbones. "With someone reliable, I can tend to my responsibilities and still have time to spend with her. Oh no." He grabbed a towel to pull a smoking, grease-laden skillet from the oven. He set it on the stove top and turned his attention back to the biscuits. "Guess that'll teach me to check the oven before I fire it up. I normally cook outside in this heat, but I can't get the biscuits to brown right."

"Can't I help you there?" she asked.

He shook his head. "No, I won't hear of it. Besides, I need something to do with my hands. Now where was I? Oh yes, we have two extra bedrooms upstairs, and I'm prepared to pay an adequate salary. I also think it best to give the lady who takes this position every Sunday afternoon and evening free. I like the idea of spending the Sabbath with my precious wife."

His gaze rested upon her face. "I was praying over the matter when you rode up today. My Sarah's a gentle lady, and she doesn't complain about her ailments. She simply needs someone to care for her, keep her comfortable and the like. There's medicine for the pain, except she rarely asks for it unless it's unbearable." He took a sip of coffee. "Miss Flanagan, would you consider a position as a nurse and housekeeper?"

Casey couldn't believe what she'd heard. With her thoughts flying like a flock of geese headed south, she found it difficult to concentrate as the reverend continued.

"I understand if you can't give me an answer right away, but do you mind meeting with Sarah and visiting for a spell?" He paused for a moment. "I can't say how long nursing Sarah might last, because she isn't getting any better. The doctor says she could live six months or six weeks. . . ." He placed the biscuits atop the hot oven and seated himself across from her.

"What do you think about my offer, Miss Flanagan?"

CHAPTER 11

Casey had practiced the art of hiding her emotional responses for many years, and Reverend Rainer's offer required her to use all those skills. While she scrambled for words with the sheriff's face still fresh in her mind, she realized this good man would lose his faith if he knew he sat across from Casey O'Hare.

"I'm afraid my beliefs aren't as strong as yours," she said.

"Are you interested in following Jesus and getting to know Him?"

"Yes, sir. I have a Bible. Been reading it."

The reverend nodded, while she fought the urge to squirm in the chair.

"If this arrangement is satisfactory to you and Sarah, I could answer your questions about God." He took a drink of the coffee. "I want the time my wife has remaining to be as pleasant as possible. Her nurse must be someone who will love her and tend to her needs. Sarah has looked after many folks in her day, and she loves the Lord unlike any woman I've ever known. She deserves the best of care, and I aim for her to have it. I've been looking for someone to do this but haven't had much luck."

An awkwardness filled the room. "But you don't know me," Casey said. The prospect of deceiving a man of God left a huge lump in her throat. "And what would the members of this community say about me—a single woman—living here?"

"My congregation suggested I find someone to help me. I plan to take the matter up with them come Sunday morning. That is, if you and Sarah are in agreement." He heaved a deep, weary sigh. "Miss Flanagan, you're a stranger, yet I feel God has sent you here for a reason." He stood and refilled both of their coffee cups.

She deliberated his offer. He really did need help, and from the looks of the kitchen, cooking and cleaning weren't among his finer qualities. Upon further deliberation, she thought looking after Sarah Rainer could be an opportunity to make up for the heartache and suffering the Jenkins gang had caused so many people. She couldn't right the wrongs, but she could make life easier for this couple. Yet the prospect of facing the town's sheriff needled at her. She should have kept right on riding after talking to the boy on the mule.

"I don't know what to say."

"It will take a special person to care for her. Frankly, she needs a friend. I know only too well how difficult it is to appear cheerful when she's dying right in front of you." He attempted a smile despite the morose look on his face. "But I'm not giving up until God decides to take her home."

"I understand." She thought back over the men she'd watched die. She hadn't lacked courage then, and those men weren't God-fearing.

"What do you want to know about me? I don't carry any letters of introduction or references." She'd heard one of Rose's girls talk about these before. That girl didn't have any, either.

She sat still, her heart quaking, while Reverend Rainer studied her. She wanted to do this, but the thought of it drove a fist into her stomach. Lying to a preacher would surely send her to hell, but getting caught by Jenkins or the law because she helped a preacher sounded better on her tombstone.

"It's sufficient to know you want to know more about the Lord," the reverend said. "I think you feel awkward with what I'm suggesting, and the truth is I do, too. All I can say is God spoke to me today, and I'm following like a blind man."

Her mouth went dry. Why didn't she simply leave and forget about the whole matter?

"Would you like to meet Sarah? Then we can talk. After all, she's the one who needs to be happy with the arrangement." He rubbed his floured palms together. "I'll see if she is awake. May I escort you to the parlor?"

They walked past a room that Reverend Rainer said was his study. Casey gazed at the shelves. She wanted to touch the floor-to-ceiling leather-bound volumes. *So many things to learn. . .about God and the world around me. I surely wish my words were better. Hearing and talking nothing but curses for seven years makes me ashamed.*

"You like to read?" he asked.

She nodded.

"If you decide to nurse Sarah, you're welcomed to any of these."

Casey caught the scent of roses blooming just outside the study window. She could have reached out and plucked one of the deep red blooms. Instead, she admired them. "How beautiful."

"Thank you. Sarah's roses have always flourished under this window. I'm not as faithful as she in keeping them looking their best."

"I can't imagine them looking more beautiful than today." She meant every word.

The parlor invited in sunshine as though the room were merely an extension of the outdoors. Through the windows, she saw a garden area and an assortment of greenery and colorful blooms. What a wonderful place to live.

Simple and modest furnishings made way for deep shades of

blue- and cream-colored lace pillows, a blue and gold sofa, and a pair of overstuffed golden tapestry chairs. Casey sat on the sofa and admired the oaken tables.

Curiosity nipped at her while she waited for the reverend. What good would it do to start over if everything became a lie? Suddenly she felt dirty, as though the bath she'd taken earlier hadn't done a bit of good. But she had to start somewhere, didn't she?

What kind of illness did Sarah Rainer have? Was she sweet like the reverend said, or bitter with the sickness? Those thoughts shouldn't matter. She'd been around enough surly men to learn how to handle mean-spirited folks.

A short while later, the reverend ushered Casey upstairs. The staircase needed a bit of dusting, but the house had a fresh smell. She followed him to Sarah's room. Plants of all sizes lined the walls, with smaller ones sitting on the windowsills. Some folks claimed plants made people sick, took away their air. She doubted if a preacher kept things that weren't good for folks. Casting aside the worrisome thought, she turned her attention to Sarah Rainer. Lines etched into the woman's face made her look much older than the reverend.

Reverend Rainer bent to kiss his wife's head. "Sweetheart, this is the young lady I told you about, Miss Shawne Flanagan." He propped her head with pillows and tucked a thin coverlet around her shoulders.

Sarah smiled, and it seemed as if heaven's gates opened wide. "Good afternoon, dear. What a pleasure to meet you. My, but you remind me of our granddaughter who lives in Oregon. Just as pretty, but she doesn't have your beautiful auburn hair." She touched her own gray-white hair, and a look of horror crossed her face. "John, I forgot to have you pin up my hair. And in front of a guest."

"You look lovely, Mrs. Rainer. No need to fret, and it's a pleasure to meet you."

Sarah talked on, even teased her husband about finding a pretty young lady to care for her. She told Casey about their children and grandchildren—and oh, how she missed them.

Her peaceful spirit and a stubborn determination not to be pampered impressed Casey. Sarah didn't ask about Casey's family or her past experiences. Rather, she talked about plants and how she cherished spring with the blooming of flowers and trees, and summer with all the vegetables ripening. Mrs. Rainer also enjoyed fall, the season of harvest and preparation for winter.

"Shawne, did you know a tree must shed all of its leaves in order for it to grow new ones in spring?"

"I never thought about it, but you're right," Casey said, more than a little apprehensive, as though Sarah knew all about her outlaw past.

"It's one of God's miracles. The old dies to make way for the new."

Casey didn't know Sarah Rainer well enough to question her way of thinking. Her words sounded peculiar. Something dying made something live? One day she'd ask what that meant. The reverend stepped from the room and allowed the two women to visit.

Once his footsteps no longer sounded on the stairs, Sarah sighed deeply. "Can you take care of an old lady until she dies?" Her weak brown gaze captured Casey.

"Yes, ma'am, I believe I can."

The woman reached for Casey's hand. She caught a glimpse of the thin, wrinkled hand—soft and frail. Deep violet veins rose from parchment skin. Although Ma had been much younger, near the end her hands had looked the same.

"Both of us need you. John wants me to have the best of care, and I resent the illness tearing him from his ministry. God's work should never go neglected."

Casey's gaze rested on the small, delicate figure nestled deep in the bed. The undeniable colorless pallor of death rested on her face, but when she smiled, her countenance cast the sweetest glow. Casey savored the moment; it was as though a sense of acceptance shone from Mrs. Rainer's face.

Sarah lifted her head from the pillow and allowed thinning hair to fall around her shoulders. "Tending to me won't be easy. I simply cannot do anything for myself. I'm like a baby, only worse. A baby is coddled, and the mother lives in expectation of the growing new life. In my case, you'll live with the certainty of death. I'm not afraid to speak of dying, but I refuse to give up without a fight. I can't dance through life in this old body, but I can make the most of every moment. In the days remaining, I want to live every breath of life. I have to be sure you can deal with me, knowing the outcome and understanding the burden."

Such strength for one woman. Casey hadn't seen any of this from outlaws. She realized the longer she spent away from Jenkins, the more she became sensitive to the things going on around her. "I took care of my mother before she died, Mrs. Rainer." Casey stroked the fragile hand.

"Well, I'll do my best to display a sweet temperament and not be too bothersome. And, dear, please call me Sarah. We'll spend many hours together, and the intimacy of friendship is necessary." She smiled. "Would you mind reading to me now and then?"

"I would love to, but I'm not real good. And would you teach me how to care for your plants?" She swallowed an inward gasp. In her last words, she'd agreed to nurse the woman.

Sarah closed her eyes. "I see we're going to get along just fine." Her hand fell limp in Casey's grasp. Pulling a thin coverlet up around Sarah's neck, Casey tiptoed from the room.

A twist of fear settled upon her, and she shuddered. She glanced about the upper hallway from the picture of two children posed in an oversized chair to the layer of dust on the floor. Already she had become involved. What if the Rainers learned the truth?

This is nonsense. Picking up her skirts, Casey stepped to the stairway. *I've agreed to my own death.* Except something about helping others sounded good. Morgan might even approve. She shook her head. Would he ever stop plaguing her thoughts?

"I'll do my best with the position you've offered, providing the folks in your church think it's all right," she said to Reverend Rainer. "Be certain of this: If you ever have any questions about me, I'll answer them honestly."

"Fine, Miss Flanagan. I think I'll pay a visit to a couple of my deacons this evening to see about you getting started right away."

The walk back to the boardinghouse brought a wagonload of hope. No one would suspect a woman living at the parsonage and tending to the reverend's wife to be an outlaw. Maybe her reading the Bible had brought good luck.

Back at the boardinghouse, the smell of food led her into the dining room. She slipped into a chair near the corner of the room and wondered how long it would take before she felt comfortable among decent folks. Within moments, the owner brought her a plate piled high with roast beef, potatoes, green beans, and corn bread. The sight of it nearly made her dizzy, and the food seemed to melt in her mouth. She forced herself to eat slowly and use the manners she'd seen from Maude. At that thought, she smiled. Soon she'd write them of her good fortune.

Midway through her meal, the sheriff walked in. The corn bread seemed to stick in her throat. She coughed, then reached for a glass of water. The only way out of the dining room was right past him. She'd made enough foolish moves today without one more. He seated himself on the other side of the room at a long table with some other folks. Relief flooded through her. Once he started to talk with the others, she'd leave.

The moment the owner set his food in front of him, the sheriff stood and walked her way. He carried his hat, and his black mustache twitched.

"Ma'am," he said, "I'm Sheriff Kahler, and I want to welcome you to Kahlerville."

"Thank you."

"Do you have people here?"

"No, sir."

"Well, if you need anything, just stop by my office."

"I'll do that very thing. Thank you again."

He turned around, took one step, then faced her. "Have you ever been to Kentucky?"

"No, sir." And she hadn't.

"You look powerful familiar. I thought I might have remembered you from home."

Trapped. If she left Kahlerville now, the sheriff would figure out where he'd seen her face and have a posse hot on her trail. She didn't know this part of the country well enough to risk it. She'd have to stay, at least for a little while.

For the first time, an idea began to take form.

CHAPTER 12

"So you're heading out?" the preacher asked Morgan.

"It's time. If I'm serious about starting over, then I need to make a few amends, beginning with my family."

"You'll do fine."

"Thanks to you and the Lord. Forgiving Jenkins is the hardest thing I've ever done." Morgan picked up his hat. "But I sure feel better."

"And what about Casey?"

"I have to find her. If the law gets her first, I can represent her. I used to be a good lawyer. But if Jenkins does, well. . ."

"God has a plan for both of you, and I'll be praying. Thanks for all you've done here. I'll miss you." The tall, lanky preacher grinned. He still looked more like a cowhand than a man of God.

Morgan stepped out into the warm morning. He shook hands with the preacher, a man who would never be forgotten.

The first few nights at the parsonage, Casey fell into bed bone-tired.

She'd always been accustomed to hard work and little sleep, but not the ache that settled in her heart as she cared for Sarah Rainer. By the third day, Casey admitted the necessity to schedule household chores around nursing. After a week, she established a routine, and her duties became easier. Not once did she regret the work. Still, she figured she'd signed her death warrant when she learned Sheriff Kahler was a deacon.

A strange, almost strangling hold kept her at the parsonage. She tried to reason why she simply didn't saddle up Stampede and leave Kahlerville. Perhaps it was the sense of purpose she'd found, more powerful than the fear of dying.

As the reverend had said, Sarah didn't complain even when the slightest movement caused her to wince. Sarah's wishes to stay neat and clean invited intense pain, but she wouldn't hear of anything else.

"I can bathe you later," Casey said on Sunday morning after Sarah had spent a miserable night. "I'm sure you'll feel better after resting."

The lines deepened in the woman's face, and her eyes clearly told of the suffering. She fought for every breath and displayed more courage than Casey had ever seen from hardened outlaws.

"No, please do it now. It's—it's important to me." Sarah closed her eyes. "Today is the Lord's day, and I want to go to church."

"Oh, Sarah, are you sure?" A frown tugged at Casey's lips. "You know how hard the afternoons are for you."

"Afterwards doesn't matter. John and I have a commitment to God and our flock. Why, the Petersons have a new baby, and I'm sure they'll bring her this morning. They named her Sarah, after me. And we want to show our congregation what a blessing you are. Now how could I stay home?"

"But—" Casey thought she'd met her match in stubbornness.

The woman shook her head. "And today will be the first Sunday

Mrs. Heilman will be there without her husband. God rest his soul. So tell me, sweet girl, how can I not go?"

Casey realized she'd been defeated. "I understand, but I don't agree."

Sarah's smile brightened. "If we hurry, John can carry me inside before the others arrive. I hate all the fussin' made over me. Besides, I want him to go over the last part of today's sermon. His message seemed to lack something when I heard it yesterday."

Casey gingerly bathed and dressed her. She understood the price the dear woman paid for attending church.

The Andrews family was among the early arrivals that morning. Casey had met Jocelyn and her daughter, Bonnie, and her son Grant the first day she lived at the parsonage. Something about the son triggered a memory, but she soon tossed the thought aside.

This week's sermon spoke of love and forgiveness as demonstrated in Jesus' story about the prodigal son. Sarah had been concerned about the part where the son wanted to come home. According to her, a family in the church had a similar problem, and she wanted to make sure the sermon included both the love and the forgiving nature of God.

Reverend Rainer talked about God's grace and mercy. Every word seemed to linger in Casey's heart and hold her spellbound until the next one was spoken. What she'd read in the Bible now had clearer meaning. Even the words to the songs touched her.

When the sermon ended, Reverend Rainer stepped away from the pulpit and made his way closer to the people. "The Bible says that Jesus is the way, the truth, and the life. Through Him we have eternal life in heaven. If you have not thanked Jesus for dying on the cross for you or asked Him to forgive you of your sins and to live in your heart forever, now is the time. Please, let us all bow our heads and pray. For those of you who have already chosen the precious gift of life, pray for those here who may not know Him. If you want the Lord in your life, now is the time to step forward and make that decision."

Casey felt the tears splash over her cheeks. She was the prodigal, and she desperately wanted to be with the perfect Father. Now she understood, and in the quiet of her heart, she reached out to Jesus. But Reverend Rainer had instructed folks to step forward, and no one ventured in that direction.

Her insides twisted. Sheriff Kahler stood beside the reverend. His reputation for keeping Kahlerville clean of outlaws exploded across her mind. Did she save her skin or save her soul?

She stood on shaky legs and made her way from the second pew up to Reverend Rainer. With her gaze fixed on the reverend, she took a deep breath. "I'd like to give my life to Jesus."

He smiled and took her hand. The prayer was short, her breathing ragged, but she'd made the decision of a lifetime. No matter what the future held, she no longer faced it alone. The derringer in her pocket must be put to rest with the Colt and Winchester under her bed. Later, she'd put together the right words to tell the Reverend and Sarah about her past. In the meantime, she'd pray for Morgan and Tim. Both needed the hand of God.

❧❀❧

Monday morning dawned brighter than Casey could ever remember. She set Sarah's breakfast of oatmeal sweetened with apple butter in front of the woman. "I feel so good today."

"That's because you're thinking of the fine time we'll have in heaven."

Casey hadn't considered that aspect. Yet it sounded wonderful. "I wanted to be a part of God's family, but I didn't know what it meant until I heard the reverend yesterday."

"Bend down here and let me give you a hug," Sarah said.

Hearing the reverend and Sarah praise her about the decision to follow God made life seem a little richer. But dealing with the possibility of the sheriff recognizing her was another matter altogether.

Morgan watched his mother pace the kitchen floor. Light brown wisps had slipped from her pinned-up hair and now framed her face.

"You don't think it's a bad idea?" she asked.

He laughed. "No. I think it's wonderful. You should have purchased the bull and told me about it later."

His slender mother ceased her pacing and grabbed the back of an empty chair. "I want to develop our own line of beef from the best of stock. Bringing that bull from South Carolina is a start."

He contemplated the risk. Investing a large amount of money in one animal made him a bit anxious, too, but he refused to dampen his mother's spirit. "Look at the figures. We have the money, and beef prices keep going up." He pointed to the ledger. "Looks like you've spent a lot of time keeping that straight. I'm more than pleased."

"Your brother does the bookkeeping now and oversees the ranch. He works alongside the others, then tends to the books after dark."

"He's too young for all that responsibility."

She said nothing but moved around to sit in the chair beside him. "Don't criticize your brother. He's smart and can work like a man twice his age. Remember what you did at seventeen?"

Guilt caused his face to grow warm. Grant might still be young, but he did more than Morgan in taking care of the family. "I should speak to him."

"Morgan." Mama's voice raised a notch.

"I mean to let him know he's doing a fine job."

"Are you sure? I won't have you undermining him."

Morgan leaned back in his chair and tipped on the back legs. "I'm doing exactly what I promised myself I wouldn't do. When I left, he was thirteen years old, and his voice had barely started to crack. Now he's grown, and I'm still treating him like a kid."

"I agree."

He offered a faint smile. "No wonder he takes off when I show up. Can't say I blame him." He hesitated, trying to figure out the best way to apologize. "Mama, I made my peace with God. I'm finished chasing after Jenkins. Time I went back to living."

She touched his cheek. A callus on her finger reminded him of the hard work required to run the ranch while he'd chased the country looking for an outlaw. "What brought this about?" she asked.

"A woman and a meetin' with my Maker."

"Both are good things." She smiled and withdrew her hand from his face.

"I intend to apologize to Bonnie and Grant and hope they see a change."

"Oh, Morgan. Our prayers are answered." She dabbed at her eyes with the corner of her apron. "Then you're home to stay? No more leaving in the middle of the night and causing us to wonder if you're dead or alive?"

He winced. "You never hold back the words when I need a scolding."

"That's what a mother's for." She eased into the chair. "Tell me more, Morgan."

"I need to find this woman. I'm not sure where she is, but I'll do my searching from here as much as I can. I'd like a couple of weeks to make inquiries; then I'll be back."

Mama nodded. "You must love her."

"I think I do. Felt something right from the start, but I can't rightly say why. I know God put her in my life for a reason, but it's been a hard lesson. I want to bring her back here, if she'll have me."

"Any woman would be honored to have you."

"Until she got wind of my temper." He sighed. "I'm a stubborn fool." He stood and gazed out at the green hills where cattle and horses grazed. He'd done enough wallowing in self-pity. "Tell me what's going on. How's Bonnie?"

"Good. Growing up some. Has more to go. We've spoiled her, and I'm afraid she's not strong enough to grab hold of this rough country."

Thoughts of his small, frail sister danced across his mind. "She can't get through life by relying on her pretty face."

"I agree. She's an Andrews, and that means she has to be strong."

"How's Reverend Rainer's wife?"

"She keeps getting worse. There for a while, the reverend tried to do it all. Even with women from church bringing food and cleaning now and then, it wasn't enough. He loves Sarah dearly, and her care is what's important."

"Sounds like he needs help."

"And that very thing has happened. He's hired a young woman to live there and tend to Sarah and the house."

Morgan considered the matter. "A relative?"

"No. She's new to town. Just showed up one day. Some of the folks at church complained that he hadn't done right, but I told them to either move into the parsonage and take care of things or hush. She's a fine young woman, and from what I've seen, she dotes on Sarah just like the reverend does. When I visited this week, the house was spotless, and Sarah was happy."

Morgan listened to his mother's every word. In times past he would only half-listen—another one of his faults. "When I get back, I'll pay the Rainers a call."

"I'm heading over there in the morning. Want to join me?"

"Monday morning. . . I guess I could before moving on. Probably wouldn't hurt for me to visit with the reverend. I owe him an apology for all the times I threw God back at him."

"Good." She patted his hand. "He had good sermons today. I wish you'd been here in time to go with us. By the way, Son," she said, her voice softening, "the wildness is gone from your eyes."

"Thanks, Mama. God has a lot of work to do with me—my temper, my pride, the past."

"He has a lot of work to do in all of us. I'll continue to pray for you and your friend."

"Pray she'll be surrounded by those who'll love her." Casey's face floated through his mind, along with a stab of fear. "And keep her safe."

❧❧❧

Casey bustled about the kitchen to make sure everything was in order for guests. One of the church members, Jocelyn Andrews, planned to visit Sarah midmorning.

"You should become acquainted with Jocelyn's daughter, Bonnie," Sarah had said earlier. "She's about your age."

Casey remembered the petite blond with the dimpled smile, but making friends invited trouble. "I really don't have time for socializing. You're my friend."

"Nonsense. Young women need each other."

"Yes, ma'am." *But I can't, Sarah. I can't allow anyone to know who I am, and I don't want to put anyone in danger.* The thought suddenly struck her that Jenkins wouldn't hesitate to harm the reverend or Sarah.

"I know you're shy, and I'm sorry," Sarah said. "Are you troubled?"

Casey fussed with her quilt. "You are what's important to me."

Promptly at ten o'clock, a rap sounded at the door. Guests had stopped by before but none with a potential friend. The thought filled her with dread. Casey took a deep breath and smoothed a green flowered dress that one of the deacon's wives had given her. Someday soon she must learn to bake. Life on the trail hadn't taught her those things, and on occasions such as this, she wanted to have something to serve the Rainers' friends.

"I'll greet the guests," Reverend Rainer said, but they met each other at the front door.

"Go ahead." Casey laughed.

The reverend opened the door. "Mornin', Jocelyn. Good to see you, Bonnie. Sarah is so looking forward to your visit." He paused. "Do I see an old friend?"

Bonnie giggled, a sweet laughter that dripped with honey. The sound reminded Casey of innocence. "Yes, Reverend."

The reverend stepped out onto the porch, then down the steps. "Son, you have just made this day a little better."

"It's been a long time."

Casey's gaze flew beyond Jocelyn and Bonnie. She shivered. Heat flooded her face.

"Sarah and I sure have missed you."

"Well, I couldn't let a visit go by without seeing the both of you."

Casey's stomach curdled. This couldn't possibly be happening. Then she saw his face.

CHAPTER 13

Casey's heart pounded until it ached, and the ability to speak escaped her lips. Finally she took a deep breath. She'd let Morgan set the tone between them, and she'd respond accordingly. The truth of her own emotions nearly staggered her. She *had* allowed this man to steal her heart.

"My, we're forgetting our manners," Jocelyn said. "Shawne, this is my son Morgan. He came in yesterday afternoon and plans to leave tomorrow, but not without a visit to the reverend and Sarah. "Morgan, this is Miss Shawne Flanagan. She takes care of Sarah."

"And helps me, too," the reverend said. "Thanks to Shawne, I've been able to return to my ministry and still have plenty of time to spend with Sarah."

Morgan smiled, but she couldn't bring herself to peer into his eyes. *They can't find out about me this way.* Her commitment to Jesus and all that meant slapped against her mind like a wanted poster.

Jocelyn took her hand and squeezed it gently while Casey scrambled for composure. "I've already told him how special you've become to the church community during the short time you've been here."

"Thank you." Slowly Casey calmed and regained control of her senses.

"It's a pleasure to meet you, Miss Flanagan," Morgan said with a slight curve of his lips. His words sounded flat, as though he forced himself to be cordial.

Uncertainty swirled around her. "I believe the compliments are exaggerated, but I do appreciate the kind words."

Morgan hesitated, then a broad grin swept from ear to ear. "This is not fair, Shawne." He turned to his family and the reverend. "The lady and I are friends." He reached for her hand. No warmth. His touch matched his eyes. "I'm glad you've found a home."

"I'm very happy to be in Kahlerville." She mentally erected a wall between them. Her knees felt like jelly.

After all we went through, and Morgan is ashamed of me. Of course, could I really fault him. . .considering? What did she want Morgan to say? *"Do you keep your guns under the bed at the parsonage?"* Casey felt Jocelyn's attention on her and feigned a smile. "Would you like coffee?"

"No, thank you," Jocelyn said. "We simply want to visit with Sarah."

"And to invite Shawne to our home next Sunday after church," Bonnie said.

The reverend grinned. "Good. I was afraid Shawne might not get out and make friends. I gave her every Sunday afternoon and evening free, but yesterday she refused to leave the parsonage."

Casey continued to smile, but her insides screamed in protest. She'd have to find an excuse to refuse the Andrewses' invitation.

"Perfect. We can ride home from church together," Jocelyn said. The tall, slender woman was so kind. . .if only she knew the truth.

"But I really don't want to leave Sarah." All the while Casey felt Morgan's scrutiny.

"I took care of her before you arrived, and I'm looking forward to it again," the reverend said. "Now who would like to visit Sarah first?"

"May I?" Morgan asked.

Thank you. Gives me time to pull myself together.

The other four sat in the parlor, and Casey attempted polite conversation. All the while, her mind raced with what Morgan had said to her before they parted in Vernal. He said the area between Austin and San Antonio was the prettiest part of Texas. She'd assumed that was where he lived, not here. Had he lied on purpose so she'd never invade his territory? And what of her past? Her lies? And his family wanted to befriend her? She thought her head would burst with all the problems stemming from her staying in Kahlerville.

I'm the outlaw. . . . I'm the fool.

She remembered the decision she made yesterday for the Lord. How could life be so happy one minute and so horrible the next? She thought of asking God to help her again, but she was new at this prayer business. Maybe she had a limit—

"Shawne, are you all right?" the reverend asked.

She startled and gave him her attention. "I'm sorry. Are you talking to me?"

Concern etched his face. "Jocelyn asked where you were from."

That she could answer and not lie. "Missouri. My mother died about eight years ago."

"I'm sorry. Is your father living?"

He's a drunk. "I'm not sure, ma'am." She felt herself redden. An awkward silence followed.

"We'll have simply a wonderful time on Sunday," Bonnie said. "Do you ride?"

Sidesaddle? "I have a horse at the livery."

Bonnie clapped her hands, and she didn't look a bit silly or childish.

"We could fetch your horse after church, if you like. I can't wait to show you our ranch. My other brother, Grant, might want to join us, but he's quiet and won't bother us."

Casey nibbled at the inside of her mouth. That probably wasn't proper ladylike behavior, either. When would this morning end?

"Sarah is anxious to see the rest of her visitors." Morgan's wide shoulders took the span of the parlor entrance. "We talked until I was afraid I'd wear her out."

The reverend made his way to Morgan's side. "Then let me join the two ladies so I can bid her good-bye before I leave for a few calls."

Casey's head pounded so hard that it hurt. She'd be alone with Morgan. He'd probably threaten to run her out of town. Dare she blame him? He was probably best friends with the sheriff.

"If Shawne doesn't mind, I'd like to take a walk," Morgan said. "It's been awhile since we last spoke."

Everyone looked to her for a response. She'd felt more comfortable facing a mountain cat. "That would be fine."

Morgan opened the door, and the two walked into the sunshine. He favored his left leg. Memories. So many of them. "Warm already," he said.

"Yes, and I think it's getting hotter."

"What was I supposed to do in there? I'm sorry, Cas—Shawne. Where did you come up with that name?"

She stiffened. "My middle and my mother's maiden name. Look, Morgan, I had no idea you lived here. I can be gone in the morning."

"I don't want you to leave." He rubbed his chin. Gone were the amber-colored whiskers.

"So you want an outlaw spending Sunday afternoon with your family and nursing the preacher's wife in your hometown?"

He didn't answer.

"I understand," she said.

"No, you don't. This is hard. Too many things you don't understand."

"So you still need me to find Jenkins? How do you plan to go about it this time?"

"I put that vendetta behind me."

Casey stopped in the middle of the pathway. "I don't believe you. Why?"

"I got right with the Lord." His expression softened, and for a moment she lost herself in the depths of his turquoise eyes.

Despite her uneasiness, the thought of Morgan striving to live like God intended warmed her. "I'm very happy for you. I did the same. . .yesterday."

"Good. We're both heading in the right direction."

She glanced down at the grass beneath her feet. What should she say? All her fanciful thoughts about him seemed simpleminded. "You healed fine?"

"Thanks to you and Doc, this leg is getting better all the time."

"I'm pleased." Frustration inched through her. "How about the hole near your heart?"

"Guess I deserve that." He pointed to the back of the house. "Do you mind if we walk there?"

She nodded and strolled beside him. Hadn't she dreamed of seeing Morgan again, talking to him, having him so close that she could touch him? "Morgan, I'm wanted in more states than I can count, and Jenkins wants me dead. Every person I touch is in danger. I don't want that for you, your family, or the reverend and Sarah. If you found me, so will the others. In fact, the sheriff says my face is familiar."

"My family, my friends are precious to me," he said.

The truth clung like a cold, damp morning. "Which is why I have to leave."

"No." He spoke so loudly she looked to see if others were watching. "I can't let you go."

"What am I supposed to do?" She raised her fist, then dropped it. Anger wouldn't solve the problems between them.

"Stay here for a little while. We can work this out."

Casey rubbed her shoulders. "I'd do better in Mexico." She shook her head. "That's not what I want to do at all. I want to clear my name, prove I didn't do all those things slapped across those wanted posters—except the shooting in Billings."

"I was there, remember? Let me help you."

"How? You're leaving tomorrow."

Morgan shook his head. "I was heading out to find you."

Bewilderment roared through her veins. She'd heard enough. Her life was filled with enough trouble without trying to figure out Morgan. "Are you a bounty hunter?"

He grabbed her shoulders. "No. And running won't solve your problems."

His hands on her ushered in memories of Jenkins—the times he'd hit her, bruised her. "Don't touch me." Her head roared in her ears. She gathered up her skirts and ran to the front of the house and up the porch steps. She turned the doorknob and stepped inside. Safe. She didn't need Morgan. He most likely wasn't any different from the others.

❧❧❧

Morgan waited in the wagon until his mother and Bonnie were ready to leave the parsonage. He wiped the sweat from his face. His chest ached. His leg throbbed. But the pain of watching Casey walk away hurt more. Those weeks laid up at Doc's, those weeks trying to run down her trail, all he could think about was how she'd risked her life to save his. From the moment he'd shoved his rifle under her chin and seen her courage, he'd realized she possessed what most women never imagined. So strange when he considered what brought them together. The truth. The horror. He had to think, pray. Find answers.

On the way back to the ranch, Mama didn't pressure him to talk, and Bonnie understood his bad temperament. Both of them had put up with his ill moods for the past four years. So had Grant. Looked like he needed to do a lot more changing.

Once he unhitched the wagon and turned the horse out to pasture, he led his mare, Twister, from the stall and saddled her up for a ride. Racing against the wind always helped relieve whatever worried him. A slight breeze stirred from the south and cooled his face.

"Where are you going?" Mama leaned against the top railing of the corral.

He loved her. She'd seen him through the worst of it. "I need to think."

"Shawne is the girl you were going after." She turned to face him. "What's going on, Morgan?"

He clenched his jaw. "I can't talk about it just yet."

"Does it have anything to do with why you favor your left leg?"

"Nothing gets by you, does it?"

She smiled. "It came by me naturally when you, Bonnie, and Grant were born. Now are you going to talk to me?"

"Once things are sorted out."

She patted Twister. "Love and hate almost destroyed you once. I saw what happened between you and Shawne today. Which will it be this time?"

"I'm praying God will carry me through."

"Are you in trouble?" She moistened her lips. "Or is she?"

He swung up onto the saddle and grimaced at the strain on his leg. "Mama, I'm fine. Casey will be fine."

Not a muscle moved in her face. "Are you leaving tomorrow?"

"No. I'm staying right here. I've changed, or have you forgotten? God will lead me in the right path."

Mama's eyes moistened. "But you have to let Him."

From her bedroom window, Casey stared out into the inky blackness of night. The outline of trees silhouetted against a silver slice of moon. Some folks feared what they couldn't see; others welcomed the opportunity to hide. Tonight she could relate to both. Her new faith said to fear nothing and to trust God. She shook her head. With her limited knowledge of the Bible, she imagined God had something to say about not putting people in danger. The law wanted her for crimes, most of which she hadn't committed, and Jenkins wanted her because she refused to be his woman. Shouldn't she be asking what God wanted?

Dare she leave the reverend to tend to Sarah alone? In the short time that Casey had been at the parsonage, she'd grown to love this woman of courage and faith. Leaving her would be difficult, and she'd lose her chance of making up for some of the things she'd done.

I like being needed by the Rainers. Makes me feel less dirty.

Tears filled her eyes, and she swiped them away. Morgan. Uncertainty was all she could muster. He'd spoken honestly. *"My family, my friends are precious to me."* She didn't know him at all, and always the unanswered questions plagued her like a case of poison ivy. He'd hated Jenkins and trailed him into the snow-covered mountains to find him. Then when danger struck, he had led Casey away from the outlaws.

Morgan hinted at feelings for her, but what about those he loved? What about those she loved? The tears flowed more swiftly, and her stomach knotted. All of her reflections brought her to the same question. Should she leave and find another town to start over, save some money, and find a lawyer she could trust?

Oh God, I don't know if You're listening, but please tell me what to do. I've lost hope in trying to figure out what is going on here. Sometimes I wonder if I'm to turn myself in to Sheriff Kahler and face whatever a judge says. My life is a pigsty, and I keep wallowing in it. All I've ever known is running and hiding. I think it's what I do best, but I despise it.

Casey opened her eyes from her prayer and blinked away the wetness. Did the urging inside her spirit mean God had provided an answer? It didn't make sense, but she was fresh out of finding answers on her own.

CHAPTER 14

Morgan couldn't sleep. He hadn't said the right things to Casey, and he wasn't sure he could if he started all over. The wounds of his life weren't healed; they still seeped with bitter memories. He craved a complete cleansing of his soul, but obviously God wanted him to learn something along the way. Every day he braved forward with one hand in God's and the other grasping for peace. Forgiving Jenkins was the hardest thing he'd ever done. No longer did he burn with a passion to kill the outlaw, only that the man be stopped.

"God either takes away the ugliness in our lives or walks with us through it," Mama had said on many occasions. For the first time, Morgan understood, and he firmly believed his spiritual journey included Casey.

What were the chances of the two of them ending up in the same place? He wasn't a gambling man, but he understood the odds. God had purposed this for something, but what?

God, what do You want me to do? I beg You to stop Jenkins. I beg You to keep Casey safe. I beg You to guide me through this.

Casey would leave Kahlerville, and he'd never be able to find her again. His feelings for her made no sense, but they were there just the same. He craved the sound of her voice, to touch her red-brown hair and gaze into her wide blue eyes. A part of him longed for a life with Casey, no matter how crazy the thought.

The clock in the parlor chimed twice. He had to stop her, and that meant riding into town and keeping vigil over the parsonage. She'd leave before dawn—a remnant of her past.

Morgan swung his legs over the side of the bed and ran his fingers through his hair. If she stayed, he could protect her from Jenkins and the law without folks finding out her identity.

"I want to clear my name, prove I didn't do all those things slapped across those wanted posters."

He had the resources to help, and it was about time he turned his profession into something good.

Casey lit the lantern on the kitchen table. Soft shadows reached to the ceiling and cast a warm glow about the kitchen, as though welcoming her to the morning. She added kindling to the cookstove, then struck a match against the side. A small flame came to life, and she laid it atop the kindling. She blew on it gently, causing it to lick at the dry wood around it. The small task reminded her of the reverend's Sunday evening sermon. He'd compared sin to a small fire that raged out of control.

Within minutes, the comforting scent of burning wood and the nutty aroma of coffee filled the room. She lifted the heavy iron skillet onto the stove to fry up bacon and eggs, and this morning she'd try her hand at biscuits. The reverend's tasted wonderful, and he'd showed her how. This morning, she wanted to try mixing them herself. Besides, the sun hadn't risen, and she needed to keep busy.

Midway through cooking sizzling bacon and kneading biscuit

dough, she heard a knock at the kitchen door. Sensing the reverend might be needed, she dried her hands on her apron and opened the door. Morgan stood before her, hat in hand. She inwardly gasped.

"Good morning," he said. "May I come in?"

Her gaze met his haunting stare. He would not see how her heart languished over the differences separating them. "Yes, of course. Is something wrong? Do I need to wake the reverend?"

He shifted from one foot to the other, clearly not the confident man she'd viewed in the past. "I came to see you."

The logical side of her said to slam the door in his face.

"Please," he added. His clothes looked like he'd slept in them. "I have a few things to say."

She moved from the door, and he stepped inside. "The coffee's done, if you'd like a cup." She determined to be pleasant.

"I could use something to get the cobwebs out of my head."

Perhaps if you would answer my questions about Jenkins instead of leaving me to wonder. . .

He glanced about the kitchen while she poured the coffee. "Sure smells good. Would you like some help?"

"If that will make it easier for you to talk."

"Remember the breakfast we had along the Green River?" he whispered.

She nodded, afraid to look at him. "You fished while I tried to figure out how I could get my guns back." She picked up an extra apron.

He chuckled. "I had one eye on the fish and another one on you."

How well she remembered that morning. "Would you like to break the eggs?" When he nodded, she tied the apron around his waist. Too close. She must not get this close. A longing to touch him crept through her, but she refused to give in. "The basket and bowl are sitting on the table."

Morgan picked up an egg and tossed it in his palm. "I'm glad you're still here. I was afraid you'd be gone before I got here."

"I thought a lot about it, but for now I'm staying. What is it you want to say?" Her hand trembled.

"I make you nervous. You scare me to death, Cas—Shawne. . . ." He hesitated and reached for her hand, but she drew it back. "I know my word is worthless. I can't ask you to trust me when I haven't given you any reason to. But I'm going to show you I'm a different man. . . different from the one you met at your campsite in the mountains."

Casey scrutinized every line on his face, afraid to believe him for fear of being hurt. "Trust you about what?"

"I've spent the night searching my soul for the right answers about you and me—and everything else. My mother frets over me when I should be taking care of her. I know what I am, and how I intimidate those I love. Grant is a fine man, but I can't bring myself to tell him what an excellent job he's doing with the ranch. Instead, I treat him like a schoolboy and criticize every one of his decisions." He broke the egg into the bowl. "He runs the ranch better than I ever did. And poor Bonnie, I won't let her grow up, either. They need much more from me than they're getting."

He whirled around to face her. His jaw tightened. "I'm rambling on like a schoolboy. I've asked God to forgive me. Only He can mold me into a man of peace and integrity." He picked up another egg. "Then there's you and me."

"I'm not a part of your life." She cut perfectly rounded pieces of biscuit dough and placed them on a pan bathed in melted lard. If she dared to catch a glimpse of him, she'd relive the tears from the night before.

"But you are, whether you want to be or not. I want to help clear your name."

The mere words caused her to shake. "How?"

"I'm a lawyer."

She caught her breath. A hundred thoughts played through her mind. *Why would a lawyer track down Jenkins?* Best she keep that question to herself since her face was on so many wanted posters. "I never took you for a lawyer." She shrugged. "Bounty hunter or lawman sounds reasonable. Besides, I don't have the money to pay you."

"I'm not asking for payment."

"That's the only way it can be."

He peered into her face, then managed a laugh. "I think I've met my match. This bounty hunter, lawman, lawyer will name his price."

His laughter caused a smile to tug at her lips. "And what will that be?"

"Time."

"Time?"

"Yes. Accept my family's invitation for Sunday, and let me. . . " He paused. "Let me ask the reverend's permission to come courting."

Casey could only stare, afraid to utter a word and afraid not to. She swallowed the lump in her throat. "You know who I am, Morgan. You know my past. We can only speculate the future. I'd like to think I'm safe, but that's craziness. But what you're asking me. . .well, it's frightening."

"For me, too."

"I thought I recognized that voice," the reverend said. "My, you're here early, Morgan. Anything wrong?"

"No, sir. I'm visiting."

"At five thirty in the morning?"

Morgan took in a breath. "I had to talk to Shawne."

Casey poured the reverend a cup of coffee. She added a dollop of cream and handed the reverend the steaming brew. Listening to Morgan sputter through the reason why he was there nearly made her smile.

The reverend took a sip. "Are you trying to court my Shawne?"

Morgan's eyes widened. "As a matter of fact. . ." He glanced at her. "I am."

Hearing Morgan repeat his request made her shiver. Had they both turned into a pair of fools? Jenkins would kill them both, just like he had planned to do months ago.

The reverend cleared his throat, but she saw the merriment in his face. "Do you want this man to come courting, Shawne?"

She hadn't formed an answer yet. All the confusion since she'd visited with Morgan the day before crowded around her. He'd help her in return for her spending time in his company. Like a real lady. . . as if she weren't an outlaw who knew more about living in the wilds than about keeping a home, more about horses and guns than about baking pies and cakes. As if a man might enjoy her company, might even think of her as pretty.

"I want to think about it."

The following Sunday morning, Casey fretted over her appearance and what to say; she even rehearsed conversations in front of the mirror. Jocelyn, Bonnie, Grant, and Morgan arrived at the parsonage shortly after the worship service. She glanced at Morgan, and he tossed her a smile. Good. She hadn't spoken with him since Tuesday morning. She wanted him to come courting, but that invited feelings she didn't know how to handle. My, but he looked handsome in a clean shirt and trousers. Even his boots shined like glass.

"Are you sure you don't mind me leaving?" she asked the reverend for the third time.

"Nonsense." He peeked under a towel-covered dish from a church member. "I stated in our original agreement that you were to have every Sunday afternoon and evening free." He pointed a finger at her. "Now off with you, and don't you dare return before dusk or after evenin' church."

Before she could deliberate further upon the matter, the Andrewses whisked her off to the buckboard. Morgan had ridden his horse, and Bonnie rode in the back of the wagon. Stampede trotted along behind the wagon, although Casey was the only who could handle the stallion.

She stole a peek at Grant, who urged a pair of dapper mares down the road. He didn't look twenty years old yet, and with slightly deeper coloring than his mother and sister, he had the makings of a fine man. He resembled Morgan, except taller, and his almond-shaped eyes were green, not turquoise. Yet Casey noted his youth—his eagerness to embrace manhood, something Tim had once possessed and lost.

Rolling countryside with a choir of singing locusts and grass-hoppers slowly led them to the ranch. Casey loved this country, rich and green in the heart of summer. Tall pine trees sometimes darkened the dirt road and then faded in bright sunlight. At first the deep groves of trees troubled her, for they brought back reminders of rough men, lying in wait for an unsuspecting traveler. But her companions remained at ease, and she forced herself to relax.

Out of habit, she touched her dress pocket where her derringer used to hide. Her strength needed to be in God, not in a weapon. Guns had a place and a purpose, but not pressed against her body like a lady's corset.

The wagon stopped on a knoll where the landscape gave way to a breathtaking view of a valley below. *Like a dream.* Casey noted a large stone-and-frame farmhouse, a barn, several sheds, and a bunkhouse, all neatly kept. Beyond the buildings, a creek glistened in the sunlight like a satin ribbon winding through the valley.

The farm Casey remembered from her childhood had been a

mixture of dirt and sweat. Nothing for her to miss; nothing for her ever to want again. She never had enough to eat in winter and worked from sunrise to sunset during the spring, summer, and harvest.

Casey craned her neck to see the magnificent show of land. In the distance, specks of grazing horses and cattle sprinkled the fields—so many she couldn't count them. "Is this your ranch?"

"Yes, it is," Jocelyn said. "We call it the Double H. My late husband's name was Hayden, and when we first homesteaded the land, I referred to it as Hayden's Heaven. He liked the name so well that he chose the Double H as our brand. Together with Morgan, we cleared it and built our first home." Jocelyn pointed. "See the cabin far off in the western corner? That was our original home and where Bonnie and Grant were born. We have hundreds of acres for grazing and just as many in heavy timber. If you look to the east, you can see hills and forests, untouched except to hunt and fish. My husband left a legacy of the land he loved, many acres for his children to raise their own families."

"You are truly blessed," Casey said, using one of Sarah's words.

"You wouldn't say 'blessed' if you had to get up before sunrise and work until the sun went down," Grant said, then shoved a grin her way.

"But it's yours." Casey watched a horse race across the valley. "You must be very proud of it."

"Oh, I am." Grant narrowed his eyes. "When I'm not dog-tired."

Bonnie poked him in the ribs, and they both laughed. "Try cooking for all of you. Ranch hands eat like horses! It's a good thing Sheriff Kahler couldn't come today. There wouldn't have been enough food."

Sheriff Kahler. Casey clenched her fists. Was Bonnie sweet on the town's sheriff? She knew keeping company with these people was a mistake, and this proved it. She must have heard God wrong.

Staying now invited a noose around her neck.

Morgan rode up alongside them. "Grant does a better job running this ranch than most men twice his age."

Shock registered on Grant's face, but an even wider grin replaced it. "Thanks."

Once they arrived at the two-story home, the three women busily prepared the midday meal. Casey marveled at the homey feeling. Jocelyn sliced thick pieces of fresh bread, and layered smoked turkey in between. A pot of beans laden with bacon and onions had simmered on the cookstove since before sunup. Newly made applesauce, spiced with sweet-smelling cinnamon, topped the meal. She needed to learn how to cook something besides beans and corn bread. Every time she stirred up a batch of either, memories of the past crowded out the present.

Bonnie rang the dinner bell. Its *clang* broke the silence like unexpected rifle fire. Casey shivered in its wake and shoved the old haunts to the furthermost part of her mind. She felt leery of the rough looks from the hands trailing in to eat, but the men were polite and undoubtedly hungry, proving Bonnie's statement.

"I'm heading up to the old place," Morgan said after lunch.

Casey wondered if he wanted her to go with him. She said nothing. Being alone with him brought on feelings she didn't know how to handle.

"Soon as we clean up, if Mama doesn't mind, I'm hoping Shawne and I can take a walk. We might go riding later on," Bonnie said.

"Go ahead. I have some reading to do," Jocelyn said. "You girls get acquainted."

"Maybe I'll join you for that ride later," Morgan said, "unless Grant needs me."

The younger man shook his head and waved his hand to the ranch hands. "We have a few things to tend to."

Jocelyn frowned. "Son, the Sabbath is a day of rest."

"It will be right after we take care of moving the herd to make room for your Caroliny bull."

"That doesn't have to happen today."

He laughed. "Then when, Mama? In the middle of fence mending?"

Casey listened to the conversation, wishing that someday she might have a family of her own. These dear people had no idea of lawlessness, and she had no intention of informing them. At least not today.

CHAPTER 15

When the dishes were washed and the kitchen tidy, Bonnie and Casey walked toward the pasture where the horses grazed. The hot sun beat down on their sunbonnets, making Casey's head much too warm. For a moment, she considered tossing it aside, but her face was already brown from the sun. According to Rose, ladies were supposed to have milk-white skin.

She picked up the unmistakable smell of horses, and a longing to ride free tugged at her heart. If there was ever anything she missed about the past, it was riding as fast as the wind and breathing in nature.

Bonnie talked incessantly, first about poor Sarah and her illness, then on to the topic of the women at church. Only at Rose's place had she ever heard one woman talk so much. Casey always thought those girls talked so much because they were lonely.

Casey wanted to ask what had happened to Morgan's wife, but the right words never seemed to form. Perhaps she'd see a family cemetery while they were here, but even that wouldn't tell her how the woman died.

"Don't you think Sheriff Kahler is handsome with his black hair and all?" Bonnie asked.

Hard to think of a man being handsome when you're afraid of him. "I hadn't time to think about it."

"I really wanted him to join us today. He and Morgan are old friends, which still left us plenty of time together."

An invisible knife twisted in the pit of her stomach. She felt as though she were at the top of a cliff and had to find a way down. "Are you and the sheriff courting?"

"Not really. Ben wanted Morgan's permission, but he hasn't been around. But Mama says Morgan's changed and wants to talk to Grant and me. My dear Shawne, our oldest brother chases away every man who looks this direction." Bonnie attempted to sound light, but frustration laced her words.

"What does he do, run them off with a shotgun?"

"Almost. He's. . .oh, very protective. Seriously, he loves us all. I'm sure of it. He simply has a difficult time showing it." She shielded her eyes from the sun.

Bonnie stopped to gather a bouquet of daisies. Not far away, horses grazed. They lifted their noble heads, shook off a few pesky flies, and promptly ignored Casey and Bonnie.

"What are you looking for in a husband?" Bonnie gave Casey a sparkling smile.

She pondered the question. She wanted to keep the mood light, but she saw Morgan's face, heard his voice, and recalled his rugged features. Then she remembered her past and the unanswered questions about him.

"I'm not looking, but all teasing aside, I'd like to have a man who's my friend. I'd want him to lean on me when he has a problem, and I'd go to him with any problem. I want a man who will love me and make it a pleasure to keep his house and bear his children. Above all, he has to love God." The latter was a new addition to her list but very important.

Bonnie tucked an errant blond lock behind her ear. "When you find him, see if he has a brother. How did you meet Morgan?"

The sound of horse hooves shattered any answer Casey might have formed as a rider galloped toward them. Behind him two others rode slowly. Bonnie studied the approaching men. Her face suddenly blanched. Casey saw the alarm, and a thousand fears flashed through her mind. "What's the matter?"

"One of those men has been hurt." Bonnie gasped.

The first man pulled his heaving mount to a quick stop. "A bull got Rafael. Gotta get the wagon." He spurred his horse on to a dead run.

Casey stared at the two other riders lagging behind. One man hunched over his saddle. She picked up her skirts and raced toward them. Already she could see red staining his shirt. "Hurry, Bonnie. We need to help."

"I can't," Bonnie replied in a near whimper. "The blood. . . I can't stand the blood."

Casey ignored her. Only the injured man occupied her thoughts. The bull had gored him through his shirt and vest. She'd seen enough knife wounds to know how quickly a man could bleed to death. His head lay on his chest. One of his arms dangled alongside the horse's neck, and another clutched his pierced side. Blood oozed through his fingers and dribbled down over his shirt and chaps. The second rider held the injured man's reins.

"Let me help. He's bleeding way too much," she said. The two lifted him from his horse and onto the ground.

He moaned and struggled to breathe. How often had she heard the anguish of wounded men? His hand slipped aside, and she instantly covered the puncture with her hand. "We've got to stop the bleeding."

She glanced about. Bonnie stood at a distance, quaking at the sight. "Bonnie, rip a strip of my petticoat for a bandage."

Bonnie shook her head.

Casey wanted to scream at her, call her a coward. "Bonnie, please!"

Still, she refused to budge.

Casey stared into the face of the Mexican man kneeling beside her. Jocelyn had introduced him earlier during the noon meal as Jesse. "I need your help."

"What do I do?"

"Tear my petticoat into a long enough strip to go around him at least once." She turned her attention back to Rafael, not once giving Jesse an opportunity to refuse.

"*Gracias*, senorita, for helping my young friend."

Rafael's boyish face twisted in pain. "You're going to be just fine," she said in Spanish. "What did you say to make that bull so mad?"

Rafael attempted a feeble smile. Casey lifted her blood-soaked hand and placed the makeshift bandage over the wound. "Can you lift him?" she asked Jesse.

Wordlessly, he obliged. She slipped the cloth under and around Rafael's chest, covering the puncture. Thankfully, his slight frame permitted her to double the remaining portion of the bandage over the wound. Already, the bandage seeped red.

Gratitude radiated from Rafael's dark eyes, and Casey grasped his hand, knowing the touch of another often gave hope. "I will pray for you," she said.

A rider raced toward them.

"Senor Grant," Jesse said. "He help us."

Casey heard the respect in the man's voice. She realized he considered Grant an equal, not a boy.

Soon Grant knelt at the injured man's side. He spoke to Rafael in Spanish and reassured him that a rider had gone to fetch the wagon. "You bandaged him?" Grant asked, then glanced at her. "Of course you did. You have blood all over you." He peered up at her. "I wonder if I should carry him. The jostling of the wagon might do more harm than good."

"Can you manage?"

"He's small, wiry. I could at least meet the wagon midway. Better than sitting here doing nothing." Grant bent to examine the bandage before picking him up. "Looks good and tight. Jesse, would you bring back my horse?"

"*Sí,*" he replied.

Grant swung a gaze over his shoulder. "Thank you, Shawne. You probably saved Rafael's life. Are you all right?"

"I'm fine." She glanced ahead several feet to Bonnie, who hadn't taken a step since the ordeal began. "Your sister's not well, though."

Grant hoisted the man into his arms. "She can't tolerate anything." His voice echoed in disgust. "Can't depend on her at all." The rumblings of a wagon came from the distance. "Guess I won't have to tote him far."

"I'll take care of Bonnie." Casey wiped some of the blood from her hands onto the grass, then stood and ventured toward Bonnie. The stains on her dress would have to stay until she got back to the parsonage.

Bonnie's lips quivered, and she glanced beyond Casey's face. "Will he live?"

"I believe so," Casey said. "Although he's lost a lot of blood. Take a few deep breaths until you feel better." *God, help me. I'd like to slap her, and I know that's not the way You want me to be.*

"I'm sorry. I simply couldn't move." Bonnie wrung her hands. "How ever did you take care of him?"

"Comes natural, I think. Are you able to walk back?"

Bonnie nodded and avoided Casey's scrutiny. "Usually I faint, but this time I didn't look at what was going on." She broke into sobs. "Oh Shawne, if left to me, poor Rafael would have died. Mama will be so angry and disappointed. I am so weak—and the rest of the family will be frightfully upset with me."

At the sight of Bonnie's tears, Casey's heart softened. She had no right to judge the younger woman's reaction to the injury. What if Bonnie knew the life she'd led with a gang of outlaws? "Some folks handle things differently than others."

Bonnie lifted her dainty chin. "I'll tell Mama about what happened. Not that she'll be surprised."

The two walked back to the house in silence. Obviously the sight of blood still shook Bonnie, for she quietly wept. How odd for a girl who grew up on a ranch to become so upset over a little blood.

At the house, Bonnie told the story to her mother word for word, leaving out nothing. Casey listened with no desire to add any of her own reflections. Later, after Jocelyn had tended to the wounds and Grant had rode after the doctor, Jocelyn pulled Casey aside.

"Thanks for what you did out there."

"I'm glad I could help."

"I believe Rafael will be all right. Frankly, my daughter worries me. Do you know what I'd have done?"

Casey eyed the woman squarely.

"I'd have made her help whether she wanted to or not. That boy could have died."

She nodded, knowing full well what Jocelyn meant. Managing a ranch the size of the Double H and rearing Bonnie and Grant took a strong woman. Casey wanted to be just like her. For a moment she wondered if Morgan wanted that kind of woman, too.

On Monday morning, Morgan rode into town to see Ben Kahler. He hadn't heard about Rafael's injury until late Sunday afternoon.

Pride nearly caused him to explode with what Casey had done. The praises from his family and Jesse fortified his belief in her ability to live a life free from those who wanted her dead. He regretted not telling her himself, but by the time he returned from the cabin, she'd elected to ride into town with Grant and Rafael to meet the doctor, who had been out on another case. *That's my Casey, tending to those who are hurt.*

Now, as he made his way down the streets to Ben Kahler's office, he deliberated how to handle seeing his old friend. Amends needed to be made with Ben, but Morgan also needed to find out about the Jenkins gang. Using friendship to help Casey ground at his resolve to live for the Lord.

He tied Twister to the hitching post and glanced around at the town. If Jenkins discovered Casey was here, he'd tear the place apart. Innocent people would lie dead in the streets, people he knew and cared for. Whether Casey agreed with him or not, Morgan intended to start working on her case. He no more believed she was guilty of all the crimes credited to her name than he doubted God's hand in bringing the two of them back together.

Stepping into Ben's office, he found his friend at a clean desk, reading a newspaper.

"Is this town so quiet that you have to find things to keep busy?" Morgan asked. "Your desk is clean except for that stack of wanted posters."

Ben dropped the paper, and a wide grin spread across his face. He stood and grabbed Morgan's hand. "Why didn't you tell me yesterday you were heading into town? We could have gone fishing."

"I'm right. Kahlerville is much too tame for you. Of course, the folks here owe that to you."

"I think a few other folks had a hand in it, too. Sit down. How long are you home?"

"Permanently. I left the old Morgan behind."

"So seeing you in church yesterday wasn't to please your mother?"

"Nope. Me and the Lord are back on speaking terms, or rather I started listening."

"Good. I'm glad, real glad."

"Well, Sheriff Kahler, I have a question for you."

Ben raised a brow. "Fishing? Hunting? You name it."

Morgan laughed. "Are your intentions honorable when it comes to my sister?"

His face reddened. "How'd you know?"

"I'm a lawyer, remember? I'm supposed to look for signs of guilt. And by the way you two were eyeing each other yesterday, I doubt if either of you could recall the sermon."

"Guilty. And, yes, I have honorable intentions. I want to come calling on Bonnie."

"You didn't need my permission. We've always been like brothers. Couldn't think of a better man to come courtin'."

"Thanks. I might just ride over your way tonight. Want to head over to the boardinghouse for some coffee, catch up on old times?"

"Sure, but first I want to know if you've heard anything about Jenkins and his bunch. I may be finished chasing after him, but he still needs to face a judge."

Ben nodded. "I read everything I can get my hands on about that gang. The last I heard he was spending most of his time looking for his woman."

"I heard she left him. Can't blame her."

"She has a price on her head, too. I'd like to get both of them."

"I'd rather find him."

Ben shrugged. "And I'd like to be the one to catch the whole gang. You know, I found myself studying every redheaded woman in this town. I even took a second look at Miss Flanagan, the woman who's taking care of the reverend's wife. Makes me ashamed of myself."

"You're just wanting to be the lawman who ends the Jenkins gang. You probably want a dime novel written about you." Morgan forced a laugh while his insides churned.

Ben leaned across his desk. "It has crossed my mind."

CHAPTER 16

Morgan left Ben's office and made his way down the dusty street to the telegraph office. Doc needed to know what was going on. His meeting with Ben had reinforced what Morgan feared: Casey wasn't safe. Kahlerville had not been a good choice.

Or had it? His mind jumped from one alternative to the other. Ben had a reputation for being a tough lawman. He'd soon put aside any thoughts of Casey's looks because it would be stupid for her to settle here. Also, Morgan and Casey were keeping company. No one would ever expect him to have connections with her. Or would Ben figure it out? Casey and Ben were clever as foxes, but who'd outsmart the other?

He sent Doc a telegram stating he had their problem under control. *Who am I fooling?*

Before he realized what he was doing, Morgan had walked to the parsonage. Maybe she'd have time to talk. The reverend sat on the front porch with his Bible and some paper, no doubt working on his next sermon.

"Is Miss Shawne free to speak to me for a few minutes?"

The reverend chuckled. "Did she agree for you to come courtin'?"

"No. I hoped to persuade her a bit."

"She's inside, Morgan. Go on in. Last I saw of her, she was working on a peach cobbler."

He found her in the kitchen. "I smell peaches. Are you baking something for me?"

She startled and smiled. "You might be risking your life."

"Wouldn't be the first time."

She glanced away, then wiped her hands. "How's Rafael?"

"Doing fine, thanks to you. The doctor patched him up, but he'll be down for a while."

"Are you here to see me?"

"I am. Got a matter to discuss with you." He looked about. "Is it safe to talk?"

"I believe so." Suddenly she paled. "There's trouble. I can see it in your face."

"Maybe. I've just come from the sheriff's office."

She stiffened. "And what did he say?"

"He's determined to catch the Jenkins gang."

"That could be good as long as he doesn't recognize me. Or has he?"

"Not yet, and I don't know if he will. He'd never suspect you as long as the town knows we're friends."

"That makes sense. I suppose they all know you were after Jenkins." She sighed. "I think I need to leave town. By the time Sheriff Kahler realized I was gone, I'd be miles away."

"Still running."

"Suppose so."

"Then let me help you clear your name. Forget about me courting. I'd like it, but saving you is more important."

"I don't know, Morgan. The more I think on it, the more I wonder if my choices are to either ride out of here or turn myself in."

He stepped closer and took her hand. "Please stay. We can make things right with the law."

She sighed and shook her hand free. "It's not you that's fixin' to swing."

Sarah and the reverend introduced Casey to countless people over the days that followed. Occasionally ladies from the church stopped by to bring gifts of food or flowers and visit with Sarah. Unfamiliar faces soon became friends, and Casey learned to relax and make sure she had something to serve them. Slowly the woman she wanted to become emerged from the shell of doubt and despair. But the lingering shadows of Sheriff Kahler and Jenkins clung to every thought. She desperately wanted to leave Kahlerville, but each time she prayed, God impressed upon her to stay. She didn't know why. One thing she knew for certain: She must find the strength to tell the reverend and Sarah the truth.

"I see the Subtle Matchmakers Society has arrived," Reverend Rainer said to her one afternoon when several ladies visited with Sarah.

Casey felt her cheeks grow warm. "They didn't bring anyone for me to meet today." She glanced about for fear one of the well-meaning ladies might overhear.

He chuckled, and his gray eyes twinkled. "Now was it two or three young men who escorted them last week? I believe they were out-of-town guests of one of our church members."

She grinned and stared at the stairway. "Just two, and they were very polite."

"Ah, one of them looked like he'd been run over by a herd of stampeding buffalo."

"Reverend!"

John Rainer roared. "Well, he was a bit homely."

Cautiously, she peered up the stairs to the balcony. "Hush, his aunt will hear."

"Yes, ma'am."

They both laughed.

He leaned in closer. "I don't believe Morgan has a thing to worry about."

He didn't. They hadn't talked since the day he told her about Sheriff Kahler's ambitions, and that was over two weeks ago. But the thought lingered. Every time she saw him, her heart did a little flip.

❧❦❧

Morgan stood outside the parsonage. His boots were shined. His clothes were clean, and his insides rumbled like a thunderstorm. He'd rather face a courtroom of wolves. Taking a deep breath, he knocked on the door. Nearly three weeks had passed since he'd asked Casey about courting. She'd had long enough to think about it. Seeing her in church and when she came to visit the ranch drove him to the edge of taking a plunge over a cliff. Today he had to find out.

The reverend greeted him with a firm handshake. "Won't you come in?"

"I can wait out here. Is Casey free to talk?"

"You two." The reverend chuckled. "She's with Sarah. Let me check with her. Sure you don't want to wait inside?"

"No. This'll be fine."

Once the reverend disappeared, Morgan paced the front porch. He scared off a black cat and nearly knocked over a plant. His insides hadn't been this shook up since he tried his first case. Casey O'Hare had no right to stir up his mind like this.

I'm being selfish here. Sarah may need her. But Sarah doesn't know the danger her Shawne is in.

The door opened. Casey's smile made him tongue-tied—Morgan Andrews, the lawyer who had all the confidence. She wore a light blue dress that matched her eyes. Her hair was swept up loosely in the back except for a few curls that framed her face. God could not have created a more beautiful woman. She stepped onto the porch and shut the door behind her.

"The reverend said you wanted to talk to me. Sarah's sleeping, so I have a few minutes."

"How is she?"

"About the same. Some days are good, and others are hard." She kept her distance. Perhaps she'd already made up her mind.

He wet his lips. "Have you made a decision about us?"

"I have." She paused. "I believe if you want to call on me, after all the things I've done and with the understanding that the law or Jenkins could ride up to the parsonage today, I'm willing."

Morgan felt himself smiling from the inside out. "Could we start with a picnic after church?"

"That would be fine."

"And I'd like to discuss the other item we spoke about."

"All right." Her slender shoulders lifted and fell. "I'll have the food ready after church."

"I was going to ask Bonnie."

"No need. Consider the picnic a payment for our other discussion."

On Sunday morning, Casey woke before five to fry chicken, boil corn, roast potatoes, and bake a blackberry cobbler. She cooked plenty so the reverend and Sarah didn't have to concern themselves with dinner. All during church, her mind wandered. She dreamed about spending the afternoon with Morgan; then she'd mentally shake herself and give the reverend her attention. She'd heard him give the sermon yesterday for Sarah's review, but that wasn't an excuse to ignore him today.

When the service dismissed, Casey whirled around to find Morgan at her side. She laughed; he seemed as excited as a little boy finding a litter of puppies. Once they said their proper good-byes, he escorted her to the parsonage.

"I forgot to tell you one very important thing about picnics," he said as he loaded the back of the wagon with the picnic basket.

"What's that?" She started to add that she'd never been on a picnic before, but decided against it.

"You have to let me kiss you."

"Morgan!" She glanced in every direction. "What if someone heard you?"

"I'm only being honest." He chuckled and helped her onto the wagon seat. "I might have to apologize."

So he wanted to tease? "No point in apologizing for something that won't happen." Her heart raced, but she willed it to calm. *With a kiss, you'd steal a bit more of my heart.*

"If you want to eat, it'll cost you a kiss."

"But I cooked the food." They laughed together, which began talk of familiar matters from the weather to the latest rumors on the outlaw trail. Neither of them mentioned Jenkins or the sheriff. No point in ripping open old wounds. They headed out of town over a winding road that led over rolling hills.

"Did you like Arizona?" Nervousness had set in, causing her to search her frenzied mind for something to say.

"Naw, too dry and desolate for me and a lot of hard riding. But the desert does have a beauty all its own. The sunset reminds me of the color of your hair."

Casey blushed crimson and couldn't think of a single reply.

He laughed. "I don't recall any wanted posters mentioning the many shades of red in your face." He paused. "Do you miss any of the old life?"

Her skin chilled with irritation. "No, I don't miss any of it except racing my horse across a flat stretch of land. Why?"

"No reason." His eyes fixed on the road—unreadable.

Silence rode between them.

"I'm starved." He avoided her gaze. "I know a good spot down to the right. It's near a creek, lots of overhanging trees covered with moss."

He suddenly sounded cold. What had happened since leaving the parsonage?

"I'm hungry, too."

Morgan jumped to the ground and reached to help her from the wagon. The moment his hands grasped her firmly by the waist, a shiver raced from her head to her toes. Their gazes locked as he fairly swept her up into the air and down onto the soft earth. She remained motionless and dizzy beneath the cool shade, not wanting to break the spell or allow her feelings to rule the moment. He lifted a wisp of a curl from the side of her face and wound it around his finger while he searched her features. She questioned his thoughts, for his brow wrinkled in a curious manner.

With an inward sigh, she wondered if her eyes told what she could not say. His thumb traced the outline of her mouth, then lifted her chin. A slight curve played upon his lips as he descended upon hers, gently tasting, as if she were a fine porcelain doll ready to shatter into irreparable pieces. The touch, the unspoken feelings, everything she ever dared to believe in his kiss soared far beyond her deepest dreams. As his kiss deepened, her first real kiss, the reality of being alone with Morgan cautioned her, and she pulled herself away from him.

"I told you I might need to apologize." He released her, yet his attention stayed focused on her.

"There's no need." She glanced away.

"I don't understand why God put you in my life." He took her clammy hands into his and inhaled deeply. "We are the two most unlikely people in the world to be together."

"I think this has more to do with your past than what you're telling me." Was now the right time to ask about his deceased wife?

"Someday I might be able to talk about it."

"Until then?"

"We'll see what God brings." Morgan touched her cheek. "I care about you, Casey. Don't you know that by now? I've ridden miles looking for you. I've dreamed of you for weeks on end. And now. . . now you're here in arm's reach, and I don't know what to do."

"What do you mean? You're talking in riddles. I agree for you to come courting; then you tell me we're an unlikely couple. Now you tell me you care." When he reached for her, she shook her head. The tension between them blazed like a hot prairie fire.

He stepped closer, and again she stepped back.

"You tell me what you expect from me, and I'll abide by it. I'll even take you back to the parsonage, if that's what you want."

I should demand it this very minute. Casey peered up into the trees and listened to the rustle of the branches woven with the gurgling of the stream beside them. She refused to let him see what his nearness did to her. "Morgan, I don't want this afternoon to end before it begins. I want today to be perfect, to spend it with you. Let's not talk about unpleasant things, not now."

She stopped herself before uttering another word. Too much had already been said, and she suspected Morgan already knew the love she held in her heart. Her vulnerability with him would get her into trouble. She'd heard the promises of men before and understood that their physical needs guided their words. Morgan seemed different from them, or maybe she just wanted to believe he was unlike any man she'd ever met.

"You're right. We're supposed to have a picnic." He stared out over the creek where the sun cast diamondlike patterns across the water. The light scent of wildflowers wafted in the still air.

"I want to understand." Casey had long since realized he had a secret. She couldn't ignore the pain in his eyes.

He shook his head. "Not today." He waved his hand around them. "Look at this beautiful day."

"When you're ready, I'll listen to every word." She hesitated. "Is it my outlaw past?"

"Casey, you were never really an outlaw, just a naive young girl. How could you have known the price for following Tim?" His fingers brushed against her cheek, and his eyes softened. "You're beautiful and wise—a rarity and a treasure. You deserve a good man who'll treasure you with affection and tenderness." He turned and ambled toward the creek, the brush crackling beneath his boots.

Whirling back around, he captured her gaze. "A few moments ago, I saw the passion in your eyes, but then it changed to fear. I realize you're afraid to trust, and I'm afraid to love. We're a peculiar pair." He picked up a stone, then skipped it across the water. "I can't explain why I trailed Jenkins, and I can't ask you to wait until I'm able to tell it all. The hatred for him was with me for so long that sometimes I wonder if I'm no better than he." Taking a labored breath, he continued. "But with God's help I'll see this through." The circles spread across the creek, ever circling, ever widening.

"I'm to blame for my own actions, Morgan. That much I know. Maybe we're not such a peculiar pair after all."

"The wounds are deep, and the years haven't healed them. They are a part of me, ugly and cruel. Ask my family. They've seen my worst."

"But I've seen your best."

Casey studied the creek, quiet and peaceful, all the while remembering the time in the shelter of the overhanging rock along the Green River. She and Morgan were still running.

He slammed his fist into his palm. "You'll always be looking over your shoulder for Jenkins or the law." He seized her shoulders and forced her to look straight into his eyes. "No woman should live this way." Instantly he lifted his hands from her. "I'm sorry. I had no right to grab you."

Casey massaged her shoulders. "I don't want to read your epitaph on the side of a tombstone. If you help me, then you're in as much trouble as I am." She bent and picked up a yellow-petaled wildflower. She had enough experience in veering the thoughts of men, except this time it was to help Morgan, not herself. *Talk of something else. Leave the past behind.* "I'm still hungry."

"And the lady shall eat." He walked past her and on to the wagon, where he lifted out the basket. "There's a spot over there." He pointed to a huge oak with branches low enough for them to sit and enjoy the afternoon.

"Good choice." She smiled.

The hours passed quickly and without further incident. Neither spoke of what brought them together or the future. Croaking frogs, noisy blue jays, and a picnic lunch spread out on a red-checkered tablecloth absorbed all of their attention.

Late in the afternoon, Casey reluctantly gathered up the remains of their picnic. The sun dipped low in the horizon, painting the sky in yellow and pinkish orange as if holding on to the last bit of day. They'd laughed and teased, yet she knew nothing more about

Morgan, except that he was clinging to God for help.

Task completed, she grasped the basket's handle as Morgan's hand slipped over hers. Their fingers touched, then slowly entwined, and she felt the fervor between them again burst into flame.

"You are a precious angel," he said. "Too bad you were thrown into a den of lions."

Not quite sure if she wanted to lose herself in the depths of his eyes, she watched a fat squirrel scamper up a tree. "I learned how to live with those lions," she said, "and I survived. Those days taught me how to read a man by his actions rather than his words."

"Is that why we get along so well?"

"No. It's why we don't. We're both trying to outthink the other."

"I believe you're wrong, Miss Casey Shawne. What are my actions telling you now?" He inched closer, and his dimple deepened.

She took a deep breath. "I'm not sure."

He chuckled. "I'm trying to convince myself that I don't need another kiss."

"Keep trying, and you'll believe it." But inside she began to waver.

"I'm losing." He gathered her up in his arms, and she suddenly knew what it was like to be a snowflake and melt with the first hint of spring.

"You're a better man not to give in to temptation," she said.

"Give me *one* good reason why I can't have *one* kiss?" He bent closer.

"Because one won't be enough."

"Exactly." As his lips tasted hers, her arm slipped around his neck, and she wove her fingers through his thick hair. He pulled her closer, tighter. They both abandoned the grip on the basket and let it fall to the soft earth. Her senses reeled. All that mattered was the soaring in her heart for a man she'd grown to love.

She lifted her fingers from his hair and stopped the kiss, not wanting the moment to end but understanding where the passion led. Visions of Jenkins. . .his dirty hands. . .his vile breath. . . "We need to get back before church."

"You're right." Morgan took a deep breath and smiled. "What you do to me isn't fair."

He helped her onto the wagon seat and placed the basket on the wagon bed. They said little on the return trip. The birds and insects serenaded them and broke the tortuous silence.

"This has been a lovely picnic," she said. "My first, and it will always be the best."

He took her hand into his. "God willing, I want to make every day a picnic much finer than today."

She heard the longing in his voice. "Morgan. That's not real life. Ignoring the ugly things doesn't make them go away. The things I've done. . . Someday I must pay."

"Did you ever rob anyone?"

"No."

"Ever shoot anyone except for the man in Billings?"

"You and I shot at a few when Jenkins was after us."

"That was self-defense."

"Morgan, I've read the newspapers and seen the wanted posters. I rode with the Jenkins gang. No matter that he threatened to kill me or Tim if I left. No matter that he threatened to sell me to a brothel. No court of law will ever believe me. Then. . ."

"Then what?"

"I want to be free of all this. Some days, I don't care if it's Jenkins who finds me or the law."

CHAPTER 17

"Let's all go riding this afternoon," Jocelyn suggested one Sunday afternoon. Casey sat outside with Jocelyn and Bonnie while Morgan and Grant discussed a problem with one of the ranch hands.

"Yes, I'd love to," Bonnie said. "What do you think, Shawne?"

"I didn't think it was, well, proper for a lady to wear men's clothing," she said, all the while thinking how she missed riding her stallion.

"It's not." Jocelyn laughed. "We wear riding skirts. It's so much easier and takes care of those ladies who fret about being proper."

Casey had no idea what they were talking about. Women were either ladies and wore skirts and dresses, or they weren't and wore trousers like a man. "I'm not so sure what you're talking about."

"I'll show you mine." Bonnie hurried into the kitchen and up the stairs. Moments later she presented the skirt. "See, it's split like a man's trousers but very proper. You can swing up into the saddle easily without the nuisance of a dress or sidesaddle. I thought you rode here on that monster horse of yours."

"I did, but I wore men's clothes." No point in lying about it. She'd not yet had an opportunity to ride Stampede, but Morgan had insisted the stallion pasture at the ranch.

Casey examined the article of clothing. "I think I could make one with the sewing lessons I've been taking."

"Of course you could," Jocelyn said. "But today you can wear one of mine. They're so sensible for ranch work."

The thought of riding again without regard to dress thrilled her.

Once they all changed clothes and prepared their horses, Casey climbed into the saddle of her stallion.

"Shawne, how do you control such a strong-willed horse?" Jocelyn asked. Stampede reared and snorted.

"My brother taught me." She sensed the old twist in the pit of her stomach.

"And you rode that animal to Kahlerville?" Jocelyn swung up onto her own mare. Casey caught her breath. *Please, no more questions.* "Yes, ma'am."

"From where?" Bonnie asked.

I will not lie. "West Texas."

Bonnie's eyes widened. "By yourself? Weren't you afraid?"

Casey forced herself to look at her new friend. "It's a long story, and one I'm not ready to talk about yet." She took a ragged breath and saw Jocelyn stare at her intently.

Jocelyn's features shifted to concern. "When you're ready, we'll have a good old-fashioned lady's talk over a cup of coffee. This afternoon we're off to have a good time."

How much longer can I keep the truth from this precious family and dear Reverend Rainer and Sarah? Every day brings more deceit. Every day puts them in danger. What kind of a woman am I?

Galloping across the countryside reminded Casey of days gone by. She relived the wild freedom of the wind blowing through her hair and the excitement of a powerful animal racing beneath her. When Stampede lunged forward, living up to his name, she felt at one with his strenuous pull. And when he lifted her over ditches and fences, she felt like a bird in flight.

Riding always brought back memories of Morgan and their race from Jenkins. As much as her feelings had grown for Morgan, she still wondered if he was a bounty hunter along with being a lawyer. No one had said, but why would he tell his family? His secrets cautioned her every move around him, and his comments about the past ofttimes frightened her. It made no sense at all. Why did he want to come courting when he had his choice of any woman around? Plenty of single women were interested in him; she'd seen the longing in their eyes. And he still hadn't told her about his wife.

On she rode, as though racing against the demons plaguing her life. A childlike passion to keep one step ahead of the things she couldn't change challenged her to ride faster.

"Shawne," Bonnie called. "We're having a hard time keeping up."

Casey whipped a glance over her shoulder and saw her friends were struggling. Obviously her idea of riding was a little different than that of her friends.

"You are such a good horsewoman. I'm envious," Bonnie said once she rode alongside her.

"Thank you," Casey said. "Riding comes natural."

"You've exhausted me." Bonnie shook her head. "I'm heading back."

"I'll join you," Jocelyn said. "But, Shawne, you go ahead."

"Are you sure?" Casey hated to end her ride, but she didn't want to appear selfish.

"Nonsense. If I see Morgan, I'll send him your way." Jocelyn smiled beneath a low-brimmed hat, revealing a few wrinkles and some tiny lines etched around her eyes. "I'm glad you two are getting along well."

Casey returned the smile, but she wondered how Jocelyn would feel if she knew the truth. "Will all of you be available before Morgan takes me back to town? I'd like to share the cup of coffee that you spoke of earlier, but I want to talk to all of you."

"Grant, too?" Jocelyn asked.

"Yes. I'd like to talk to everyone."

Jocelyn shook her head. "Grant is heading out to the north pasture to mend fence with two of the hands. He may have already left. I'm sorry. Can't seem to get that boy to take a day of rest. Maybe next Sunday?"

"Of course. Our talk can wait a little while longer."

"We all care for you, Shawne. If this is urgent, I can send a rider after Grant."

"No, ma'am. Next week is fine."

Jocelyn and Bonnie turned their horses and left Casey praying for courage. Next week, she'd tell the truth. With a deep breath, she dug her heels into Stampede. Next week, she'd decide if Morgan could help her—ever. She had a little money saved but not enough. Morgan said he didn't want payment, but Casey refused to be beholden to anyone. She fought her feelings for him every moment of the day.

She raced over the grazing land until her horse heaved and she was forced to bring the animal to a walk. In the distance, she saw a rider and shielded her eyes from the sun. *Morgan. How can I love him from a distance and keep him and those I love from danger? I'm selfish, purely selfish.*

As he rode nearer, she pondered one more time the idea of turning herself in.

"Someone after you?" he asked.

She blinked and caught a mischievous sparkle in his eyes. "Yeah, I heard you were looking for me."

"And you didn't want to get caught?"

She wondered how much truth lay in those words. "Not today. You can walk with me if you like." She swung down from the saddle and grabbed Stampede by the reins. "I'll make my horse mind."

He chuckled, the familiar deep-throated sound that tickled her toes. The September heat was sweltering, but she didn't really care. Being safe took precedence over any kind of physical comfort.

They stopped to enjoy a view of the valley from a hilltop. "Are you remembering the last time we rode together?" Morgan asked.

His glance sent her emotions into a whirl. Away from his family and the ranch hands, she saw him unmask his normally controlled exterior to reveal one of desire.

"How could I forget?" Casey asked. "I can safely say we're two different people now, thanks to the Lord." She paused and drank in the beauty around them. "What was it like when you first arrived here with your parents?"

"Well, we cut down more trees than I cared to count. Worked from sunup to long past sundown, but it was all worth it when my father purchased the first spread of cattle and later on added good horse stock." He gestured across the valley. "Just look at the winding streams and pastureland. You know, Mama worked right beside us and not once complained."

"I can see her working as hard as a man."

"I remember the day we finished the cabin, after spending the spring and summer with only the wagon as shelter. She wanted to celebrate by having my father bring out his fiddle, but we were all too tired." He paused. "I don't think I'd trade those early days for anything." Morgan lifted his hat and brushed back the hair on his forehead. "We had lean winters and fights over barbed wire, and I remember when Bonnie and Grant were born." He paused, obviously deep in thought.

"Sounds like the memories that make a man." She studied his face, and the realization of her growing feelings nearly staggered her.

"The other day, I gave Grant full rein of the ranch until he's ready to head east for school." He grinned. "My little brother wants to be a doctor."

She recalled how he handled the young man gored by the bull—and compared the traits of Doc in Vernal. "He'll be a fine doctor."

"I agree, and I'm lucky he doesn't despise me for the rough times I've given him."

"He loves you, Morgan." She craned her neck to see the outline of the log cabin in the distance. "And you plan to live in your parents' first home? Seems fitting."

"I don't think so. Do you still carry a derringer?" Morgan asked.

Startled, she glanced into his face, but his hat hid his features. "No, not since I came to Kahlerville and found the Lord. I don't carry a knife, either. Why?"

He shrugged. "Just curious." When he looked her way, a haunting, faraway look spilled into his turquoise eyes. "This life rests well with you."

"Thank you. I feel like I belong here, even if the future is so uncertain." She sighed. "I'm so glad you suggested Texas."

"It's God's country, for sure."

"I'd probably be dead if I'd stayed in Arizona. A part of me will always long to be in the open spaces, but sleeping in a feather bed definitely has more advantages. My, I'm beginning to sound like a woman." Embarrassed, she ceased speaking.

Morgan chuckled, and she felt her cheeks flush. "You're happy, and I enjoy hearing you talk."

They walked on in silence. Casey sensed something wrong with Morgan, but she couldn't figure out what. So many things swept through her mind. "I read in the newspaper that Frank James walked into the governor of Missouri's office and surrendered." She paused.

"Do you know what happened? I'm not sure the article gave an accurate accounting."

"Ben said Frank got too nervous after Bob Ford shot Jesse. Of course, Governor Crittenden stood behind both deals."

"Bob and Charlie Ford aren't any better than Frank and Jesse."

"I disagree," he said. "Jesse's dead, and Frank won't be holding up any more trains. They were the worst. There's nothing left of the James gang and the infamous brothers but history."

"All I'm saying is Bob and Charlie Ford rode with Frank and Jesse. That makes them the same."

"Do you know any of those men?" Morgan's face hardened.

She stiffened at his abruptness and slowly formed her words. "I've met them. Jenkins originally rode with a lot of men who later turned outlaw after the Civil War." She shrugged. "They belonged to Quantrill's Raiders. The story goes they raided Union forces along the Kansas-Missouri border. After the war, Frank and Jesse gathered up what was left of the guerrillas and formed a gang."

"Why didn't Jenkins stick with the James brothers?"

His sharpness piqued her, and she regretted mentioning the newspaper article. "He probably couldn't take orders from anyone else. Jenkins has a way of taking over. He's persuasive when it comes to having men do what he wants. Tim told me he was a young officer in the Civil War and never accepted losing. Anyway, with the James gang broke up, Jenkins won't last long."

His gaze bore into hers—the same look she'd seen in the mountains. She despised this side of him. The intensity brought back the old feelings of alarm and mistrust.

"What's the matter?"

"Don't you miss the excitement?" he asked.

Casey attempted to bite back her anger. "Morgan, you've questioned me about this before, and the answer is still no. There's no satisfaction in seeing men take what isn't theirs or in the bloodbath that follows."

"Then why did you stay with them for so long? You must have liked something about it."

Casey clenched her fists and dug her fingers into her palms. Suddenly it didn't matter if Morgan knew her fury. He'd insulted her, and she'd done nothing to provoke him. He cast a seething glare, and it echoed with disgust. "I don't have to explain my life to you. It's none of your business why I did anything at all. I have better things to do than allow you to take out your bad temper on me."

Morgan shook with anger, and fear raced up her spine, but she managed to maintain a placid demeanor. Just like in the old days. No man would steal her confidence.

"All right. You can have your piece," he said. "But I tell you this. I will never understand why you stayed with Jenkins for seven years, unless you really liked that life." He grabbed his reins.

She faced him squarely. "I don't want you to ever come near me again. Who are you to judge? Aren't you the man who admitted his thirst for blood? Aren't you the man who planned to use me to get to Jenkins? How do I know you aren't still planning to do the same thing? You're no better than Jenkins."

"You don't know anything about it."

"Whose fault is that?" Casey refused to look at him. She turned away to the wide, green pastures and the rolling hills in the distance. She heard the sound of the saddle creaking under his weight just before hoofbeats. She was alone again. The safest place to be.

Shaking, she took a deep breath. *Pray. I need to pray.* How could Jocelyn have birthed a son who could change his moods in the blink of an eye? Sinking to the ground, numb and drained of strength, she couldn't stop the tears that spilled uncontrollably over her cheeks. She buried her face in her hands. She intended neither to hear his accusations again nor to allow him to tug at her heartstrings. Leaving

Kahlerville seemed like the best thing to do. She'd invited trouble by staying this long.

Casey loathed her weakness when it came to Morgan. More so, she hated losing control of her temper. Too many times she'd seen men make foolish and deadly choices in the heat of anger. Her past resolve to allow only God to rule her emotions lay shattered and broken, just like her dreams of Morgan.

Something from his past must have driven him to what he said today. Frustrated and confused, she felt the same deep sense of betrayal that she'd experienced whenever Tim allowed Jenkins to beat her. The bruises finally healed, but the hurt of Tim's turning his back stayed with her. She despised Morgan's temper and his reasons for not telling her the truth about himself. Furthermore, she didn't care.

She'd tell the reverend and Sarah the truth before she rode out. In about six months' time, she'd have enough money to hire a lawyer. Then she could hold her head high.

Casey wiped her cheeks. Stampede nuzzled her neck. Her dear stallion was more faithful than the man who claimed to care. Blinking back the wetness, she slowly walked across the grassland. The ways of violence. . . Would she ever be free?

CHAPTER 18

By the time Morgan had ridden back to the barn, he'd worked through most of his anger. But what had he done to his relationship with Casey, if he really had one at all? He stared at the cabin in the distance. That's where it had started. Sometimes he wanted to burn the place down, but the memories would still be there, tearing away at his soul like a flesh-eating animal.

What had happened at the little church where he prayed for God to remove the hate and bitterness? When he'd walked out of there, he'd felt clean again. It was a new beginning, or so he thought, and he believed he'd left it all at the altar—until today.

Frustrated, he sat atop his horse, and his gaze swept the horizon to where he'd left Casey. No point in heading back her way. He didn't deserve her forgiveness, not for the spiteful things he'd hurled at her. None of this was her fault.

Doesn't matter if she forgives you or not. What's important is that you ask.

Morgan lifted his hat and wiped the sweat from his brow with the back of his hand. He'd rather face a she-bear with cubs than apologize to Casey. The old Morgan allowed hate to consume him.

The new Morgan fought those flames of bitterness. True, he couldn't ride back there alone, but Jesus rode a white horse beside him.

He blew out a ragged breath and raced back to Casey. She hadn't ventured far from where he'd left, and her red eyes and splotchy face told him exactly what his words had caused. She carried her hat, and her long auburn hair lay in waves about her shoulders. It glistened in the sun like spun gold. He remembered the newspapers describing Casey O'Hare: *Hair the color of fire. The face of an angel, but beware of her trigger finger and her lust for whatever you own.* She'd stolen Morgan's heart, and he didn't have the sense to treat her like a human being. Casey kept right on walking as though she were alone.

"Casey."

"You heard me earlier."

"Casey, would you give me a chance to apologize?"

"If you don't stop using my name, someone will hear, and I don't have a hankering to be hung or shot."

"I'm sorry."

She whipped around like a trapped animal ready to strike. Hurt more powerful than hatred penetrated her gaze. "Are you?"

"Yes," he said. "I love you. I realize it's too late, but it's the truth."

"Love? How do you treat your enemies?"

Her words stung. "I love you, and I don't know what to do about it."

Casey sucked in her breath. "Maybe you should learn what love means." She lifted her chin and glanced straight ahead. "I don't claim to know, but I don't think it causes what happened today."

"It's not you." He desperately needed to convince her, but how? Reveal a tale so horrible that no one around him ever hinted of it?

"Jenkins used to say the same thing."

Morgan felt his blood run cold. "Don't compare me—"

She waved her hand in his face. "Jenkins used to say the same thing," she repeated. "When Tim wasn't around, he'd swear his love and promise me anything I wanted. Then he'd beat me because I refused him. Later he'd say I deserved it for not wanting to be his woman. I'd hurt for days from those beatings." She tightened her chin. "Funny thing, none of those beatings ever hurt like I feel now. Guess I'm feeling sorry for myself. I'm an outlaw. Trash. And you just proved it." She brushed past him and mounted her stallion. "I'll ride my horse back to the parsonage."

Morgan didn't try to stop her. All thoughts of earning the woman's love had vanished. And it was his fault.

❧

Casey managed a smile for Jocelyn and Bonnie, then explained she needed to get back to the parsonage. Her head ached and her emotions were spent after the ordeal with Morgan. "I'm not feeling well," she said. "I'd like to rest a little before tonight's church services."

"Sorry you're feeling poorly," Jocelyn said. "Let me find Morgan, or I can take you myself."

"I'll ride my horse. Really, I'll be fine. Do you mind if I wear these clothes? I'll wash them and give them back to you."

"Fine, Shawne." Jocelyn tilted her head. "I do hope you'll be all right."

Casey hurried inside the house and up the stairs to Bonnie's room.

Forgive him.

The small whisper shook her senses, but she pushed it away. She bundled up her Sunday clothes and made her way downstairs. How could Morgan tell her he loved her after what he'd said? Did he think she'd swoon like some lovesick girl? Jocelyn waited for her on the front porch.

Forgive him.

Casey shivered. *Never. I'm not a fool.*

"Are you feverish?" Jocelyn asked. "You're pale."

"No, ma'am, but I'm tired."

Jocelyn pointed in the distance. "There's Morgan now. He'll want to make sure you get to town."

Casey started to protest, but that would have meant explaining. "I think Grant needs him."

Jocelyn ignored her and motioned to Morgan. "Shawne's not feeling well. Would you mind escorting her to the parsonage?"

"Really, I can take myself." Humiliation snaked up Casey's spine. "I don't want to be a bother."

"It will only take me a minute to hitch up the horses." Morgan made his way to the barn without giving her an opportunity to protest again.

The whispers to forgive still clung to her mind, but her heart felt as though it had been snatched from her body. Casey had endured Jenkins and the gang for a lot of years. She could endure a ride into Kahlerville with Morgan.

Soon Casey and Morgan eased across the dirt road to Kahlerville.

"I'm sorry," Morgan said. "I had no right to say those things to you. What I said would make anyone ill." He fixed his gaze on the dirt road. Clouds rolled across a gray sky. It reminded her of the day she left Jenkins.

She took a deep breath. Thoughts of the outlaw trail floated by with all of the horrible crimes that Jenkins and his gang had committed. God had forgiven her. "I forgive you."

"Thank you." He raised the reins and urged the horses a little faster. "We're going to get caught in a storm if we don't hurry."

"We've been in a storm since the day you walked into my campsite." She avoided his stare. The only sounds were the moans and groans of the wagon. Suddenly a gust of wind cooled her face.

"I do love you," he said. "I want to make things right between us."

"It's impossible," she said. "Once, you said that I was afraid to trust and you were afraid to love. Now you tell me you love me, but you act like you don't trust me. From the way I look at it, you don't know what you want."

His face hardened. "Yes, I do. I'm just going about it wrong."

"Are you a bounty hunter?"

Crimson rose from his neck. "How many times do I have to tell you that I'm a lawyer?"

"Now you know how I feel when you ask me if I miss the outlaw life. I didn't mean to sound unfeeling; I simply want to know what Jenkins did to you."

A huge droplet of rain landed on her riding skirt.

"I can't, Casey. Not yet."

Exasperation caused her to shudder. "Then how can you expect me to believe you love me?"

The rain started, pelting her body like tiny bits of hail. Let it rain, for now Morgan wouldn't see her tears.

"Shawne, didn't John bring a newspaper from Houston?" Sarah asked one mid-September morning. She'd insisted Casey prop her up in bed, declaring how much better she felt.

"Yes, he did." Casey looked down to the left of her. "In fact, I have it right here under my mending basket."

"Would you mind reading it to me?"

"I'd be delighted." Casey pulled out the folded newspaper. "Is there anything in particular you want to hear?"

Sarah paused thoughtfully, then smiled. "Not really, dear. Just read the articles you know I'll enjoy." Her voice sounded stronger than usual, and for that Casey praised God. She moved the rocker closer to Sarah's bed.

Casey scanned through the *Post*, quoting the latest prices on French shoes, millinery wear for women and children, and a new opera opening soon. She avoided the various advertisements for doctors and medicines guaranteed to cure every disease imaginable.

"Oh Sarah, here is a picture of the most beautiful gown I've ever seen. Listen to how it's described: 'This gown is composed of Venetian cloth and velvet. The plain underskirt is of golden green velvet as is also the greater part of the bodice. The cloth drapery is a medium shade of fawn and is open the whole length upon the left side to show a velvet petticoat. It is elaborately braided with green and gold mixed braid and has a border across the front and right side of stone marten. The high, flaring collar is edged with a narrow roll of the fur, below which is a braided design. The close sleeves are of cloth, braided to match above the velvet cuffs.'"

"It sounds magnificent." Sarah's eyes met Casey's gaze. "That gown would look lovely with your auburn hair. Someday you must find a rich husband to dress you in fine things."

She laughed. "I'd settle for much less, believe me." An image of Morgan drifted across her mind. They'd talked some, but she'd held him at a distance, fearful of his next outburst.

"Do read on. What about social gatherings?" Sarah entwined her fingers gracefully and waited.

Casey reported on activities and events pertinent to the fall days. Some of the names Sarah recognized, and she expressed delight in hearing about traditional get-togethers. The last few days had been good ones for the older woman, and Casey wanted desperately for the gaiety to last. She continued to read the news from the latest CATTLEMEN'S REPORT. Her eyes swept over the FARM NEWS, and then an article caught her attention. Her senses paralyzed.

A man and his son had been murdered on their ranch west of Houston. The report concluded that Davis Jenkins and his outlaws were responsible for the killings. It neither cited a reason for the crime nor explained why the paper accused the gang. The article merely reported the outlaws were far from their usual route.

Casey felt Sarah's gaze piercing through her. "Shawne, what's wrong?"

"Nothing." Casey promptly folded the paper. *Dear God, can't Jenkins leave good people alone?*

"Are you ill?"

Whatever happened to the days when she disguised her feelings? Casey laid aside the newspaper and smoothed the quilts around the woman's thin shoulders. "You worry too much about other people and not enough about yourself." She kissed Sarah's wrinkled forehead. "I'm perfectly fine, except I think you should rest a little. I won't leave the room. I promise. Later I'll read the rest of the paper."

"You don't lie well, dear. It doesn't become you."

Casey felt her insides churn. "I read something about a father and son murdered for no apparent reason. The thought of innocent people killed disturbs me. . .that's all."

Sarah lifted herself slightly from the pillow, her gray-white hair properly pinned except for a few stray tendrils. "Does anyone know who did it?"

"The paper says an outlaw gang." Her heart hammered against her chest.

"Which one?"

Casey hesitated. "Davis Jenkins and his bunch."

"The Rangers will be on it, I'm sure. Even though their work has diminished for the last few years."

Casey took a deep breath. Dread needled at her. "I hope so.

This country needs to be tamed. Lawless men shouldn't be allowed to take over."

Sarah studied her. "Shawne, let's talk about you."

The silence proved deafening.

"Why me?"

"Because I want to tell you what I see and what I feel."

Casey felt her head throb, and drops of perspiration gathered around her temples. "Are you sure this is necessary when you should rest?"

"This is a perfect time. My dear child, you can run from the past, but until you reckon with it, yesterday will haunt you."

"What do you mean?"

"I don't intend to pry or make things painful for you, but I'm your friend. I think you need to talk about this with an old lady who loves you very much." Sarah reached to take Casey's hand. "God does put special people in our lives—to be our friends, to help do His work. You have been such a comfort to me. Let me repay you by helping with whatever troubles you."

"I'm the one who's blessed." Casey couldn't lie to Sarah, not the woman who lived as a beacon of patience and courage.

"I've often seen a strange look in your eyes. It tells me you're afraid. Shawne, my feelings are rarely wrong. Who or what are you afraid of?"

Casey pulled away from Sarah's scrutiny. The truth longed to be set free. "You're right. I'm afraid."

"Would you share with me your heavy load?"

"Isn't God supposed to carry all our burdens?"

"Yes." Sarah smiled. "But we have to allow Him to work through other people, too."

Hopelessness swelled inside her, and she fought the tears threatening to flood her eyes. "I'm so ashamed of my life." She hesitated to gain control. "I despise it, and I couldn't bear to see the hurt in your eyes if you knew the truth."

"You've read the Scriptures." Sarah smiled so sweetly, as though the angels in heaven painted her face with love. "The truth is what sets us free, and neither God's love nor mine comes with any conditions."

Casey eased her hand from Sarah's and rose to face the window. "I don't know where to begin." The morning sun had climbed nearly to the rooftop, and in its place spread a sky so blue. . .perfect. . . innocent. She took a deep breath. "The outlaw gang in the paper, Davis Jenkins and Tim O'Hare, do you know much about them?"

"Only what I've read about in the newspapers. I guess I know as much as the next person."

A plea for help sped silently to the One who could provide the courage she needed. "Well, they're looking for me. At least they used to be. I'm Tim O'Hare's sister, Casey."

When she heard no response from Sarah, Casey continued. And in the peaceful stillness of the room, surrounded by green plants and purple violets, the story unfolded.

". . .After the problem in Deer Creek, I took off again and ended up here in Kahlerville. Again, I have lied to protect myself. I feel dirty and ashamed. Sarah, I realize my sins are worse than others, and the more I deceive people, the more I hate myself." She rubbed her arms as though she could eliminate the filth corroding her life.

"God doesn't see sin in degrees," Sarah said.

Casey shook her head. "How could my sins not be worse than someone who has no idea about life with an outlaw gang?" She resumed her position in the rocker. The pain and suffering of those years apart from God took form in the agony ripping at her heart.

"Perhaps I can explain it to you in a different way," Sarah said. "Do you recall seeing animal tracks in the snow?"

She nodded, wondering what Sarah was about to say.

"Birds make tiny tracks and small animals make bigger ones. Larger animals leave their prints in the snow. Then along comes a man in his wagon that leaves huge wheel tracks. So the perfect blanket of snow becomes covered with all types of imperfections. When spring arrives and thaws the ground, all of the tracks are melted away. That is what Jesus did when He died for our sins—not just for some sins but for every single one of them."

No longer could Casey contain the sobs, and she buried her face in her hands. All of this time, she had read of God's endless love and mercy, but not until this moment did she fully understand. He *had* forgiven her. The realization rang through her head—wonderful, startling, and incredibly freeing. She sucked in a breath. "How do I rid myself of this horrible guilt?"

"Just ask God," Sarah said. "The guilt you feel is not from Him, so give Him those feelings."

"But I need to settle up with the law."

"Indeed you do, but I know God will help you. Have you considered having Morgan work in your behalf?"

"He wants to, but I'm not sure how I feel about it."

"I can tell he loves you. I imagine the thought of Jenkins after you must drive him nearly mad. That dear man."

Sarah knows what Morgan will not tell me. "Thank you so much. You have no idea what your words mean to me. Every Sunday, my thoughts wrestle with avoiding Sheriff Kahler and worshiping God. If you don't mind, I'd like to go to my room for a little while."

"Go right ahead. I think it's time for me to rest, too."

Casey stroked the older woman's face. "I love you, Sarah." The woman's words were engraved forever in her heart. Life didn't promise any reprieve from Jenkins or the law, but she was free of the guilt. Without a doubt she must pursue a lawyer and face what a judge and jury decided. Her deeds would be reckoned with, and her life finally put at rest.

The next day, Casey approached the reverend. She found him in his study, preparing Sunday's sermon. As she sat across from his massive desk, she found it difficult to begin. He'd been gracious enough to give her employment and a place to live. At last she spilled out the words like a waterfall tumbling over rock.

"Don't you remember telling me if I ever had any questions I should simply ask?" he asked.

The birds sang outside the open window, and the delicate fragrance of roses scented the air. "Yes, sir, but I deliberately lied to a man of God."

"Don't you think I suspected something amiss when you rode in here that first day?" He eased back in his chair. "When we stood by the well and shared the cool water, God spoke to me. He told me you were the one to nurse Sarah. I've never regretted it. You've made peace with God, and I am happy for you. Sarah and I love you, and we will support you as you strive to make things right with the law."

"I don't deserve your goodness, and I thank God for putting you and Sarah in my life."

"Let's pray together for God's guidance." The reverend held her hand and prayed while Casey listened. The tears slipped from her eyes, cleansing drops of thankfulness to the One who sustained her. "Heavenly Father, thank You for drawing us all closer to You in times of distress. Thank You for bringing this precious young woman here so we could help her through these difficult circumstances. Guard her safely, Lord, and show us Your will in all things."

No matter what, Lord, help me to tell the Andrewses.

CHAPTER  19

Morgan swung his ax through the top of the log and split it deftly in two, then tossed it to the side with the others. Keep this up, and he'd have enough firewood for the next year. Sweat poured from his face and into his eyes like a stinging waterfall. The muscles in his shoulders ached not so much from the work but from the speed with which he lifted the ax and sank it into one piece of wood after another.

Strenuous work was an old habit when he needed to hash out whatever had crawled under his skin. He stopped long enough to wipe the sweat off his face with the back of his hand. Nothing was working today. He'd ridden long before dawn, helped Grant move a hundred head of cattle, and now the wood. With sunset dimming his light, he should have had a few ideas about how to mend his relationship with Casey. But he was fresh out. Accusing her of missing outlaw days had been cruel. He even knew it at the time, yet he didn't have enough sense to shut his mouth.

God, why didn't You stop me? I ruined what I craved the most—to start life fresh with Casey. I thought You and I had made our peace that day in church. Seems like every time things are going good, I set out to ruin them again. Guess I deserve whatever happens.

He picked up the ax and slammed it into another log. Splinters flew in all directions. His mood reminded him of those years gone by, and he despised the thought. Casey didn't understand his moods, and he didn't have the guts to tell her.

You know what you have to do.

Morgan recognized the voice, although the commands he'd heard all day set like a bad fever. There had to be a better way to explain his vendetta with Jenkins than the truth.

And where has not telling her got you?

He glared up at the sky beginning to fade from gold and orange to bluish black. Clouds covered the heavens with only a sliver of the moon blurring through, indicative of his faint hope of ever calling Casey his own.

I can't do it to her.

Who are you trying to protect, Casey or yourself?

The words echoed against the fast-approaching night. He told himself the sounds he heard were really insects calling out to each other and not God pressing him to tell Casey the whole story. She'd run so far he'd never find her. He released a labored sigh. She might do it anyway. No guarantee with Casey; she was a hard woman to read.

"Son, don't let it eat you alive."

He swung around to see his mother. In the faint light remaining, he saw her shadow; then a wistful touch of wind blew at her apron. "I'm doing the best I can." He turned back to the wood and leveled another piece.

"I see a bit of the old Morgan, and I don't like it at all."

He lifted his head, unable to look at her. "This time I'm talking to God about it."

"Shawne loves you, and you love her. I pray God makes a way."

"If I haven't destroyed it."

"I don't know what has happened between you two, but I wonder if your stubbornness is the root of the problem. Are you going to punish yourself forever?"

He picked up the ax and raised it over his head. "Maybe it's what I deserve."

"Morgan."

The harsh sound of her voice caused him to lower the ax and face her.

"Self-pity never solved a thing. It makes you weak and mean."

"I'll think on it some more."

"For sure, Morgan, God understands what it's like to lose someone you love."

"But what if it happens twice?"

"Shawne doesn't strike me as the kind of woman who'd run from bad news."

In the days ahead, Casey considered how she'd tell the Andrewses about her past, but she couldn't bring herself to confess the truth. When she finally collected her courage, either the time wasn't right, or someone was missing.

She saw Morgan at church, and they talked when she visited his family on Sundays, but she kept her distance. His words were forgiven, but the damage had been done. Everywhere she looked, a remembrance of him rattled her senses, surfacing when she least expected it.

She'd wake in the middle of the night with his turquoise eyes burning into the blackness. Treasured memories and cherished words flooded the darkness surrounding her, but his black moods reminded her of ruthless men. She forced herself to consider the likelihood of his not changing. Love was a powerful emotion, but it couldn't alter a man's personality unless he truly wanted to change. He claimed God now guided his life, but not every part of it. Casey knew it best to forget him. Time and again, she gave the matter to God only to pull it back. Maybe she and Morgan were too much alike.

During this time, Reverend Rainer wrote a doctor in Dallas, requesting a visit to examine Sarah, but it would be weeks before the man could leave his practice. In the meantime, the local doctor prescribed laudanum to ease her pain.

True to Sarah's initial accounting, Casey cared for Sarah as if she were a child. She bathed her, dressed her, combed her hair, and rocked her when the pain seemed unbearable. Some days, Sarah cried for her husband, who watched her suffer helplessly. In those moments Casey wept with her. She saw a steadfast love and commitment in the couple soaring beyond her own comprehension of what true love meant between a man and a woman.

At times, the couple lovingly teased each other and acted as though the illness didn't exist. But when the two separated, telltale agony clouded their eyes. Casey questioned the fairness of God in allowing two good people who loved and honored Him to experience such anguish.

"Reverend Rainer, why does God permit Sarah to hurt so?" she asked one evening at supper. The day had proved exhausting for all of them, especially Sarah, who had sunk her teeth into her lower lip until it bled to keep from crying out.

"He doesn't want any of us to suffer." The reverend pushed aside his full plate. "This present life is difficult to understand, and surely none of us know the mind of God. He permits adversity for a reason, and God will use this for good." He sighed. "Sarah's illness seems so wrong, but her pain does bring blessings to others. Think about all of the ladies who visit and bring gifts. If she were well, they would be denied the joy of giving. They share from their hearts, and God honors their love. Sarah prays with each one and allows them the opportunity to voice their own trials and prayer requests. God is using her to reach and teach others."

Casey chose not to respond until she carefully weighed the reverend's words. "Are you saying Sarah should be happy with her illness?"

"Not happy, but her heart is filled with the joy of the Lord. And folks remember the good she did for them. I need strength from God to keep me from becoming bitter and angry. I want my wife to be the woman of her youth, but God has a different plan—and it's a struggle."

"Surely not you?"

"I'm a man who loves his wife and isn't ready for her to be taken from him. But in all of my soul-searching and in all of my Scripture reading, I'm certain of one thing: I must accept God's will for her life. . .and mine." He smiled. "This is probably none of my concern, but I'm going to say it anyway. Don't give up on Morgan. He has a posse of devils chasing him every minute of the day."

She blinked. "He won't tell me what happened."

"Patience, dear. Have patience. I know you care for him as surely as I see he cares for you."

"Are you asking me to give him another chance? Reverend, some of the things he says are hurtful."

"I'm not surprised. He's been where no man should ever walk. Much like you, I imagine."

On October 1, the Rainers' daughter and son-in-law arrived with their family for a month-long visit. The daughter wanted to tend to her mother. She didn't resent Casey's nursing, but she realized her mother's days were limited.

"Come stay with us," Jocelyn said to Casey. "Morgan can move into the cabin or bunkhouse, and you can have his room."

Casey hesitated. She still hadn't told them the truth. "I don't feel comfortable chasing Morgan out of his bed."

"Nonsense," Jocelyn said. "He'll be delighted that you're here." In the end, Jocelyn won out. She and Bonnie wasted no time in visiting the parsonage and whisking Casey away to the Double H for the month. If the reverend felt it was important for her not to give up on Morgan, then she needed to honor his request. A month at the ranch would give them an opportunity to talk—really talk.

As soon as Jocelyn and Bonnie helped her settle into the assigned bedroom, Casey took a glimpse out of the window. Strange, being in Morgan's room. How did he feel about it?

"Grant and Morgan are busy branding cattle," Bonnie said, as though reading her thoughts.

"So they don't know I'm coming?" she asked.

Bonnie laughed, that glorious infectious sound that always made Casey smile. "Oh yes. We told them before we left. Morgan acted strange. Are you two having another spat?"

"I'm not so sure that's a question you should be asking Shawne," Jocelyn said.

How do I answer this? "I don't mind." Casey offered a faint smile. "Maybe he and I will have time to mend our differences. Time has a way of making the past not so important."

"I hope so. The idea of you and me someday being sisters sounds wonderful."

But you have no idea who I am. "Only God knows what He can do with two stubborn people like your brother and me." Casey adored Bonnie, her treasured friend who'd never known the ugliness that could strip a heart and mind of all hope and goodness.

"Let me save Shawne from any other unnecessary questions here." Jocelyn nodded at Bonnie. "How is Sarah really doing?"

She deliberated her response. She wanted to sound optimistic despite Sarah's failing health. "Her spirits are good, especially with her family here to visit."

"Every time I ask the reverend about her, he says 'much better' and thanks me for asking. She doesn't seem to be getting any better," Jocelyn said.

"I do hope the doctor from Dallas comes soon. The reverend hopes he may have more knowledge about her condition than Kahlerville's doctor."

Bonnie sighed. "I wonder why God lets terrible things happen to such good people?"

"Many folks have asked the same question. I suppose that's something we'll have to ask the Lord one day," Jocelyn said.

Bonnie frowned. "Life can be so hard. Makes me wonder if you believe in God and care for other people, then you're certain to die a painful death. If that's true, then it would be better to live an outlaw's life."

Casey felt her knees weaken and the familiar sick churning in the pit of her stomach. Shame and the lies she'd told hung over her like a storm-filled cloud. She had no right not telling them the truth.

❧⁓◉⁓❧

"I thought you were courtin' Shawne?" Grant asked Morgan the afternoon following Casey's arrival. They stood by the corral while Jesse and some of the other ranch hands worked on breaking horses.

Morgan winced as Jesse fell from the horse—the third time since he'd decided to take on a high-spirited mare.

"Did I hit a sore subject?" Grant asked.

More than you know. Morgan motioned toward Jesse. "I was watching that mare toss Jesse again. In answer to your question. . . well, things could be better."

"Thought so. I talk to her more than you do lately."

Morgan tossed his brother a sideways glance. It was obvious Grant more than liked Casey, and the idea of his younger brother falling for her needled him worse than a bee sting. "She's a little older than you."

"Not by much, and besides, she's your girl, not mine." Grant kept his eyes on Jesse, who'd dusted himself off and was ready to mount the mare again. "Does she know?"

"What do you think?" Morgan's reply snapped a little harder than he intended.

"Thought so." Grant kept his attention on Jesse and the mare. "Don't chase her away. She doesn't deserve that."

Those words repeated in Morgan's mind until he had to do something about them. "I'll tell her after I get back from taking Mama to town."

Grant nodded. Strange how a seventeen-year-old perceived so much. But he was right. The ache and the longing inside kept Morgan awake at night and surly during the day.

He couldn't blame Casey. His pledge to the Lord looked like pig slop, and it seemed his love for her bordered on conditional—when he felt like being generous. He hadn't always been this way. The past four years had changed him, and he didn't know if he'd ever be a good man again. He needed God's help for every breath he took.

CHAPTER 20

"What did you think of my brother when you first met him?" Bonnie asked with girlish interest. They'd seated themselves around the kitchen table in the lull of the early afternoon. Morgan and Jocelyn had left sometime earlier for town, and the two girls had talked all morning.

"I didn't care for him much."

"That's understandable considering his moods. I will say he's done so much better since he's come home for good."

"I'm real glad for all of you."

"When did you two start being friends?"

Casey hesitated. Perhaps she should tell her friend now. "After Morgan and Jocelyn return, I'll tell you everything."

Bonnie looked at her thoughtfully, as though questioning herself before speaking. "Shawne." She folded her hands on the table. "As much as I want to know about you and Morgan and your life before you came to Kahlerville, I can't help but wonder if he has told you about his wife."

Casey often wondered if his ill temperament had something to do with his marriage. Had she been unfaithful? Died during childbirth or gotten sick? "Not yet, but I'm going to insist on it tonight after I explain a few things to your family."

Bonnie stood from the table and clasped her hands behind her. "Those days were a nightmare. We thought he'd never get over her death." She shrugged ever so daintily. "Our whole family is grateful for what you've done for him."

Casey reached for her hand. Morgan should tell her this part of his life. "Enough of this gloom. What do you say about stirring together a batch of sugar cookies?"

A sharp sound cracked in the afternoon silence. Gunfire. A mixture of alarm and old memories sent Casey to her feet. "I wonder where that's coming from."

"Oh, it's most likely Grant." Bonnie sipped at her coffee.

"What's he doing?"

"Target practice. He doesn't bring out the rifle and revolver when Mama's around. She says it's a waste of ammunition and time."

"Why does he do it?" Casey peered through the kitchen window in the direction of the shots.

"Probably has something to do with his curiosity with outlaws. I mean he reads the dime novels—everything he can find about the Dalton Brothers, Jessie and Frank James, Cole Younger, Billie the Kid, but not Davis Jenkins."

"You mean he wants to be a lawman?"

"Maybe. Mama and he fussed about the revolver until he told her he wouldn't bring it out again. He still wants to do everything as well as Morgan. And Morgan is fast."

Casey's stomach knotted. "Being fast with a gun doesn't make him more of a man." Uneasiness about Grant's obsession crept around her heart. A whirlwind of outlaw faces—dead and alive— swept across her mind.

"I agree, but he's up there practicing with it now." Bonnie smiled.

"I don't see any harm in target practice, but Mama says the gun leads to other things."

"She's right." Visions of Tim swept across Casey's mind. "I've never seen any of his friends."

"That's 'cause Mama and Morgan ran most of them off. Grant had a wild streak for a while, but he's doing much better. Mama didn't realize how Morgan's tragedy had affected him."

What had happened to Morgan and his wife? A thought struck her. Did Morgan accidentally shoot his wife? "I have to talk to Grant. Can you tell me where to find him?"

"He won't like you interfering." Bonnie's eyes flashed a warning. "My brother can be as bullheaded as Morgan. Mercy, Shawne, I really think you should stay here. I'll talk to him about stopping, I promise."

Casey headed for the door. Grant worried her, for she'd met his stubborn nature a time or two, an admirable trait if led in the right direction but harmful if not controlled. She knew Jocelyn and Grant argued at times, and Casey thought their arguments had to do with a young man seeking to become a man.

"I don't know who's more headstrong in this family. All right, he's on the southwest ridge. Let's get our horses, and I'll take you myself."

"I need to talk to him alone."

Bonnie expelled a heavy sigh. "All right. I'll show you where he is and then ride back."

Casey hurried to the barn with Bonnie close at her heels. It marked one of the few occasions when the younger woman had nothing to say. Each time the gunfire echoed, Casey quickened the motions of saddling Stampede. She glanced at Bonnie struggling with the cinch on her saddle and wordlessly assisted her.

How could she stop Grant? Perhaps she could reason with him. He liked her; she'd have to be blind not to see that. The whole idea of him pumping bullet after bullet into a target infuriated her. And his interest in outlaws? But not Jenkins? So much she didn't understand about this family.

Too well she recalled the squeeze of the trigger and the feel of metal against the palm of her hand. She remembered the smell of gunfire smoke and the best-forgotten nightmares of riding with an outlaw gang.

Grant must be made to understand the severity of his private game.

Oh God, please help me convince him of this foolishness. Help me to speak the words of wisdom.

The two women mounted their horses and spurred the animals on toward the ridge. Casey realized she must end Grant's folly no matter what the cost.

"Over there." Bonnie pointed and pulled in the reins on her horse. "You can see him from that grassy area near the top of the hill," she said. "There's a clearing just beyond it."

"Thanks." Casey surveyed the hilltop. "Pray for me. I don't want to say the wrong things."

"Shawne, I'm confused about your concern over Grant's target practice."

"I know you are." Casey's gaze swept over Bonnie's face. "But on this matter, you need to trust me until we have a chance to talk. I've waited too long to tell you and your family about me. I'll be back as quickly as I can."

She sunk her heels into her horse's sides and left Bonnie behind. At the clearing, Grant spotted her and waved. "Afternoon, Shawne." His wide smile revealed his infatuation with her. "What brings you out here?"

"To see you, naturally." She dismounted and wrapped the reins around a sapling. "When I heard gunfire, Bonnie told me what you were doing."

"Do you want to watch? I'm getting pretty good. Almost as good as Morgan." He lifted his chin and gave her a half smile.

Now I see Morgan in him. "No, I'd rather talk." She moved closer, wanting to see every muscle in his young face. He used a Smith and Wesson revolver, and a rifle leaned against a tree. "I can't believe you're doing this."

"You disapprove of me learning to shoot?" Grant filled the revolver with cartridges.

She sickened. "Depends on your reasons for doing it. There's a rifle match going on next week to raise money for the town's orphans, but nothing was said about a revolver."

"Oh, I already entered. Mama signed me up."

"Why are you doing this today?"

"Did my sister send you up here, or is she going to complain to Mama and Morgan?"

"Neither. I came on my own. Grant, guns can hurt people. . .kill people. . .and make men selfish and greedy."

He scowled. "In this country, a man needs to know how to use a revolver." He set the target for the next round of shots.

"For what purpose?"

Grant chuckled. "You women are all alike." He turned and fired into a burlap bull's-eye nailed to a tree. The bullet lodged a few inches from the center.

"What can I say so you'll see the mistake you're making?" She feared angering him, but desperation for him to see the problems ahead urged her on. "This country is getting safer all the time. The time will come when none of us will have to worry about protecting ourselves."

He laughed and spun the cartridge. The sound grated against her nerves. "Shawne, I might listen if I thought you knew what you were talking about. But you're a woman and know nothing about a man's world. Morgan of all people should have told you what happens when faced with dangerous men."

"You mean outlaws? Don't be too sure of that. I've lived most of my life where wits took over every breath I took."

He turned, and she noticed his shoulders were already as broad as Morgan's. "Can't possibly be the same. A man has to do what he feels is right. My brother's fast with a gun, and I don't intend for him to outdo me."

She took a deep breath and pushed aside the danger signals going off in her head. "If I proved to you I could handle myself with that Smith and Wesson, would you leave the revolver alone?"

"I might." Amusement spread across his face. "Except I'm sure you can't."

A wagonload of ugly memories burdened her. She'd do anything to keep Grant from experiencing such nightmares. "All right, Grant. Give me the gun, and step back from the target." She purposely backed up several feet from where he stood.

A smile played on his lips as he positioned himself to the side of her. "Don't hurt yourself, Shawne. Do you want me to show you how it's done?"

Casey ignored him. She raised the weapon and squeezed off five shots dead center in the target. With the revolver empty, she held out her hand for more cartridges. Grant strode her way and silently gave her a handful more. She skillfully filled the cleared chambers. His gaze focused on her, but she refused to look at him. Casey turned her back on the target, then whirled around and fired four more shots into the bull's-eye.

"I dare you to match that," she said. "But I know you can't. Of course, it's a little different looking into the face of a man who wants to kill you. If you're fast enough, you can watch the blood ooze the very life out of him. It's not a pretty sight, Grant, and you're too smart to get in the middle of gunslingers." She stared into his startled face and braved on. "Maybe the first time you shoot a man, you think it's over. You've had enough, but what you've done spreads like wildfire. Someone else wants to call you out, and the list goes on."

"Shawne—"

"Please put this crazy passion aside. I've heard you say you want to be a doctor. Make something worthwhile of yourself. I beg you. Leave the revolver alone."

Grant glanced at the target, then back at her. "Where did you learn to shoot? Morgan?"

"Years of practice." She pressed her lips together. "I had nothing better to do while my brother rode with Davis Jenkins."

"Casey O'Hare," he whispered, as though someone might hear. "You ran off from the Jenkins gang. Neither he nor the law has been able to find you."

She eyed him squarely. "Yes, that's who I am. I've lied to you and everyone else here in Kahlerville to save my own skin. I escaped from Jenkins, dodged the law and bounty hunters. My face is on more wanted posters than most men can count. It's an awful life, Grant. I figure it's my own hell."

"This can't be." He swung around as though the truth hit him in the stomach. "But you're nursing Sarah Rainer? You're living at the parsonage? You and my brother. . ."

"The Rainers and Morgan know about me." She was more shaken than she cared to acknowledge. "Where do you think I learned how to take care of dying people but through nursing outlaws?" she asked. "That leg your brother favors? Do you really want to know what happened?" She took a ragged breath. "I've seen enough blood and heard enough screaming men to last forever."

He shook his head. "You took a big chance by telling me all this. Why?"

"Because God gave me a second chance, and now I want you to

have the same. I couldn't ignore what you're doing any more than I could deny Jesus Christ. Some might think this is harmless, but I saw my brother turn from a good young man into a killer." Suddenly she felt at ease. A sense of peace flowed through her veins.

"Morgan knows." Troubled lines creased Grant's brow, and he frowned. "Now I understand so much more."

"Will you give it up?"

Grant sighed deeply and ran his hands through his hair, just as she had seen Morgan do on so many occasions. "I'm not sure I can."

Morgan's brother, a boy with grandiose dreams of becoming a man. Oh, dear Jesus, make him see how wrong this is. "Do you want to give up on your future for a wanted poster—or an early grave?"

He hesitated while she stared into his face. Taking a deep breath, he slowly nodded. "Yes, I'll give it up. I'm not sure what I've been thinking. Guess I've been jealous of Morgan all my life and wanted to do everything like him."

"You're a fine man all by yourself." She offered a grim smile. "I think I know how you felt. The gun gives you a sense of power. It is, or can be, the one thing you can do better than anyone else. I never had anyone tell me differently. I never had anyone who cared enough to put me on the right road. Your family loves you dearly. They are so proud of you." She opened her palm to reveal the revolver glittering in the sun. "Putting your faith in this will destroy you."

Grant shook his head. "I've been a fool, and I even told Mama I'd quit."

"It's not too late." She looked at the gun in her hand. "Do you want it back?" Holding it out to him, she waited for a response.

"What's going on here?" Morgan asked. In the intensity of the moment, she hadn't heard him ride into the clearing. He glared at Casey. "Can't get it out of your system, can you? Now you're trying to turn my brother into one of them."

CHAPTER 21

"No, Morgan. You're wrong." Heat flooded Casey's face.

"Hold on." Grant clenched his fists. "Let me explain."

"I'm not blind." Morgan's lip curled. "The young lady here is demonstrating her skills with a revolver, and she does it quite well, I may add."

"I said, let me explain." Grant's voice rose.

"Don't defend her." Morgan dismounted and stomped toward them. "I've seen what the likes of her can do."

"I will defend her, and you'd better listen to what I have to say! You're a fool, Morgan. You haven't the sense of a mule."

"Don't quarrel," Casey said. "Morgan, give us a chance to tell you what happened."

"Shawne, get back to the house." Morgan's stonelike glare told fathoms. "I've got to talk to my brother."

"You're making a terrible mistake." She stepped between him and Grant.

"Let me be the judge of that," Morgan said.

She shook with the fury rising in her blood. Turning, she offered the revolver to Grant again, but he shook his head. "I don't want it."

"I don't, either." She handed the gun to Morgan and stared into his rigid face. "You always believe the worst about me. Always."

"Go on back," Grant said. "This is between him and me. Morgan's going to listen to me whether he likes it or not."

She shook her head.

"Go, please. You gave me something today to hold on to. Let me do this in return."

She swallowed a lump in her throat and climbed onto her stallion. Morgan's words had slashed her heart for the last time. *Why, Lord? Are You punishing me for the past?* Stinging tears blinded her. She must leave the ranch. Look for a new home, if such a place existed. She'd have to abandon Kahlerville, and this time ride to where no one would ever find her.

Behind her raged the sounds of arguing brothers. She imagined Grant pushing his brother into a fight, and Morgan growing angrier with every word. Their voices roared above the peaceful late afternoon, and she prayed the two didn't resort to fists. She couldn't stop them. Neither did she want to hear their heated quarreling. Morgan believed outlaw blood flowed through her veins, and the proof shouted from the gun he'd seen her offer Grant. One more time, he'd succeeded in reaching his own conclusions.

Nearing the house, she saw Jocelyn and Bonnie watching her ride their way. How much should she say? Let Morgan tell them the truth.

"I've got to pack." She swung from the saddle with no thought to her dress and climbed the porch steps. *I'm no lady. Never have been.* Her eyes burned, and she refused to look their way. She despised this horrible display of emotion.

"Why are you so upset?" Jocelyn followed her into the kitchen. "Can we talk first? I'm sure there must be a misunderstanding."

Casey shook her head in an attempt to walk past them as though nothing of importance had occurred. "Was it Morgan or Grant?" Bonnie asked.

She paused to answer. "Neither. It's me. I need to stay at the boardinghouse."

"But we want you here." Concern resounded in Jocelyn's tone.

"I can't. I don't mean to be rude or unappreciative of your hospitality, but this is how it must be."

"Won't you tell us what brought this on?" Jocelyn asked.

"Probably Morgan," Bonnie said. "He spoils everything."

"Morgan's fine." *Please leave me alone, so I can do what I have to do.* "He and Grant should be along shortly." She started up the stairs, then whirled back around. "Jocelyn, they aren't fine. Maybe you should see if you can stop them from fighting."

"I was afraid they'd fight over you," Bonnie said. "Stupid men."

"It's not what you think. I only wish it was." Casey climbed the stairs to her bedroom and hoped the two women didn't follow. She'd wept more for Morgan Andrews than he deserved. All of his promises, his words of following God and of loving her, were lies. She hated him, and she hated herself for falling in love with him.

With a choked sob, she pulled her clothes from the small chest and stacked them on the bed. Never would a man hurt her like this again. She'd said it before, but this time she meant it.

Once she finished with her packing, a knock at the door interrupted her dilemma over how to get back to town. "Please, I'd like to be alone." Casey snatched up a handkerchief and blew her nose.

"It's Grant. May I come in?"

"I'd rather you didn't." She wiped the wetness from her cheeks. "I'm not good company. Would you mind taking me back to town?"

"Sure. Can we talk first? I won't stay long."

She didn't want to be inconsiderate of him. After all, he'd done nothing but stand up for her. She tucked her undergarments beneath a dress. "Come in, then."

The younger man walked in with Morgan behind him. "You didn't say he'd be with you. I don't want to see or talk to your brother."

"Don't blame Grant."

Morgan stood in the doorway. "I knew you'd throw me out."

I wish I could really hate you.

The tension could have been split with an ax.

"I'm sorry." Grant shoved his hands in his pockets. "But a matter needs to be settled, and I'm here to see it's done."

"Apologies are useless words to your brother." Casey focused her attention on the younger man. "He uses them as he sees fit."

"I'm not referring to apologies," Grant said. "My brother owes you an explanation for his bad temper, not just for today but for a lot of things. What happens afterward is out of my hands."

For the first time, Casey glanced Morgan's way. Lines creased the corners of his eyes. "I'm not in the mood to hear long stories that mean nothing or promises that belong in a spittoon."

Morgan's hand rested on the doorknob. "Five minutes, Casey," he said. "Then, if you still want to go back to town, Grant will take you. And I'll never bother you again. I promise."

Her gaze rested on Grant. He silently begged her to listen. For him, she'd give Morgan five minutes. "All right." Crossing her arms, she sat on the bed.

He closed the door. "I need to tell you about Kathleen."

Casey studied the violet flowers painted on the pitcher and basin on the washstand.

"My. . .my wife."

I've never heard her name before. Sitting motionless, she waited for him to proceed. Did she really want to know the story, supposedly the reason for Morgan's bitterness?

"She died over four years ago. . . . Kathleen was murdered."

Casey's gaze flew to Morgan's face. She sensed an explanation more horrible than any evil ever conceived.

Agony gathered in his turquoise eyes. "Jenkins forced himself on Kathleen and killed her."

Casey gasped and covered her mouth.

Morgan took a deep breath, the nightmare vividly depicted on his face. "The scar on Jenkins's face? Kathleen put it there just before he used the knife on her. I got to the cabin in time for her to tell me his name." He stood and moved toward the window. Outside, one of the ranch hands called for another. A horse neighed. "She died in my arms."

Casey covered her face in her hands. A sob from deep inside rose until she could no longer disguise it. All the words Morgan ever uttered now held undeniable meaning. The many times he'd lost his temper. The hostile looks, his stalking of Jenkins, and his initial plan to use her to get to the outlaw. No wonder Morgan fought any feelings for her. No wonder he warred with himself to drive her from his heart and mind.

"Why didn't you tell me? You should have told me right from the start. If only I had known. If only I had known."

"And what could you have done?" he asked. "I wanted to tell you. I tried, but the words hung in my throat. I hated Jenkins with everything I could possibly feel. I hated him and wanted him dead. I wanted to kill him with my bare hands. The thought lived with me day after day until it became the reason I breathed." He paused and took a deep breath. "Laid up in Vernal, I found something that I thought I'd never find again. I fell in love with you in a matter of hours. It made no sense. Still doesn't. But I loved you more than I hated him. The realization that I had to give up one or the other made me furious. You made me want to live. Jenkins made me want to die. I selfishly thought I could keep the truth from you, never thinking

I'd hurt you time and time again." He turned from the window. She'd never seen tears from a grown man.

"Take the time you need, Brother." Grant placed a hand on his shoulder.

Morgan shook his head. "I have to do this now. I never wanted to catch Jenkins. The chasing and hating pushed me on. My only purpose in life was to kill him, and the chase carried me nowhere except to my own private hell."

Casey waited, numb and in more misery than she could ever remember. Silence lingered.

"Just when I thought I'd made a turnaround—"

"Stop it, Morgan." The truth fluttered like a banner across Casey's heart. "You don't understand. It's my fault Kathleen died." Her gaze swept across the room, not really seeing Grant or Morgan but the glaring face of Jenkins. Everything about her whispered *murderer.* Thoughts of the calamity between her and Jenkins tore at her heart.

His madness was aimed at me. I lived while an innocent woman died.

"How can you possibly take the blame?" Morgan stepped toward her.

Several moments passed before she could speak. "I remember a time when we camped near Fort Worth. The rest of the gang had ridden into a town, and Jenkins stayed behind. When he tried to force himself on me, I pulled a gun on him. He rode out drunk and mean. He didn't return for over a week, and when he did, he had the gash on his face."

Morgan's face paled.

"Don't do this to yourself." Grant kneeled at her side. "You're not to blame for what he did."

Casey looked into the young man's sea-green eyes, gentle and compassionate. "And you wouldn't?" She wept uncontrollably and didn't know who the tears were for—Morgan, Kathleen, the

Andrews family, or herself; perhaps they were the culmination of all the suffering. Grant wrapped his arms around her and held her while she wept. She wanted to drown in the truth.

After several minutes, Grant released her and rose to open the bedroom door. "I think I'd better leave you two alone. Casey, I'll be waiting for your decision about going to town."

Morgan faced him. "Tell Mama and Bonnie—"

"What has happened." Grant stuck his hands into his pockets. "They deserve to know everything, and neither of you are in any shape to tell them." He shut the door without another word.

Stay, Grant. I can't bear to be alone with your brother.

Morgan took Grant's place where his brother had knelt on the floor beside her. He lifted her chin to meet his gaze, but she turned away, not wanting him to see her red-splotched face or the sorrow she'd caused. She didn't know what to feel or think. She was dirty. Vile.

"Please look at me," he said. "I honestly never intended to hurt you. Falling in love with you seemed to be a terrible joke played on me by some ugly twist of fate. It took losing you in Vernal to see that God had given me back my life by calling me to forgiveness. I had to give Kathleen's death to God and forgive myself for not being there when she needed me. Craving Jenkins's blood wouldn't bring her back. Neither would trying to punish you."

Casey finally forced herself to look into his face and saw his eyes welled with tears. The longer she stared, the more both of them wept. She reached out to him, and he gathered her up in his arms.

"Oh Morgan, I'm so sorry."

"You have nothing to be sorry for. I'm the one who couldn't be honest with you or myself. I don't know what I was thinking today. I knew better." He paused as though to gain control of himself. "I know I've asked you this a hundred times, but can you ever forgive me?"

She pulled herself away from him. "I love you. Nothing can

change those feelings. I may have been ready to end our relationship, but my resolve didn't mean my love ended, too."

"I can't imagine another day without you."

"I have a long road ahead of me, and as much as I want to be strong, I'm scared."

"Please let me walk it with you. We can win this battle to clear your name so Jenkins can be found."

She nodded, not really agreeing but attempting to comfort him. He'd been through enough.

"There's something I need to do." Morgan stood and pulled her to her feet. He swept a wispy curl from her damp cheek. His eyes searched hers, and she saw his love more clearly than ever before. "Years ago, I watched a young girl's face turn from innocence into harsh reality in Billings, Montana. I never forgot that girl. Often wondered what happened to her." He paused and squeezed her hand. "I've made many mistakes in my life, but I will not make another one where you are concerned. I'm asking you to forgive me for all the things I've done to hurt you. I love you, Casey, and I want to spend the rest of my life loving and cherishing you. Will you marry me? Will you allow me to take care of you for as long as I live?"

His words fell on shattered emotions. She'd dreamed of those words, tarried over them. Morgan had asked her to be his wife, but she couldn't. Friends, yes. Anything else was impossible. Love had nothing to do with it. She'd go to her grave loving him. She quivered like a blade of grass shaken by the wind. "It's not right. Too many things are spinning around in my head."

He drew her close, and she heard the dance of his heart. "I've never been so sure of anything in my life." He brushed his finger across her lips and traced her mouth. "If I could only say the words for you."

Casey touched the finger resting against her lips. She refused to agree to marriage with her own life in such turmoil. "I love you, Morgan, but I can't be your wife until we've had time to work through the ugliness of our lives." She hesitated before speaking again and waited for his reaction, to see whether it was a display of temper or control.

"I understand more than you might believe," he said. "Trust is what we're talking about here."

"And. . .I must clear my name and take whatever punishment a judge decides."

He shook his head. "I don't think there's a judge anywhere who would find you guilty. You and I both know the warrants for your arrest are fictitious. The law has no evidence, only newspaper reports." He played with each of her fingers, then grasped her hand gently.

"I must prove my innocence of all those charges and confess to the shooting in Billings."

"Casey, you're innocent until proven guilty, not the other way around. I've seen those warrants. Some are alleged crimes that happened in another part of the country after you left Jenkins—while you were here."

Casey touched his cheek, searching his eyes for some type of understanding. He must see the reality of their lives. "I watched Jenkins and his men rob that land office in Billings. I held the horses. I shot a man—a good man who was only trying to protect what was his. I don't know if he lived or died."

"You wounded him. Remember, I saw the whole thing."

She wondered if he spoke the truth. "No matter. I was barely fourteen, stupid, didn't really see what was happening there. But the fact is I still shot him while breaking the law. One of these days, a federal marshal will show up in Kahlerville and arrest me, or maybe Ben Kahler will put it all together. We've talked about this before. Do you want your family to face that humiliation? And what of Jenkins?

Do you think he's given up finding me?"

He sighed deeply. "I *can* help you. You won't ever be free—whether to marry me or to live your life without fear—unless this is done."

She shrugged. "I've thought a lot about what to do. I know the location of some of the outlaw hideouts, which might help my defense. I know the names they use in various parts of the country. Is it possible to trade information for a lesser charge?"

"It would look favorable in your behalf, but unless it's handled properly, your life won't be worth a nickel." His words sounded flat, distant.

"I've considered all those things and twisted the outcome over and over in my mind. I really think I could help the law find some of them."

"And what about Jenkins?" His jaw tightened.

She hesitated. Satan took the form of Jenkins every time she thought about him. "I don't know. I guess I'll deal with him when the time comes." She thought about the outlaw's threats. "There was a time I probably could have ridden away, and he wouldn't have cared."

"But what you're proposing is too dangerous."

"I can't hide forever. Besides, too many people know who I am. It puts all of you in terrible danger. Now your whole family will be a part of this. We haven't even discussed their feelings. Jocelyn and Bonnie *will* have a difficult time with the truth. Morgan, I knowingly deceived them. They trusted me, and I deceived them."

He gently grasped her shoulders. "Honey, Grant would have been right back up here if Mama and Bonnie were upset."

Casey stood and reached for matches to light the kerosene lamp. Glancing into the mirror over her dresser, she smoothed her dress and tried to straighten her disheveled hair. Her eyes were red and puffy. She detested looking so unkempt. Weak.

"I want to talk to your mother and Bonnie," she said. "We've been too close for me to allow Grant to handle this. I may be ashamed of the things Casey O'Hare has done, but I'm not too proud to admit I've been wrong in not telling them the truth."

"I want *us* to talk to them," he said. "You and I are in this together. In the days to come, we're going to face more problems than you can imagine. Some may be legal. Some may be threats from Jenkins, and others may be misunderstandings from the past, but we must be committed to seeing this through."

He took the comb from her hand and smiled. "I won't always behave as though God is holding my hand. With me, He needs to seal my mouth. But God hasn't brought us this far to abandon us in the middle of a fight. I know He's with us, and I know He's for us."

She nodded, her mind a haze of fog. Oh, how she wanted to believe him.

Morgan continued. "Before we go downstairs and discuss our plans with *our* family, I'd like to ask God for guidance and protection."

She bowed her head, and again her tears flowed. Morgan's words strengthened her resolve to no longer let the past rule her every action. But one thing she knew for sure: Only God could work out the future, because she was fresh out of ideas.

CHAPTER 22

Morgan and Casey descended the stairs to the kitchen. They stood amid the shadows of evening and fears of the unknown to face whatever lay ahead. Morgan's body craved rest just like the day he'd talked with the preacher about Jenkins and made his peace with God. Odd, how the mental and spiritual aspects of life were more demanding than the physical.

The tantalizing smells of supper greeted him. He'd long since forgotten the hour. "I'm suddenly starved." He hoped his words lightened the heaviness threatening to strangle them.

Casey offered a shaky smile as they made their way toward his mother.

"There you are." Jocelyn lifted a pan of corn bread from the cookstove to the table. He smelled the jalapeños and beans, and his stomach growled.

"Supper's ready. I hope you're hungry," said Jocelyn.

"Mama, we need to talk to all of you." He clutched Casey's hand firmly. He sensed she needed strength as much as he did.

Mama waved her hand as though nothing could be of importance, but he saw her watery eyes. "Why don't we eat supper first?"

"I know Grant told you what happened."

Jocelyn faced both of them with a strong determination ever present in all of her dealings. "Yes, he has, Son. I know the truth. All of it."

"I'm so sorry." Casey's words nearly broke.

"You forget I consider you one of my own." She reached for Casey and hugged her close. Morgan held firmly to her hand as much for himself as for her.

"You always knew something wasn't right." Casey dabbed at her eyes. "The way you looked at me when I stumbled over why I'd come to Kahlerville."

"You tried many times to tell us. I never imagined. . . I never thought it could be this." Her eyes held the pain of past remembrances. "This is hard, but we can work through it. My dear girl, the burdens you've carried." She turned to Morgan. "Once, when you and I were talking, you called her Casey. I wondered then if she was linked to Jenkins. Perhaps the same person. Except the woman I read about in the newspapers was not who I saw in Shawne."

"I'm sorry for the deceit." Casey hesitated. "I told the reverend and Sarah. No one else in Kahlerville."

Not a hint of condemnation creased Jocelyn's features. "We'll find a way to make this right. God always has a plan."

Casey blinked several times and touched the wetness under her nose. She must have left her handkerchief in the bedroom. Morgan reached into his pocket for a clean one and saw Bonnie standing in the doorway. Her face was mottled red. Morgan knew the truth had been quite a shock for his frail sister.

"What about you, Bonnie?" he asked. "I know you're shaken, and I hate to think we caused those tears."

Bonnie lowered her head, as though denying her emotions. "I don't know what to say." She paused, and he knew she was trying desperately not to cry.

"I haven't forgotten that you saw Kathleen right after it happened and that you're still suffering from it," said Morgan.

"When Grant told us, I wanted to believe Shawne could not possibly be Casey O'Hare. . .the outlaw." Bonnie's lips quivered. "I want to say the right things and be forgiving, but I feel as though Kathleen's grave has just been opened, and it hurts all over again. Shawne, I mean Casey, is my best friend, and I do see why she lied to us, but this is so hard."

Bonnie turned to Morgan. "Now I see why she's so different from me, and I understand why sometimes you treated her so badly. I guess I need time and prayer to love you both the way I should."

Morgan stroked her pale tresses as though she were a child. "Bonnie, I don't expect any miracles, but I know God will help us. I'm asking you to consider one thing as far as Casey and I are concerned."

Bonnie nodded. "I'll do anything."

"God needed to hit me hard with something powerful, something that would get my attention. He used Casey to make me realize I was selfish and indulging in my own self-pity."

"And I should have told the truth right from the start," Casey said. "I thought I could start all over my own way. Please forgive me, Bonnie. You are the first real friend I've ever had, and I don't want to lose you. You are all I ever wanted to be—a godly woman, a real lady. I really understand if you need time. . . . I'd do anything to change the past."

"I'll try," Bonnie said. "I want it all back the same, too." She brushed away her tears, then held out her hand to Casey. "I'm afraid we have another problem."

"What?" Morgan's thoughts flew in a dozen directions.

"Ben. . .he's asked me lots of questions about Casey. Where she came from. Her family, and does the reverend know anything about her. I'm afraid he might suspect the truth."

Casey inhaled sharply. "I've wondered the same thing—nearly left town because of him."

"Perhaps I shouldn't see him anymore."

"No. Bonnie, I won't stand in the way of your happiness." Casey spoke with the strength Morgan remembered in Vernal when she announced she was leaving him and Doc. "I've seen the way you look at him, and I won't have it."

"I could never forgive myself if he arrested you," Bonnie said.

"If he does, it's because of what I've done—not because of anything about you."

"I think we all need to put ourselves in Morgan's and Casey's places," Grant said in a way that was uncharacteristic of his manner; he normally resorted to silence in matters of emotion. Yet today he'd displayed traits so much like their father. "Who knows how we might have reacted in the same situation? We've always had each other to lean on. But Casey didn't have anyone, and Morgan refused our help." He jammed his hands inside his jeans pockets. "I believe the only part I can play in this family is to support my brother and Casey. We have too much at stake to risk splitting our family. Remember how Pa used to talk about the war? He said most folks were against the North and the South fighting and killing each other, but what he felt was important was the common goal of preserving the Union. Isn't that what we have here? We're a family, and if we don't stick together through this, well, then we have nothing."

Admiration, respect, and love for his brother seized Morgan. "If Pa were here today, he'd be so proud of you. And I'm honored to say you're my brother. I hope I can make up for the past, because there are some lessons I need to learn from you."

Long after the evening's conversations ceased and silence ruled through the house, Morgan weighed the words, feelings, and reactions of those he loved.

One matter convicted his soul. Casey had to be cleared of the charges against her without delay, and that meant the information he'd started compiling for her case had to be put to use. With Ben calling on Bonnie and asking questions, this whole thing could explode. Tomorrow Ben would be there for dinner. Could his old friend be trusted, or would he see this as an opportunity to advance his reputation as a lawman?

The following morning, Morgan left the cabin at daylight for Kahlerville. He hated staying at his old home. Ghosts from the past still haunted him every second he was there. More and more, the idea of moving his things into the bunkhouse made sense.

Today he wanted to see about reopening his law office and continuing with his work on clearing Casey. He planned to send a telegram to Doc in Vernal. . .for more than one reason. Foremost, he had to talk to Ben. His old friend needed to be on Casey's side.

When Ben wasn't at his office or at the boardinghouse eating breakfast, Morgan sought out the owner of the newspaper. The sound of the printing press and the smell of the machine reminded him of the constitution's guarantee of freedom of speech.

"Mornin', Thomas. I see you're getting the news out."

Thomas lifted his gaze from the typeset. A wide grin spread over the man's face, and he reached out to shake Morgan's hand. "Good to see you. What can I do for you?"

"I'd like to take up practicing law again," he told the balding man. "Is my old office still available?"

"Everything's just how you left it. Just a mite dusty." He opened up a paper-laden desk and pulled out a key. "I've been looking for the day when you'd walk in here and ask for this."

Morgan pulled out a wad of bills. "Here's six months' rent and a little more for all the trouble I've been. Can you mention what I'm doing in the paper? I plan to open in about a week."

"Sure can. Folks will be mighty happy to know they have a lawyer again." He handed Morgan the key. "You look good, Morgan. Real good."

"Must be the clean living."

Thomas laughed. "You forget your pa and I pulled you out of more trouble than I care to recall."

"That's why I ended up in law school."

"Better there than jail."

Ouch! The sound of that curdled his stomach. He'd waited too long to work on Casey's problems. Once outside, the sun seemed to light a faint path through the center of town to the small building beside Kahlerville's general store and post office. Hard to remember the last time he'd called the place his. He stuck the key in the door and stepped inside. A flood of memories rushed in, but they weren't all bad as he had anticipated. A lot of good times and good things had happened here. Helping folks. That's what he enjoyed doing the most. The ranch had its roots in what made him an Andrews, but his heart lay in practicing law.

He glanced around the office. Stale air met his nose, and dirt from the street covered the outside of the window. Beneath a thick layer of dust sat an oaken desk that the reverend had helped him build. A bookcase leaned against the wall on one side of the room, and two chairs sat against the opposite side. His law books and plaques were stored away at the ranch. Mama had taken care of packing up his office after he'd taken off after Jenkins. Immediately, he envisioned everything neat and clean. Somewhere at home was the sign he'd once hung above the outside door: MORGAN ANDREWS, ATTORNEY AT LAW.

A sense of pride and humility for how he could help Casey and the community rooted deep inside him. This afternoon he'd pull out the books and start compiling research. Tomorrow, providing Grant didn't need him, he'd clean up the office. *Casey might want to help.*

The next item on this morning's list, before trying to find Ben again, was to send a telegram to Doc. This time of day, the telegraph office was usually empty. He didn't need folks listening in on his business. Furthermore, he had to be careful how he worded the message in case the clerk couldn't be trusted.

Inside the small establishment, Morgan greeted a young man barely old enough to shave. After a few pleasantries, he pulled out a piece of paper from his pocket. "Can you send a message for me?"

The clerk took the paper and read through it before tapping out the words.

> *Doc. Need a referral letter for our friend. I'm taking the case.*
> *Back to practicing law. Time crucial.*

Morgan waited until the clerk finished, then tucked the piece of paper back into his pocket. He'd follow up with a letter. Someday the price of a telegram wouldn't be ten times the cost of sending a letter. But in this case, time ticked away. The door behind him creaked and captured his attention.

"Mornin', Morgan." The cold, hard look on Ben's face spoke fathoms.

"Mornin'. I've been looking for you."

"That's what I heard." Ben nodded at the clerk and then turned back to Morgan. "You finished here?"

"Yes. Can I buy you a cup of coffee?"

"I'd rather talk in quiet."

Morgan followed him out of the telegraph office and down the empty street. "What's wrong? Do you need to talk about Bonnie?"

Ben threw him a hard stare. "I'm through being a fool, Morgan. Why don't you tell me what's going on between you and Miss Shawne

Flanagan?" He spat the name like it was venom.

"That's what I wanted to talk to you about."

"Little late, don't you think?"

"Not for old friends."

"You've got some tall explaining to do on this one. Outlaws won't be taking over my town. I have a reputation here."

"It's not your town. It's everyone's town."

"I'm not in the mood for your lawyer-twisting words."

"And I'm not in the mood for you sending an innocent woman to her death."

"You of all people should see what this woman has done to you. What about your family and the people in this community? And the reverend? Maybe I already know. Prostitution has been linked with Casey O'Hare a time or two. I imagine she has her ways."

Morgan fought to keep from slamming a fist into Ben's face. He took a few deep breaths and formed his words. "Do you honestly think I'd be involved with anything that would desecrate the memory of Kathleen? Or for that matter desecrate God?"

"I don't know." Ben's words softened. "You've been gone a long time, and nothing I've learned makes sense. Have you forgotten that I've sworn to uphold the law?"

"Would you hear me out first? I need your help."

"Need my help? Do you think I'd sacrifice the safety of this town over some lovesick, half-crazed lawyer and a wanted killer?"

"I think you'd give me a chance to state the truth."

Ben fumed. His face had long since reddened. "Guess I owe you that much."

CHAPTER 23

Casey trembled the moment she saw Morgan ride into view with Ben Kahler. She wanted to believe the two of them together meant something good. Then again, it could mean nothing at all. A coincidence. Morgan had left early this morning, according to Grant. He hadn't said a word to anyone about where he was going.

How can he stay at the cabin where Kathleen was killed? She shrugged and massaged her arms.

"I've been praying all day," Jocelyn said. "I've made Ben's favorite fried chicken and creamed potatoes, hoping it will make a difference."

"And I baked his favorite peach cobbler," Bonnie added.

"So you two think Morgan is going to tell Ben everything tonight?" Casey asked.

Jocelyn wrapped her arm around Casey's shoulders. "Morgan's a good lawyer, and he thinks things through. I bet he stayed up all night working on your case."

"If this doesn't work—"

"Hush." Jocelyn squeezed her shoulders. "Who is in control here?"

"I know. But I can't help but feel the day of reckoning is coming much too fast." Casey watched the two men make their way from the barn toward the house. "Remember to call me Shawne until this matter is settled, probably forever." She couldn't think clearly when her mind was muddied with emotion.

The men's boots pounded on the steps and onto the porch, shaking Casey's resolve to relax. *Read Ben's eyes. Remember who's in control.* She snatched up a glass vase full of the wildflowers that Bonnie had picked earlier and set it on the table. A few deep breaths and she transformed herself back to another day: Jenkins had ridden back from a job gone bad and was drunk. He called out for her, then cursed. Back then she depended on her wits and her weapons. Now she depended on God.

"Good to see you," Jocelyn called to Ben. She hugged him and wagged her finger at Morgan. "You took off this morning, and I had extra breakfast on the stove."

He kissed his mother's cheek. "Sorry. Had business to tend to."

Ben stole a look around Jocelyn. "Evenin', Bonnie, Miss Shawne."

Bonnie's dimpled grin would have melted ice. "Glad you came, Ben."

He doesn't know. Casey nodded a silent greeting and caught the grit in his stare. Yes, he *did* know. "Did you and Morgan spend the day together?"

"Fishing?" Bonnie laughed.

"Yes and no." Ben couldn't have disguised his love for Bonnie if he had to. His eyes held a certain light that she'd seen in Morgan's. "Hmm, something sure smells good, and I'm starved."

"We're putting it on the table right now," Jocelyn said. "It's just us tonight. We took the hands their dinner before you rode up. But someone needs to round up Grant."

"I'll get him." Morgan glanced at Casey with a grin. "I could use a little company."

Outside, she waited until they were clear of listening ears. "You told him."

Morgan wrapped an arm around her waist. "Didn't have to."

"Are you giving me an opportunity to ride out of here?"

"No, not yet, anyway. Tonight I want you to tell Ben everything."

She shivered and watched the sun slowly make its way beneath the horizon. "Do you have any idea how many times I've wanted to leave Kahlerville? But I'm so sick of running that it doesn't matter anymore."

"If Ben is on our side, we're a step ahead of Jenkins and able to move ahead on your case."

"So now Sheriff Kahler is going to protect an outlaw from an outlaw? And make her look lily white in the process?"

"Trust me, I believe in your innocence, and I think he will, too."

Casey didn't have any more appetite for supper than she'd had for breakfast. More than once over the last few weeks, she'd called herself stupid. Now the word rang in her ear. Bonnie and Jocelyn did their best to keep the talk light, but heaviness clouded them all.

"That's it." Ben pushed back his plate. "I can't eat another bite. Can't think of a better way to end a meal of fried chicken and potatoes than peach cobbler and cream. In fact, I could use a walk." He smiled at Bonnie. "If you don't mind, I need to talk to your friend."

Bonnie paled. "Of. . .course, Ben."

Casey patted her hand and rose from the table. She caught Ben's scrutiny, but then again, she'd felt it all evening. Without a glance at the rest of the family, she made her way to the door. This was between her and Ben.

With the sounds of night and the rapid beating of her heart, Casey breathed a quick prayer. "When did you figure it all out?"

"Yesterday. I'd suspected it for a long time, but I couldn't imagine Morgan with—"

"Jenkins's woman?"

"Uh, yes."

"Are you arresting me?"

"No. Morgan told me a strange tale today. I want to see if your story matches his."

"And if it does?"

"Then I promise to help him clear your name and protect you from those who want you dead."

She heard the respect in Ben's deep voice. "I know this has to be hard. Morgan's your friend, and I see how you care for Bonnie."

"I'd do anything for this family but sacrifice my principles."

"I understand, and I respect that."

"You're a strange woman, Casey O'Hare."

"I've been called a lot worse."

He laughed. "Morgan is like a brother to me, and he loves you very much."

"And I love him, but I want you to know this: I'm more concerned about risking the lives of the dear people of Kahlerville—the reverend and Sarah, all of them—than I am about saving my neck. Today I realized without a doubt that God brought me here to this place to settle up with the law. I can't run anymore."

"Well, I have all night to listen. It wouldn't be the first time I rode back to town in the dark."

"Do you need an armed escort?"

Ben laughed, and that eased the tension between them for her to start at the beginning, when she and Tim had left their drunken pa and eventually fallen into company with Jenkins and his gang. . . .

"I know my story doesn't fit with the newspapers or wanted posters, but it's the truth."

He shook his head and stared up at a full moon. "What I find rather odd is that Morgan's story matches yours exactly."

Her pulse quickened. "Then you believe me?"

"Guess I do. I'll keep what I know to myself and give Morgan a hand in clearing your name. But if Jenkins rides anywhere near my town, I'm calling for help. The good people of Kahlerville will not be put in the middle of this."

"I wouldn't expect anything less from you."

After Ben left, Morgan spent another sleepless night. Living at the cabin was like living inside a nightmare. Morgan thought he could conquer his fears, but they were winning. Thankfully, Grant had made it a habit to stop by each morning.

"Move into the bunkhouse until Casey leaves," Grant said at the cabin door. He touched the worn curtains over the kitchen window—the ones Kathleen had made. "Staying here is crazy."

"Maybe I'll take a room at the boardinghouse. I'm reopening the law office. Haven't told Casey yet, but, little brother, you don't need me here."

"An extra hand is always good, but you do what you feel is right." He drew out a long breath. "If Pa hadn't built this place, I'd help you set it on fire."

"I've thought about it, but destroying a sound cabin won't change the past." Morgan stepped out into the morning air, a little cooler than the torrid days of summer. "I thought I had to prove something by living here. All I'm doing is reliving it again and again."

"This is not a home." His brother's gaze swept back inside the cabin. "I don't think you need the past staring you in the face," Grant said.

Morgan didn't say it, but at times he could hear Kathleen's voice asking him where he'd been when Jenkins attacked her. "You're right. I want a permanent place with Casey."

Grant said nothing. Morgan knew he had to clear the uneasiness between them. "I know you care about her."

"She's your girl. Told you that before." He scuffed the toe of his boot into a knothole on the floor. "I just looked out for her until you came to your senses."

Morgan chuckled. "More truth there than you might think."

"Take good care of her."

Morgan heard the conviction. A different man would have called it a threat. "I will. If and when she decides to have me, I'll need a best man."

Grant grinned. "I know a fella who might be interested."

"Thanks. You know, when I'm with Casey, I forget about Kathleen. They are two different women. Kathleen accepted me just as I am with all my faults. Sort of put me on a mountaintop." He paused. "Casey challenges me to be a better man. She's strong, like Mama in a lot of ways."

"Someday when I'm done with school, I hope to find a woman who makes me feel the same way."

"You will. I'm sure of it. I have the letters drawn up to a few medical schools. I'll get them posted this week."

"Thanks. Glad to hear Ben is helping."

"I gambled with that one." Morgan watched the wind pick up a ragged curtain from inside the cabin and cause it to sway. He shuddered in remembrance. "I refuse to lose."

❧

The morning after Ben agreed to help with her case, Casey awoke with more hope than she could ever remember. Surely with both men's belief in her, there'd be a way to clear her name.

Since sunup, she'd worked on the washing with Bonnie while Jocelyn made breakfast for the hands. In the late morning, Morgan stopped at the house while she hung the last load of sheets and

229

pillowcases to dry. They'd smell very fine when she crawled into bed tonight. Odd how little niceties could mean so much.

"Would you take a ride into town with me?" Morgan smiled like a little boy who'd played hooky from school.

"I think so, as long as Jocelyn doesn't mind. Can we stop by the parsonage? I'd really like to check on Sarah." He nodded and kept on grinning. "What are you hiding?"

"It's a surprise." He took her arm and linked it into his. "I'm one lucky man to have the prettiest girl in Texas. Nothing better than a curly-headed, red-haired angel."

"What did you do, buy another bull? A horse? A whole herd of cows?" She laughed.

"None of those. This is more of a surprise for us."

She chilled. His words of marriage paralyzed her. *I can't let him know my fears.* "Did you buy the whole town?"

"If I could get you to marry me, I'd buy the whole state."

The wagon ride was pleasant with a fall chill that proved refreshing after the summer's heat. She'd given up questioning him about the surprise, but when they pulled up in front of a small building beside the general store, she instantly knew what had him so excited.

"Are you going to practice law again?" she asked. "For folks other than me?"

"I am. I made the arrangements yesterday. Tomorrow I'm cleaning up the place, and in a few days, I'll move into the boardinghouse." His grin refused to go away.

"Now all of Kahlerville will have a lawyer," she said. "But what about the ranch?"

"Grant doesn't need me until he heads east for school; then I'll do both or get a law partner."

She glanced around at the dust and dirt. "I'd like to help you get things ready."

"I didn't bring you here to clean."

"Looks to me like you need a woman's touch." She pointed to the cobwebs in the corner of the ceiling.

"I'm not so sure about that."

She caught the mischievous twinkle in his eye. "Are you saying you resent a woman's touch? We do have much to offer."

"Miss Shawne, you have the wrong idea about me. I'm thinking as sure as I hire a sweet young woman to tidy up, she'd up and get married on me. Where would I be then?"

Casey crossed her arms and swept her gaze about the office. "I think better than where you are now."

"I have a better idea," he said.

She raised a brow. Oh, how she loved moments like these. "And it is. . ."

Her wrapped his arms around her waist and kissed the tip of her nose. "I think I'd be better off to marry me a sweet young woman."

She laughed lightly. "Just to have someone clean for you? I think I remember Doc offering me a deal like that once, but I turned him down."

"I'm glad you did. Now I have you all to myself." He lifted his hat and sent it soaring across the room. His lips brushed across her cheek and slipped just above her lips.

"And this would be one of the sweet young woman's duties?" she whispered.

"Hmm. Lots of these. Several times a day." His lips descended upon hers, warm and tender.

"How would you get any work done?"

"We'd live on love."

She should have stepped away and not let him see how his nearness caused her to forget what was right and proper. Instead, she slipped her hands to his face and wove her fingers into his hair.

How many days had she waited for this intimacy? Yet she feared the depth of her love for Morgan. As his kiss deepened and she gave into the feelings swirling through her mind and body, all the doubts and mistrust faded.

Morgan's arms tightened around her. Suddenly a swarm of memories blackened the moment. She remembered Jenkins grabbing her and bruising her lips with his vile mouth—the same mouth that had ordered good people killed.

Casey struggled to press her hands into Morgan's chest. She trembled. Her gaze flew to his face, and her heart begged for understanding. She loved this man, but she was afraid of what passion might do to him.

His face flushed, and he released her. "What's wrong?"

The words refused to form. "I'm afraid." She shook her head. "I'm sorry."

"Jenkins." He spat the word like rotten food.

"Yes." She picked up his hat and handed it to him.

"What else?"

I can't tell him I'm afraid of him—that his good temperament might not be true. He'll think I'm throwing him in the same lot with Jenkins. "Isn't that enough?"

"I love you," he said. "I will not let Jenkins or anyone hurt you."

She stole a glimpse of his face, a mixture of sadness and tenderness. She despised herself, for she knew real love did not embrace fear and distrust.

CHAPTER  24

After the Rainers' family traveled back to Oregon, Sarah steadily declined and grew totally dependent upon Casey and the reverend. Casey applied salve to the bedsores and did her best to keep the woman comfortable. She brewed herbal teas and tried every medicinal herb she'd ever learned from Franco, but nothing eased Sarah's discomfort.

No one spoke of it, but they all sensed the disease had progressed far beyond any cure.

On a damp and dreary November day, the doctor arrived. A small, wiry man with a red-gray beard, he spoke in terms that Casey and the reverend understood. His past successes with patients who had diseases similar to Sarah's had earned him a reputation of distinction.

The doctor spent nearly two hours with Sarah while the reverend paced the parlor and Casey sat stiffly on the sofa watching him move from one emotion to another. His shoulders appeared to droop farther with each crossing of the room. Never had he looked more vulnerable.

A silver teapot, Sarah's best gold-rimmed china, and an intricately carved silver tray filled with lemon cakes sat on a small oaken table.

Neither Casey nor the reverend felt the pangs of hunger or thirst. It was merely a form of hospitality extended to the physician.

When at last the doctor joined them in the parlor, the lines on his face clearly indicated the diagnosis. "Let's sit down and discuss your wife's condition."

"Would you like for me to leave?" Casey rose to her feet.

The reverend motioned for her to stay. "No, I'd like for you to hear this, too." He turned his attention to the doctor. "I've known for a long time my Sarah was dying. I just need for you to confirm it. From the look on your face, I see there is nothing you can do."

The doctor cleared his throat. "As a man of God, you already know the Lord doesn't always answer our prayers the way we'd like."

"I want her free of pain. If she can't be healed, then let her die without suffering."

The doctor folded his hands and leaned closer to the reverend. "The disease has progressed rapidly since the first time you wrote me. The only alternative is to use medication to numb its effects. I talked with Sarah for quite some time about this, and she prefers to refrain from taking anything until the pain becomes unbearable. She doesn't want to spend her remaining days asleep."

The reverend nodded, and his hands trembled. "How long do you think she has?"

"It's difficult to say, two to three months at the most. Your wife is a fighter, and she will hold on to every drop of life for as long as she can. I am sorry, sir. It would have been much easier to give you good news. I'd like to leave laudanum for those times when she desperately needs relief. After all, peace is what we all want for her."

"Is there anything else we can do?" The reverend's drawn features tugged at Casey's heart.

"I think you and the young lady are already doing everything possible. Sarah loves you both, and the decision concerning the medication took much deliberation. She understands the extreme tension existing here in the home and feels guilty for causing it. I admire her courage and faith, as I believe you do." The doctor shifted his bag to the other hand, then stood.

The two men shook hands, and the reverend thanked him for coming. Casey excused herself, knowing the fee and payment needed to be addressed. The grandfather clock chimed its harsh reminder of time slipping away.

She mounted the stairs to Sarah's room and knocked lightly. When no response came, she slipped her fingers around the door and gently pushed it open. Sarah lay sleeping, her face calm with no trace of pain.

Poor thing, the examination must have hurt her terribly. Casey folded the quilt around Sarah's neck and bent to kiss the pale, wrinkled forehead. *My life has been a long, strange road. I never imagined nursing outlaws would lead me to nursing a godly woman like Sarah.* She pulled a rocker close to the bed and remembered doing the same for Morgan when he nearly died in Vernal.

Her mind wandered to what Morgan was attempting to do for her. Clearing her name. . .a pardon from the state of Texas. . . freedom. At times it all sounded like a dream. He worked night and day on her case. He never complained; he never demanded anything in return. His bad temperament vanished the same day he told her about Jenkins killing his wife. But she waited as though he might explode at their next meeting. The old fears about violent men had taken root and seemed to overshadow her every moment with him. It wasn't fair to Morgan, but they were there nevertheless. If only she could trust him. Why couldn't she accept the changed man and stop holding back on her love?

Shaking her head in an effort to rid her mind of the past, she concentrated on her prayers for the reverend and Sarah.

I will never forget all the wonderful things the reverend and Sarah have done for me. Casey leaned back in the rocker and massaged her arms. *Oh, how I want to see Sarah and the reverend to the end before anything else happens.*

Morgan wrote until his wrist throbbed and his arm felt like tiny splinters had embedded in his skin. For days he'd muddled through law books and made notes of the items pertinent to Casey's case. He'd posted correspondence back east to renowned attorneys who had tried similar cases and cleared their clients' names. A letter went out to Doc and explained what was going on. Another letter was sent to Hank and Maude Stevens in Deer Creek.

Casey. Her defense, her acquittal, haunted him night and day. He believed in her innocence with all his being, yet something was still missing in her defense.

He went to sleep deliberating the case and woke as though he'd been up all night. His nightmares about Kathleen now bore the image of Casey. And for that reason, he could not sit idle for fear this might be the day Jenkins rode into town.

He'd caught up with her before. He could find her again. And what of Tim? When Morgan's thoughts and worries overwhelmed him, he dug into the work, and when he could do no more, he rode out to the ranch and helped Grant. Seemed like he and God were having a constant conversation.

One evening, Casey and Morgan spoke quietly in the parsonage's parlor while Sarah slept and the reverend read in his study.

"You're wanted for a train robbery and a bank job with Jenkins during the time after you left Vernal."

"Ben pointed that out to me. I was far from civilization during those holdups. I wonder if Doc's testimony will help."

Morgan smiled. "I think he'd do just about anything for you. Made me jealous a few times. He'll vouch for you risking your life to keep me alive and your desire to start fresh. As soon as we get the letters, I'll stick them in a lock box. And don't forget the reverend. A character reference from him is crucial to your defense. Mama is writing one, too."

"What about the seven years I rode with the gang?" Casey asked. "That's fact, Morgan, and I don't believe any judge would believe I did nothing during that time. Besides, I simply ignored what they were doing."

"I'm researching those things. Give me time. Our case has to be perfect, no room for error. I'm looking at the charges from every angle."

"I'm just nervous. The only other person who could testify on my behalf is Rose."

"Rose?"

"She owns a brothel in Denver. Not exactly a model citizen." She stood from the parlor sofa and walked across the room. "I tried life her way once, but I couldn't handle one night. I should be glad Jenkins didn't sell me to her."

"You don't have to tell me any of this."

"I know, but I'm sure the thought has crossed your mind."

"What I want is you and me as man and wife. And you won't marry me until I have your name cleared and Jenkins behind bars." He attempted to sound light, but so much weighed on his mind.

What about the other crimes of which Casey had no proof of innocence? The whole explanation surrounding her alleged criminal acts rested in her own credibility. And he had to prove it. He'd lost Kathleen. He couldn't lose Casey.

Casey finished ironing the last shirt for the reverend. She inspected it once more before hanging it with the others. The overflowing basket stacked with clothing for Sarah, the reverend, and herself had taken most of the morning to finish. Glancing around the kitchen, she laughed aloud at the articles hanging from every peg and knob available. A bit of breeze blew in through the back door and played with one of Sarah's gowns as though some invisible lady danced inside. *My, how Sarah would love to see this.*

Periodically she checked on Sarah, who had tossed fitfully during the night. Earlier, she'd requested laudanum and now rested under its soothing effects. Casey saw her friend's strength dwindle and the need for pain medication increase. True to his word, the reverend remained close by his wife's side. Together they savored their precious remaining time together. Even now, he wrote his sermon by her bedside, where he waited for her to waken and share whatever dream had lured her from the sleeping hours.

Stepping out onto the back porch, Casey drank in the fall freshness. Yellow mums nodded in the late morning sun. She loved this time of year as though it were a resting time before winter. She wondered if Sarah felt the same.

More than eight months had passed since she'd left Jenkins. She wanted to believe he'd given up on finding her and that some other woman had replaced her and caused him to forget his hatred.

A knock at the door interrupted her musings, and she hurried to answer it.

Ben stood in the doorway, hat in hand. The lines around his eyes indicated his weariness. "Can we talk?"

"Yes, of course. Come on in."

Apprehension washed over her. She stood back as he made his way inside and on to the parlor, where she offered him a chair. "I'd rather stand, if you don't mind."

"Ben, am I in trouble?"

"I'm not sure. Got word on recent activity of Jenkins and his gang."

"Where are they?"

"Last seen in New Mexico. Rumor is Jenkins and Tim split. A couple of the men went with Tim."

A few faces crossed her mind—those loyal to her brother. "I'm not surprised. Jenkins and Tim barely tolerated each other. Tim doesn't like taking orders. Never did. Where did you hear this?"

"Lawman from Austin. He's staying at the boardinghouse tonight. Probably best for you to lie low until he rides out."

She studied his face and the way he worried the brim of his hat. "What else, Ben?"

"Rumors are Jenkins refused to give up his search for you. Tim wanted it ended."

"So I'm no safer from Jenkins than I was eight months ago."

Ben moistened his lips. "Looks that way. And Tim's not riding with him to protect you."

"He has his own priorities. My guess is he saw Jenkins passing up too many chances to bring in money. Where did your friend get his information?"

"A fella who used to ride with the Daltons." He glanced about the parlor. "When's Morgan going to have your case ready?"

"We're meeting on Friday morning to go over it all."

"I'm afraid we're running out of time."

She nodded. "Does your lawman friend suspect I'm in these parts?"

"He thinks you might be in Galveston. I haven't told Morgan."

"I will." She swallowed hard.

"I'm wondering if you need to hide out until all of this is over."

"And desert Sarah? She hasn't long for this world, and I can't leave her."

"Even if it costs you your life?"

Casey forced a smile. "I'd rather go to my grave knowing I did something decent than run again."

"There's something I want to say. Now is as good a time as any." His black mustache lifted in a half smile. "When you came down front that Sunday in church, I thought it strange that a woman nursing the preacher's wife was not saved. Then when I figured out who you were and heard your story, I realized you had left that part of your life behind. Folks who know you respect you. And I'm one of them. I intend to write a letter testifying on your behalf for Morgan." He shrugged. "It might make a difference."

Casey felt a surge of emotion. She blinked several times. "Thank you, Ben. I'm sure it will make a difference. Right now I'm trying to convince Morgan to let me share what I know with the federal marshals."

"Every outlaw in the country will be after you then."

She shook her head. "Only one."

CHAPTER  25

The Friday morning that Casey was to meet with Morgan to review his findings for her state pardon brought all of her misgivings to the surface. Sarah had spent a miserable night with severe vomiting. The poor woman had withered away to nearly nothing, and the constant sickness did not help.

Both Casey and the reverend were exhausted. Sarah's bed had to be stripped each time until there were no clean bed coverings left. Before sunrise, Casey managed to hang the wash out to dry. She already dreaded the morning with Morgan, certain his position as a reputable attorney was about to be challenged by his taking on an outlaw. She needed a little rest to perk up her spirits. Before returning to her own room, she checked on Sarah and found her crying. Wet vomit coated her hair and body. Casey put aside her own needs and bathed her dear friend. She brewed a cup of ginger tea to stop the retching, but the woman couldn't drink it. Finally she slept.

Much later, Casey entered her own room only to discover Morgan's arrival stood just moments away. She heard the door open downstairs and listened to the reverend greet him. Her entire body felt as though someone had given her a beating. The reverend needed his breakfast; she smelled of vomit, and her Bible hadn't been opened. After peeling off her dress, she washed up and hurriedly dressed, then pinned up her hair. All the while, she stole glances at the clock racing ahead.

Emerging from her room shortly after nine, she cringed at the late hour. *Morgan will be furious with me.* She shuddered at the memory of his cold, hard stare. *He's gone to so much trouble for me, and I can't even be on time.*

"Good morning," Morgan said as she hastened down the steps. "Whoa, girl." He frowned.

"I'm so sorry." Her heart pounded. "I didn't mean to keep you waiting."

He held up a cup of coffee that had been made hours before. "My concern is you. Slow down. The reverend and I have been talking and drinking coffee."

"Reverend, you haven't eaten breakfast." She brushed past the two men to the kitchen. If Morgan was drinking the reverend's coffee, he'd have a surly disposition for sure.

"I'm fixin' it now. Have the biscuits all ready to set in the oven. You're the one who needs something to eat. I just told Morgan how you were up all night with Sarah."

"We both were."

"Maybe so, but I don't have an appointment with the best lawyer in town. Why don't you sit down for a little while, drink some coffee, and at least eat a biscuit and apple butter?"

"Oh, I can't." She glanced at Morgan, desperately needing to read his mood. "We're already late."

"Casey, calm down a bit." Morgan reached for her hand. "I'm the fancy lawyer here, and I'm waiting on one of the reverend's prize-winning biscuits. I don't have anything scheduled except you."

"I think I'd rather get it over with." Her stomach twisted.

"And we will, honey. A few more minutes won't make any difference. I think you will be pleased with what I have to say." He sounded so sweet and caring that she believed every word.

"All right." The coffee did smell wonderful, even if the reverend's strong brew tasted like prairie dirt, and she'd felt the pangs of hunger long before dawn.

"By the way, you look beautiful," Morgan said.

The reverend chuckled. "I believe those are the words spoken by a man in love and looking forward to his wedding day. Mmm, wouldn't a Christmas wedding be nice?"

Casey shook her head. "You two are a matched pair." *I'm not ready to get married. There's too much left unsettled in my life.*

"I'm taking my coffee up to Sarah's room," the reverend said. "I'll be praying for you two this morning."

Once the reverend disappeared, Morgan turned to her. "I'm sorry you had such a bad night. You look exhausted."

"I really am all right. Tired mostly, and nervous about my case."

He traced his finger on top of hers and grasped the cup. "Are those feelings why you're avoiding me?"

"I haven't been avoiding you." But she had.

"Honey, something has had you upset since that afternoon at my office."

"The problem isn't you." *I can't tell him I'm afraid of him.*

He raised an eyebrow. A worry line etched across his forehead. "Are you having second thoughts about marrying me?" He breathed deeply. "You're expecting the old Morgan to lash out at you without warning."

While she scrambled for words, he must have realized the truth. He lifted her chin, and her gaze met his. "I'll earn your trust, Casey. I won't have you afraid of me."

She turned her head. "Maybe I'm just like some scared cat with all that's happening. It's so hard to be cheerful around Sarah when I see her dying in front of me, and it hurts to see the reverend struggle with his emotions. Then I worry about Bonnie and Ben, afraid they will get caught in the middle of my problems. And you're spending all your hours on this case to clear my name. Well, my jumpiness can't possibly be your fault."

He brushed a kiss across her fingertips, and she swallowed the lump in her throat, which lately seemed to accompany every waking moment.

"One day," he began, "you and I will be able to put all of the misunderstandings and problems of today behind us. Until then, we must talk. I can't possibly know how you feel or what you're thinking unless you tell me. Agreed?"

She nodded, and he patted the hand still within his grasp.

"It's easier posing as Shawne Flanagan." She attempted a smile.

"We're about to remedy any more pretense. I believe you're going to be pleased with what I've put together."

At ten thirty, Morgan ushered Casey into his law office. By then, they'd taken time to pray, and she'd relaxed a little—or so he hoped. He saw the fear in her eyes, and it had nothing to do with clearing her name. Perhaps a year ago, she might have hid it better. Back then, the wall she'd built around her didn't leave a weak spot for emotions to take over. But she was incredibly strong, much more than she realized.

I'm to blame. He'd seized her trust, then threw it back in her face without explanation. He'd waited too long to tell her the truth about Kathleen, and he may have lost her for good. Perhaps battling for Casey's love was Morgan's most difficult struggle, but first he had to set her free from those who chased her.

She removed her shawl and laid it over a chair. With a sigh, she studied his few furnishings, then walked behind his desk to the bookcase filled with law books. Her fingers traced the engraved gold lettering along the spines as she moved from one to the other. "It's dusty again," she finally said.

"Sorry. I raised the window." He studied her, wondering what was going on in her pretty head.

"These books teach you the laws of our country?"

He smiled. "Yes."

She whirled around and returned his smile. "Morgan, you must be very smart."

"I'm glad you think so."

She wore a dark blue skirt and a white blouse. Her swept-up red-brown hair and the curls framing her face gave her the appearance of a fine lady—no hint of an outlaw.

"I believe God is our hope and strength, but having this much knowledge at your fingertips has to make you feel confident."

He chuckled. "Not always. I sure felt better when that friend of Ben's left town yesterday."

"Have you and Ben talked about a pardon from Governor Ireland?"

"I had a feeling you'd bring that up." Morgan lifted a chair from behind his desk and moved it beside hers. "I've compiled information I want to go over with you." He opened a leather satchel and removed letters and documents pertaining to her case. "I've recorded your story in detail. You'll find dates, places, and types of crimes that the Jenkins gang committed while you rode with them. Remember the night at the parsonage when I questioned you about the role you played during his robberies? Note"—he pointed to items of interest—"you stated specifically your whereabouts during each one of them. He had you posted as a lookout with the horses or back at the campsite. Also, I have a signed statement from Doc about risking your life to help me. He added a lengthy portion attesting to your good character. In the past six months, newspapers and wanted posters report you've been involved with gang activities while you were living at the parsonage." He handed her the various documents and studied her reaction to each one.

"Everything has been signed or witnessed and dates verified," she said once she completed reading each one. "So this is what you've been doing these past weeks." She read both of Doc's letters as a result of Morgan's request and hers. "I know the problem is where there's no proof of my innocence." She straightened up the stack and handed the papers to Morgan. "If you don't contact the federal marshals for me, then I'll have Ben do it." She clasped her hand over his, sending tiny shivers up his spine. "Don't try to talk me out of this. I've thought of little else for months."

This would seal her coffin. I can't let her do it. "What you're telling me is dangerous. I'm not so sure it's necessary."

"I have to do this. Will you arrange it, please?"

Morgan studied her placid face, the one he first saw in the mountains of Utah. "I'm sure I can secure your pardon without endangering your life."

"Have you forgotten all of the things Jenkins has done? What good does it do me to ask for a pardon and not give something back in return? And do I need to remind you that he has not given up his search for me?" She tilted her head. "Did you speak with Ben's friend from Austin?"

"I met him. He's determined. Of course, I made sure I came across as a small-town lawyer. He wasn't interested in me." Morgan tapped his pen on the desk as though the distraction might alter her stand. He grappled for words—not a normal problem for him, but the woman he loved wanted to step into a viper pit. "You might have to change your name again and move to some obscure town far from Texas."

"I wouldn't ask you to give up your home and family, Morgan, but to me, any other way is selfish." She turned to him and tilted her head, her face a vision of peace. Yet he knew her deepest need. She had to free herself from running and hiding. Or she would die trying. "You know I can't do anything less, not only for me, but for all the Kathleens and Morgans of the world."

"I want to stop you, but I don't know how. What can I say or do to change your mind?"

"Nothing. The price of freedom is not too dear to me." Her words swept over him like a soft breeze. "Simply help me do what must be done. You have no idea what it's like to constantly look to see who might be behind you. There's no safe place. All I can do is stand and fight."

His heart swelled with emotion, causing him to say nothing for several moments. She was right. He hated to admit it, but the state would look favorably on her offer.

"I've been called a lot of things," she said. "You've heard them, everything from Jenkins's woman to a she-devil. I want it all to end."

He studied her, the woman he loved. From her stubborn stance, he knew she'd have Ben help her if he refused. This way he could still protect her. *Casey, my love, must it be this way?* He leaned back in his chair and folded his hands behind his head. "I'll need to follow up on a man in San Quentin who rode with Jenkins for a while— Leroy Wilson. I want to see if he'd consider backing up any of your statements."

"Leroy Wilson? How did you know about him?"

"Honey, I put him there. He despises me for sure, but he may not feel the same way about you."

"I don't understand."

"After Leroy was shot, I found out about it. Hate drove me to track down every man who ever rode with Jenkins. I went to the railroad folks and said if they'd let me represent them, I'd not charge for my services. I worked hard to get him into prison, and I doubt if he's forgotten it."

"So much I never knew. I'm so sorry."

"It's in the past, remember?" Morgan asked. "Do you recall anything about him that might help us?"

Casey nodded. "He's not a smart man, but I'm not so sure anything he'd say about me would be good."

He leaned toward her and directed his words straight to her heart. "Then we'll find out together. The risk is someone may find out what we're doing. You didn't ride all of those years with Jenkins and not comprehend exactly what I'm saying. Those men might understand if you received a pardon. They know you aren't guilty. But every outlaw around will be after you once they got word you sold them out to the law." He hesitated. "They'd cut you down in front of a town full of witnesses."

She smiled. "I'm too tough for you to scare."

CHAPTER 26

Stepping into the fresh, crisp air, Casey felt better about the path Morgan had chosen to clear her name. They'd prayed together again, asking God to lead the way and asking for help to accept whatever He chose for them. On the way back to the parsonage, she found it easier to talk about what she could do for the federal marshals. Her burden seemed lighter, as though her dreams were not impossible.

"How long will it take to arrange the meeting with them?" she asked.

"I need to speak with Leroy Wilson first. Then I'll make a trip to see Governor Ireland. Considering how that goes, I can request a meeting with the federal marshals." He paused. "I don't like this at all."

"It has to be this way." She linked her arm into his, and they both waved at a wagon passing by. "The more I think about Leroy, the more I remember conversations and what he did for the gang. The last time I saw him, he was in his fifties. He smelled worse than the others. Looked like dirt had gotten under his skin and stayed there. His hair and beard were always greasy and scraggly looking, and he drank too much."

"Why did Jenkins put up with him?" Morgan asked. "I thought he booted out drunks."

"Leroy proved to be the exception. He played up to Jenkins—praised him about how smart he was. That he'd never be caught and one day he'd be the richest man in Mexico. Bragged to the others that there wasn't an outlaw around who could measure up to Jenkins."

A lady and her small daughter walked by. Casey and Morgan greeted them and continued on.

"Anyway," she said once the two were out of earshot, "too much liquor slowed Leroy's reaction time during a train robbery, and a passenger shot him."

"He was lucky to get a jail term and not a hanging. I'm afraid he won't cooperate with me, but maybe he'll talk to you."

She didn't have much hope that the old outlaw would help her receive a pardon. Not that she recalled anything unpleasant in her dealings with the craggy old man. But why should he? "I wish I had a guarantee that all you're doing will be worth it to you in the end. You've worked so hard."

"Who's in control here?" he asked. "Have faith, Casey. Don't fret so."

"Hush. Don't call me Casey in public."

"You're right. I've told all the others to call you Shawne. Then I slip up."

They walked on in silence, while her world spun with the possibilities of total freedom. A crow called, and another flew from a treetop. She'd never cared for those birds. Their feathers reminded her too much of Jenkins's black hair. Many times she wondered if being caught by the law or Jenkins would end the turmoil raging inside her. A moment ago, her hopes heightened. Now she questioned it all again.

"Oh Morgan, when the gunfire is over and the smoke clears, where will you and I be?"

"Together."

His firm words nearly shook her. She had to trust. That caused her to shudder, too. The ways of men. . .

"Will you go with me to California?" Morgan asked.

"San Quentin? What's going to stop the guards from arresting me? Or one of the prisoners from recognizing me. I'd—" She stopped her sentence in midair. *I have to go. Old Leroy hates Morgan.*

"I'm sorry. That's selfish of me."

"No. Leroy won't talk to you without me. I'll make sure I look like a lady and wear a bonnet that shields some of my face."

"Honey, you always look like a lady." He sighed heavily. "This is too dangerous. I don't know what I was thinking."

She laughed. "You were being smart. Walking down the streets of Kahlerville is dangerous for me." The idea of walking into San Quentin was madness, but she didn't have a choice. Morgan needed Leroy's testimony, and she'd do whatever was needed to get it. "I'll have to find someone to tend to Sarah. She's so fragile, and I hate leaving her."

"We'll talk to the reverend."

"And we need a proper escort."

This time Morgan laughed. "We rode down a mountain in the dead of night without the proprieties of society. As well as I can remember, we had someone chasing us."

"This is different." She punctuated her words with a nod. "When the word finally gets out about you and me—and it will—it'll be bad enough that you're keeping company with an outlaw. We don't want the town gossiping about anything else, especially if a federal marshal starts asking questions." She gave him her best smile. "Do you suppose Jocelyn would take the trip?"

He studied her for several moments with a grim look she didn't quite understand. "I'll see what I can do."

A week and a half later, Casey and Morgan followed a prison guard down a damp, dark corridor to the visitation room, where they were instructed to wait for Leroy. She didn't feel like talking. Too much rested on the convict's cooperation. The mere thought that she might not walk out of there or that she might end up in a prison like this one brought about the familiar churning in her stomach. Her breakfast threatened to come back up, and her head began to pound. She smoothed her dress and adjusted her bonnet. Repeatedly she deliberated over Leroy's loyalty to Jenkins and his hatred for Morgan. What had the past few years behind bars done to him?

"We've traveled to San Quentin for a reason," Morgan said. "And we won't go home without what we need. A statement on your behalf from Leroy Wilson adds that much more to your defense."

The *clang* of keys beating against the metal door rang like a bad omen. The guard unlocked the area separating the prisoners from the visitors. *I hope I never hear the same sound against a door for me. Oh Lord, is it wrong to ask Your help? I understand I should have left Jenkins when Tim and I first joined up. I understand a whole lot of things now. Sometimes my life is so horrible that I wonder if I can ever be respectable.* She shook her head. She had God right beside her, and she had Morgan.

A sideways glance revealed his confidence. A tousle of amber-colored hair fell across his forehead, and he brushed it back. She took a moment to appreciate his calm and handsome face and the square chin that gave him a determined look. His eyes were what she treasured most—the color, the brilliance. She loved this man. If only she could rid her memory of what men had done to her in the past. She loved him in her heart, but her body felt frozen, unable to respond to his love.

A much-aged Leroy and a guard entered the small area. The old outlaw looked tired and more hardened than Casey remembered. Line upon line dug in around his face as though his deeds had branded him. From his sunken jawline, she gathered he must have lost the rest of his teeth. Four years hadn't affected his memory, because his small beady eyes immediately reflected a strong dislike for the lawyer who had led his prosecution and proved instrumental in his sentence at San Quentin.

"I ain't got anythin' to say to you, Andrews." He spit through the metal bars dividing him from Casey and Morgan. For a moment he leered at her—the cold look of lust.

She'd nearly forgotten his crude mannerisms. Strange how being among respectable folks caused her to forget outlaw ways. Rose and her girls weren't much better. They swore, drank, and ate like the hardest men.

"Sit down," the guard said. "They've come a long way to see the likes of you."

"You can't make me talk to him." The old man snorted like a pig. "What do you want to do now? Get me hanged?" He peered up at the guard. "Might as well take me back to my cell."

Leroy failed to glance her way. *He has no idea who I am. Do I interrupt? Expose myself to the guard? Or let Morgan handle this?*

"Calm down, Leroy. Just hear me out." Morgan's voice rang smooth and even. "All I'm asking is a few minutes to talk."

"I ain't talkin' to you 'bout nothin'. Leave me be, Andrews. Yer wastin' yer time." He pulled his bent body up to stand.

Morgan glanced at the guard, but the stoic, uniformed man didn't offer any assistance. Leroy faced the lawyer defiantly and again asked the guard to take him back to his cell. Jerking the outlaw around to face the door, the guard escorted him from the visitation area. The door creaked and slammed shut, echoing as though it sealed Casey's fate.

Morgan pounded his fist on the narrow ledge before him. He clenched his hand until his knuckles glared white. His face reddened. Fury threatened to explode through the pores of his skin. He took a deep breath, and for several minutes he paced the floor until the frenzy of the moment no longer creased his face.

Casey waited. He had to calm down before she could help him reason through what had happened. He'd been so sure about battling it out verbally with the old outlaw and leaving the prison with a signed document, but Leroy never gave him an opportunity. All this way for nothing.

Watching Morgan sink back into the chair, she deliberated what to say. Perhaps nothing until he was ready. The room smelled musty, nearly suffocating. Telltale odors of unwashed prisoners lingered in the room much like the cheap, sickly sweet perfume of the soiled doves who worked the pleasure palaces. Old sounds and smells and the taste of whiskey washed over her. She'd do anything to keep from being locked up in a place like this. She'd rather be dead.

She glanced at the ceiling and studied the spiders in the corners. Their lacy webs continued on and on in an endless pattern. Their weaving was purposeful. They didn't allow anything to stop them.

Once more she considered the brief meeting with Leroy Wilson. The prisoner needed an incentive to listen—or rather a bribe so enticing he'd be a fool to pass it up. *Some things naturally require more effort than others.*

Morgan had never been a man prone to give up easily. Today his efforts had failed, but what about tomorrow? She flatly refused to walk out of San Quentin beaten and depressed without a fight.

Leroy could be convinced to talk to them.

"Don't give up." She studied Morgan's face. "We need to ask God for wisdom."

"I'm not beaten. That old man thinks he won today, but he hasn't seen the fighting side of me." He rose from the hard wooden chair. "I'm taking you to the ferry, and then I'm heading straight for the warden's office. Tomorrow he'll talk to me or face the biggest regret of his life."

The next morning, Morgan and Casey again seated themselves in the visitation room and waited for a guard to bring Leroy into the area. After the experience of the day before, Morgan had requested a different guard who had the reputation of keeping the convicts in line. This time Leroy would sit there until Morgan finished.

The old prisoner took one look at Morgan and stopped in the doorway. "Told ya yesterday, I ain't talkin' to ya. I'll send ya an invite if I change my mind."

The guard, a stocky man who looked no better than most outlaws, shoved him down into a chair. "Wilson, you'll stay here and listen to this man, or I'll make it real tough on you. Do you understand?"

Morgan thanked the guard and settled back in his chair. "I may need you to make sure he listens to what I have to say," he said to the guard.

"Or what?" Leroy asked.

"You might break this partition between us and try to slit my throat or harm this lady." Morgan smiled.

"I could, providin' I had me a knife." Leroy wiped his whiskered chin. He glanced at Casey and squinted.

I do look familiar to him.

"Maybe so." Morgan was unbelievably calm, reminding her of how still the prairie lay just before a twister. "But we're going to talk first. I've got a proposition for you."

"Like what?" Once again the old man's attention swerved in Casey's direction.

"You help me, and I'll help you."

"How can you help me?" Irritation wrinkled Leroy's brow.

"By talking to the warden and recommending parole if you cooperate with me."

Casey saw the confidence in Morgan's face, but she knew he feared the same outcome as the previous day.

Leroy cocked his head. "You're lying. Somethin's in this for you."

"How will you know unless you hear me out first?" Morgan leaned back in his chair.

Leroy blew out an exasperated sigh. "State your business, Andrews. I ain't got all day." He sat sideways on the straight-backed chair, as though he might spring from the room like a trapped animal.

"Well, since you're such a busy man, I'll get right to the point. I need your help in getting a pardon for one of Jenkins's gang."

"Where were they when I needed 'em? Now yer wantin' me to help ya? Yer crazy."

Not a trace of emotion touched Morgan's features. "This person is innocent. Wasn't even around during the train robbery or some of the other jobs you pulled."

"Who is it?" The convict peered down his nose.

Morgan glanced up at the guard. "Could you let me have a few moments alone with Mr. Wilson?"

He nodded. "The warden said you might ask for that." He stepped through the metal door. "I'll give you five minutes. No more."

"Agreed." When the guard disappeared, Morgan leaned in closer to Leroy. "I want to prove Casey O'Hare is innocent of robbery and murder. Don't you recognize her?"

Leroy squinted at Casey and chewed on his lower lip. "Is that really you, Miss Casey?" The soft manner in which he spoke her name eased the anger etched into his face.

"Yes, Leroy, this is me. I haven't seen you in a long time." Her heart thumped faster than a hummingbird's wings.

Leroy grinned and displayed a toothless mouth. He whipped his attention to Morgan. "And what did you say you're gonna do for me?"

Morgan cleared his throat. "Told you before, recommend parole. I've already talked to the warden, and he'll draw up the papers if you'll agree to help Casey."

"I want it in writin'." Leroy rubbed his chin with the back of his hand.

Morgan opened his leather satchel for pen and paper and waited until the guard reappeared. "If you can write all this down for Leroy to witness, I'll sign it, too." The uniformed man unlocked the door separating them and took the writing material. All the while, Morgan continued to talk to Leroy about the latest news from the outlaw trail.

"I'm tired of your jawin'. Now what did you want me to say about Casey O'Hare?" He gave Morgan his full attention. "What they pinnin' on her?" Thank goodness he understood the risk she had taken in coming there. Her stomach still felt strange.

"Murder, train robbery—a whole list of things. You've seen the wanted posters."

Leroy whipped his gaze around the drab room. "She ain't never done nothin', at least not while I rode with Jenkins."

"What did she do for the gang?" Morgan's implication startled her. A surge of anger trailed up her spine. What did he mean by that?

"I thought you wanted a pardon for her," Leroy said.

"I do, but I have to know what she did do for Jenkins."

Morgan, didn't you believe me? The old hurt caused her to ache all over. Surely he had a reason for this.

"Just like I said, nothin'. Most times she just rode with us, so's folks would see her with all that purdy hair and face. Jenkins liked that, 'cause he claimed she was his. But when it came to jobs, she refused to help. Why, she stayed back at the camp most times unless Jenkins was in a fit. Then he made her ride along to watch the horses or somethin' like that. Miss Casey was a good girl, yes sirree. She never shot nobody or stole nothin'. All she did was bandage us up and cook." Leroy stared at Morgan triumphantly. "So if you're figgerin' to get me to say somethin' bad about her, forget it. I'm no fool, Andrews. You're trying to get her in prison, too—or hung."

Morgan shook his head and tilted back his hat. "I can't trick you, can I? I have a hard time believing a woman riding with Davis Jenkins all those years wouldn't earn her keep, but of course she was Jenkins's woman."

She clutched her hands tightly in her lap. She desperately wanted to believe Morgan had a good reason for the questioning. Later she'd find out why. Now she needed Leroy's statement.

Contempt spread over Leroy's face. "Jenkins just thought he owned her, but I knew better. She hated him."

"Would you be willing to write a letter stating what you just told me?" Morgan asked.

Bless you, Morgan. I'm so sorry.

"I don't read or write good."

"The guard will write down what you say, word for word. Then he'll read it back to you. You can make a mark, and he'll witness it."

"Got it all figured out, don't you?"

"I meant what I said. I'll tell the warden you helped me. He's already assured me of recommending parole," Morgan said.

Leroy swung his attention toward her. "Ma'am, I don't know what you see in this lawyer, but if I were you, I'd stay away from the likes of him."

Thank you, Leroy.

A short while later, Casey and Morgan took in the fresh, fragrant air of a California winter day. For a while, she thought the stagnant smell of the prison had penetrated her whole body. And Leroy Wilson—she'd forgotten how he never bathed. But right now she could kiss him.

"I'm sorry about the questioning," Morgan said. "We simply needed additional character references. He hates me for a good reason, and he got a full measure of my bitterness." He paused. "I made sure he got a stiff sentence. At the time I felt hanging was too good for any of Jenkins's gang. I wanted them to suffer. . .for Kathleen." He patted her hand. "But yesterday's gone. We have today and all the tomorrows we're allowed."

The sun seemed to shine a bit brighter, or maybe it was God's blessings illuminating their souls. Morgan whistled a nondescript tune while they walked to the ferry that would take them across the bay to San Francisco. There, Jocelyn waited at a hotel. Casey leaned into his strong shoulder. "I admit I was ready to come after you myself. I shouldn't have gotten so upset without waiting for an explanation. You were wonderful."

He chuckled. "Wonderful, huh? I thought you might tear me apart right in front of Leroy and the guard."

She smiled. "I strongly considered it. Fought it really hard."

He planted a kiss on her forehead. "We'll wade through this mess, and it will be worth it."

"I can't wait to tell your mother."

"Yes, ma'am, anything for my lady."

The train ride back to Kahlerville proved uncomfortable. The black soot settled upon their clothes, and the food tasted terrible. But for Casey, it was a time of victory. With Leroy's testimony safely tucked in Morgan's satchel, she had hope.

"I think we're having an early Christmas," Morgan said one

morning midway through the journey home. "I think we celebrated early."

"I agree," Jocelyn said. "I'm anxious to get back home and start baking, but what you two received from Mr. Wilson is the finest gift."

"Thanks, Mama." Morgan turned to Casey and gathered up her gloved hand. "I wanted a Christmas wedding, like the reverend suggested, but I guess I'll have to wait."

Casey felt her pulse race, not in anticipation of the wedding, but in eagerness for all of the legal matters to be over. Perhaps someday she'd busy herself with thoughts about Christmas baking, gifts, and family celebrations. But not yet.

CHAPTER  27

The few days before Christmas brought a chill to the morning, and sometimes the crispness lasted all day. The difference in the weather left a feeling of anticipation in the air. Or perhaps it was the time of year. Casey realized so many things in her life were about to change. She wasn't convinced the changes would be for the best, but for now she'd celebrate all those blessings that God had given.

Sarah grew worse. Every day that ticked by drew her closer to the end. Casey prayed she would not pass away before Christmas. *Just a few more days, Lord. Let her have this one last Christmas with the reverend.*

Casey pasted on a smile and looked for things to brighten the ill woman's day. She made sugar cookies and let the smell waft through the house, although dear Sarah could not eat even one. The reverend spent more time in his wife's bedroom. Every day the lines in his face increased.

Morgan had decided to wait until after January 1 to visit Governor Ireland. She realized Morgan knew best, but each day that passed chiseled away at her hope.

Christmas arrived quietly at the parsonage. The reverend and

Casey had decided that Sarah needed rest and that an abundance of celebration and visitors would only weaken her.

"It's enough for me to have Sarah this last holiday," the reverend said at Sarah's bedside. "God blessed me with this extra time to share the celebration of Jesus' birth with my precious wife, and I refuse to leave her side today."

"I was hoping you'd say that," Sarah said. "I'm being selfish, but I can't think of anything better than you right here with me." She leaned back against the pillow, her hair pinned properly and her face a beacon of light.

"I want to prepare a good dinner for you," Casey said. "I'll bring it upstairs as soon as it's ready."

"No pumpkin pie for me," Sarah said with upturned lips. "Often wished I liked it, but never acquired a taste for it. John here loves it. 'Pumpkin pies and roasted pumpkin seeds make my day,' he always said." She smiled up into his face. Her skin looked and felt like paper. "Tell her, John," she said.

"We do have something for you," the reverend said.

Casey shook her head. "It's not necessary at all."

"I know, but Sarah and I decided upon this some time ago." He excused himself and brought her a fairly large package wrapped in brown paper and tied with red cotton ribbon.

"I've never had a gift this large for Christmas." She glanced into his face. "In fact, I haven't celebrated this time of year since I was a little girl." She swallowed a lump. "I'm getting more like a woman every day."

The reverend laughed, and Sarah smiled. Casey immediately set the package down on the rocker and touched Sarah's cheek. She bent and kissed the woman. "Merry Christmas, Sarah. I love you."

"And we love you." Sarah's eyes sparkled as though all of heaven radiated through them.

Feeling a bit giddy, Casey opened the package. She gasped. A dress, a beautiful green velvet dress fit for a queen. "This—this dress was featured in the newspaper." Her gaze flew to Sarah. "The day I told you about my past."

"Indeed it was," Sarah said.

"But it's so expensive." Casey smoothed her fingers over the fine fabric. "You shouldn't have done this."

"But we wanted to," the reverend said. "You are like one of our children, and this is a small token of our devotion."

Casey lifted it from the package and held it up to herself. "I don't know when I will ever be able to wear something so fine."

The reverend chuckled. "If you would ever say yes to Morgan, I imagine he might take you someplace fancy after the wedding."

She didn't breathe a word of the misgivings mounting in her mind about marrying Morgan. This was a day of celebration, and she would not spoil it. "I have something for each of you." She excused herself to retrieve the small gifts from her room. For Sarah she had a shawl that Jocelyn had helped her crochet, and for the reverend she had handkerchiefs embroidered with his initials, also with the help of Jocelyn.

In the middle of the afternoon, Morgan arrived bringing gifts from the Double H. The two sat in the parlor, side by side on the sofa. The clock in the hallway ticked away peacefully, as though blessing their time together.

"Is your tree beautiful?" she asked, feeling a twinge of regret for not being a part of the festivities.

"Nearly touches the ceiling," Morgan said. "Yesterday Grant and I took the wagon and found it. Took us a couple of hours because we couldn't agree." He laughed. "Anyway, Mama and Bonnie brought out the decorations, and Grant and I strung popcorn."

"How much popcorn did you eat?" Casey could almost smell it.

"More than we strung." He sobered and brushed a wayward curl from her face. "Sure wish you could have been there. We all missed you."

"Me, too, but I need to be here. Besides, I don't think it would be a good idea with Ben enjoying the day with Bonnie. There will be plenty of other Christmases for me to share with friends." She tried to envision the decorated ranch house. "I have gifts for you to take back to your family." She nodded toward a basket on a table near them. "I baked a few things, and there are some jellies and jams." She took a breath. "And I have a little item for you."

Morgan rubbed his palms together. "Is it a year's supply of kisses?"

She glanced at him before standing from the sofa. "Not exactly." She reached among the gifts and handed him his.

He opened it slowly, not at all like she expected. She watched his face, hoping to see a favorable response.

"A journal," he said and turned the book over in his hand. His features lost all manner of teasing. "This is perfect, Casey. I needed one of these to record these—these days of securing your freedom. Thank you."

She nearly wept. He was obviously moved by her choice, and it pleased her very much.

"Now, my turn," he said a few moments later." He reached inside his jacket and pulled out a small box.

Casey stared at it and then at him. *Please don't propose marriage now, Morgan. I can't give you the answer you desire, and I don't want to spoil Christmas.*

"Go ahead and open it," he said.

Casey lifted the lid of the box to see a delicately carved gold and ivory broach. It nearly took her breath away. "Morgan, it's beautiful."

He smiled. "I found this in San Francisco. Remember when you and Mama rested at the hotel?"

She nodded. He said he'd gone for a walk. "Thank you so much."

He sighed as though relieved that she was pleased. "I knew the reverend and Sarah had purchased you a dress, and I wanted you to have something special to go with it."

"Perfect," she said, brushing her fingertips across the broach.

"But you are my real gift." He drew her into his arms and kissed her lightly, his lips tasting of the peppermint candy from a bowl in the hallway. The sweetness reminded her of what life with Morgan might be like. If only she weren't so afraid.

CHAPTER 28

On January 2, Morgan left for Austin to see Governor Ireland. Casey should have been excited; instead, worry knitted her insides. She wanted it finished. Now. The three days Morgan was gone seemed like forever, but when he did return, the wait continued.

Marriage. Morgan brought up the subject so often that she hated to see their conversation veering toward his love for her. She used to look forward to his visits. When did her love for him turn into such agony? *When I remember how Jenkins hurt me over and over again. . .*

In the evenings when Sarah drifted off to sleep and Casey had the remaining hours to herself, Morgan arrived at the parsonage. She believed he stood outside in the street and waited for her to blow out the lamp in Sarah's bedroom. Night after night, his pattern continued. Many times she wished the reverend would stay seated with them in the parlor, but he always excused himself to his study after a brief conversation. This particular evening, she sensed a lighter mood about Morgan the moment she opened the door.

"I have a surprise for you." He closed the door behind him. He grinned, and the way he rubbed his palms together made her wonder what had happened.

"From the look on your face, you'd better tell me soon before you burst."

"Evenin', Morgan," the reverend said. "Did you have a good day?"

"A busy one, which is good," he said. "I saw you this afternoon coming from the barbershop. Thought about inviting you to my office, but a couple of ladies stopped you."

The reverend chuckled. "I needed rescuing. Did you want to discuss something?"

"Just to talk a spell," Morgan said.

"Here I thought you and Shawne had set a date. Sarah'd love to hear that."

I hadn't thought of Sarah wanting to see us marry. How could I ever disappoint her? But I just can't face getting married.

"You'll be one of the first to know." Morgan wrapped his arm around Casey's waist. "Soon, I'm sure."

Casey forced a smile. "Things need to calm down around here first."

The reverend sobered. "I understand. Hard to set up housekeeping with all this upheaval. Glad I started calling you Shawne right from the start. Seems like I look twice at every man who enters town. Want to make sure it's not a stranger."

Her smile this time was genuine. "Thank you. We should have word any day." She turned to Morgan. "Right?"

"Well, I did receive a letter this afternoon."

She gasped. "From Governor Ireland?"

"Possibly."

"I'm leaving you alone." The reverend laughed. "This sounds like something just the two of you need to share."

Morgan took her hand and led her into the parlor. She trembled from the excitement. He moved one of the cream-covered lace pillows and sat on the sofa. Her heart pounded and her pulse raced. He pulled out a folded piece of paper from inside his coat pocket.

"Is it good news?" A fluttering in her stomach reminded her of butterflies—hatching.

"What do you think?" he asked. "Do you honestly believe I would interrupt your evening if I didn't have good news?" He shrugged. "Of course, I interrupt most evenings."

Casey tried to ignore the anxiousness rippling through her body. "Morgan, I can't wait much longer. Please read it to me."

"I have two items to report."

She held her breath.

"Can I have a kiss first?"

She leaned over and lightly touched her lips to his. "Please." She immediately caught her cross words in midair.

"I'm sorry," he said. "This is important to both of us, and I'm teasing. First, I found my old marriage records from Billings that place me there the same day the land office was robbed. So the records seal my testimony. And this letter came." He opened the folded piece of paper. "Would you like to read it?" He handed her the paper.

She pushed it back to him. "No. You do it. I'm too nervous."

"To tell you the truth, I have it nearly memorized. Governor Ireland has taken into consideration all of the documents we presented. He deliberated over them for several days before making a decision. With your willingness to reveal confidential information about the outlaws, he has agreed to drop all charges against you in the state of Texas."

Casey laughed and cried at the same time. "I can't believe it finally happened. And this means I won't be wanted for any crimes in this state?"

Morgan nodded. "I didn't want to bring this up before, but the problem lies in the alleged crimes from other states. You could still be forced to stand trial for each charge. By law, a state has a legal right to demand extradition. In other words, a state has the right to demand that you be turned over to them."

"If they find me." That thought brought little comfort even in light of the pardon.

He picked up her hand. "Understand once the word is out about your pardon, lawmen from all over will be swarming like angry bees to find you."

"But I don't understand. I'm willing to work with them." Depression welled up inside her. Had Governor Ireland's pardon made matters worse?

"The governor knows this and recommends we take your file to President Arthur as soon as possible. A meeting has been arranged with you and a federal marshal. In fact, a marshal is due here in three weeks. The governor feels we will be successful in receiving a full pardon from the president with your willingness to help end the lawlessness."

She shivered. "I wanted the opportunity to help. I prayed for this. But I'm afraid for you, your family, and our friends. I know it's selfish, but I'm afraid for myself."

He lightly squeezed her hand and looked into her face. "Not if this is handled properly."

"Do you think meeting with the federal marshal is a better way than standing trial for each accusation?"

"Definitely. Standing trial and casting your fate upon a jury is like throwing dice. Who knows what kind of mood they'd be in or who may have bribed them? The whole thing could last months, even years. This way, the marshal can hear your sincerity. He will already have viewed the testimonial letters. Also, he won't have any idea you live in Kahlerville. I'd prefer you lead your conversation toward whereabouts in another part of Texas. I don't want you to lie. Just not offer every bit of information." He paused. "I want to protect you, so don't say anything that could be twisted around against you unless you're asked specific questions."

"I understand." She sensed warmth rise from her neck to her cheeks. This had to work.

"When this is over, you'll have a clean record with the law. You'll be a free woman."

The mere thought of freedom tempted her enough to do anything the president or the governor or the federal marshals asked of her. Morgan slipped his arm around her shoulders as though he read the many thoughts racing through her mind.

"Will Ben's effort to help me look like he kept an outlaw from being exposed?"

"Not at all. Ben's reputation for keeping the law in this part of the state cannot be disputed. He's highly respected."

"Then Jenkins will be the only one left," she said. "My last battle."

<hr>

The next day, Sarah showed signs of improving. She sat in bed propped up with pillows and talked clearly of days gone by. She arranged her funeral while her husband took careful notes and wrote letters to their children and grandchildren. Her funeral would be a homecoming, a celebration of life rather than an ending.

With her renewed strength, Sarah saw an immediate urgency to have things done. The plants needed their leaves cleansed with milk, and Casey hurried to complete the job. A new family within the congregation needed a visit, so the reverend saddled his horse and paid them a call. Countless other tasks were completed to Sarah's satisfaction, and still she had more for them to do. She made a list of those who needed food and clothing. Her bed was covered with books and papers while laughter poured from her very soul. She ate with an appetite not seen since the past spring. A time of rejoicing rang through the parsonage.

Sarah stared longingly outside and questioned the condition of her roses. In a few more months they'd need pruning. Did Casey know how to do that? Perhaps tomorrow she'd feel well enough to sit outside wrapped in a blanket.

After a restful night, Sarah woke cheerful and alert. She shooed the reverend out of the bedroom and on to his church responsibilities. "Your work is lagging because of tending to me. Go on and get caught up."

About midmorning, Casey detected a change in Sarah's physical and mental disposition. A certain sadness or longing prevailed in Sarah.

"Is something wrong? Are you in pain?" Casey touched Sarah's pale cheek, but she was cool.

"Not in pain; I just have a yearning to go home." She offered a weak smile.

Casey caught her breath. "You're not giving up, are you?"

"Yes, I believe so. I felt strange yesterday, and this morning the urgency is still with me. I'm content in Jesus' presence. I feel Him all around me saying it's time to go home, and I'm ready."

Casey knelt at Sarah's bedside and took the woman's withered white hand into her own. Now she understood the surge of renewal from the previous day. She'd seen it in the dying before. But she hated to let Sarah go. The dear woman stood for all that was good and genuine in this world. "Are you sure?"

"Precious girl, I'm so tired, and I do want to see Jesus. Angels were here around my bed last night. They're still here waiting for His word to carry me home." Sarah's gaze swept all around the room before resting again on Casey's face. "Oh, I feel such peace. I wish I could describe it."

"Should I go fetch the reverend?" Casey wanted to weep, but the joy in Sarah's pale face refreshed her.

"Not yet. I want to spare him all the heartache I possibly can. This will come as a blessing. And for John, I want my death to be swift. When it's all over, he can go on with his life and his ministry. The relief and strain of caring for me will be gone. I'm so glad I said good-bye to the children in October. Everything is finished." She rose slightly from the pillow. Some of her white hair slipped from her bun. "I worry about you, dear. Some things aren't resolved, are they?"

Casey tilted her head. She realized Sarah could see through any falsehood. "Do you mean the legal matters?"

"I mean with Morgan." She laughed lightly. "Don't you know by now that you can't keep anything from me?"

Casey refused to burden Sarah with her own turmoil. "Morgan loves me and wants to marry me."

"And what is wrong with that? Don't you love him?"

"Oh yes, Sarah. I've loved him since the beginning." Casey smiled and kissed her cheek. "You shouldn't be fretting over me. I'm fine."

"If you truly love him, why are you so unhappy?"

Silence filled the room.

"I don't know how to put my feelings into words," Casey finally said. "I feel so selfish discussing myself."

"But you must. . .talk to me. This is the old woman who loves you so very much."

Casey hesitated a moment more. "I don't trust him. I'm afraid his wildness and bad temperament will return. And marriage frightens me. This is hard to explain. It's uncomfortable for me to talk about things that a good woman like you would find unpleasant. . . . Jenkins hurt me in the way only a man can hurt a woman."

"I understand without you explaining more. Any woman would be afraid of what marriage requires after an experience like that. Has

Morgan given you reasons to doubt him?" Sarah asked.

"No. Since he told me what happened to his wife, he hasn't lost his temper or done anything to make me think otherwise. But I keep waiting for his temper to flare up, and I'm afraid of marriage. So I'm always. . .well, prepared for the worst. Sometimes I want to touch him or tell him how much I do love him, but I'm afraid. I hate those awful moments."

"You're protecting yourself," Sarah concluded and closed her eyes.

"Let's not talk of this. You need your strength."

With her eyes still closed, Sarah offered a weak laugh. "I will soon be dancing in heaven, but I can't leave until I feel you're going to be all right."

"You are such a loving, beautiful lady," Casey said. "I don't know what to do but pray about the situation with Morgan. I can't marry him with unsure feelings, and I've put him off until the legal matters are settled. I could insist Jenkins be found. But what then?"

"You're right in not marrying him until you're certain. If the Lord wants you to marry, He will tell you if Morgan is the right man. Just listen for the quiet voice of God. Sometimes we are so busy praying that we forget to hush and simply let Him speak." Sarah moistened her lips and took a labored breath.

Casey fussed with the quilt around Sarah's neck. "Please just rest now. You can talk to me later."

Sarah shook her head. "There may not be a later. Sweet girl, remember this. It's our nature to fail. Morgan will disappoint you from time to time, as you will him. He cannot be perfect, but will he try? There lies your answer, and only you can know his heart." The last of her words came between gasps.

Casey leaned over and tearfully kissed her pale cheek. "I love you, Sarah, and I will miss you. You've been my mother and my friend. If I live a hundred years, I'll never be able to replace you."

The day progressed slowly, and the older woman's anguish heightened. She refused to suppress the incessant pain, and her strength wavered. When the supper hour approached, she asked for the reverend. Before the parlor clock struck seven, Sarah died, cradled in the arms of her husband.

Kahlerville had lost a fine woman of God.

The day of Sarah's funeral service dawned cool and sunny, just as Sarah would have wanted. The church and yard were filled with people who loved her and were not ready to let her go. Many folks had stories to tell of her goodness, and the accountings were told well into the night.

Casey wanted to save her grieving for the quiet solitude of her room. She needed to be strong and help comfort those who mourned Sarah's death. But in spite of her resolve, she felt a flood of her own tears. The death had been inevitable. Since the moment Casey agreed to nurse Sarah, the outcome had never been in doubt. Yet reality rarely found folks prepared.

She stepped into the kitchen and rearranged the mounds of food that appeared each time someone paid a call. Repeatedly she swallowed hard to keep from weeping.

"My sweet lady." Morgan eased up beside her. "You can cry. There's no reason to be brave."

"But someone might need something." Her voice quivered, and she took in a breath. "I've changed so much since I started my life over. I can remember moments of sadness from before, but never the grief I feel today."

"You have God's Spirit in you, honey." He turned her to face him, and the tears slipped from her eyes and down her cheeks. Morgan pulled her to his chest. And as she gave in to the comfort of his arms, she heard his heartbeat, firm and strong.

"You loved her and have every right to grieve," he whispered.

"She was like a mother to me. I miss her so."

"Go ahead and cry. I'm here. I'll always be here."

And she did until his shirt was soaked and not a single tear remained.

She'd learned the true meaning of humility and selfless love. She vowed never to forget Sarah's wisdom and her striving always to put others first. Casey prayed for the same characteristics to show in her life, especially in her relationship with Morgan. She truly loved him. There had to be a way of ridding her mind of the fear.

I must distance myself until I know what I'm supposed to do. I don't want to hurt Morgan. He's endured so much already.

CHAPTER 29

After the funeral, Morgan helped Casey pack up her belongings from the parsonage and move to the ranch. He understood she had to live somewhere, but he regretted not having her nearby. When he had come to live at the boardinghouse, the answers to the problems between them looked easier to solve. He could see her every day, court her properly—bring her flowers, tell her how beautiful she was and how much he loved her. Now they were separated again. He struggled with how to talk to her about the way she distanced herself from him. Most days, he suspected he'd chased her off for good. If he could figure out what to do, he'd do it. But this way, he felt helpless. And frustrated.

Two days later, Morgan volunteered to help his mother, sister, and Casey assist the reverend in going through Sarah's things. He sensed it was his last chance to rekindle what he and Casey once had. Casey didn't look pleased to see him. She rarely did anymore.

"You're an answer to prayer," the reverend said at the sight of the group. He led them to the kitchen, where Casey made coffee. "If left to me, I'm afraid none of this would get done. Every time I think about it, I feel like I'm destroying her memory."

"She lives inside you, Reverend. Nothing will ever destroy that," Jocelyn said.

"It's better this way. I remember what it feels like." Morgan shrugged, then offered a smile. "Reverend, I'll make sure these women get everything in order."

Bonnie poked him in the ribs. "Who's going to make you work?"

His mother and Bonnie pointed at Casey, but she took a step back. "I don't own a whip. Besides, I have plants to move."

"Morgan, I think you and I are at the mercy of these women." The reverend laughed, but it sounded forced. "Do you mind if I take these pies and cakes to needy families? I'm afraid they're going to spoil if something isn't done with them soon."

"By all means. I don't think you'll ever eat them all." Jocelyn waved her hand over the table. "It's a shame to let it go to waste."

"I thought I might wait until you ladies are finished sorting through Sarah's clothes, but you could be busy all day." He obviously needed something to occupy his time.

"We'll be done in about three hours if you want to deliver the extras now."

The reverend agreed, and Morgan quickly loaded much of the food into the back of the wagon. Once he had the reverend headed down the road, he made his way up the stairs to find Casey. She bent over a plant and scooted it out of the bedroom.

"I think you need some help there." Morgan slid into his teasing mode in the hope that she'd tear down that barbed-wire fence around her heart.

She stood and massaged her back. "Oh, kind gentleman, I accept your offer."

He lifted the plant through the doorway, and the two carried it into the upper hallway.

"Do you need another pair of hands?" Bonnie asked.

"I think we can manage." Morgan turned his attention back to Casey. "What is this called?"

"I don't know. It looks like a stalk of corn or a small tree to me. I meant to ask Sarah, but I kept forgetting."

"Well, it's fixin' to grow right up through the ceiling."

"That's why it's going outside. Hopefully a heavy frost won't damage it. Sarah said if it did, all I'd have to do is cut it back." Casey tilted her head. "I may trim it a bit today."

"Shawne, where are the other plants?" His mother stepped into the hallway with Sarah's few dresses draped across her arms.

"The African violets are sitting on a kitchen windowsill. I've written the reverend a note explaining how to take care of them. The soil has to stay moist, and he shouldn't let water touch the leaves. The ferns are in a shady area on the front porch along with the ivy."

"I guess you have it all taken care of," his mother said.

"Do you think the plants will sadden him? They're a constant reminder of Sarah." Bonnie stepped into the hallway. She, too, had her arms laden with clothes.

"Perhaps," his mother said. "We'll check in on him now and then. I'd think keeping them alive and healthy would be in fond memory of Sarah."

Morgan felt as out of place as an armless man in a milking contest. What a bad idea to help the women. He should have gone with the reverend or worked in his office. "Is this the biggest plant to move?"

When Casey affirmed his question, he glanced about. "I'll get this corn-looking plant outside, and then you can tell me what I need to do next."

Casey sighed and smiled. He wanted to put that pleasure on her face for the rest of her life. "I think that's a splendid idea. We should pull out Sarah's mattress and replace it with the one I used."

She walked with him to the front porch, where she pointed to the perfect spot for the plant. "Thank you. I thought my back would break in two."

"You could ease the pain in my heart by agreeing to marry me." He regretted the words the moment they left his lips.

"I can't." She fussed with a brown spot on one of the leaves. "I can't even talk about it until all of this is over."

Why can't I keep my mouth shut? Casey wrestled with the nightmares that he wanted to destroy. "I'm sorry. Leave it to me to spoil a good morning."

"Nonsense. You made it a wonderful morning."

But he didn't believe her. Casey was slipping through his fingers, and all he could do was watch.

Casey watched Morgan walk toward the shed in back of the parsonage. Her heart ached for what she could not give. She wanted to say what he craved to hear, but she couldn't. She tarried awhile, examining the rosebushes and pulling a weed here and there. Appreciative notes needed to be written to those who'd brought food. Housework awaited her attention. Sarah's room had to be aired. She didn't feel like accomplishing any of it, but it had to be done. Praise God, Jocelyn and Bonnie were there to help.

She blinked and allowed a tear to slip onto her cheek. She wished folks wouldn't question her about setting a wedding date. No one really understood her reluctance to get married. No one sympathized with her but Sarah. Granted, Morgan was a changed man, and he never seemed to tire in proving his devotion to her. His efforts made her feel guilty of the doubts plaguing her mind, but she simply could not agree to marry him until her misgivings were gone. Not a day passed without a reflection upon Sarah's last words of advice. God always answered prayer, and Casey simply needed to listen.

When all the plants had found new homes and Sarah's clothes were sorted, Jocelyn and Bonnie chose to clean Sarah's room while Casey cleaned the kitchen.

The sound of Morgan's voice diverted her attention. He waved and made his way toward her. She stepped onto the front porch, and her pulse raced at the sight of him. Some things never changed. She didn't understand her own emotions. How could she want something and be afraid of it at the same time?

"I'm ready for digging fence posts or whatever you need." The late-morning sun picked up the light in his eyes—filled with love for her. Yes, she did love him dearly.

"I know of a farmer who needs a new barn. Looks like a lovely day for a barn raising, doesn't it?" she asked.

"Yes, but I'm powerful hungry. I've worked hard this morning."

She picked up her skirts and made her way to his side.

Morgan leaned against the front gate. "Do I smell coffee? Is there any of that apple cobbler left?"

"Morgan Andrews, you haven't helped me carry out the old mattress yet. I think you're trying to get out of a little work."

Shock spread over his face. "I wouldn't think of it. Why, when it comes to your coffee, I'd ride halfway around the world."

"So what's your price to finish up the work here?"

"A cup of coffee, a big bowl of apple cobbler with fresh cream, and a hug." He reminded her of a schoolboy reciting his lessons.

"You certainly know how to try a woman's patience."

"That's my price." His grin looked permanent.

She tried to glare at him, but she laughed instead.

"You're beautiful when you're angry." He touched his hand to her cheek. "But you always look beautiful."

"Thank you."

"And I love you."

How long had it been since she'd told him she loved him? She took a deep breath. "I love you, too." *But I'm not ready to get married.*

"Thank you. Those are the words I needed to hear." His hand lingered on her cheek. "So what do I get first?"

Casey sighed. "Coffee, cobbler, and then a hug."

"Wonderful. Are you bringing it out here, or am I permitted to come inside?"

"Inside, Mr. Andrews. Let's not give anyone a thing to gossip about, and let me remind you that your mother and sister are in the house."

Once the back door closed behind them, Morgan reached into the bucket of water that she'd used to water plants and splashed her. She reached into a pan of water that she planned to use for cleaning and splashed him back. For the moment, she relished in their game and pushed aside Sarah's death and all of her misgivings.

"Would you two please settle down?" Jocelyn called from the upstairs. "The neighbors will wonder what y'all are doing."

"Yes, ma'am," Morgan said. "Your favorite Shawne won't let me work."

"Me?" Casey covered her mouth to keep from laughing. "Your son is pestering the life out of me."

"You two are worse than a couple of kids," his mother called.

"I agree," Bonnie said. "Mama needs to take you to the woodshed."

Morgan shook his finger at her. "See what you've caused."

If only these wonderful times would last. "All right, I'll give in this time."

After she served the cobbler and a light kiss was given to sweeten his coffee, Morgan grasped her hand. "I want to make you laugh like this every day for the rest of our lives."

And she knew he did, but a lump in her throat the size of the Double H refused to let her utter another word.

Casey slept little over the next week. The meeting with the federal marshal consumed her. Her appetite vanished, and she fought hard not to tear into her friends like some wildcat. She needed logic rather than worries to rule her mind.

The federal marshal could decide that her information was no better than what they already had in their possession. Another outlaw could have offered the same deal. A hundred things jumped in and out of her musings, and none of them were good. The what-ifs curved and turned with every fleeting thought. Her accountings of events and people might not be enough to sway the president of the United States. The man in charge of the country had many critical matters before him. Her request might appear insignificant or troublesome. Casey had never believed in fairy tales or grandiose ideals, and she didn't intend to start now. But she prayed for a miracle.

CHAPTER 30

Casey faced the day of the meeting with the federal marshal with a mixture of dread and expectation. For months this meeting had been what she wanted most. But a twinge of fear twisted at her insides. She could walk away with the hope of the president pardoning her or be handcuffed and face a hanging. Fear wrapped its cloak about her, and she fought the urge to run.

Morgan arranged the meeting at an abandoned ranch house about five miles west of Kahlerville—away from those folks who knew her. There, questions and answers would determine her fate.

Casey took great pains in dressing. She didn't want to appear like a member of the ladies' aid society. Neither did she want to look like she'd just ridden in off the plains—or stepped out of a brothel. After much thought, she chose a simple brown street dress with a waist-to-foot inset of cream and brown print, which she had often worn to church. She tucked her unruly hair into a chignon at the back of her head and selected a dark brown hat trimmed in cream and green ribbon. The costume also gave the impression that she'd traveled some distance to Kahlerville in order to meet with the federal marshal.

She read through notes she'd carefully penned about various

outlaws. Not knowing what might be asked of her, she fretted over the information. *I could ride to the border and live out my days in Mexico.*

A whisper of an ambush rode the wind, a trap set by the federal marshal to lure her into their jurisdiction. She wished she knew more about the law. She wished she knew more about a lot of things. Was she properly prepared for the upcoming ordeal? Had she dressed so Morgan would be pleased?

Run, you fool. You'll hang.

Just when she began to doubt, she realized the tiny voice shaking her resolve had not come from God. *I can do this or I will die trying. Living a lie is no life at all.*

Casey recalled all those times when life had challenged her to the fullest and she'd used a mastery of wit as her strength. A jury held in its hands the life of anyone charged with a crime. A judge had the authority to sentence her to a hanging or prison. But God had given her eternal life with Him. She trusted Him, not anything else. *My thoughts sound courageous, Lord, but You see the panic that staggers me.*

She took a ragged breath and descended the stairs to find Jocelyn, Bonnie, Grant, and Ben in the kitchen. Through the window, she saw Morgan waiting by the wagon.

"You look beautiful this morning," Jocelyn said.

"Thank you." She forced a shaky smile.

"We just prayed for you." Jocelyn gave her a hug. "This is the day you've waited for. We're on your side."

Casey glanced at those she'd learned to love. If a bullet found her today, she had no regrets in her decision to leave Jenkins's gang. "I appreciate you all. Promise me if something goes wrong today that you'll not let Morgan suffer alone. He'll need you."

Jocelyn nodded. "We promise. But that won't happen."

Casey thought of all the ways the meeting could go wrong, but she refused to state them. Instead she bid them good-bye and once more thanked them for all they'd done.

Outside, Morgan waved. "You look like you're headed to the city. Very beautiful."

"Then you approve?"

His attention on her held a gentle glow. "Oh yes."

Their gazes met, and a host of memories passed between them. Some folks lived a lifetime without sharing what they'd been through. Words could not have defined the bond.

He helped her onto the wagon, and he climbed up beside her. "Are we ready, pretty lady?"

"Not sure." She trembled. "How is it that I can want something and not want it at the same time?"

He picked up the reins. "Sounds like how I felt when I first met you. Odd, I didn't have a choice."

"Neither do I."

He urged Twister away from the ranch. Each creak sounded like a warning. Casey took Morgan's hand and held on to it tightly, as though having his fingers entwined with hers symbolized God's presence.

The last few days had brought in a very warm spell, so unlike the usual Texas February. The sun beat down mercilessly, reducing her to a puddle of liquid heat. She worried if the high temperatures might cloud her thinking. Her defense held no room for half-truths, and any wrong facial expression might threaten the attempt to prove her innocence. Neither the heat nor Morgan's attempt at conversation stopped her heart and mind from racing. As the wagon inched toward the secluded site, she fretted about everything all over again.

Morgan had spent hours deliberating every twist of her case, and she didn't dare shatter any of his expectations. Suddenly her thoughts turned to the sacrifice he had made on her behalf. He'd committed to clear her name and had worked long and hard for this moment. She recalled the late hours, the times of prayer, and the heated debates when they disagreed on what should and should not be said. Now it all lay behind them. Every part of her must convey the truth and honor God with assured confidence. Only He knew the outcome of today, and she desperately needed His peace.

She reached for the canteen of water and allowed the liquid to dampen her lips and slowly trickle down her parched throat. Immediately her mind soared back to the past when long rides brought the taste of dirt, and she kept her eyes peeled for anyone who might be trailing her.

Morgan squinted at the sun directly overhead and took out a gold pocket watch to check the time. Reaching for a handkerchief from inside his suit jacket, he wiped the sweat from his face and neck.

"Having second thoughts about your Sunday suit?" Casey felt a deep desire to speak of anything except the obvious.

He tugged at his jacket, no doubt to send a breeze up his dampened back. "Perhaps," Morgan said. "Can you believe this heat? Feels like August." He flashed a smile her way. "But you still look beautiful."

With a sigh, she wondered what kind of picture she painted on this hot afternoon. "Talk to me, Morgan. Anything to help me get through these miles."

"I wish nothing more than to take your place. Today marks the day Casey O'Hare publicly announces her allegiance to the laws of this country. Few men have the courage I see in you, and certainly none are as pretty or as feisty. Sweetheart, we can turn this wagon around right now and head back to the ranch. You understand that once you're finished with the federal marshal, every outlaw in the country will be after you."

She nodded while perspiration trickled over her forehead and stung her eyes. "You've warned me of this before, but I have to tell what I know. Running is no life at all. If the president grants me this pardon, I can rely on the law's protection from Jenkins." She rubbed the top of his knuckles with her gloved hand. "I'd be a liar if I didn't admit how much this scares me."

"Let me pray for you," he said, and she nodded. "Oh God, help us to say the right words today. I pray we find favor in Your eyes and our mission will be acceptable to You. I thank You for this courageous woman who is putting her life on the line to bring the truth to light. I am so unworthy of her, and I thank You every day for her. Whatever happens today, I know You will be beside us. I thank You for Your guidance and Your hand on our lives. Amen."

"Thank you," she whispered. With all of her other self-doubts, why did she still question marrying Morgan? *Not now. I'll have hours to consider this once today is over.*

She drew a lace handkerchief from her handbag and patted beneath her eyes. Where had this heat come from? Had Satan set foot into the day? Sensing Morgan's gaze upon her, she turned in his direction and silently reassured him of her composure. The remaining two miles were ridden in silence.

Up ahead at the abandoned ranch house, two horses stood tied to a hitching post, and two men waited on a decaying porch.

"Are there two marshals?" Casey whirled around to see if others were there. Had she been led into a trap? Had Morgan betrayed her?

He glanced about them. "I was told one, but this is good. Both men will hear your testimony."

She refused to tremble. The marshals might see her fear. "Yes, you're right." If one didn't believe her, the other one might.

The closer the wagon drew them to their destination, the more apprehensive she felt. The unknown tugged at her senses. She wanted the confrontation with the federal marshals to settle all of the accusations against her. But it could all go wrong. Raging fear threatened to seize her.

"I feel your trembling," Morgan said. "Remember who's in control."

Once they stopped in front of the deserted cabin, Morgan assisted Casey down from the wagon and escorted her to the darkly tanned federal marshals who stood like statues against the rickety cabin. She eyed them evenly and tried to imagine what preconceived notions lay in their heads.

Morgan greeted the nearest man and shook his hand. "Morgan Andrews."

Both marshals looked as though their faces had been carved in stone. Casey had seen the lean, hungry look before. She wondered if their ambitions were for justice or to seal their reputations.

"Zach Bennett, federal marshal," the rail-thin man said. "And this is Joe Henderson."

The other man nodded, and Morgan shook his hand. "This young woman is Miss Casey O'Hare."

Casey stepped forward and lightly grasped each man's hand. Pushing aside any visible signs of emotion, she forced pleasantries. "It's a pleasure to meet you. I trust you haven't been waiting long in this heat."

"No, ma'am. We were here but a few minutes before catching sight of the wagon." Zach's beady eyes reminded her of a hawk. Could he see her soul?

"Shall we get down to business?" Joe asked. "It's mighty hot, and we have a lot of work to do."

"First I'd like to see your credentials," Morgan said. Both men produced identification for him to examine. When he finished, he handed their papers to Casey.

Once convinced Zach Bennett and Joe Henderson were indeed federal marshals, she handed their documents back to Morgan, and he returned them to their owners. "Thank you, gentlemen," he said. "Your papers appear to be in order."

Morgan gave Casey his full attention. Compassion emitted from his turquoise eyes. "Are you ready?"

"Yes. Let's get this done." And for the first time, she relaxed.

Inside the cabin, it took several minutes to wipe the dust and dirt from a roughly constructed table and find suitable seating. They opened doors and ripped frayed cloth from the windows to let in light and fresh air. The stuffy odor plus the stale scent of tobacco reminded Casey of days best forgotten. Still, the atmosphere would aid her in recollecting sights, sounds, and smells of another time.

She sat on the only chair directly across the table from Zach and Joe, who swung their legs over a rough-sawn pine bench. Morgan pulled up a wobbly stool next to Casey. Out of habit, she gauged how quickly she could get to the door. Some things from her former life never changed.

"We understand you're willing to help us locate wanted men," Joe said. "Is this true?"

"Yes, sir." She observed paper and pen before Zach. His penetrating gaze nearly unnerved her. "Is Mr. Bennett writing down everything I say?"

"Yes, ma'am. The questions and answers will be recorded exactly as they are spoken," Joe said.

Casey studied the man's leatherlike face. No emotion. She well knew that stance. "May we see them when we're finished?"

"I'll take notes for us." Morgan already had paper and pen in hand. "But I want to see what you've recorded at the close of our meeting."

"We can do that." Joe cleared his throat. "We understand you've received a pardon from Governor Ireland of the State of Texas for criminal activity, and you want to request the same from President Arthur."

"That is correct." Casey sat erect with the perfect posture she'd seen from the town's ladies. *Be with me, Lord. I can't do this alone.*

"Upon the completion of this meeting today, the governor has entrusted me with your official pardon, signed and sealed. He will then instruct his secretary to file the proper papers with the president. Let us begin with a few formalities. Would you kindly state your name?"

"Casey Shawne O'Hare."

"And are you the same Casey O'Hare who rode with the Jenkins gang for seven years?"

"Yes, sir. I joined them when I was fourteen with my brother, Tim. At the time, Jenkins thought I was a boy. When he discovered otherwise, he forced me to continue riding with them."

She detested the time it took to record the questions and answers. Her patience ran thin each time the two men painstakingly wrote each word. She hadn't told Morgan about the two weeks that Jenkins didn't know she was a girl. Everything changed when he caught her bathing. . . . She shook her head to dispel the thought.

"How were you forced to ride with them? This is no longer a country of slaves."

"Davis Jenkins threatened to kill my brother if I left the gang. He also threatened to sell me as a. . .prostitute."

"What's your brother's full name?"

"Timothy John O'Hare. He still rides with Jenkins." She hesitated. "Although I heard he and Jenkins split." Her voice sounded faraway as if it belonged to someone else.

"Didn't you just state Davis Jenkins threatened to kill him if you left?" Joe's eyes narrowed.

"I've witnessed what Tim has done." She took a deep breath. "My brother chose his path a long time ago. If I thought he'd change, I wouldn't be here today." Why did her heart have to pound so hard? "It took me a long time to see that my brother had become just like the rest of them."

Joe removed his bandanna and wiped the sweat from his brow. "So why did you finally leave the gang?"

"I hated how they lived and what they did. My life seemed headed nowhere except a hangman's noose or a bullet. I chose to take my chances and run from Jenkins rather than stay. I realized I would someday have to face charges for the crimes held against me, but I had to take that gamble." Was she rambling?

"It says here that although you held horses for the gang during holdups, you did not commit any of the crimes we've listed, except the shooting of a man in Billings, Montana."

"The man recovered," Morgan said.

Joe nodded. "I've read the letters written on Miss O'Hare's behalf. Each one will require an investigation. Your statement given to us by your lawyer, Mr. Andrews here, indicates a strong desire to lead a decent, respectable life. Is this also true?" Joe had not moved since they began.

"Yes, sir. The statement also says I'm a Christian. Jesus Christ is now the Lord of my life."

The federal marshal coughed and shifted his feet. "Yes, ma'am. It does state your—your newfound religion. Now. . ." Zach handed Joe a map of the western United States and territories. He turned it for her to see. "We've been unable to penetrate a good many of the outlaws' hideouts. Are you willing to give us a hand?"

"Yes, sir. I made mention of this in my statement to Governor Ireland."

"Would you kindly indicate how we could get into the Hole in the Wall?"

Couldn't you have asked me something easier? Casey found no need to examine the map. "You can't. There's only one way inside—through the opening. Two men with Winchesters can easily hold off any posse. Most likely you'd have to bribe another outlaw to gain access."

"What about Brown's Park?" Joe pointed to the familiar area in the far northwestern corner of Colorado and the Utah Territory.

She didn't need to take a look at his map there, either. "It will take a long time before lawmen can cleverly outdo the outlaws in this area."

"Why?" Joe's question sounded angry, even hostile.

Casey carefully picked her words. "Outlaws are clever. They aren't afraid to take a gamble on the odds against them. This is serious business for them. Not only are they getting rich, but they're also working on their reputations." She hesitated and clenched her fists in her lap. "Most lawmen—forgive me, gentlemen, for being blunt—form a posse and take off after them without any forethought or plan. Now I can show you trails leading out of the various hideouts." She leaned over the table and pointed to Brown's Park. "But it won't assist you in finding outlaws. It will only help your men get out alive."

Joe continued the lengthy process of questions and answers. At last he folded the map and handed it back to Zach. "Your information will definitely help us. We also have several wanted men who've disappeared. Possibly headed north to Canada or south to Mexico and South America. Given the list, can you help us locate them?"

"I'll do my best," Casey said. "Please understand, the locations may be outdated. Usually outlaws return to the same hideouts to rest up and plan their next job. But with a hint of trouble, they move on. An outlaw changes his name as often as respectable folk say their prayers."

The meeting lasted until early evening. They broke once for water and continued on. Casey and Joe were tense with the tedious questions and answers, and the other two who had labored over the written portion were equally tired.

"I believe we're finished, Miss O'Hare," Joe finally concluded. "I want to thank you for your cooperation. It will be rewarded. I promise."

"I appreciate the government giving me this opportunity to tell the truth and possibly clear my name." She watched for movements in his face. None. No help at all. "How long before I can expect to hear from the president?"

"Six weeks, I'm sure. Since the governor's office researched your other documents, the process should not be any longer than that." He pulled a folded piece of paper from his saddlebag on the table. "Here's the governor's pardon just as I told you at the start of the day. I know you heard his decision before our meeting. This is the official document."

Casey took the paper and read it slowly. She savored every word. Her eyes dampened upon completion, and she held it firmly in her grasp. "Thank you, sir. God bless you for delivering this to me."

The two federal marshals stood. "Good luck, Miss O'Hare," Joe said. "I wish you the best. Is there anything else you'd like to say on your behalf?"

Casey didn't need to deliberate the matter. "Only that I would be forever grateful if you could stop Davis Jenkins." Even the name of the dreaded outlaw upon her lips caused her to tremble.

"Yes, ma'am. With your information, I hope we're able to find him and a lot more like him," Zach said. "And I want to thank you for your patience while I recorded your statements. After listening to your answers, I plan to write my own recommendation to the president."

Afterward, the wagon creaked and groaned away from the deserted house and back toward the ranch. Twilight shadows darkened to evening against a three-quarter moon and the first hint of stars.

"It went well," Morgan said. "Casey, you displayed considerable control the whole time."

"It wasn't me." The emotional strain of the day left her exhausted. "God must have stood right behind my chair with His hand on my shoulder and directed it all. And I couldn't have done nearly so well if you hadn't been there to support me."

Morgan lifted his hat and wiped his wet forehead. "I'm so proud of you, and I'll make sure Ben knows about the official pardon. Most likely he'll sleep easier knowing he's not bending any laws."

They laughed. It felt good. Casey's gaze swept over the silhouette of the man she loved. "This was a hard day, wasn't it?"

"I felt as though each drop of sweat was a prayer in itself. Between the heat and the tension, I lost track of time. Recording every word was like being in law school again. But it's over, and we did our best."

"I don't know whether to laugh or cry." Casey sniffed and reached for her handkerchief. "In one breath I want to shout, and in the next I'm so relieved it's over that I want to cry a bucket of tears." She stretched stiff, aching back muscles. Suddenly a realization hit her. "Morgan, they're making the recommendation for a full pardon."

He laughed again. "I knew they would."

"Now we wait." She attempted to sort out the inquiries and her replies from the afternoon. Both men had asked numerous questions, and she didn't always have an answer. She offered information and drew maps, especially in the area of the lower Colorado Plateau and on south through the canyon lands.

Six weeks. Seems like forever. Surely I gave them enough information. Both of them said they were grateful for my statement. Still, I'm impatient. I want it over, but all I can do is allow God to work out His plan. She felt Morgan's attention on her and met it with a weary smile. His devotion never ceased to amaze her. If only she could reveal her own devotion to him.

CHAPTER 31

Three weeks passed, and Morgan sensed Casey moving farther and farther away from him. He tried to ignore her black moods and the way she avoided being alone with him, but how much was he supposed to take before he confronted her? He had no intention of ever turning back into the old Morgan who resorted to behavior that looked like a three-year-old's temper tantrum. Telling her he loved her never seemed to be enough. Many times he thought she didn't believe him, or maybe her feelings had changed.

Morgan's selfish attitude made him angry. He needed to be thinking more about her and less about his wounded pride. Confusion etched his every waking moment and haunted his dreams.

The problem lay in waiting to hear from Washington. He knew how much Casey looked for the official pardon. The worry and wondering had to be driving her nearly crazy.

Davis Jenkins. . .he hadn't given up. The man held a grudge against anyone who crossed him. If Morgan let his mind dwell on the way the outlaw had pursued Casey from the time she was barely a girl, the old fury threatened to take over. If he chose to dwell on her brother, Tim, who had done nothing to help Casey, he grew angry again. Morgan could only imagine what he'd do if faced with Jenkins or Tim.

Don't dwell on it. You can't change the past.

Tonight he planned to ride out to the ranch and ask her straight out if she'd changed her mind about him. He shrugged. Maybe she'd met someone else. After all, Grant was right there at the ranch ready to step into his big brother's shoes. The age difference wasn't that much. *I am really pathetic to be jealous of my own brother. If she was happier with Grant, I'd have to walk away.*

With a deep breath, Morgan decided to sidestep his own feelings and ask her what he could do to help. He'd join his family for dinner and hope for the right words—and the right answers.

❧

Casey wondered why Morgan showed up unexpectedly for dinner, but she didn't ask. Lately she'd treated him shamefully, and she didn't really mean to. He simply irritated her with his constant urging to spend time with him. She wanted to be left alone until this whole ordeal was over. The idea of being touched or kissed repulsed her. Then she'd remember all Morgan had done and how much she really did love him.

"What can I do to help you through this?" Morgan asked while they sat alone on the front porch step.

"Nothing. This is my war." She listened to the singing insects and fought the unexplained anger rooted deep inside.

"It's *our* war." Morgan's voice rang tenderly against the approaching evening shadows. "Casey, don't shut me out."

"I'm not. I'm simply tired of waiting on something that probably won't happen."

"I love you—"

"Morgan, please, must our conversations always lead to this?"

She turned her attention to the lights of the bunkhouse. Not that she cared at all about what went on out there.

"I sense the cool night air is getting to you," he said much too cheerfully.

"Not the air. Just you."

He rubbed his palms over his jeans and stood from the porch step. Without a glance in her direction, he walked toward the corral, where the faint light of dusk cast a golden shadow on a single horse.

"I'm sorry." How could she be so cruel? When he failed to reply, she ran after him. "I didn't mean to snap at you."

His eyes stayed fixed on the horse grazing nearby. "What did you mean?"

"Oh, I don't know. The waiting to hear from President Arthur. Not having any money to give Jocelyn for living here. Tim...Jenkins." She dared not say more.

"I want to hear the rest of it." In the fading light, Morgan turned to face her. He didn't appear angry, but she recalled the same tone from the time he questioned her in the mountains of Utah.

She took a deep breath. "I'm not sure I want to get married."

"Why? Have you decided you don't love me?" His words were laced with hurt.

"You're not being fair."

"I'm not? You tell me you love me, but you don't want to marry me? I want the truth."

"I do love you, Morgan. I'm scared."

"Of what? I thought we were going to see this pardon through together."

I'm not afraid of not getting the pardon as much as I am of living the rest of my life with a man who might turn on me.

Silence echoed around them. The horse walked to the edge of the corral where they stood, and Morgan reached to stroke the animal's head. Several long moments passed.

"You know, Casey," he said without looking her way, "the ranch hands said this mare couldn't be broken. They claimed she was too wild, even *loco*. Jesse told me the horse ought to be shot. He gave up on her. Then one day, Grant decided he'd break her. He worked long and hard, gentle-like, until the horse felt confident of his voice and touch. She's now tame enough for children, but the ranch hands still won't ride her. They're afraid. Can't see past the mare's old ways."

A chill snaked up her spine. Tears stung her eyes, and she touched Morgan's shoulder. "Can I have a little more time until we hear from the president?"

He blew out a sigh. "All right. I'll not mention another word of marriage till the pardon arrives. And I'll not be coming out to the ranch, either. You can have all the time you need to think about us. I love you, Casey. Nothing will ever change that, but I'm a man, and my pride won't let me beg."

He turned and walked into the house. She felt numb and miserable. An emptiness settled in the pit of her stomach. A short while later he rode off toward town.

What have I done? I love him so much, and now I've hurt him. Maybe lost him.

No one pressed Casey and Morgan about the problems between them, but she saw the dejection and worry in the whole family. Her restlessness coupled with unhappiness caused her to stay to herself. Day after day she searched the Scriptures for God's answer to her quandary. She hated herself. She was fickle. Whatever happened to the godly woman she craved to be? Sarah would be so disappointed.

Morgan attempted to focus his attention on drawing up a land sale for a nearby rancher, but he couldn't concentrate. Frustrated, all he could think about was Casey. Her words and actions made no sense to him. He wanted to understand; he really did.

Shaking his head, he tried reading the document before him again. The door opened, and his mother stepped into the office. He stood and embraced her.

"Afternoon, Mama. What brings you into town?"

"I stopped in to see the reverend and you."

"Thanks. How's everything at the ranch?"

She nodded. "Busy. Do you have a few minutes for me?"

"Sure. Sit down. Is something wrong?"

"As a matter of fact, yes."

He raised a brow and waited for her to continue.

"I want to talk to you about Casey."

"We're not seeing each other right now."

"I don't need a lawyer to tell me that." Her eyes narrowed.

"Mama." Morgan startled at her sharp tone.

She moistened her lips and removed her bonnet. "I think I should explain something to you."

"I wish somebody would. This is making me crazy."

"I know, Son." She hesitated as though searching for the right words. "What do you think her experience with men has been like?"

He shrugged. "Not good. Her brother mistreated her, and Jenkins is an animal."

"Do you really understand what that means to her?"

He scratched his stubbly chin. "I suppose."

"Her pa was a drunk, and he beat her. You know the situation with her brother and Jenkins." Mama leaned in closer. "She's never known anything but fear when it comes to men. Jenkins forced himself on her when she was nothing more than a girl. He hurt her, Son, over and over again. What do you think that did to her?"

Realization flooded his entire body, and he swallowed hard. "She's afraid I'll be the same way. I—I hadn't thought about it that way before. She's afraid of me."

"I believe she loves you, but fear is pretty powerful."

"What can I do? I make her angry every time I come near her."

"I'm not sure, but I think prayer is a good beginning. And don't give up."

He didn't answer. Jenkins still had a hold on her. As much as forgiveness had been crucial in his relationship to God, most days he'd like to see the man dead. "I can't give up, Mama. I love her too much."

❧❧❧

One Sunday afternoon just after the midday meal, Casey borrowed the Andrewses' wagon and drove toward town. She was so tired of the confusion about her feelings for Morgan, and she desperately needed direction. Prayers went unanswered. When nothing but silence came, Casey decided to turn the wagon around and head back to the ranch. Perhaps she needed to talk openly and honestly to Jocelyn and Bonnie about her doubts in marrying Morgan. She didn't want to disappoint her friends any longer. Besides, she was consumed with guilt for the ugliness raging in her soul.

The longer Morgan's kindness and devotion ruled his emotions, the more suspicious she became. She felt his caring covered for something else, and that something would be hidden until she spoke her wedding vows.

She tried to listen for God's voice, but the only thing she heard was the clamor of her own doubts. Surely all of this wasn't due to her impatience with the pardon or her fear of Jenkins. Or was it?

The reverend had spoken this morning on man's insistence in

judging others. *"Judge not, lest ye be judged,"* repeated in her mind like a newspaper headline. She pondered the sermon and wondered if God meant those words especially for her. Then she saw Morgan's face and heard his voice. Oh, how she loved this man, but things weren't right between them. Might never be. She felt awkward seeing him at church, as if he were a stranger. Grant stood beside him and nodded when they walked by, while Jocelyn and Bonnie looked on with sadness written in their eyes. None of them were unkind. . . simply distant like a patch of wildflowers on a mountain pass just beyond reach.

Glancing about, Casey stared up at the sky. It had turned a dismal shade of gray. She studied the sky for possible rain clouds. Suddenly the wagon hit a hole in the road and sent her bouncing on the rough wooden seat.

"Stupid horse!" she shouted to no one but the animal pulling the wagon. Closing her eyes, she heard the reverend's words with sudden clarity. The wagon wheel rolling over the rut wasn't the horse's fault. *It's my fault for not paying attention to the road. I'm judging a horse for my shortcomings. . . . I'm judging Morgan for my shortcomings. . . . I'm judging Morgan because I'm afraid he's like Jenkins.*

The turmoil about Morgan suddenly made sense. His actions weren't separating them. Her refusal to trust had caused the problem. All this time, Morgan had been trying to please her and show his love. And all of this time, she'd been running from what she wanted most. God had put Morgan in her life for a reason. They belonged to each other. She knew that now. Sarah's words echoed across her mind. Morgan would always try; that's what mattered. She had to tell him now. She must tell him how wrong she'd been.

Casey reined in the horse. *Forgive me, Lord, for not listening and for being so stubborn.* The immediate necessity to see Morgan overwhelmed her. She'd barely come two miles. Was this foolishness? Certainly not.

She needed to talk to him right away and ask him to forgive her. He deserved to know she would marry him. That is, if he hadn't changed his mind.

She turned the wagon around and headed to Kahlerville with a sense of urgency that chilled her to the bone. Once in town, the proprietor of the boardinghouse checked for Morgan, but he'd left earlier.

"Miss Flanagan, I believe I heard him say he was heading over to talk to Reverend Rainer."

Should she visit the parsonage and interrupt them? Casey fought the urge to race down the street to the whitewashed parsonage beside the church. What if the two men had business matters to discuss? One more time, she'd look selfish.

"Did he say how long he'd be gone?"

"Most of the afternoon, I think. Is there anything I can do for you?"

"No, thank you." Perhaps she'd wait until he returned. Still, she had the Andrewses' wagon, and they'd need it to return to church tonight. "May I write him a note?"

The man pulled a pad of paper from under the counter and pointed toward the pen and ink beside the register. "You go right ahead, and I'll shove it under his door."

She smiled and hoped she disguised her disappointment. The proprietor walked away, giving her much-appreciated privacy. She composed her thoughts and wrote:

Dear Morgan,
 Today God spoke to me about my terrible actions toward you.
I'm so sorry for the way I have treated you. I do love you, and
I will marry you tonight if that is what you want. I know the
future is uncertain, but I can't imagine one more day without you.

She blinked back a tear and regained her self-control.

> *I hope to see you at church tonight. Morgan, you've done so much for me, and I do feel badly about the heartache I've caused. I love you.*
>
> *Casey*

Saddened by Morgan's absence yet filled with the joy of her new understanding, Casey realized she must get back to the ranch and apologize to Jocelyn and Bonnie. They had put up with her brooding long enough. She'd confess her self-centered heart to everyone and ask them to forgive her.

She climbed back into the wagon and for the first time did not feel the immense burden that had been a part of her for weeks. The ride back to the ranch sped by quickly. She remembered all the precious times with Morgan—the many times he'd proven his love. How she longed to make up these weeks to him.

"I love you, Morgan Andrews," she said, and the horse picked up its pace. Casey laughed. Nothing could dampen her spirits.

Jocelyn and Bonnie were seated on the front porch, reading, when she returned. Grant had seen her coming and stepped down from the step to take the horse and wagon from her.

"You were gone such a long time. I worry about you, dear. So many bad things can happen." Jocelyn took a breath. "Bonnie and I were just talking about spending tomorrow planning our garden. We'd love for you to help us."

"That sounds like fun. In fact, we can start tonight after church if you'd like. We can even bake bread while we're talking about the spring planting." She laughed at their questioning stares and proceeded to tell them about the early afternoon.

"So Morgan still doesn't know?" Bonnie pressed her palms

together as though she planned a prayer—which wasn't a bad idea.

Casey shook her head. "I didn't want to bother him at the parsonage, and I've been so self-centered. I've hurt him, and I want to make up for it all."

"He will be so happy." Jocelyn brushed back a strand of her amber-colored hair. "We've been praying for you."

"Do you think I'm too late? Maybe he has grown tired of waiting for me. Not that I blame him."

"No, my dear. I know my Morgan, and he loves you. He would have waited for as long as it took," Jocelyn said.

Casey climbed the steps and embraced the older woman. "I never intended to cause this much trouble."

"When it comes to the heart, decisions are always difficult," Jocelyn said. "The thought of sharing a lifetime with someone shouldn't be taken lightly, and both of you have been through so much."

"I realized a lot of things today. We've had some hard times, but together we can build a future."

"Now isn't this a bit of luck," uttered a man from behind the left side of the porch.

Casey swung her attention in the direction of the voice. Terror swept over her, reminiscent of the cruelest of nightmares. "Jenkins," she whispered.

"That's right, Casey girl." He pulled a revolver from his hip, and she heard the sharp *click* of the hammer. "Inside, all three of you. No one makes a sound, or you're all dead."

CHAPTER  32

Casey's and Jocelyn's glances met in clear recognition of the danger. Any pleading or display of emotion from the women invited a taste of Jenkins's fury. Bonnie, her face pale, stood as if her small body were frozen to the porch. *Do not open your mouth, Bonnie, or it's all over for us.*

Jocelyn gently took Bonnie's arm and escorted her inside.

Jenkins smelled of whisky, and his right eye twitched. Killer mad. Someone always ended up dead when he was like this. *God, please help us.*

"Your quarrel is with me," Casey said once the four of them were inside with the door closed. "Let these women go."

"Maybe I will, and maybe I won't." His glare sent a flash of alarm up her spine. "Here, girl, let me take a look at you." He ripped off her bonnet and yanked on her hair, sending hairpins flying. "My, you sure look fancy. This new life must be agreein' with you." He pointed the revolver at Jocelyn and Bonnie. Casey immediately planted herself in front of them. "It's a pity I have to kill all of you."

Horror for her dear friends penetrated her soul. She'd caused this. "Leave them alone, Jenkins. This is between you and me."

He appeared to think over her request while Casey stared into his reddened eyes. He hadn't bathed in days. Images from the past gripped her. He had no sense when he'd been drinking. They were as good as dead unless she thought of something fast. How many times had she seen him this way? How many folks had he killed in a drunken stupor?

Jocelyn. Bonnie. Poor Bonnie, who saw Kathleen's bloody body after her murder.

"There's rope by the wood box," she said. "I'll tie them up for you. Gag them, too, if you like."

"Why?" He appeared to weigh her words.

"So they don't cause trouble."

"They're Morgan Andrews's family." Jenkins wiped his dirty mouth and slapped his right leg. "I have him to thank for this. Seems only fair for me to kill his women." He stepped toward Bonnie. "This pretty little thing needs a good man first."

Bonnie stiffened and lifted her chin in an uncharacteristic display of strength.

"Morgan is on his way here. He's right behind me," Casey said.

"You're lyin'."

"Why should I? You could pick him off when he comes riding in." Her eyes never left his face. "You've got both of us, Jenkins. We're all trapped." She gambled on Jenkins's having to seize control of every situation. He'd planned her death for a long time. Any interruption would bother him.

Jenkins angrily knocked over the coffeepot resting on the stove. His right eye jerked. "Tie 'em up, and be quick about it before I change my mind. I've got my own way of handling this. I sure never thought him stupid enough to bring you here. What did you promise him?"

"Nothing."

Jenkins waved his gun in her face. "I know what you are, Casey girl. Hurry up. We're getting out of here."

Casey captured Jocelyn's gaze and mouthed the word *pray*. Bonnie saw the exchange and nodded slightly. She seemed to be in control of her emotions. Casey bound both women with loose knots and gagged them. She sent silent messages of hope to her precious friends. She needed time—time to think. The door flew open, and Grant walked in.

"What's going on here?" Grant's gaze swept to his mother and Bonnie, then rested on Casey.

Jenkins whipped around and raised his revolver.

"No, please." Casey's words died in the blast of gunfire.

Grant fell back against the door. Blood spurted from his shoulder and dripped down his shirt. He grabbed his upper arm and stared dumfounded at the thick red liquid oozing between his fingers. Pain and shock spread over his face. He swayed toward the table.

The nightmare had begun.

"Let me take care of him." Casey moved toward Grant.

Jenkins grabbed her arm and pushed her toward the door. "We're getting out of here before that shot brings any more uninvited company." The outlaw knocked her to the floor and delivered a savage kick to her side. "One more word, and I'll kill 'em all."

Grant grabbed his bleeding shoulder. "My brother will tear you apart with his bare hands."

Casey looked up, her eyes glazed from the sharp bruise to her body. She sent a silent warning to Grant.

"Not likely, kid," Jenkins said. "You've got a lot of guts, considering I've already shot you once."

Casey forced herself to stand. "I'm ready."

"Get outside and on my horse," he said.

Once outside, she managed to pull herself up onto his saddle.

The outlaw climbed up behind her and drew her to him. His touch brought back too many memories—the many nights she'd slept with her Colt beneath her blanket and her fingers wrapped around a knife. The nights he'd wrenched the weapons from her and used her until he was satisfied.

He cursed and threatened those inside who might venture out after them. He took a quick look around and spurred his horse into a dead run. Casey saw a couple of ranch hands emerge from the bunkhouse and shout at the two as they raced away. Jenkins whirled around with an explosion of lead. She couldn't tell if any of them were hit, but she prayed for their safety.

At first she had no idea where they were headed, but it soon became clear just where Jenkins planned to take her. They were riding in the direction of Morgan's cabin.

This can't be. Morgan will go mad. This can't happen to him again.

She prayed for wisdom. Jenkins had wanted her once. "We can ride together again," she said. "It can be just like you want it."

He tightened his grip around her waist until she choked back a scream. She'd do anything to spare Morgan the horror of finding her dead in the cabin. Anything.

❧❦❧

"I'm ashamed of myself, Reverend." Morgan paced the kitchen of the parsonage. "A rider brought Casey's pardon late last night. I wanted to tell her this morning, but she left church before I had a chance to talk to her. I know I have to accept whatever she says about us, and that has my insides feeling like curdled milk. Guess I needed to talk to you before I head out to the ranch." He shook his head. "I'm sorry. I've really gotten prideful about this. I should have chased her down this morning. She's waited too long to be free."

"You're being honest. I've seen her the past few months in church, staring back at me as though she wanted to cry."

Morgan crossed his arms and stopped in front of the window. He remembered all the times when Casey had been afraid of him. "I think I ruined it between us, and it's my fault. I shoved my bad temperament at her one too many times. Mama reminded me that she's never known a decent man. No wonder she's afraid to trust."

"I'll be praying you two will be rejoicing with the good news."

"We both worked so hard on this pardon." He turned from the window. "Lots of folks did. I think I'll head back to the boardinghouse and get a clean shirt."

"Facing our problems is the best way to solve them. If you two make it to church tonight, I won't ask you about my sermon. Something tells me you'd have a hard time concentrating."

"Maybe so, but I need to listen more instead of stepping into life each morning like a stubborn mule."

The two said their good-byes, and Morgan made his way down the street to the boardinghouse. He thought about how he missed the ranch. Even the bunkhouse was more homelike than his room here. The proprietor waved at him.

"I have a note for you from Miss Flanagan. It's under your door."

Taking two steps at a time up the stairs, Morgan rushed down the hall to his room. He opened the door and snatched up the folded piece of paper. With the door open, he read each word, then read it again. He shut the door with his boot. "Thank You, Lord!" His words bounced from the walls inside his small room. In two minutes, he had on a clean shirt. Cramming the note inside his shirt pocket, he grabbed his hat.

At the livery, he saddled his horse, all the while frustration creeping through him. He couldn't get to the ranch fast enough. But as he swung up onto the saddle, Ben walked in.

"Morgan, we need to talk."

"I'm in a hurry. Need to ride out to the ranch."

"There's trouble."

Alarm sounded through Morgan's body. "What do you mean?"

Ben made his way closer. "Tim O'Hare was seen earlier this morning riding toward your land. He was alone. But what about Jenkins?"

～◌6◌～

In all of Casey's days at the ranch, she'd never been this close to the cabin—the scene of Kathleen's murder. Morgan wanted to burn it to the ground, but it was also the cabin his father had built. Recently he'd cleaned up the weeds and underbrush with the idea of asking Jesse and his family if they'd like to live there. All of that stood starkly against what Jenkins now planned.

Jenkins rode up behind the cabin, dismounted, and tied his horse to an oak. Casey started to swing her leg over the saddle, but he pulled her to the ground onto a patch of prickly thistles. She waited for him to empty his revolver into her, but that would have been too easy.

"Didn't I tell ya not to ever leave me?" Jenkins bent down to her face. His foul breath reminded her of a hundred other times he'd come after her. "Were you fool enough to think I'd never catch up with you? I don't ever give up, Casey girl."

"I guess I knew it. Expected it." *How stupid I've been. I shouldn't have stopped running. Morgan, I haven't told you in so very long how much I love you.*

Jenkins yanked her up from where she'd fallen and dragged her around to the front of the cabin. Forcing her to her feet, he grabbed her waist and limped inside. Even with his bad leg, his strength was something to be reckoned with. She recalled how fighting him only made matters worse. He slammed the door shut, and the cabin shook. Shadows from the overhanging trees intensified her fear of what Morgan would find. She blinked and searched for a way to defend herself.

As though Jenkins knew her thoughts, he pinned her arms behind her. White-hot pain shot up her fingers to her shoulders. He wrapped rawhide tightly around her wrists until it cut into her flesh. All the while he cursed. Casey understood his game. She refused to give in to any semblance of anguish that would spur him on to inflict more agony. He shoved her onto a chair and reached for a nearly empty bottle of liquor on the table.

"Casey girl." He swayed with the effects of the alcohol. "We've got us a reunion—you, me, and Andrews. But I ain't killin' you now. Not until he shows up. Why, we've got ourselves a party." He took a gulp from the bottle. "Been resting and drinking all mornin', thinking how I was going to make you pay for all the trouble you've caused me. I should have sold you to Rose since you couldn't handle one night there. You always were uppity." He sneered. "And I loved you, too. I'd have given you anything you wanted. But you lit out."

He took another swallow. "Purdy dresses. A ranch in Mexico. Anything. But I wasn't good enough for you."

Jenkins paced across the wooden floor. She calculated how fast she could get to the door before he caught her.

"Let me tell you about the things I learned about making folks pay," he said. "There's a lot of fun we're gonna have with a knife and a little fire. But most of it will wait for Andrews. That man has bad luck when it comes to women."

Panic ripped across her mind. Living meant enduring his threats. . . his torture. . .or whatever he chose to do to her.

"Do you remember all the promises I made you? Do I have to remind you? I'm a man of my word, Casey girl. You'll see. I'm going to take care of you and Andrews together. Seems fittin', doesn't it? And that no-count brother of yours is miles away."

With each threat, he lifted the bottle and drank until he sent it crashing to the floor. Bits of glass splintered about the room. She held her breath and understood that the shards fueled his mind for what he planned to do next.

Jenkins's eyes narrowed, and his laugh grew louder. He moved her way. As long as his garbled, deranged shouts of insanity spun around her, she had time to think. The ranch hands saw what happened. They'd help Grant and send word to town for the doctor and Ben and Morgan. Watching Jenkins swerve and bump into the side of the cabin, she prayed he would pass out.

I can't even fight back. If only I could get away long enough to make a run for it.

She tried to work her hands free, but the rawhide knots only tightened. Casey clung to a prayer for deliverance as soundly as she clung to life.

She heard a horse. A rider? A man called out. She strained her ears and tried to move. That voice. *Tim.* Jenkins stomped outside. With his back to her, Casey made her way to where Jenkins leaned against the open door of the cabin.

"Jenkins," Tim shouted from the small clearing in front of the cabin. "What are you doing in there?"

"O'Hare, I thought you had better things to do than trail me."

"I wondered where you were headed. I hadn't been in this part of Texas before, so I thought I'd find out what you were up to." Tim sounded friendly. "You're a hard man to find."

"Well, now you found me. Get on out of here. I want to be alone."

"Who do you have in there with you?" Tim dismounted from his horse and slowly ambled toward the cabin. His right hand rested on his gun belt.

"Nobody. Just me and my bottle."

"I think you're lying. This is Andrews's land. Morgan Andrews."

"What do you mean?" Impatience seemed to mount with Jenkins's every word. Casey wanted to warn Tim, but Jenkins would shoot him.

"I want to come in and take a look. I wouldn't want you to be drinking by yourself. I've come a long way." Tim stared at the drunken outlaw.

Jenkins raised his revolver. "I don't think so."

The *click* screamed at her mind. "Tim," Casey cried, "he'll kill you for sure. Do what he says."

The muscles in her brother's face tightened. "Jenkins, I told you too many times to leave my sister alone. I've been trailing you for a long time, knowing you'd not give up on finding her. Casey, come on outside."

"She stays put," Jenkins said.

"Then you and I will settle this for good."

"I could shoot you where you stand." Jenkins limped off the porch.

"But you'd rather fight me square. You've wanted to for a long time," Tim said.

"Yer pushin' me."

"Come on out in the open, Jenkins. Show me what you're made of. This business with my sister has to stop here. I told you to leave her be. She ain't no good to you alive or dead."

"I'm faster than you." Jenkins spit tobacco between them.

"Prove it." Tim whirled one quick glimpse her way.

Casey gasped. Her mind scrambled. *Is Tim faster?*

"I don't want to kill ya," Jenkins said.

"Then let my sister go."

"She's mine. Always has been. You're not giving me any choice but to gun you down, O'Hare."

She realized Tim allowed silence to strengthen his challenge. She well remembered his tactics. "Are you afraid of me?"

Jenkins made his way into the clearing. She followed, no longer afraid that he might swing his gun back her way.

Tim met Casey's gaze. One brief moment of compassion. "That's my sister you're treatin' that way. I'm ready, Jenkins."

In the midst of anger's fury, two men fired. And two men fell.

Casey screamed as her brother's body slumped to the ground. He rolled over on his back. Blood rippled over his chest and onto the dry ground. She stumbled to his still form. "Tim. I'm coming." She struggled with the rawhide binding her hands. "I can't touch you." She stared in horror at the sight of his ashen face. "Why did it have to come to this?"

He groaned and opened his mouth to speak. She tried to stop him, but he ignored her pleading. "Cas, I'm sorry. . . . I never did right by you."

She blinked back stinging tears. "It's all right. Save your strength and rest. I'll go get help."

"Not this time, little sister," he whispered. "Jenkins's bullet did me in."

And with the red pool at his side, she saw his words were true.

"Tim, do you still remember Jesus?" Sobbing broke her words.

"No. . .only through Ma."

"It's not too late to ask Him into your life." All of the things she wanted to tell him about Jesus flowed through the recesses of her mind, but time stole them from her heart.

He struggled to breathe. "Someday, when you see Ma again, tell her I'm sorry. I never kept the promises I made to take care of you proper."

"You did keep. . ." Her words fell on lifeless ears. Casey heard the *click* of a revolver. Her gaze bore into the crippled, mangled outlaw who had stalked her and killed her brother. He'd crawled to her. He aimed his revolver directly at her face. If she hadn't been on her knees, she could have kicked the gun from his hands.

"Go ahead, Jenkins," she said. "Do it now. I dare you."

He raised the weapon to fire, but movement caught her eye. Morgan raced from the trees beside the cabin and slammed into Jenkins. In the shuffle, the gun slipped from Jenkins's fingers.

Morgan grabbed the revolver and towered over him. "Don't try anything." He shoved Jenkins aside. Blood oozed from Jenkins's side, and he groaned. Morgan whipped around to her and pulled a knife from his pocket to cut the rawhide binding her wrists.

"Are you all right?"

All she could do was nod.

"Shoot me." Jenkins's words sounded more like an animal begging to be put out of its misery.

"Not this time," Morgan said. "That's what the law's for."

Morgan knelt at Casey's side. "It's all over. No one will hurt you now. No one will ever hurt you again."

"Tim tried to stop Jenkins," she said. "He died trying to save me. . . . He died without Jesus."

Morgan stared at Jenkins, who clutched his bleeding side. He pulled her closer. "There was a time I'd have filled you with every bullet I had," he told the outlaw. "But a judge and jury will make this decision."

Horses and riders approached them—ranch hands.

"Jesse, get this man to the house. The doc can look at him after he sees to Grant. Then Ben can have him."

"Grant? Is he all right?" Casey's tears refused to stop, but she didn't care.

"He'll be just fine. It's not too deep. Rafael went after the doctor and the sheriff."

Casey wet her lips. "I'm so sorry for not trusting you. I love you. . . .

I never dreamed you would come."

"Oh, my dear sweet lady, how could you ever think such nonsense? My nightmare was that I wouldn't make it in time. Thank God, I found you."

"Do. . .you still want to marry me? I don't care about the pardon."

Morgan planted a kiss on her forehead. "Honey, the papers came yesterday evening. President Arthur granted the pardon. You're free. Free from Jenkins. Free from ever running again." He gathered her up and carried her away from the sight of Tim's body. "I'm taking you home, sweetheart. It's all over."

EPILOGUE

"Into this holy estate this man and this woman come now to be united. If anyone, therefore, can show just cause why they may not be lawfully joined together, let him now speak, or else forever hold his peace." Reverend Rainer smiled out over those sharing in the marriage celebration.

Casey longed to look out at her friends, too, but gazing into the eyes of her beloved Morgan was where she always wanted to be. She saw the love radiating there and silently promised her devotion.

"Morgan Andrews, wilt thou have this woman to be thy wedded wife, to live together after God's ordinance in the holy estate of matrimony? Wilt thou love her, comfort her, honor, and keep her in sickness and in health, and, forsaking all others, keep thee only unto her, so long as ye both shall live?"

"I will." Morgan nodded his head to affirm the fact.

The reverend turned to Casey. "Casey O'Hare, wilt thou have this man to be thy wedded husband, to live together after God's ordinance in the holy estate of matrimony? Wilt thou love him, comfort him, honor, obey, and keep him in sickness and in health, and, forsaking all others, keep thee only unto him, so long as ye both shall live?"

Thank You, Lord. "I will." Casey swallowed a sob. *I will not cry. This is a day of happiness. Too many tears have been shed in the past. Oh Sarah, I pray you are watching this.*

Casey stood confidently beside Morgan, their hands firmly locked in the midst of their vows. A bouquet of Sarah's vibrant red roses trembled in her hand, and a single tear slipped from her misty eyes. Bonnie managed a quivering smile beside the bride, and Grant grinned broadly from his position as best man. The reverend stood like an old Indian chief whom Casey had known in years gone by. The same white hair and dignified stance characterized both men. She longed to find Jocelyn, but not at this moment. This moment belonged to Morgan.

A wide smile spread over the reverend's face. "I don't think anyone here objects to me pronouncing you man and wife," he said. "Morgan, you may now kiss your bride."

A whoop and a holler rose from Grant. Others began to clap. But Casey's attention focused on her husband, the only man she'd ever loved or would ever love. As his lips touched hers, sealing their commitment for a lifetime, she remembered the words of Sarah. *"He cannot be perfect, but will he try? There lies your answer, and only you can know his heart."* Morgan would always love her, and he'd always try to be a godly husband. What more could she want?

Morgan smiled and with featherlike softness brushed away the dampness on her cheeks with his finger. "I love you, Casey Andrews. I'm not a perfect man, but with God's help, I will do my best to cherish you always."

"I love you," she whispered. "The past is behind us. We have today and tomorrow."

Award-winning author, DiAnn Mills launched her career in 1998 with the publication of her first book. Currently she has sixteen novels, fourteen novellas, a nonfiction book, and several articles and short stories in print.

DiAnn believes her readers should "expect an adventure." Her desire is to show characters solving real problems of today from a Christian perspective through a compelling story.

Five of her anthologies have appeared on the CBA best-seller list. Three of her books have won the distinction of Best Historical of the Year by Heartsong Presents, and she remains a favorite author of Heartsong Presents' readers. Two of her books have won Short Historical of the Year by American Christian Romance Writers for 2003 and 2004. She is the recipient of the Inspirational Reader's Choice award for 2005 in the long contemporary and novella category.

DiAnn is a founding board member of American Christian Fiction Writers and a member of Inspirational Writers Alive, Chi Libris, and Advanced Writers and Speakers Association. She speaks to various groups and teaches writing workshops. She is also a mentor for the Christian Writers Guild.

She lives in sunny Houston, Texas, the home of heat, humidity, and Harleys. In fact, she'd own one, but her legs are too short. DiAnn and her husband have four adult sons and are active members of Metropolitan Baptist Church.

Some Other Books by DiAnn Mills

Texas Charm

Nebraska Legacy

Footsteps

When the Lion Roars

AVAILABLE WHEREVER GREAT
CHRISTIAN FICTION IS SOLD

Visit DiAnn's Web site at www.diannmills.com